COME INTO MY WORLD

ALFRED L. BOLING

WINTERS
PUBLISHING

winterspublishing.com

Thank You

Thank You to Rita Martin for her endless hours of work transcribing the original stories to a document I could edit. I could not have done this without her.

Come Into My World

© 2021 Alfred L. Boling

Photos from the collection of Mary Mead

Cover and interior page design by Tracy Winters

Published by:
Winters Publishing
P.O. Box 501
Greensburg, IN 47240
812-663-4948
www.winterspublishing.com

ISBN 13: 978-1-954116-05-4

Library of Congress Control Number: 2020950629

Printed in the United States of America

Table of Contents

Alfred, with children Max and Mary.

Foreword

Alfred Boling (October 15, 1914–November 9, 1968)

Who was Alfred Boling? He was a loving husband to Stella and father to Max and Mary Elizabeth. He was also grandfather to Sean, Chris, and Angie. He never met Heather because he died before she was born. Six other great-grandchildren would follow. Alfred would have been very proud of all his children, grandchildren, and great-grandchildren. Every grandchild displays the qualities that he valued so much: honesty, kindness, caring, hard work, and love of animals.

But he was so much more. He was a soldier in WW II, serving in the 7th Army, 200th Battalion, as a Supply Sergeant. He served from 1942 to 1945. He was overseas for almost four years. He didn't see his son Max until he was three years old, except in an occasional picture sent by my mother. Letters were the only means of communication. His journey started in South Africa and ended in Germany. He never saw battle because he was a supply sergeant. However, he still experienced all the cold, the endless rain in South Africa, hunger, emotional pain, loneliness, and homesickness that the other soldiers experienced. Probably his worst experience was toward the end of the war, when he, along with hundreds of other soldiers, were on scene when the concentration camp of Dachau was liberated. He writes about this in a letter to the editor of the *Indianapolis Star* in the following stories.

After the war, he came home to Salem and continued to live there until his death in 1968. Conservation and love of animals, especially coon hounds, were his primary focus during those years. He was instrumental in starting the Blue River Coon Hunters Club and the County Conservation Council. At some point, he was their chairman. When Washington County joined the 12th District Conservation Council, consisting of twelve Indiana counties, he eventually served as their secretary-treasurer. He wrote articles for the "Hoosier Conservation" paper and worked very hard to get legislation passed that would protect hounds from being stolen and abused.

Sometime in the early sixties, he began to write. He was the first fiction writer for the magazine *Full Cry*. As you will see in the following stories, they almost always involved a dog. He owned several coon hounds over the years, but I think his favorite was Old Red. Red is buried at the house on Walnut Street, where Max and I grew up.

Over the years, he wrote numerous letters to the editor of different publications, always on a subject that he believed to be unjust. He loved his family and friends and would do anything to protect them.

Our mother also played a part in his love of writing. She must have spent many hours alone, while he sat in the basement pecking away at his typewriter, but I don't ever remember her complaining.

One final note, on the night before he died, he was going coon hunting and experienced a stroke. He died the following morning, but at the end, he was doing what he loved.

Mary (Boling) Mead and Max Boling

Let Me Take Him Home

The pleading tones of a boy's voice cause a hardened police lieutenant to risk the loss of thirty years' retirement pension in a feeling of compassion for the youth's efforts to aid an aging hound.

The Commissioner glared at me across the desk that had suddenly become ten feet wide. I knew that I deserved anything he might say. But I also knew that if it was to do over again, my actions would be no different. The Kid had gotten to me and I wasn't sorry.

Finally, he jerked a well-chewed, but unlit cigar from between his teeth and ground it out viciously in the ash tray. Even then, I could feel some sympathy for him. The boys out front had tipped me off about the Mayor's stormy visit. He was in a bad situation and I was responsible.

"Well, Lieutenant," he bellowed, "I want an explanation, and it had better be good."

It all seemed a bit hazy now, the morning after. My reason was good enough to suit me, but I could hardly expect him to buy it, being city-bred and city-raised like he was. While he waited impatiently, I desperately attempted to rally my thoughts; groping for words with which to explain something that I couldn't possibly expect him to understand.

There was one thing, though, that was clear in my mind. Right then, after the evening before, I knew that I didn't like the city. That may sound strange coming from one who had spent thirty years as a member of a Midwestern police force. I really didn't know before, but now there was no doubt. There was a feeling of shame, too, for having been a part of the cold, mad, and greedy rat race that has become such a part of everyday metropolitan existence.

But as I stood there lost in thought, the boy's strained white face flashed before me and everything fell into place. Just him against the city. And for a while it had been that way. Then his voice pierced the density of my thinking; penetrated the hot roaring in my head; dragged me up from the abyss of big city indifference. I was once more a boy back on the farm, looking down in disbelief and horror as my old Shepherd dog, the victim of a careless hunter's gun, bled to death at my feet.

All he had said was, "Please, let me take him home." And I placed thirty years' retirement on the line.

I had been at the desk talking to the Sergeant when the call came in. Just routine, we get many such calls every day, but for some reason or other I heard myself saying, "I'll go with Harmon."

While he tooled the squad car through the heavy homebound traffic, I thought again of that one terse statement from the dispatcher. *Vicious dog attacking people at 52nd and Oak. Investigate.*

It was, I thought bitterly, probably the other way around. As we turned the corner at 51st, we saw that the entire lower half of the block was jammed tight. The siren got us nowhere, so dismounting, we proceeded on foot. Now the wild hootings and derisive laughter of the crowd pounded our ears, while several men could be seen darting back and forth. I was suddenly sick with hatred for all that their heartless action implied.

An aged Black and Tan hound stood in the middle of the intersection, surrounded by the howling mob. Reeling, he pivoted slowly around, in an effort to face as many of his tormentors as possible. Angrily, I tried forcing my way through the circle.

Harmon growled disgustedly, "So this is the vicious dog? My God, what gets into people?"

"Not surprised, are you?" I grunted, as I set my shoulder into the back of a middle-aged, red-faced howler and shoved violently.

He didn't answer directly. "Yellow-bellied cowards," he gritted, as he grabbed a wild-eyed youth by the collar and slammed him to the side. "They'd do a human the same way, if they only had the guts."

Progress was painfully slow. Flashing my shield made no impression. It was just as if they had gone blind. Blind to anything but that poor frightened animal in the center. Sickened by the look of wild hysteria in their eyes, I knew that the thin veneer of civilization had been stripped completely away. They didn't even recognize us as police officers.

The old dog was waging a losing battle to stay on his feet. With sides heaving and head down, his eyes burned from beneath drooping lids. Only grit was propping him up; nothing else. As he heeled and almost went down, some of the braver ones edged a little closer. A deep growl rumbled in his throat and they instantly pushed back in panic.

A wild cry of "Mad dog! Mad dog!" went up from all sides.

Oh, how I hated them all. Man's inhumanity toward God's lower creatures, as intensified beyond all reason. Every effort to stiffen his legs brought a shudder throughout the old dog's pain-wracked body. Only his deep growl held them off.

Harmon unsheathed his blackjack and looked at me beseechingly. But I shook my head. Not yet. Not yet. There might yet be another way.

But time was running out. A large bushy-haired, burly youth was advancing upon the now completely prostrate dog. I guessed him to be about twenty. In his hand, he held a long club. My fingers closed over the butt of my gun; maybe I could deter him by firing into the air. But I never even jerked it free; there was no need.

A hush had fallen over the crowd. The brave one, now in striking distance, had raised the club over his head. They held their breath; licking their lips in anticipation.

The would-be killer, enjoying his moment of heroics, paused in apparent joy of his glorious stance. For an instant, the club hung suspended in the air. Then the muscles of his big shoulders tightened, and I knew that I would be too late.

Before I could reach the man, a piercing yell split the silence and the bushy-haired man went flying through the air. A hurricane in the form of a lanky red-haired boy had blown upon the circle and they parted like uprooted palms.

The crowd stood in open-mouthed amazement. Not a movement rippled through them as the boy stood beside the dog. He appeared to be about eighteen, but those blazing blue eyes in that taut white face placed on him the mark of centuries. Right then, he was as old as all men, and as time itself.

Scornfully, his eyes slowly swept the circle, then he deliberately spat at their feet. Still, he said nothing. Many, in which the mob hysteria was quickly dying, looked shamefacedly away, refusing to meet his eyes as they began to push back; to broaden the circle around those lonely two in the middle.

Then, with one last contemptuous look, he turned his attention to the figure at his feet. Kneeling, he placed his hands upon the scarred head and stroked it gently, speaking softly as he did so. The old fellow responded with a whine and weakly began to lick his hand. Spellbound by the quick events, I had remained where I was at the interruption, and because of that, I must blame myself for what happened next. I had been a policeman too long to take for granted that it was all over. But I did.

The big guy, whom he had knocked down, suddenly climbed to his feet. Quickly, he scooped up the club and moved to attack. Too late, I saw that he was going to strike the kneeling youth from behind. Crazed with rage at being denied his moment of triumph, his only desire was revenge.

Then I saw something else and realized that my troubles were only beginning. I hadn't recognized the bushy-haired man before, but now there was no doubt; he was the obnoxious, over-bearing, and ultra-spoiled son of the Mayor. He had given us trouble before, but this was swiftly turning into something a lot different. I had only time to shout a warning.

But that was enough; God, how it was enough. I never saw anyone move quicker. Like a flash the redhead shot to his feet and whirled on the balls of his feet. Disdainful of the partially raised club, he calmly executed the old one-two. The big knobby knuckles of his left hand were planted in the midsection of the other, and as the air went out with a whoosh, his looping right fist landed flush on the side of the jaw. It was beautiful. Out of the corner of my eyes, I saw a big grin split Harmon's face from ear-to-ear. But the unmistakable crack of a broken bone, as the blow landed, at once enshrouded the encounter with a deadly seriousness.

But the fallen one was not alone. As he went down, a half dozen friends who had been egging him on let out an angry howl. Their hero down, on top of being robbed of the sadistic pleasure of seeing the old dog's brains bashed out, was just too much. As a group they surged forward, intent on finishing that which their fallen comrade had failed to do. And then a cyclone went to work in the middle of that circle.

There was blood upon the street when it was finished. Again, I must blame myself. I never moved, and I'll never know why. Maybe I'm getting old and slow. Maybe I sensed that the redhead could handle it very well by himself; or did I hesitate because I felt as he did about the mob? Did I let him go ahead because I enjoyed seeing him do that which I could not? I'll never know.

Swiftly, he scooped up the club dropped by the big youth, as the crowd closed in. Briefly then, he was out of my sight. And then the hairs on the back of my neck prickled at the wildness of the war whoop that rang out from the center of the circle, and they went reeling backward like tenpins.

My skin crawled at the sound of wood against flesh, as the club landed with deadly impact. The boy was spinning in a circle with the club held at full length. And those nearest the center went down with the rapidity of grain before a scythe.

It was over as quickly as it began. What a mess. Three lay moaning on the ground, while three more stood with pain-wracked faces, clutching obviously broken arms.

Red Head stood there, calmly surveying the carnage, as the light of battle slowly died in his eyes. Then the club dropped from a hand suddenly gone limp, and a shudder swept him. For an instant he looked as if he was going to be sick and then his eyes lifted to mine. I saw the dismay mirrored there in their blue depths, and the sorrow and regret.

As Harmon and I pushed through the slack-jawed crowd, relief flooded the boy's face as he recognized us for what we were. The composure he reflected told us that he knew he had done only what he had to do and that he was ready to take his punishment. I was not going to enjoy what I must do.

The arrival of the ambulance, summoned by Harmon, took my mind off the boy for a moment. After a brief examination by the doctor, it appeared that things might not be as bad as I feared. In his opinion, the ones with the skinned heads, barring possible concussions, would be none the worse for wear after a few stitches here and there. It was a distinct relief to see them loaded and on the way to the hospital.

But the big one, the Mayor's son, was a different story. He was still out cold. And his jaw was definitely broken. The Mayor was going to cry for blood and I knew whose it would be.

Red Head stood waiting, with a calmness that was, for the moment, infuriating. While the crowd stared in awe, I pushed angrily through to him. Even then I knew the anger I felt wasn't at the boy, but just everything about the city that made people like they were. But, for that instant, he was the focal point for all my misery, something solid before me; an object to grasp, to feel, and on which to vent my wrath.

I don't remember a word I said, but only that I was aware that my voice trembled with fury. The face of the boy grew whiter with every word. But even under my tirade he was unshaken, for with one piercing flash of those intense blue eyes he suddenly ignored me completely. My words hung in the air as he knelt once more to the side of the dog.

Tenderly, he took the old head in his hands and as he spoke softly, the raging but aged old lion became a lamb under his touch. No other sound broke the stillness as he crooned to the dog. His words were too soft for the rest of us to hear, but that was as it should be. For it was only between them.

Slowly, he raised his face to mine and a knot formed in my stomach, only to travel rapidly into my throat, for those terribly angry eyes of only moments before now glistened with unshed tears. Wretchedly, I waited for him to speak.

Finally, in a voice strained with emotion, he began, "It's all right, Officer. I know I'm under arrest and I deserve it, but I couldn't … I just couldn't stand by and let … let them mistreat this old fellow."

Harmon asked softly, "Is this your dog, son?"

For a moment the boy didn't answer as he looked down into the luminous eyes of the old hound. Whimpers of delight arose in the old fellow's throat at the touch of his hand.

Then raising his head, he said, "No, sir, I never saw him before in my life. He was just a hound that needed help."

Compassion such as this was indeed strange to a lifelong city resident such as Harmon. He found it all a bit incredulous. Silently, he shook his head as he stared at the boy.

I forced myself to say, "Son, you sure did get yourself in a mess."

He nodded. "Yes, sir. I know. But I had to do it."

My attention was drawn to the old hound, who had gotten shakily to his feet. Pity for him swept me, accompanied by instant fury at whatever lack of compassion within someone had brought him to this spot. Still governed, though, by years of impersonal training as a cop, I said, "I'll have to book you, son. I must warn you that there's no telling what the charges may be after the report from the hospital."

He only nodded. But at my next words, his eyes widened in dismay. "We'll have to send him to the pound to be put away," I said.

"Oh, no, sir! You can't do that," he said, his voice rising.

Again, I was suddenly angry. I struck out at him in my frustration. "Obviously, there's nothing else to do," I said acidly. "Come along now, and don't give us any more trouble."

Harmon was turning to walk back to the car to call the animal shelter truck, when all at once, the sickness in the eyes of the boy, for some reason or other, caused me to ask him to wait.

"You got a better idea?" I said to the youth.

The relief that flooded his face was easy to see. "Let me take him home."

"But," I spluttered, "you said you didn't know him."

He smiled with a maturity beyond his years. "Beg your pardon, sir. That's not what I said exactly. I said I had never seen him before. But I know him, as I know all hounds. I know he deserves some decent treatment, for God knows, he's had little enough of that lately."

This kid was upsetting what should have been merely routine business. For the moment, thoughts of my pension going down the drain drove away all other feelings.

"Sorry, kid," I said harshly. "It can't be done. Don't argue any more now. Let's go."

But he wasn't giving up so easily. "Please, sir, he only has about a year to live. Maybe two, at the best. He deserves a chance to die back in the hills where he came from. I don't know how he got here, but I know how he can get back."

I could feel my pension slipping. Desperately, I grasped for it. Scathingly, I barked, "So, now you say that he came from the hills."

Again, that brief smile flickered across his face. "Not only that," he replied gently, "but I know he has been a good coon dog."

He hadn't struck me as a liar, but he had gone too far. "Now, see here," I exploded.

He didn't answer, only flipped back one of the old dog's big long ears. His fingers traced a pattern of small narrow scars on the underneath side. "Those scars were made by the claws of many coon," he said, matter of factly. Then pointing to similar ones across the muzzle, he added, "Those, too."

But he hadn't made good on the rest of his statement. "That doesn't prove he's from the hills."

Now he pressed the old dog down on his side. "No, sir, they don't," he said calmly, "but these may do."

Indicated by his fingers were three or four much larger and longer scars on the upper part of his belly and a couple more across his chest. "Now I could be wrong about these, but I don't think so," he continued. "I think they were made by cats and what few cats we have in this state are found mostly in the hills. There aren't enough cats for a dog to get much experience in fighting them so that's why he got cut up."

Harmon was looking at me in bewilderment. I knew what he was thinking. I had lost control. Instead of making an arrest, I was only putting off something unpleasant by listening to the spiel of a wise kid, who was probably pulling my leg. It had gone far enough.

"That may all be true," I said gruffly. "And maybe you can take him home after this is all over with, but not now."

"Later will be too late," he rasped angrily. Then more softly. "Please, sir, let me take him home now down to my farm, a hundred miles south of here where he can run free for the time he has left. Then when his time comes ... there's a little hill ... out back of the barn ..."

Then to my horror, I heard myself saying, "Can I trust you to come back by tomorrow morning to answer the charges?"

Steadfastly, his eyes bored into mine. "Yes, sir. I'll leave at once and be back whenever you say."

While depressing thoughts of what it would be like to start building a new retirement plan at my age nagged at me, I nodded at the kid in agreement. It took a few minutes more to get the information I needed. His name was Jody Hawkins. He was a freshman at the university, and was from Richmond, county seat of Webocco County. He had only his mother alive and owned a small farm left to him by an old man who had passed on. Then, telling him to report to the address I gave him at nine the next day, we watched him load the old dog into an ancient Chevrolet and head south.

I was suddenly very tired as I flopped into the seat beside Harmon. I had finally done it, something for which I would have chewed him out plenty. Harmon's interruption of my dark mood was a pleasant break.

A sardonic grin wreathed his face as he said, "Congratulations, Lieutenant."

"For what?" I grunted. "Maybe kicking thirty years' retirement down the drain?"

He shook his head. "No, sir, I mean for being a human being, and for doing exactly what I would have done if I had the power."

All at once, I felt good. Harmon was a veteran cop, levelheaded and well thought of on the force. Subordinate or not, right then, his approval meant a lot to me. But he had better news.

"Don't worry about losing that retirement," he said. "I'll back you up one hundred percent. And while you were talking to the boy, I got the names and addresses of five people who will testify as to just how it happened."

Right then, I knew that boy was going to be a sergeant before long. I knew something else, too. The redhead would be back just like he said; and that he and I were in for a long talk, all about those hills of his, and a little piece of ground off that farm of his, where I could build my house. Maybe soon enough to have the old hound for company for a year or two.

Suddenly, the harsh jangling of the phone on the Commissioner's desk snapped me back to the present and the hard facts of reality.

He listened briefly and hung up. Slowly, the scowl on his face gave way to a grin that preceded a deep chuckle by only a second or two. "Relax, Cal, I just couldn't resist that one last chance to needle you. It's all here in Harmon's report. And" … his grin grew broader, "the boy and your five witnesses are outside."

When I would have spoken, he added, "That must be quite a boy. I want to meet him and to shake his hand. I've had a belly full of people standing around refusing to lend assistance when it's needed. Maybe there's a chance for the human race, after all."

It's funny how everything can fall into place all at once and the answers stand out so clear. The boy wouldn't be held, my judgment of character had been upheld, and it didn't matter where you were raised, if you were the right kind of person, you could feel compassion for weaker things anywhere.

Canine Justice

The brakes on the old panel truck squealed, grabbed, and squealed again as Uncle Bob pulled over to the side of the gravel road and came to a stop just short of the Beam's Bridge. In the glow of the dash lights, I could see the grim look on his lean, tanned face and the worry in his eyes. I always felt secure being with my Uncle Bob, but a shiver of apprehension ran over my skinny thirteen-year-old body. Something about this night was different, and I knew that this was a part of coon hunting that I would never like.

Little Queen whimpered at the empty space beside her, in the back of the truck where King ought to be. My uncle reached back and put his hand on her head and rubbed her soft ears. "You could tell us what happened, old girl, if you could only talk, and how I wish you could."

I, too, reached back and let her nuzzle my hand, as I ran it down along her side. "Uncle Bob," I said, "she is still trembling."

"Yes, Jody, I know. Something scared her real bad and that something is what happened to King; you wait here, I'm going to walk up to the bridge to see if I can hear anything, but I'm afraid he's been stolen."

I answered, "Okay," as he opened the truck door and got out. His lanky sixty-year-old frame soon outreached the shine of the parking lights and he was lost to my view, as he climbed the small incline to the arched concrete bridge.

As I sat waiting, the events of the last hour kept running through my mind. It just didn't seem possible that what had started out as a very pleasant evening only an hour ago, could have turned into such an unpleasant and frightening one in such a short time. I had been looking forward to a few hours in the woods with my favorite uncle and his Treeing Walkers, and now here I sat, engulfed in a feeling of foreboding and disaster.

Uncle Bob owned a hardware store, and of course, this had been my favorite hangout for just about as long as I could remember. Also, it was the regular meeting place of all the coon hunters in town. I never seemed to get enough of listening to the talk of coon hounds and coon hunting that flowed knee deep in the back of the store, whenever a bunch of them got together. For the last year I had accompanied my uncle on a coon hunt every Friday evening, unless my mother thought the weather was too bad. We did have a few arguments about that, with me on the losing end, naturally. But even that was taken care of, because this afternoon, Uncle Bob had sent word for me to come past the store on my way home from school. He had something for me.

I made that eight blocks in nothing flat, and was fairly bursting with eagerness, when I reached the store. He was waiting on a customer, so I only waved to him and went to the back of the store. A couple of his coon hunting buddies were holding down a bench by the big stove, Bill Goddard and Steve Rainer. Bill, a barber, was a broad, powerful fellow in his late forties, dark of complexion, eyes, and hair. Steve, a carpenter, was almost the opposite, tall, rawboned, and fair, with blue eyes and blond hair, in his early thirties.

They both exchanged grins, and Bill said, "Now I wonder what Jody is doing in here?"

Steve shook his head, and replied, "I just can't imagine." But he slapped me on the back, and said, "How is the old coon hunter; are you going with Bob tonight?"

"Sure am," I answered, "if he will let me."

"Oh, he will take you, all right," Bill chuckled. "How else is he going to get the coons out of the den trees that his pot lickers tree up? We know that they are too slow to put one up on the outside, and he takes you along to do the climbing."

I just grinned without bothering to answer such an absurd charge against my uncle, because I knew that they were only joshing. Everyone knew how Uncle Bob felt about disturbing den trees; in fact, I knew that these fellows felt the same way, or else they wouldn't be hunting partners of his. My uncle just wouldn't hunt with a game hog.

By this time, Uncle Bob had finished with the customer, so he came back where we were. Completely ignoring me, he said, "Bill, are you sure that you didn't get those hunting clothes too small?" With that, he reached over to the top of his desk and picked up a brand new hunting coat and a pair of heavy duck pants.

"No, I don't think so," Bill said, real solemn like. "I intend to go on a diet, and besides they will probably stretch once I get to wearing them."

As he took the clothes from my uncle's hand and held the pants up to him, I began to smell a mouse, for they didn't begin to cover the broad front of his two hundred pounds. And when he picked up a cap, that couldn't have been over a size 6½ and stuck it on top of his head, I knew that he had no intention of wearing that suit.

Steve said, "Now, I don't know of any little coon hunters, but if I did, I would try to get you to give those clothes to him."

"Well, now," Uncle Bob drawled, "I just might know of one, but these are mighty fine hunting clothes; they were made for someone who would not be afraid to give them lots of wear, and in all kinds of weather, in mud and rain and even snow, if need be."

By this time, I was ready to explode and the effort to keep still was making me dizzy, but just as I was ready to split at the seams, Uncle Bob looked at me, with a twinkle in his keen blue eyes, and said, "Jody, do you think that maybe they would fit you?"

I couldn't answer. I was afraid that if I opened my mouth I would blubber, and to do that in front of these men would have ruined me for life. My father had been killed in the war, and although Mom and I lived on the pension she received and we didn't want for necessities, there just wasn't much left over to buy hunting coats and pants.

"Go on, Jody, might as well try them on." So with that, Uncle Bob held them out to me, and with trembling hands, I took them from him. In a matter of seconds, I had on the coat, a perfect fit, and was pulling the pants on over my school clothes, another fit, and Steve slapped the size 6½ cap onto my 6½-sized head.

Uncle Bob studied me for a minute, and said, "Well, we might as well do this up right," and as he spoke, he opened a desk drawer and lifted out a beautiful pair of insulated rubber boots and a package that, to my amazement, contained, of all things, a suit of insulated underwear.

I was weak with happiness, but all that I could say was, "Thank you, Uncle Bob, I will try not to disgrace them."

My uncle ruffled my head with his big hand, and said, "I'm sure you won't, Jody; now maybe you had better take them home, your mother will be worrying. I will be past to pick you up about six thirty, so that you can break them in tonight."

"I'll be ready, I'll be ready!" and with that, I took off, because if I stayed there any longer, there was danger that I might disgrace myself.

As I went out the door, I heard Bill say, "That boy will have those clothes on from now until he goes to bed and will probably put them on again the first thing in the morning."

I ran all the way home and hit the front door with a shout, "Mom, Mom, look what Uncle Bob got for me!"

She came from the kitchen with a smile. "I know, he asked me for your sizes the other day. I hated to keep it from you, but he wanted it to be a surprise. I think that he gets a lot of enjoyment out of doing things for you, partly because he and Min don't have any children. I have your supper about ready; I knew that you would just about die if you couldn't wear them tonight. I hate to think of you out in the wet woods, chasing an old hound around till all hours, but I guess it's born in you, so I reckon I can stand it, if you can."

She bent and kissed me on the cheek, and added, "Your Daddy loved a hound, too." For a moment she stood silent, seemingly unaware of my presence, her eyes moist with unshed tears, and I knew she was thinking of him, the father I had never known, and for the millionth time, I wished I had.

While Mom was setting the table, I began putting on my new clothes. By the time she called me to eat, I had everything on, even the coat, which she made me remove. That was a good thing, because with that insulated underwear and heavy duck pants, I was really beginning to get up a heat before I gulped down my last glass of milk and shoved back from the table.

It was getting on towards six, so I said, "Mom, I think I will just go on outside and wait for Uncle Bob, it's too hot in the house."

"Yes, I imagine it is with all those clothes on," she said with a smile, "but a man just has to see how his new hunting clothes fit, doesn't he?"

As I slipped into my coat, she said, "It seems to me that there should be something else to go with a new coon hunting outfit, now I wonder what it could be? Hmm, now let me see. Oh, yes, a flashlight." And with that, she pulled open a drawer in the cabinet and lifted out the most beautiful six cell I had ever seen. "Now, here is an old thing that I have lying around, do you suppose that maybe you could use it for something or other?" She placed it in my hands, and I felt like someone had just given me the greatest gift that a boy could have.

"Gee, thanks, Mom, you sure know what a boy needs," I gulped. "Can I go outside and see how it works?"

"Yes, I suppose you must." So, kissing her goodbye, I slipped into my coat, grabbed my light, and rushed out the door.

Standing in the front yard, I tested the light on everything and anything, just about putting the street lights to shame, and I have no doubt that by the time my uncle drove up, the neighbors were about ready to call the cops. Mom came out onto the porch, and, as usual, cautioned my uncle not to keep me out too late, and, as usual, he promised not to. With that over, I climbed into his old hunting truck and we were off for the Blue River bottoms.

As I sat in the truck, waiting for Uncle Bob, I thought of how we had parked at the Martin Bridge, just a mile west of where we were now, and turned Big King and Little Queen loose, heading them east up the river. They had hit on the river by the time we had traveled a hundred yards. It was a slow track that showed promise of getting better fast.

They were drifting along pretty good, by the time we had climbed to the top of the bluff and found level going, so we kept on traveling east along the top, but not more than a hundred feet from the river at any time. King's bawl was beginning to turn to a chop and Queen's yodel was sounding more often, by the time we reached the Spring Branch Hollow.

Dropping down the hill, we crossed and climbed the ridge on the other side, still keeping just above the river. About that time, they jumped him and headed out, straight east towards Beam's Bridge. "Let's move, Jody," Uncle Bob said. "They will soon be across the road and out of hearing."

We walked up the ridge, trying to keep the dogs in hearing; after about five minutes of fast walking, we stopped to see if they had changed direction. We could still hear them plain, their music sending shivers of delight up and down my spine, and they were still on the river. It sure seemed that there was one coon that would have to climb or hole soon.

Just as my uncle said, "They are almost to the bridge, Jody," something happened. That race was chopped right off in the middle; there was a yelp, and then, nothing. We held our breath and listened, until I thought my ear drums would bust with the noise of the silence. Then I heard a sound that, for some reason I couldn't explain, sent a flash of fear through me, the sound of a car motor starting up. Though we could see no lights because of a curve in the ridge that cut off the road from our view, we heard it pull up the hill from the river bottom, going north, and fade away.

In the glow of the lantern, I could see that my uncle was standing rigid, straining his ears, hoping to hear his Walkers. In about five minutes, we heard a splash in the river, and the sound of a dog rattling up the rocky bluff, then little Queen poured into the lantern light.

Whining as she came, she went straight up to Uncle Bob and looked up into his face. It didn't take a very sharp eye to see that she was scared, plenty scared. Uncle Bob knelt down and took her beautiful head in his hands and stroked her, as he said, "There, there, old girl, you're all right now, nothing is going to hurt you, but where is King?"

She tried to tell him, she tried real hard, but of course, we could only guess. My uncle straightened up and stared silently into the darkness towards the last place we heard them open. Suddenly, my new hunting clothes and flashlight didn't seem important anymore; to have King there with us right then seemed to be all that mattered.

I waited for my uncle to speak, dreading to hear what I was afraid he would say. Finally, he turned to me and asked, "Jody, do you think that you could drive the truck around to the other bridge?"

"Sure, Uncle Bob, I can handle it all right."

"Good boy, I thought you could. There won't be any traffic on that side-road tonight. You are just a short distance from the truck, go right straight back along the top of the ridge and down to the road. I'll wait until you blow the horn, then I'll go on up the river and meet you at the bridge."

Turning on my new flashlight, I headed back to the truck at a high lope, while Queen and Uncle Bob waited for me to sound the horn. In about ten minutes, I dropped down the west end of the ridge onto the gravel road, and then down the short hill to the truck. Quickly reaching the key hidden under the seat, I sounded the horn a couple of times and started the motor.

I suppose that it took me around fifteen minutes to make the circle to where I was to meet my uncle. I stopped the truck and turned off the lights. Getting out, I stared down the river into the darkness toward where Uncle Bob should be coming. There was his light, slowly approaching along the riverbank, about a hundred yards downstream. I started toward him, through the picked-over cornfield, and met him. He had found nothing, so we turned and went back to the truck, and sat down to think and listen.

After a while, Uncle Bob got out and blew his whistle, the long and short blast, that he and King had worked out between them. Again and again, that loud blast echoed through those bottoms and bounced from hill to hill, but King didn't answer.

Getting back into the truck, he said, "We will go back to where we turned him loose and wait." So we drove back around the circle to the other bridge. Uncle Bob blew more blasts on the whistle, which shook the shadows off the bluff and chased them right down my coat collar and into my stomach, where they gathered in a great kind of lonesomeness and despair.

A half hour there, and then back around to the other bridge again. My uncle walked up onto the bridge to listen. I just couldn't sit there any longer, by myself, with all those thoughts pounding through my head. So I got out and walked up to stand beside him on the bridge. As I strained my ears into that heavy, black, wet river bottom, I'll swear, that the silence was the loudest thing that I had ever heard in my life.

Finally, Uncle Bob broke the mounting tension in me as he said, "Jody, we might as well face it, that car we heard was hauling King off, but I don't see how they could have caught him. He wouldn't have let a stranger get hold of him." He was silent a moment longer, and then spoke with a heavy tiredness in his voice, "Well, let's look for signs, you take the left side and I'll take the right."

Our big light lit up the road like daytime, and it didn't take long to find the car's tire tracks where they had pulled off to the side. There was a man's track heading out from the edge, across the corner of the soft muddy field, towards the river about fifty feet away. We followed them to the bank and saw where he had slid down to the gravel bar about four feet below. There he had milled around, messing the wet sand up quite a bit.

At the edge of that maze of tracks, we found what we were looking for. Fresh dog tracks coming right out of the water, to be lost in all that extra trampling the man had done. No dog tracks led away from there, only the boot tracks going up along the edge of the riverbank towards the road.

Even I could see that King was never led away from there, the thief had to be carrying him. "Uncle Bob," I asked, "how was he able to pick him up?"

"There was only one way he could have done that, Jody; he had to knock him out some way. If he had just grabbed him, King would have taken his hand off. Come on, we might as well go back to the truck." So, back to the road to take another look at the tire tracks.

I noticed one thing right off. "Look, they had mud grips on all four wheels."

"Yes, Jody, I wondered if you noticed that. Come to think of it, that car we heard did sound like a jeep. Well, that is something to go on, at least, and there is another thing, too."

"What's that?" I asked.

"Well," he answered, "from the guy's tracks, I would say that he was a heavy man, probably just fat, and I don't think that he is used to doing much walking."

"How can you tell that?" I gasped.

"Well, the way he sank into the mud shows that he is heavy, and the small size of his feet and short steps show that he probably isn't very long-legged. From the way he turns his feet out, I can only suppose that he doesn't do much walking, or at least, that he is a poor walker." With that, he turned towards our truck and said, "Come on, Jody, we might as well go home, we can't do any more for King tonight."

"Do you think you'll ever get him back, Uncle Bob?"

"I don't know, son, I just don't know, but I sure aim to work on it. There have been other dogs stolen this winter, and I haven't heard of any of them being recovered. But starting tomorrow, I have a lot of things to do along that line."

It was a pretty dejected pair that rode back to town that night. As I got out and told Uncle Bob goodnight, I felt mighty sorry for him. At the same time, I was thinking of the pup that I would never have; the one I was to get from King and Queen's next mating. Telling my uncle that I would be down to the store the next morning, I sadly went into the house.

Mom was still up, and I guess that I would have talked all night about what happened, but she finally put an end to it by saying, "Now don't worry so much about it; Bob will probably get him back. Into bed with you and don't lie awake all night thinking about it."

It was a long time, though, before I finally went to sleep, and my last thoughts before dropping off were that owning a good dog could sure be the cause of a lot of worry, when something like this happened.

Because it was Saturday, Mom just let me sleep the next morning, and to my dismay, it was going on ten o'clock when I finally woke up. Holy mackerel, Uncle Bob had been down to the store for three hours! Jumping out of bed, I hastily pulled on my clothes, and went through all the formalities that a kid my age has to go through before his mom will let him out of the house.

That done and my breakfast eaten, I left our yard in a run and fairly flew down the street to the store. There was a consultation going on in the back, so I hurried back there to see what I was missing. I soon learned that my uncle had been back to where we had lost King, but was unable to pick up any more clues than we had seen the night before.

Steve and Bill were there and a couple more men that I had never seen before. One of them was talking when I arrived. "I'm sure glad that we stopped by, Bob, we will get word to all the clubs in our part of the state. As I said before, that sounds just like the same way Ike Pruitt lost his big Plott just before Christmas. Actually, we may even have a suspect or two, but we can't be sure yet!"

"Here's all we know so far," the other man added. "There have been eight good dogs stolen around home since we started having our hunts last fall. They have all been lost along a road or close to a bridge. We have noticed two guys that have always seemed to be at the hunts, but never enter a dog; they do, however, sometimes go out with a cast if they can find anybody to take them. They drive a jeep truck with four wheel drive and mud grips all around. It seems that the stolen dogs all seem to disappear from the same territory where the cast last hunted."

"Who are they and where do they live?" Uncle Bob asked. "And by chance, is one of them pretty fat and short-legged?"

The two men from out of the county exchanged surprised glances. "Why, yes," the one called Mose exclaimed, "but what in the world made you ask that?"

"Because," my uncle answered, "the one who stole King was built exactly like that."

"Now, we are getting someplace," Mose added excitedly, "but we don't know who they are or where they live. No one has ever thought to ask; you know how it is around a hunt, so much going on, and always rushed for time."

"Well," Uncle Bob said, "we have to try to set a trap for them, and I think I can get my club to go along. We will just throw a hunt in a couple weeks, after the season is over, and see if our ads will pull them here; they must have been to our last one. Right now, though, I'm getting a letter off to the American Hound Association with King's tattoo number, description, and picture; also, I'm having about fifty more photos made today to send out to coon hunters all over the country. I'm sending a notice to *Full Cry* with an offer of two hundred dollars reward for his return."

"We will get busy on our end, Bob, just as soon as we get home. We had better head that way right now. Keep us posted and let us know about the hunt; we will be here, and bring some more boys, too. They would all like to be in on catching those dog thieves." Mose rose as he finished speaking and shook hands all around, even with me, then bade us goodbye.

Uncle Bob looked at Steve and Bill, his expression a serious study as he asked, "What do you think of this idea? If those guys show up, we will get someone to invite them to go along on a cast; then while they are still around, we let them overhear some plans for a hunt in that same locality, on say, the following Tuesday night?"

"Sounds good to me," Steve said, "and I sure hope they take the bait."

"So do I," Uncle Bob said grimly. "So do I."

PART TWO

The fifteenth of January slipped by, and with it, the end of the open season on coon. The running season didn't start until the first of February, so my uncle spent that time driving a lot of miles, looking for King. I guess he followed up every lead, no matter how small, but never turned up much. He did find a couple of other fellows who remembered seeing two guys answering the description of the two unknowns who were under suspicion. Too, he discovered that three more dogs had been lost in an adjoining county, in about the same way that he had lost King. His ads had produced nothing as yet, but as he said, those things took time to develop. Uncle Bob was very calm about his loss, but he never was one to show much emotion. I noticed, though, that he hadn't had Queen in the woods since that night; he just seemed to have lost interest in hunting, for the time being.

The hunt was held on the second Saturday night in February. I kept at my mom day and night to let me go. She finally gave in, when my uncle told her that I could help out behind the lunch counter. So, by seven o'clock that night, I found myself a very busy boy, helping to dish up soup, and setting out coffee and sandwiches. I was so busy, in fact, that when I did get a chance to slow down and look around, I was surprised at the size of the crowd. There must have been a hundred men in the room. I saw the two men who were in Uncle Bob's store that Saturday morning talking to him and Bill over by the front door. They were all casually watching everyone who came in.

I guess it wasn't more than five minutes after that, when I saw the friend of my uncle's, called Mose, suddenly stiffen and stare intently at two men who had appeared in the open doorway. Then, as if he hadn't noticed them at all, he resumed his conversation with the others, but I saw him incline his head just a hair towards them. Just as casually, my uncle and Bill took a glance and then looked away. I'm afraid, though, that I couldn't have looked away if I had wanted to. I had built up a mighty strong dislike for the thieves who had stolen King and beat me out of my pup. I sure wanted to see what they looked like.

Maybe a dog thief doesn't have to look any certain way, but I thought they did, and in my estimation, these two fit the bill. One of them was short, fat, and dirty looking, with about a two days' growth of heavy black beard. He wore greasy overalls, an old mackinaw, and had topped his big fat head off with an old slouchy felt hat. The other guy was what I call a rat of a man, normal size, though maybe on the skinny side a little. He didn't appear to be any cleaner than the fat one, but he was wearing somewhat better clothes, or maybe his clothes just fit a little better; at least, he presented a better appearance, that is, with the exception of his eyes. They looked just like a weasel's, and were just as black and vicious looking. He, too, was wearing overalls, but with a leather jacket and cap.

Right off, I named them Hog Jowl and Weasel Face. Oh, I didn't know, of course, that they were really the ones who had stolen King, but they looked like what I thought a dog thief ought to look like. So, as far as I was concerned, they were already convicted, and I was choosing their penalty.

They eased back through the crowd, stopping now and then to look around, as if searching for somebody, but they mostly seemed to be just listening to the hum of conversation going on about them. Slowly, they made their way back to the lunch counter and each ordered a cup of coffee.

I hated to wait on them, but I hadn't much choice. I did manage, however, to accidentally spill some hot coffee on Weasel's hand as he reached for his cup, and I got a little satisfaction out of that, at least. He didn't say anything, though he did grunt a little, and turned his mean little old eyes on me for a second or two. About then, Hog Jowl muttered something about a punk kid, and steered him to a small table over to the side along the wall.

Things had let up around the feed mill by that time, so I went over to where Uncle Bob, Steve, Bill, and the other two men were standing. My uncle was saying, "Now, Bill, we will try to work it so that they can go along on the cast that you're judging. I want you to take them to the Martin Bridge and go east toward Beam's. They will know that is an easy place to get hold of a dog. While you are there, casually mention, once or twice, that you have a date to hunt those bottoms again Tuesday night. Brag your dogs up a little and don't fail to mention that they are Registered Redbones and worth a lot of money."

"Don't worry," Bill replied, "I will have them drooling for old Kate and Tom. And you know something? I'm really going to enjoy helping to set a trap for those skunks. Maybe I can just sorta bump one of them off of the slate bluff into that deep water; that fat boy would sure make a splash, wouldn't he?"

"Don't you dare do that," Steve spoke up quickly. "He might not be able to swim, and we don't know for sure that he is a dog thief, and besides, from the looks of him, he would probably contaminate the water."

"No, Bill," my uncle said laughingly, "don't do that, save him for me. Now I'll make them welcome, and see what I can do about getting them to ask about going along on a cast."

He started slowly through the crowd in the general direction of Hog Jowl and Weasel Face, stopping, now and then, to speak to others along the way.

As he left, Steve said, "Bob is sure taking this mighty easy like, but he never was one to get very excited or to make threats. Just the same, I would sure hate to be in those guys' shoes if he does get the goods on them."

I was afraid to follow my uncle to their table, for fear that I might spoil everything by my inability to hide my dislike for Hog Jowl and Weasel Face. So I went back to the lunch counter, where things were not too busy. Just then, I realized that I could hear a little of their conversation, enough to hear Uncle Bob ask them if they were going to enter any dogs in the hunt.

Hog Jowl said that they didn't have their dogs with them. They hadn't known there was going to be a hunt or they would have sure brought them along. They were just in that part of the country on a hay-buying trip, and happened to hear about the hunt while eating lunch at a local restaurant. Since they were laying over for a day or two, they had just decided to come down and soak up the atmosphere awhile.

Hog Jowl's voice was like a rasp on the nerves, too loud, and his attempts to act the good-natured fat man made me sick to my stomach. I just couldn't see how my uncle could sit there so friendly like, and listen to him bellow, when I felt as if my red hair and freckles lit up like a Christmas tree every time I looked at Hog Jowl or Weasel.

Weasel didn't seem to be taking much part in the conversation, just dropping a question now and then. Mostly, he just listened, while he turned those mean little black eyes on everybody in the room. It was as if he wanted to make sure that he wouldn't forget what they all looked like. His actions weren't lost on Uncle Bob. Every once in awhile, his clear blue eyes would grow frosty cold and he would turn his head away for a moment, until he could get some warmth back into them.

It was getting on towards 8 o'clock, and since Uncle Bob was to be Master of Hounds, I knew that he couldn't spend much more time with those two. It was nearly time to draw out the casts. As soon as I saw him get to his feet, I went over to where Steve and Bill were standing. I knew he would have to tell them the results of the conversation.

"It's all set," he said, as he came over. "They took the bait. I told them that I would try to find a judge willing to take them along. So, Bill, let's go over and introduce you."

Things happened pretty fast after that, and before I knew it, the casts were all drawn and had gone to the woods. The few who were still at the club house took a break for awhile, before starting the posting of men and dogs on the board. Uncle Bob sat down with a sigh, as if he was really tired.

"Jody," he said, "that big guy is all mouth and no brains, but that slim-faced one is the one to watch; he does the thinking for those two; he's sharp, and I sure hope that we didn't overplay our hand. Another thing, too, I have a feeling that he could be real mean if he took a notion, and that's all right, too." That was a tone of voice I had never heard my uncle use before. I knew what Steve meant when he said he wouldn't want to be in those guys' shoes, if Bob found out for sure that they were the ones.

Since it would be about four hours before the casts would be in, I accepted my uncle's offer to take me home. The only important part of the hunt, as far as I was concerned, had already taken place. Besides, if I got home early, Mom would be more likely to let me go with Uncle Bob the next Tuesday night.

Each day, I stopped at the store and learned by listening to the men just what their plans were. Bill and another fellow were going to turn loose at the Martin Bridge at 7:30 and start upriver. They would each have two dogs. They were taking a chance, of course, on hitting a coon that was going the wrong way, but for some reason or other, about nine out of ten of them seemed to run east from there, and on this, their whole plan rested.

They figured that, on a hot track, the dogs could make the Beam's Bridge in fifteen minutes or less. By turning loose at 7:30, they shouldn't hit anything too cold. They would come right upriver as fast as they could. If the thieves were there and anything did happen, it would all be over anyway, before they could get there.

Bill had mentioned, while on the hunt and within Hog Jowl's hearing, that he was supposed to meet the other fellow there at 7:30, so they knew that the thieves would be at the other bridge waiting. Uncle Bob, Steve, and Rex Homer, a deputy sheriff, would be up at the Beam's Bridge, waiting, too. They were going early, about 6:30, so as to have plenty of time to take their positions before Hog Jowl and Weasel arrived. Another club member, Glen, was to drive them there, and then take the car away, but would return at 8:30. As they unfolded their plans, I knew something they didn't. There would be one more person along that night; for someway, somehow, I just had to be there.

After thinking it over, I decided not to say anything to my uncle about wanting to go, and when Tuesday night came, I would just sort of wander over there, and act like it was understood that I was to be a member of the party. Once I was there, I felt pretty sure of my ability to talk him into letting me go. With that decision taken care of, I turned my thinking to how I was going to get around Mom. I couldn't lie to her, and yet, if she knew the purpose of the trip, she would, most definitely, not let me go. She would say that I might get hurt, and carry on just as if I was a little kid. So I would have to trick her a little bit.

When Tuesday night rolled around, I was on pins and needles. Mom and I finished supper about 5:30, so I immediately went to my room and slipped into my insulated underwear, putting my regular every day clothes back on over them. I hoped that she didn't notice that I had on my boots, but she would not be suspicious of my hunting coat and cap, as I wore them quite often, anyway. I slipped my big flashlight into the tail of my coat and prayed that it would not attract too much attention, although it did poke out some, both front and back.

Luck was with me, for as I sailed out of my room and entered the kitchen, I caught her with her back to me, as she stood at the sink, washing dishes. I fairly flew across the kitchen to the back door, and as I started out, I called, "Bye, Mom, I'm going over to Uncle Bob's a little while."

I felt a little guilty as I went out without waiting for her to answer, but as I hurried through the yard, she came to the door and called after me not to stay too long. I answered back, "Okay, Mom," and made tracks for my uncle's. So far, so good; now all I had to do was to convince him that he really needed me tonight or something like that.

The closer I got to his house, the more worried I became that he might not take me along. I didn't feel so sure now that I would be able to persuade him. By the time I arrived, and saw Steve's and Bill's cars in front of the house, I had worried myself into becoming convinced that I would not be allowed to go along. So I felt kinda sheepish, when I opened his front door and let myself into the middle of the session that was going on in the front room. In fact, after I was in, the thought struck me that maybe I ought to turn around and run right out again. All I managed to do, though, was to stand there inside the door and grin like a possum, but I hoped it was like a brave-looking possum.

The three of them just looked at me for several seconds, without expression, and then Steve looked at Uncle Bob with a grin, and Bill burst out with a big laugh, and said, "See, what did I tell you?"

My uncle didn't bat an eye, as he asked me, "Well, what took you so long? I had begun to think that we would have to go off without you."

I breathed then, for the first time since entering the room. I had never felt so grown up as I did right then. There didn't seem to be any need for me to answer, and I don't believe I could have anyway, for I was sort of choked up.

Just then, a car horn sounded out front, and my uncle said, "There's Glen now, so we might as well get started." In the car with Glen was the deputy sheriff.

Bill said, "See you at the bridge, fellows; good luck," and entered his own car to go pick up his hunting partner, Earl.

As the rest of us crawled in with Glen, the deputy, Rex, turned to my uncle, and asked, "Did you guys bring your guns?"

Uncle Bob nodded and made no comment. It was then that the full seriousness of this undertaking finally got through to me. With all my grown-up thirteen years, I had a fleeting moment of panic, and a tiny wish that I was back home with Mom. It was such a safe feeling, though, to be with these men, so I put my fears aside, and settled back to listen to their final plans.

It only took fifteen minutes to get to the river and Beam's Bridge. Glen waited long enough for us to unload, and then took off at once, saying as he left, "See you at 8:30. Good luck."

It was just getting dark, about 6:15, as I followed the others to the foot of the ridge that lay east of the road and about a hundred feet back from the river. The small trees were thick enough to conceal us, and at the same time, clean enough to move around in a little. Since they were sassafras, there were no small limbs low down to block our view of the road and bridge. The moon was already up and a little more than half full, so we were able to see pretty well all over the bottom.

As we made ourselves comfortable on a small log, Uncle Bob put his hand on my shoulder, and said, "Now, Jody, you are to stay right here, and don't move unless I tell you. Okay?"

"Okay," I answered, feeling mighty proud to have been trusted and talked to just like a grown-up.

The night was fairly warm for the last of February. I was very comfortable, as I sat there and listened to them make one last check on their plans, while we waited for the ones under suspicion to show up.

They were going to wait until the thieves were actually in the act of loading a dog, before making their play. Bill and Earl were to turn loose at 7:30. The deputy was to see that they did not drive their truck away, and to place them under arrest after they were caught. Since I was under strict instructions to stay in the thicket until everything was over, they just didn't include me in their plans, at all. Steve and Uncle Bob were to converge on the dognappers as quickly as possible, and take them without any trouble, and if not, to take them any way they could.

There wasn't much traffic on that road at any time, and tonight, there didn't seem to be any. About 6:45, we heard a car approaching from the north, and as we all sat there, it went on past; probably just a farmer on his way home from town.

About ten minutes later, we heard another one coming from the same direction. There was something different about this one, we all felt it. It came down the hill slowly, the headlights picking out the bridge as it hit the level and started across the stretch to the bridge. It was a jeep, half-ton with a boxed-in bed. We knew at once, that this was it. The thieves had taken the bait.

PART THREE

Nobody said a word, as it came to a stop just short of the bridge, and we heard the motor die. They turned out their lights and just sat there. It stayed there only a few minutes, though, and then started up again, pulling ahead over the bridge. My heart sank.

"They must be suspicious," Steve whispered. "Do you think they are scared off?"

Uncle Bob held up a hand, "Wait a minute now, they may come back." Sure enough, we could see the headlights swing around across the curve and bottom, south of the river, and back, they came.

Slowly, the truck crept up over the arched span of the bridge and down the side next to us, then to the left of the road, and to a stop. No sound for a minute. We could see the vehicle quite well, and as we all glued our eyes to its bulk, the door on the driver's side opened and someone got out; then another one from the right side, and I could tell by his size and waddling gait that it was Hog Jowl. The other figure then, being much smaller, had to be Weasel Face.

Hog Jowl went around the front of the truck to stand beside Weasel. We could see him gesturing down towards the river where it joined the bluff. We were too far away to understand what they were saying. There was just stillness in the air, blended with a slight mutter.

There wasn't anything the men could do, but sit still and watch, waiting for 7:30 to roll around, and with that, Bill and Earl would be turning their dogs loose, heading them upriver. In whispered tones, they brushed up their plans. Uncle Bob reached in a pocket of his hunting coat, and when he opened his hand, the objects in it glistened brightly in the moonlight.

"Here, Rex," he said to the deputy, "maybe you had better reload with these; they are armor-piercing."

Rex took the glistening .38s from him, and studied them a moment, before he answered slowly, "I see what you mean, Bob; if they try to get away in the truck, one of these through the block will stop it dead."

"That's right," my uncle replied grimly. "We can't take a chance on their getting away," and as an afterthought, "Steve and I will leave that up to you; we won't show our guns unless we have to."

"That's the best idea," Rex answered. "One other thing, too, when we start out there, let's move fast, the more we surprise them, the easier it will be to take them without any trouble."

I had already received my orders to stay put, so they didn't include me in their plans. I just sat there listening, trying not to notice the quivering inside me, and the fact that my legs felt like jelly.

The two guys were still standing beside their truck, talking in low tones. As we watched, though, the big fellow went around to the back end, opened the door, and lifted out what appeared to be a box. He placed it on the ground at his feet and bent over it for a moment. When he straightened up, Steve exclaimed, "Well, I'll be! I believe he has a coon." Then, in the moonlight, we could all see a small object milling around at his feet. Sure enough, from its actions, we knew that it was a coon on a leash.

"Old hands at the game, aren't they?" my uncle whispered. "Well, let's see that they don't get any older at it." The others agreed with an angry mutter, and I felt the jelly in my legs get just a little bit softer.

Rex looked at his watch, and said softly, "7:30, right on the nose; it won't be long now." The men were still, no word was uttered, as we listened and sweated out the minutes, as they dragged by, one by one.

My throat felt so dry that I couldn't have talked if I had wanted to, as I sat with my eyes fixed on that sky-lined ridge to the west, the direction from which Bill would come. Wouldn't they ever hit? I was afraid to breathe, for fear that I would drown out the sound of the strike. Then it came, from out of the vastness of that silent night, the long, deep-drawn bawl of a hound.

"Ah," Uncle Bob's low voice informed us, "there's old Tom." Then a clear tenor mouth took up the chant, and the deep mouth again. Then another and another cut in, and we knew that they had all hit and were coming upriver.

From that point on, I didn't have enough eyes to see or enough ears to hear all that went on. I sure didn't have any time for thinking, for with the first sound of the hounds, old Hog Jowl began to move faster than I would have thought possible. Scooping the coon up in his arms, he headed west across that bottom towards the point where the field, ridge, and river all joined. He covered that hundred yards in nothing flat, and then immediately started back up along the riverbank, making a couple sweeps along the river's edge, and then cut back across the field, straight towards the truck. Reaching there, he quickly picked the coon up and placed it in the box, shut the lid, and slid it back into the truck.

Weasel Face then pulled something from inside the cab. As he turned around, I saw it, even as Rex said angrily, "The dirty rats, that's a gun."

"Bob," Steve whispered fiercely, "what do you think? We couldn't just sit here and let that happen."

Uncle Bob stared at the two figures beside the truck for a moment, before he answered, "No, we couldn't do that; I'm sure, though, that we don't have to worry, a dead dog wouldn't be any good to them."

"But," Steve said angrily, "that must be a gun they have." Uncle Bob raised his hand to slow Steve down, he was about half-raised up off the log, as if he were ready to tear out of that thicket.

"Yes, I think it is a gun, all right, but a very special one, and the Lord knows that I hope I'm right. If I'm wrong, I'll never forgive myself. If anything happens to those dogs, I would never be able to make it up to Bill. It must be what I think it is, so take it easy, we will soon know."

All four dogs were opening steadily now, already about halfway to the bridge, and they hadn't jumped the coon yet. Even I was beginning to see what was going to happen. The jump would be made any minute, and the closer they came to the two waiting men before that happened, the harder they would be running when they got there, and the quicker those dog thieves were going to have to move; and that, of course, would mean that Uncle Bob, Steve, and

Rex would have to move faster, too. Ah, there it was, the jump, just about a quarter mile west of the bridge, and they were coming up that river like a tornado.

There was immediately a flurry of activity around the truck. Weasel got in and started the motor, letting it idle slowly; we could just barely hear it. Hog Jowl took the gun and slid into the roadside ditch just a short distance from the bridge, and squatted down so that his head didn't even show above the edge, on the cornfield side. He was completely hidden from the dogs' view, and directly on the line where he had led the coon back to the truck. Weasel Face was out of the truck, and standing very still, right up against it.

Here they came, out past the end of the ridge and into the stretch of open bottoms, with the bridge only a hundred yards away. They were still under the riverbank and out of our sight. Their chorusing was one continuous roll of music in our ears. It seemed to blanket the whole river bottom until every single, solitary, living thing within hearing was surely holding its breath just to listen.

Up over the bank poured two boiling geysers of dog flesh, breaking away from the others; they had found the lead coon's hot track. Sweeping wide, they made one pass at the field and then back to the bank, where they came on with a rush. A short overrun, where Hog Jowl had tickled the water's edge a little with his coon's feet, and then they were down there for a short distance, right on top of the other two, then they all came on together. A solid pack bunched close, two blues and two reds, sounding as one, with a wildness to their tone that I could liken to only one thing; something that I had once heard an Old Timer say, "Like a tom cat clawing its way out of hell."

Cold chills were running over me, and I was too paralyzed to shiver. I was as still as a knot on my log. I only half-heard Steve say, "That's Kate in front," and then they were practically overrunning the ditch. I wanted to hide my eyes, but I couldn't move.

As if in a dream, I saw Hog Jowl rise up like a big, ugly, dark cloud right in front of that roaring pack of hounds. As he stood in the ditch, only his body from the waist up was above the level of the field, as he raised the gun and fired point blank at the lead dog. I say fired, but if there was any sound, I didn't hear it, but the sharp cry of a dog in pain was easy enough to hear, and with that, the rest fell silent and swung wide away.

All, but one; it staggered but a few steps, and then collapsed not over five feet from where Hog Jowl stood feverishly trying to reload the gun. Again, through the pounding in my ears, I heard Steve's voice cry hoarsely, "Kate's down, Kate's down," and then stopped as our horror-stricken eyes beheld a red demon's wild fury to revenge the striking down of his mate. The proof of one dog's love for another. It was payment in full for Hog Jowl, for all the dogs struck down by him in the past, and in a manner that left me shaking for hours.

Though he had veered away with the others at the sight of the man, Big Tom had immediately swung back to Kate's side at her first cry of pain, and was licking her face when she fell. Standing over her inert form, he was nudging her with his nose, when the fat man's frantic movements caught his attention. His decision was made from the instant he raised that big head. Maybe instinct or maybe just the smell of that dirty figure in the ditch, but somehow, he connected Kate's trouble with the man that stood before him, and he exploded.

With a savage growl, that red devil launched his seventy pounds straight at Hog Jowl's face. There was a scream of terrifying agony, as man and dog both went down out of sight in the ditch. "My God, let's get down there," my uncle's voice rang out, and all three men left the thicket on the run.

I tried to get up, but my legs wouldn't hold me. I could only sit there, with my eyes locked on that weird scene that was to haunt my dreams for many nights to come. The roaring of Big Tom and the screams of Hog Jowl rose in high crescendo from that roadside ditch. Uncle Bob and the others closed in rapidly on the melee.

Weasel Face seemed stunned by the unexpected turn of events. At first, he didn't even move, and then, suddenly, he darted to the edge of the ditch, where he danced around a bit above those combatants in the mud. But he was to get no chance to help his partner. Though he was facing away from the running men bearing down on him, some second sense must have sounded a warning. When they were no more than thirty feet away, he became aware of their approach.

With a startled turn of his head, he took in the situation at a glance, and at once, forgot all about the plight of his buddy in the ditch. Like an arrow, he dived for the truck and slammed it into gear.

Steve, who was in front of the running men, paid no attention to Weasel or the truck, but hurtled on past, and right into the ditch, as he yelled, "Tom, Tom, let loose, boy, let loose." Somehow, that voice reached through, that familiar command, that had in the past, taken him off of many a coon, penetrated the dog's wild fury, and his attack ceased as quickly as it had started.

Some of this I got from Steve, for there was so much action at the track, that my eyes were mostly riveted there. As Weasel Face slammed the truck into gear and released the clutch, Rex, who was in front of Uncle Bob by several feet, jumped to the side. As the vehicle shot forward, it found Bob still in the middle of the road, without a chance to get out of its path.

A blast from a .38 crashed over that mad scene, and I went over backwards off my log. Terror lent strength to my muscles at last; my back had hardly touched the ground before I was up and tearing out of that thicket. I hardly realized that I was running towards the others, but before me I saw the truck motionless, steam and hot oil fumes pouring from its hood. Then the door on the right side opened, and Weasel Face shot out on the run, right towards me, just as the tall, lanky figure of my uncle dashed across to head him off.

I pulled up short, and for an instant, we were all three motionless, the two men facing each other, and me about ten feet behind Uncle Bob and a little to the side. Then there was a click and a glitter in the moonlight. A wicked switchblade knife appeared in Weasel's hand. Holding it low, he advanced on my uncle. With a snarl on that pointed face so full of hate, I mentally apologized to the weasel clan right then and there.

Without thinking, someway, somehow, I found myself pushing the switch on my new flashlight, and turning the full impact of its six batteries directly into Weasel's beady eyes. He staggered back, as if from a blow, one hand going up in a feeble effort to ward off that blinding glare, and then, he knew no more.

The break that Uncle Bob had been waiting for had come and he acted. One of those big, bony fists of his swung from the ground, and literally lifted the skinny form of Weasel off his feet and slammed him to the ground fully six feet away.

My legs gave out, and I sat down right there where I was, at the edge of the road. Dazed, I watched my uncle walk back to Weasel's inert form and kneel down beside him. Taking his face in his hand, he carefully moved the head a little, and I heard a big sigh of relief, as he said in a voice that trembled, "Thank God, I was afraid that his neck was broken. I didn't mean to hit him that hard, but I guess I just lost my head, with him pulling that knife on me and all."

Rex was standing beside him by that time and put his hand on his shoulder, as he said, "Don't worry, Bob, it's good that his neck isn't broken, but if it was, he would have gotten no more than he deserved."

My uncle shook his big grey head and said, "No, Rex, he wouldn't have deserved that, but I do believe his jaw is broken."

Rex knelt and felt of Weasel's jaw, moving it back and forth just a little. "Yep, it's broken, all right. It will be a long time before he forgets this night's work."

Feeling was beginning to come back into my legs by then, so with the second attempt, I managed to get to my feet. I was a little wobbly, but at least I was up, and I hoped that the others hadn't seen me collapse there in the road. If they did, they never mentioned it. Instead, Uncle Bob turned to me, and placing his hand on my head, said softly, "Jody, that was real smart, thinking to turn your light in his eyes. I was afraid there for a minute, when he pulled that knife, that I would have to use my gun. Thank you, son, for saving me from that; I won't ever forget that, and I'm mighty proud of you."

Such praise coming from my uncle was music to my ears. Later, when the others came around to pat me on the back, I just decided not to tell them that it really wasn't quick thinking, and that I really didn't think at all. In fact, I didn't even know that I was doing it, until it was done.

About then, Steve called from the other side of the truck, "Hey, men, this one sure needs a doctor and quick. He sure has lost a lot of blood." Rex was picking Weasel up when I walked around to Steve's side and saw Hog Jowl. I took one look and was instantly sick. As I wrenched up my insides, that terrible sight kept flashing through my mind. He lay on his back by the side of the road and was moaning pitifully. One side of his big face was laid wide open and the other side had big gaping tears on the lower jaw. Also, the right sleeve was torn out of his mackinaw, and I could see the dark pulpy, bloody mess that had once been a good, big, fat arm.

Weasel Face was still out, as the men worked feverishly over Hog Jowl, who seemed to be in some kind of coma. Removing the bulky coat, they put a tourniquet on his arm and managed to stop the bleeding, but there just wasn't much that they could do for his face. Compresses, torn from their shirts, helped a little, but he was in mighty bad shape. I could tell that the men were plenty worried.

Along about then, I noticed a light coming down the ridge towards the bottom, and realized that it must be Bill and his hunting partner. I had forgotten all about them. In about five minutes, Bill pulled up at the scene, and for a minute, didn't say a word, but just stared in awestricken silence. He looked down at Hog Jowl in disbelief. By then, I was feeling so sorry for him. I found myself wishing that I knew his real name, so that I wouldn't have to think of him as Hog Jowl anymore. It just didn't seem right to saddle a man, who was suffering so much, with a name like that. I didn't hate him anymore.

Bill let out his breath with a shudder. "What in the world happened to him?" The other men looked at each other, seeming reluctant to answer him, but finally, Steve spoke. "Don't ask me to explain, Bill, but Big Tom did that; that's all we can tell you, after he shot Kate."

"Shot Kate!" Bill yelled. "What do you mean, shot Kate? Where is she?"

"Right over there," Steve pointed, and as we all turned to look in that direction, a wonderful sight met our eyes. There stood Kate on her feet, with Old Tom beside her, nuzzling her.

Bill crossed the ditch to her, at once. Uncle Bob bent down into the ditch, and picked up the gun that the injured man had used. Turning his flashlight on it, he examined it closely before he spoke, "Well, I never saw one like it before, but I know what it is. I believe, though, that this is a homemade job; took a pretty good gunsmith to do it, at that." Rex finished handcuffing Weasel to the front bumper of the truck, where he sat slumped over, not quite himself yet, then he joined the rest of us in our examination of the gun my uncle held.

"Uncle Bob, what kind is it?" I asked. "And how come he was able to shoot Kate and lay her out, and yet, not kill her?"

"Jody," he answered, "this is a tranquilizing gun; it isn't made for killing, but only to immobilize for a few minutes. You see, it shoots a little dart that is something like a hypodermic needle. I'm not sure just how it works, but the stuff that knocks the dog out is carried in the dart, and injected into the animal when it strikes."

Steve knelt down and began going through the fat man's mackinaw pockets, as he said, "Maybe we can find one to see what they look like." Ah! He did. One hand held up a small glittering, silver-colored object, a little slim needle-looking thing, with a bulge at the back end.

Holding it carefully, he took hold of the sides and pushed back. A small amount of fluid shot from the end. "See," he said, "this one works on a spring that is depressed when it strikes and the dope is forced out."

"But what shoots it out, Uncle Bob?" I asked. "Well, now," he drawled, "I think that if we search a little further through this guy's pockets, we can find some gas shells." Sure enough, another pocket yielded up just what he had predicted, and the mystery of how they were able to steal so many dogs was solved. The answer of King's disappearance was here before us.

PART FOUR

Bill had come back across the ditch, with Tom and Kate on a leash. In his hand was one of those shiny little darts. "This was in her shoulder, and it must work just like you say. Kate is still plenty wobbly." He looked down at poor old Hog Jowl and shuddered. "I find it hard to believe that Tom did this; he is a gentle dog. Those things only happen in the movies, not in real life, and especially not with a hound."

"Well, it did this time, Bill, and that's for sure. When Tom saw what happened to Kate, he just went wild, as wild as any animal in the jungle. It was as if he had reverted, all at once, to something ten thousand years out of his past. Who knows what genes lie around in our makeup, inherited from ancestors of prehistoric times, just waiting to be called into use when some action out of the ordinary is required of us?" Rex spoke in an awed voice, that left all of us silent for awhile, as we thought about what he had said. For me, the night had taken on an added chill, and I felt the need to draw just a little closer to the others. I didn't understand much of what he meant, but the others seemed to, so I nodded my head, right along with them.

Earl, Bill's friend, had just come up to the truck. He had been up the river to catch his dogs because they had wandered off and were trailing above the bridge. He had them both, two big blues, long-eared, big-headed, and beautiful. Earl Wells was his name. I had seen him around my uncle's store a few times, but I didn't know him as well as I did the others. He only stared, at first, just as Bill had, before he croaked out, "My Lord, what happened to that man?"

When the story was told, he shook his head, and said, "I can't imagine Old Tom doing that to anybody. Why, I have never even heard him growl at anyone. I've seen men killed in combat that didn't look any worse than he does."

They had placed the hurt man's coat under his head to keep it out of the mud, but he still didn't seem to know anything. Uncle Bob spoke in a worried voice, "I wish that we had told Glen to come back sooner. I'd sure like to get this man to the hospital." Holding his watch up to the light, he said, "Fifteen after eight, fifteen more minutes yet."

It was hard for me to believe that it was not later than that. So much had happened, that it seemed hours and hours had passed, since we had first heard the dogs open down at the Martin Bridge. It had really only been a half hour.

We noticed a movement from Weasel, and all eyes turned on him. The little rat was awake at last; that mean face glared like a cobra's. He started to snarl, but with a grimace of pain, he seemed to realize, for the first time, that his jaw was broken, so he gave that up and just slumped there, glaring his hate.

Uncle Bob stepped over to him and asked, "Can you talk?" He got no answer. Kneeling down, he fastened those cold, blue eyes on that evil face and spoke slowly, in a hard, flat voice. "Listen, mister, you are in the fix you're in because you stole my big Walker, right here in this very spot. You will talk in time, for I mean to have that dog back, and you're going to help me. I don't know what the law will do to you, but I do know what I will do, if you don't cooperate. I'll wait until I know you are able, and then you will talk, one way or another." With that, he rose and turned his back on Weasel. Every man there knew that he meant what he said, and that Weasel understood, could be read on his face.

The men were growing more worried by the minute about Hog Jowl's condition. They kept looking up the road towards town, hoping, as I was, to see the lights of an approaching car. He had lost so much blood, and it was still oozing from under the compresses, but not nearly so fast now.

A little before 8:30, someone exclaimed, "I believe he's coming," and all eyes swung to the hill in time to see the first glimmer of headlights. In seconds, the car topped the crest and started down, its lights picking us out, bathing us in their ghostly glow, as we stood grouped around the truck.

It was Glen, all right, and in Rex's car. They had planned it that way, so that a radio would be available in case it was needed, and it was. No sooner had the car pulled up, than Rex was at its side, calling for an ambulance and making arrangements for an emergency at the hospital.

In the seven minutes that it took the ambulance to arrive, Glen heard the story and was shocked, just like the rest of us.

Soon the ambulance came roaring down the hill and drew to a gravel-throwing stop. Hog Jowl was loaded by the attendants, and Uncle Bob climbed in to make the trip back to town with him. It seemed only a minute from the time we saw it top the hill until its taillight faded out of sight, rushing that poor fellow to the emergency care he so urgently needed.

The truck was left on the side of the road right where it was. Steve had the gun and poor Hog Jowl's torn coat. As Rex unfastened Weasel from the bumper of the truck, Bill and Earl loaded three of the dogs in the trunk. Kate would ride inside.

Rex spoke to them, "You fellows get in on each side of him, keep him between you, and watch him close." His hands were handcuffed behind his back, but apparently, Rex didn't trust him, even then.

"It will be a pleasure to keep an eye on him," Bill growled, "but I sure hate to sit next to him."

"Oh, come on, get in," Steve said, "you can burn your clothes tomorrow and get rid of the smell, maybe."

"Yeah, maybe," Bill retorted, but he climbed in without further argument.

I was about to get in the front with Glen, Rex, and Earl, when I thought of something. Asking them to wait, I went around to the right side of the truck and soon found what I was after, the knife. It had been left where Weasel dropped it when Uncle Bob hit him.

Its blade was still open, and my hands felt dirty from just touching it. As I returned to the car and held it out to Rex, Bill asked, "What part did that play?" When he heard, the look on his face caused me to wonder if it was really safe to put him back there with Weasel, after all.

First, we had to go around to the Martin Bridge where the other car had been parked. Earl got out there to follow us to town. Soon, we were out on the highway and only five minutes away from the hospital.

I knew that I should get out at my house when we passed, but no one mentioned it, so I went with them to the hospital. Reaching the hospital, we unloaded and went inside, with the exception of Bill. He stayed by the car to watch Weasel Face. They weren't worrying much about his broken jaw right then.

We filed inside to the waiting room, where we found Uncle Bob talking to the sheriff. He looked at the bunch of us, and asked, "Will you fellows give blood to that poor devil if your type is right? I've had mine checked already, and I'm first if they need it, and the doctor thinks that they will. He hasn't come out of the shock yet."

All the guys agreed, even Earl. I knew they felt just as sorry for him as I did. I wished that I could give, too. When I mentioned it, Steve said, "Shucks, Jody, you're not big enough to have over a pint of blood altogether, and you might need that, especially when your ma gets through with you for slipping out tonight."

All the others grinned at that, and I had a sudden sinking feeling, for I had forgotten all about how I had managed to come along tonight. Uncle Bob must have seen it on my face, for he said, "Boys, maybe I had better take Jody on home and square things with his mother. I'll take Bill's car and be right back."

Somehow, that sounded mighty good to me. The peace and quiet of my mother's company looked mighty inviting, though I wondered if there really would be peace and quiet, especially after she found out what happened.

There was no light on at home, so we passed on to pull up at my uncle's, as he said, "Sarah is probably in here, Jody, so let's go in and get it over with." Sure enough, there sat Mom, and I sure didn't like that look on her face.

"Jody Hawkins," she began, "just wait until I get you home, young man."

Uncle Bob raised a hand and waved her to silence. Mom was his youngest sister, and she often looked to him for advice. She sputtered and was plenty red in the face, but she held her tongue, and waited for him to speak. "Now, Sarah, Jody hasn't done anything so wrong, has he?"

"Wrong," she almost shouted. "He didn't tell me that he was going out with you to catch dog thieves; he just said that he was coming over here."

"Well, now," Uncle Bob said soothingly, "he did just come over here, and then I just took him along, because I thought he might be able to help."

"You mean that you two didn't have that planned?" she asked.

"It's the Gospel truth, Sarah," he answered. "There hadn't been a word said about him going with us; it wasn't planned, at all."

She didn't want to believe him, but she knew, too, that he had never lied to her, so she took another tack. "Help you? Now you don't expect me to believe that you actually thought a knothead like him might be of some help?"

"No, Sarah, I really didn't expect Jody to help us, but he did, and in a way that will forever put me in his debt." Mom was looking very perplexed by this time, but from the tone of his voice, she knew that he was dead serious. "To tell the truth," he went on, "Jody disobeyed me, but I think I know why, for I would have probably done the same thing. I figured on him getting some valuable experience tonight, and he certainly did, but not in the way I had it planned."

I agreed with him there; it wasn't the way I had planned either, and I would never forget that night, not ever.

Mom hadn't given up completely; she made one more feeble attack. "You never said just how he helped you."

Uncle Bob took his time before answering, and when he did, there was silence in the room. Both women seemed stricken speechless. His tone was low and soft, "Sarah, Jody saved me from having to shoot a man tonight; but for his quick thinking, things might have been very bad at the bridge. The thieves are injured badly, but believe me, but for this boy, they would have sure been a lot worse. I have to go back to the hospital now to check on the condition of one of the wounded men. I will probably have to give him a pint of blood, so don't wait up for me, Min. Jody can give you the details."

With that, he was gone, leaving me at the mercy of two mighty excited women. What a trick to play on a little kid. Both of those women were at me at once, wanting to know everything that happened, until I couldn't think straight. It seemed that everything I said left them more confused than ever, and they fired questions at me so fast that I didn't know who was asking what.

"Did you catch the thieves?"

"Yes, both of them, only I didn't catch them, they did."

"Who are they?"

"Oh, Uncle Bob, Bill, Rex, Steve, Earl, Glen. Only they didn't catch Hog Jowl first, Tom did."

"Tom? I didn't know any Tom went along. What do you mean; he caught Hog, HOG JOWL? Who's Hog Jowl?"

"Oh, he's one of the thieves and Tom bit him through the face."

"Bit him through the face?" one of them screeched. "My heavens, what kind of a man would do that?"

"He's not a man, and besides, he didn't do that until after he shot Kate."

"Who shot Kate—Tom?"

"No, Hog Jowl."

"KATE! What was a woman doing down there?"

"She's no woman."

"Well, I'll say, she's not. Was she with the thieves?"

"Of course not, she was with Bill and Earl."

"Bill and Earl! My Lord, and them both married."

"Oh, you don't understand. Anyway, when Kate ran up to Hog Jowl …"

"I thought you said she was with Bill and Earl."

"She was, but they couldn't keep up with her."

"I guess not. They're not spring chickens anymore, you know."

"Anyway, they weren't very far behind."

"Well, they will wish they had been when their wives hear about this."

"Oh, heck! How can I tell this, if you keep interrupting me? Anyway, Tom was with her and she ran right straight up to Hog Jowl and he shot her."

"My Lord! My Lord! What a thing for a thirteen-year-old to see; a wild woman running all over the river bottoms at night; leaving two men to chase with the third, and then trying to catch the fourth one. By gosh, she should have been shot; good for Hog's Head."

"Not Hog's Head, Hog Jowl; only that's not his real name. I just made that up."

"Jody Hawkins! Do you mean to sit there and say that you made this whole crazy story up?"

"No! No! Just his head, oh, I mean his name. He shot her, but he didn't try to kill her, just stunned her, so that he could carry her away."

"Well, if she was running up to him, she surely wanted to go with him, so there was no need to shoot her."

"Oh, she came to, when Tom licked her face."

"Licked her face! Oh, you poor boy, you were down there with a crazy man."

"Oh, Mom! Well, anyway, Bill came along then, and chained Tom to the truck and picked Kate up to put her in the car."

"Well, if I ever heard of a man that needed chaining, that Tom was the one. You say that Bill put Kate in the car? After she ran off with another man? Oh, his poor wife. Where was Bob all this time?"

"Well, he was running down the hill towards them, for he got mighty mad when Kate was shot."

"Heavens to Betsy! Does he know her, too?"

"My gosh, yes, Aunt Min, he has been out with her lots of times."

By this time, Aunt Min was swooning, while Mom fanned her with one hand, and herself with the other. Finally getting control of herself, she asked in a trembling voice, "Does he seem to like her?"

"Like her? Why you should have seen the way he rubbed her ears."

This time, she passed out like a light. Mom ran for the smelling salts, and waved them under her nose, took a whiff herself, and they started in on me again.

"What happened then?"

"Well, before the others could get to where Tom and Hog Jowl were fighting in the ditch—"

"In the ditch? Well, just where they belonged."

"Anyhow, before they got there, Weasel Face saw them coming."

"WEASEL FACE! Who is that?"

"Oh, he was with Hog Jowl."

"So that's why she was running away from Tom? There were TWO other men."

"Yes, two. Anyway, Weasel jumped into the truck and tried to get away. He didn't try to pick Kate up out of the mud."

"OUT OF THE MUD! Oh, that poor woman, I mean, well, that shows she was driving her ducks to a poor market. Wouldn't even pick her up out of the mud, and after she was shot for trying so hard to get to him, too."

"OH, FOR GOSH SAKES! You're getting me mixed up. So since Uncle Bob was right in the middle of the road, he almost got run down."

"The old goat, chasing a woman at his age, it would have served him right."

"Oh, it wasn't like that. Well, anyway, about then, Rex shot a hole through the block of the truck."

"Where were you all this time?'

"I was in the thicket, but right then, I fell off my log."

"What were you doing on a log?"

"Oh, it was my ringside seat."

"A ringside seat to such carryings on, and you just a child; goodness, this young generation is always interested in the wrong things."

"I guess so, but when the truck stopped just short of running over Uncle Bob, Weasel jumped out and tried to cut him with a knife."

"Cut who?"

"Why, Uncle Bob, of course."

"Oh, my Lord! Was it because he was rubbing this Kate's ears?'

"Gosh, no, Aunt Min, she was still lying in the mud."

"There's that poor woman still lying in the mud."

"I told you she's not a woman."

"And I agree."

"Well, quit worrying about her lying in the mud. So when Weasel tried to knife Uncle Bob, I shined my light in his eyes."

"Whose eyes, Bob's?"

"NO! IN Weasel's eyes."

"You did? From behind your log?"

"NO! NO! From behind Uncle Bob."

"Oh, he was on the log?"

"No, he was in the road."

"Oh! The log was in the road?"

"No! It was in the thicket."

"Well, how did it get in the road?'

"It didn't. I did."

"But you said—"

"I KNOW WHAT I SAID. Then Uncle Bob gave Weasel an uppercut and laid him out."

"In the mud?"

"No, in the road."

"WHAT! He took time to lay that Weasel out in the road and that poor woman still lying in the cold mud?"

"I told you she's not a woman, she's a dog."

"Humph, lower than a dog, if you ask me."

"Then they found out that Uncle Bob had broken Weasel's jaw, but they were afraid that it was his neck. Uncle Bob said that he didn't aim to hit him that hard, but he got so mad when he pulled that knife, and after seeing him shoot Kate and all."

"I'll bet he wouldn't fight over me that way."

"Oh, Aunt Min, stop it. Anyway, that's about all. Glen came with Rex's car, and he called the ambulance so they could get Hog Jowl to the hospital. Then they put Tom and the others in the trunk of Rex's car and Bill held Kate on his lap."

"On his lap? If she was shot, why didn't they put her in the ambulance, too, with Hog's Head?"

"Oh, she was up and reeling around by that time."

"REELING AROUND! Was she drunk?"

"Oh, heck, of course not."

"I'll bet she was; that's why Bill held her on his lap."

"NO, NO, she was just nervous, so Bill kept rubbing her back."

"Oh, my Lord, and right in front of you, too."

"Well, what's wrong with that? I rubbed her some, too."

Mom reeled in her chair and staggered to her feet. "He's ruined for life, and all from letting him run with those coon hunters. I just knew that no good would come of it."

Then, walking kinda tottery, she grabbed my hand and started for the door, saying, "I can't stand anymore. Min, you tell Bob that I'll be over in the morning to give him a piece of my mind."

At the mention of my uncle's name, Aunt Min asked me once more, "Jody, does Bob really like that Kate?'

"Like her! Why, Aunt Min, he told Bill, that if he ever got tired of her, that he would lay out plenty of cash to take her off his hands in a minute."

That did it. Aunt Min gave one big squall and fainted clear out of her chair. Mom ran for the smelling salts again, and I headed for home, before those crazy women could ask me anything else.

PART FIVE

When I reached home, believe me, I lost no time in getting to bed. When Mom came in about ten minutes later, looked in on me and called my name, I wasn't foolish enough to answer. I knew that if I had to answer any more questions that night, I would probably end up asking her what happened. So I really snored up a storm and she must have been fooled, for she pulled my door shut, real easy like, and went away.

It was a long time, though, before I finally dropped off to sleep, to dream that I was riding old Tom across Blue River Bottoms, with a .38 in one hand and a big knife in the other. Ahead of us ran a wild-looking woman, covering the ground in ten foot leaps, while she yelled, "Bill, Bill, come rub my ears."

When I got up the next morning, I found Mom had been over to my uncle's already and had a little better idea about what happened the night before. She didn't say much, just started by asking, "Young man, what did you mean by telling us that a woman was down there?"

That's as far as she got, though, I sounded a little hysterical when I screeched, "But I didn't, you did." With that I grabbed my hat and coat and headed for school. As I left I thought I heard her say, "How could I have told you that when I wasn't even down there?"

Boy, what a kid has to go through if he has a mother to look after.

After school that afternoon, I rushed to the store to learn what had happened and found Uncle Bob in a pretty good mood. He had given blood to the injured man and so had Bill. The man would recover, but would be a long time in the hospital. His face would be horribly scarred for life. The truck that belonged to him would be sold and the money applied towards his hospital bill.

The sheriff had run a check on the pair and found out that Weasel was wanted in Tennessee for cutting a man up real bad with a knife and for robbing a hardware store. It was all arranged for the law down there to come up and get him. He would get a much stiffer penalty for his crimes there than in Indiana. Poor old Hog Jowl wasn't wanted anyplace. It seemed that he was just a tool in Weasel's hands. This was his first step into crime. He was from a little town down in southwestern Indiana and I finally found out his real name. It was Homer, Homer Eugene Catling. Someway he just didn't look like a Homer Eugene to me. Since his arm might never be just right again and he was going to have a hard time from then on anyway, Uncle Bob had decided not to press charges, but to let him go, once he was able. Weasel's name was Rafe Slater and he had spent more time in jail than out, so he wouldn't be missed by anybody. Well, as my uncle said, that sure busted up one dog stealing ring.

My uncle had saved the best news until last. Hog, I mean Homer, had been so grateful to find the charges against him dropped that he had spilled the whole story. They had been selling every dog they stole to a man over in Illinois. He paid them up to fifty dollars each, according to what they looked like. He met them at the state line and the dogs were delivered, not hauled across the state line, but forced to walk across by themselves unassisted. Homer said that they figured to stay clear of a federal charge that way. This guy was a dog dealer, so nobody saw reason to become suspicious of any strange dog that appeared at his place. He also raised dogs himself, so I guess he had himself a real nice setup.

Homer remembered that when they had sold King to this man, the man had remarked what a fine looking hound he was and what a good price he would bring. He might even keep him for himself for awhile. Homer thought that there was a chance that the man might still have King.

Uncle Bob had been mighty busy since finding that out. He had notified the American Hound Association. They had promised to start investigating immediately. He had also wired *Full Cry* for the name of some reliable coon hunters who lived in that vicinity. Once he received the names, he had wired the two most highly recommended that he would be in their town the next day and would appreciate their help. In the mail that day there had been a couple of letters from fellows from over in that part of Illinois. They reported seeing a big Walker entered in hunts there recently that looked a lot like the picture of King that appeared in the magazines.

Steve was going with him and they were leaving before daylight the next morning. He sure was anxious to get going and I found myself wishing that I could go with them, but of course, I knew that was impossible.

So I wished him luck and got out of there so that I could go home and just think about it; how he would make a quick trip, out and back, and would have old King sitting there beside him when he drove up.

It comes easy for a thirteen-year-old boy to count his chickens before they hatch; too easy, as I was to find out. Uncle Bob was gone three days, and on the evening of the third, I was waiting at his house when he and Steve arrived. I was sick with disappointment when I saw right off that King wasn't with them.

I was full to the brim with a thousand questions, but Uncle Bob looked so worried that I held them back as best I could and waited until Aunt Min asked, "Well, what happened; didn't you find him?'

His voice was tired and strained as he answered, "Oh, yes, we found him."

"Well," she demanded, "why didn't you bring him back? Is he all right?"

"Yes, he is fine and in good condition, but I couldn't bring him back this trip. It's just not that simple. Oh, I'll get him all right, but it will take time, so he will just have to stay out there awhile."

"I don't understand," Aunt Min began, but he went on to explain.

"The dealer still had him, but stood there barefaced and tried to tell me that he had raised him, and with King jumping all over all the while. He knew that he was mine. There was no doubt in his mind about that, but he had three big mean-looking boys to back him up. He even had a set of papers that he said belonged to King. I suppose that they were from a dog that is dead. Anyway, I told him that I would be back and that King had better be there when I arrived. He was so sure of himself that I was almost certain he wouldn't try to do anything with him. So we drove back into town and saw the sheriff."

"He was an all right guy. Seems that he had been suspicious of this fellow for a long time, but had never had any proof. I had him call the sheriff here to find out that I was reliable. Roy must have given me a good recommendation, for as soon as he hung up he turned to me with a grin and said, "Mr. Brown, if you will press charges against this man, I will get a Warrant out at once. We will impound the dog and slap this guy under bond until we can get him into court."

"So we went back with the sheriff this time. Over the fellow's loud protests, he was charged and arrested and brought back to town along with King. Of course, as the sheriff had said, he posted bond, but we found a good coon hunter to take care of King. He will be well taken care of until the trial and then I will bring him home."

Steve hadn't said a word until then. "I'll say that you made a friend for life out of that sheriff, Bob, when that loud mouth complained that you had knocked him down."

"Knocked him down!" Aunt Min exclaimed. "Bob, has that temper of yours got you into trouble again?"

Uncle Bob looked embarrassed and seemed a bit reluctant to answer, so Steve chuckled and filled us in.

"You see, after we had listened to this guy tell over and over just how he had raised King, Bob played his hole card, or so he thought. He said, "Mister, that dog has a tattoo in his right ear and one on his flank reading WDBB."

The guy threw back his head and laughed real big and said, "You wanna bet?" That's when Bob threw back King's right ear and that's when one of the boys leveled a shotgun at us."

"Why?" Aunt Min wanted to know.

"Why because he didn't like the looks of his old man lying there on the ground."

"What was he doing on the ground?"

"Well, you see, your husband sorta knocked him there." Uncle Bob wasn't enjoying this, but Aunt Min had to know.

"Why?"

"Now, Min," Steve grinned at her, "I expect that you would have done the same thing. When Bob turned that ear back to show the tattoo, there was nothing but a long white scar, looked like acid had been used to burn off the letters. That's when your old man got just a little peeved. He didn't say a word; just straightened up, drew back and knocked that guy colder than a wedge. Sure was a pretty sight. Wish I had done it."

"Wish I had been there," Aunt Min said, as she patted Uncle Bob on the shoulder, "I would have done it for you."

"Min," he answered grimly, "that's something that I wouldn't have let anyone do for me and I sure did enjoy it."

"You know, Bob," Steve cut in to say, "there wasn't any doubt in that sheriff's mind as to who really owned King, not after he asked who was going to pay the feed bill. This guy who claimed him said that he wouldn't pay one red cent and you pulled out your billfold and handed the sheriff the money, plus enough for a check by a vet. I was watching the sheriff's face. He was convinced, all right. You know, I wouldn't be surprised but what he just did that to test you both."

"Could be," Uncle Bob said, "so now all we have to do is convince a judge and jury."

PART SIX

Time sure did drag its feet for me after that. March faded into April and everybody began to think about the last day of school, even me. It sure was hard to concentrate on my lessons when all I actually wanted to think about was King and whether we would get him back or not.

Oh, I was confident that my uncle would manage it some way; he was a very determined man, but the anxiety was killing me. Mom said that if I didn't make all passing grades so that I would be promoted to High School, I definitely wouldn't be going to Illinois with my uncle when the trial came up. So I got busy, and by the end of May, I had managed to squeak by.

Word had come that the trial would probably come up during the second week in June, so I was really counting the minutes.

Uncle Bob was real pleased with the young lawyer who was going to handle his case. He was an up and coming young fellow, who was highly recommended, and was, of all things, a coon hunter himself. He was being retained by several other people, too. It seemed that everybody wanted to get in on the prosecution of a jobber in stolen dogs. Uncle Bob said that all concerned were agreed on one thing, that it be settled by a trial by jury.

The dog men wanted it because it would attract more attention. More people would become aware of the fact that hound owners were no longer going to take dog stealing, lying down. They were convinced that if they could convict this guy, it would make quite an impression on any would be dog thief. They would realize that it was hardly a paying proposition.

The crooked dealer, with his back to the wall, wanted a trial by jury, too. My uncle figured it must have been because it was all or nothing for him.

That was his home county, he did operate a rather large farm, and he did some legitimate dog business. He was, in fact, enjoying a pretty good living and must have decided that he would have a better chance of clearing his name by trial. He was quite active in politics and carried a lot of weight among the farming people of his community. It seems the farming community just didn't think that he was guilty.

This political angle had my uncle's lawyer worried some because he was afraid that the State's Attorney might be a little reluctant to try for conviction. It was a well-known fact that he was elected because of the efforts made by this one man.

They had expected to have Homer Eugene Catling as a witness, but since his discharge from the hospital, he seemed to have disappeared. Traced to his hometown, they found that he had hung around only a few days and then left without saying a word to anybody about where he was going. He had no family or property there, so nobody actually even knew when he left. I guess the only thing he had owned in the world was that truck, and he no longer had that. It looked like they were just going to have to get by without his help.

Weasel, or rather Rafe Slater, was doing time in Tennessee and had absolutely refused to cooperate, so there didn't seem to be any use in trying to get him here.

The coon hound magazines had given the trial a lot of publicity, and as the time drew near, the newspapers began to pick it up. The hound men had wanted publicity and they were sure getting it.

Of course, the story of how the dog thieves were caught got out and Uncle Bob's store was besieged by reporters for a while. They even came from the big newspapers.

They really played up the part about Tom attacking old Homer

Eugene. Bill had a dozen offers to buy him in one week, some of them from people who weren't even coon hunters. But he would just laugh them off and say, "Nope, not for sale; that's my insurance dog." And when talking to the ones who weren't coon hunters, he would look real sad and say, "Why, folks, if I was to sell that old hound, his mate Kate would just pine clear away. Why it would be just the same as someone selling your husband or wife away from you because it would break her heart for sure."

At that, they would look real shocked, and as they stared at Bill's sad looking face, they would become ashamed and end up apologizing for even suggesting that Bill might sell King. Bill sure had himself a time, but down underneath he was mighty proud of that old Redbone. He was most sincere in saying that he wasn't for sale.

Finally, the long-awaited time arrived. Latest word from the lawyer indicated that the trial would start on Monday, June 4. He had suggested that it would be a big help if Uncle Bob would bring along several men who could identify King. Many of his hunting friends offered to go, but some of them were farmers and it was right in the middle of a very busy time. Late spring rains had held up corn planting and he knew that every day lost from the field could very well cost them their crop, so he just couldn't let them take the chance.

He ended up taking Steve, Earl, and me, plus affidavits from several prominent people around town, including the sheriff and judge. Besides that he had several photographs of King, two of which showed him standing behind trophies he had won. Actually, that doesn't seem like very much, now that I look back on things that happened during the progress of the trial. At the time, armed with honesty and his sincere belief in the good in all men, Uncle Bob had no doubt that he carried with him sufficient proof for convincing any judge and jury that King belonged to him.

We left on Sunday morning, and I, in all the ignorance of my thirteen years, imagined that three or four hours on Monday morning would see it all wrapped up and by Monday night, at the latest, we would be headed back home.

We arrived in the town late that afternoon and took a motel at the edge of town, Steve and Earl in one cabin and Uncle Bob and I in another.

As soon as we were settled a little, my uncle called his lawyer. Soon after that, a car pulled up at our cabin and Uncle Bob went out to greet the driver. It was his lawyer and I liked him right off. A young, energetic, bouncy type of guy, stocky built and with a blond burr haircut. He had the look of an outdoor man.

He greeted Uncle Bob warmly and seemed glad to meet the rest of us. After the introductions, we all went back inside and sorta flopped around on the two chairs and double beds while he lost no time in getting right down to business.

PART SEVEN

A lot of their talk was over my head. He said the Judge who was trying the case was a very fine man, fair-minded and a pretty good judge of people and what made them tick. I'm afraid that I was sleepy from the trip and was dozing most of the time they were talking, but I perked right up when he suggested that we all get in the car and go see old King.

The fellow who was keeping him lived over on the other side of town, so in about five minutes we were there. We found the man working in his front yard and he immediately took us around back to where King was kept. I guess King had already heard Uncle Bob's voice and before we rounded the corner of the house we heard that big bawl of his. He was really going wild as Uncle Bob approached, standing on his hind feet and talking up a storm. Pulling that chain as tight as it would go, he was sure trying to meet him halfway.

Even a person who knew nothing about dogs could have easily told right off that the real owner had stepped up. It brought a lump to my throat just to see those two together, making over each other. I looked at the lawyer, and from the expression on his face, I knew that he recognized the honesty of that scene before him.

Uncle Bob stepped back then and let me make over King for awhile; he acted almost as tickled to see me as he had his master. There was a difference, of course, but I had spent a lot of time with him and he really was happy to see me.

Steve and Earl both petted him and then we started drifting back around to the car while my uncle and the attorney made final plans with the fellow who was keeping him. He was to bring him to the Courthouse the next day and wait until the trial was actually ready to get underway before bringing him over. Our lawyer had said that there might be some delay in selecting the jury, something to do with an attempt to pack the jury, whatever that means. It seems that this crooked dealer had a lot of kinfolk in the county and also plenty of money to spend. With that taken care of, we went back to the motel, ate our supper at the little restaurant,and finally hit the hay for a good night's rest.

We were all up and showered by seven o'clock and after a good breakfast of hot cakes and sausage, we got in the car and drove to the Courthouse in the middle of the town square. It was a big, spacious, three-story limestone building, surrounded by a well-kept lawn. We just sat in the car for awhile, until about eight o'clock. By that time, several men had begun to gather around the steps on the south side and after we had watched them awhile, we began to wonder about their interest in the case.

"Bob," Steve said, "let's mosey up there and see what we can hear."

"Good idea," my uncle answered, so up we went. No hurry, just kinda drifting in that direction and finally lodging on the edge of the crowd.

The talk was all about the trial. It seemed that they were about half and half in their opinions concerning the dealer's guilt. It wasn't hard to pick out the hound men from the rest; they were grouped away from the others and weren't doing nearly so much talking. We soon discovered that part of the group was from out of town and that two of them were officials of the American Hound Association. Uncle Bob introduced himself to them. From then on, they kept him busy going over every detail of the story. Before I knew it, the time had come for us to go inside.

The courtroom was on the third floor. As we climbed those wide stone steps, I felt awfully meek and insignificant amid those sober surroundings. In fact, I had felt that way ever since we had arrived, and for once in my life, I had done more listening than talking. This was so unusual that Uncle Bob had inquired if I was feeling well.

"Oh, I'm feeling fine, Uncle Bob," I answered with a grin.

I think he understood, because he patted me on the shoulder and said softly, "I guess you do at that, so just stick around, you may have to shine your light into someone else's eyes again before this is through."

As we entered the big double doors on the side of the room, I saw my uncle's attorney at a table up front and to the left. He beckoned us toward him. He directed Steve, Earl, and me to the row of seats directly behind the table and took Uncle Bob to the table with him. In a few minutes the two guys from the American Hound Association came in and took seats beside us.

The other man at the table with Uncle Bob and his attorney must be the State's Attorney. He appeared bored with the whole thing, as if trying a case of dog stealing was far beneath him. Somehow, I just didn't feel right about him from the very first. He was too smug, too dapper, and prissy to suit me. I'm sure he couldn't have been over forty years old, but he was already about half bald. From his delicate looking body, lily white hands, and pasty face, with its superior knowing smile, I formed the instant opinion that here was a man who had never been in the woods at night in his life. He would probably be scared to death of a hoot owl's cry. I wondered how such a man could be expected to understand the importance of uniting a man and his dog.

When I looked again at our attorney, I felt a lot better, for there was one who could feel as my uncle did, and would have his whole heart in the case. He was on his toes, too; they didn't get much done the first morning but select a jury, but he objected to three men whom the State's Attorney was going to accept. It was easy to see that they weren't going to agree on a lot of things.

I had been watching the man who was on trial and he didn't seem to be worried at all. He was looking around the courtroom, grinning, with a big-toothed smile and waving to someone here and there. Even his big old smart alec boys were smirking all over the place and looking like three cats that had just eaten a canary.

I even thought that I saw the accused and the State's Attorney exchange knowing looks every once in awhile, but I couldn't be sure. This man and his lawyer were at another table across the front from my uncle. His lawyer was a big-framed man, plenty active, but getting along in years. He was very reserved and all business. What a contrast from his loud-mouthed, pop-eyed, swarthy-complexioned client. I decided that it might be possible for me to like that attorney if it wasn't for the fact that he was against my uncle.

By the time they had selected a jury to everyone's satisfaction, it was time for noon recess, so we followed the crowd out and hunted for a place to eat our dinner.

Court reconvened at one o'clock, but long before that the room was beginning to fill up. There sure was a lot of interest in this case and a lot of those interested parties were hound men.

The trial seemed to drag at first. The jury was informed as to the purpose of the trial, as if they didn't already know. As the State's Attorney explained to them, the accused, Sid Howser, was charged with knowingly being in possession of stolen property, namely one registered Walker coon hound, and aiding and abetting the crime of dog stealing for personal gain. Most of this legal stuff went clear over my head and a lot of it I don't remember at all, just the important things.

Old King had been brought in at the start of things. Some guy they called a bailiff took his chain from the man who was keeping him. He fastened it to the leg of a high old-fashioned desk that sat off at one side of the front. He was, however, in full view of all present. As he was led in past where Uncle Bob sat, he almost jerked the chain from the guy's hand as he pulled suddenly towards Uncle Bob. He was whining and scratching on the old wooden floor and that little old bailiff was sure hard put to hold him, until my uncle spoke two words, very softly, but they took instant effect.

"Quiet, boy," was all he said, but King silenced at once and allowed himself to be led to the desk leg where, as I said before, he was tied. None of this little drama was lost on the jury of nine men and three women, and I noticed that they all seemed to look at each other at the same time. It wasn't lost on the Judge either, for as I glanced at this big grey-haired, elderly man, I noticed that his keen old eyes really lit up behind his spectacles.

The Judge just sat there quietly for awhile, looking at old King as he sat down, facing across the room towards Uncle Bob and managing to look very dignified as he did so.

In fact, I think that everyone in the room took time out to admire that big, beautiful tri-colored hound, with his broad tan head and ears and with that white blaze up his forehead.

King didn't look a bit more dignified, though, than Uncle Bob when they called him to be sworn in. He sat there in complete confidence, his big rawboned figure alert, his iron grey head held high, as he looked directly into the eyes of the State's Attorney and answered his questions in a soft, firm voice.

Honestly, you would have thought that this prissy attorney was the lawyer for the defendant. He was meagerly outlining the case and not giving Uncle Bob too much chance to offer proof of ownership.

Oh, he let Uncle Bob say that he owned him, that he had bought him as a weanling and from whom. He let him tell how he had found out where King had gone after he was stolen and all that kind of stuff, but the questions were asked in such a disinterested monotone, and in such a feeble manner, that even I knew that not a single point was being driven home. The answers that my uncle was allowed to make just weren't the kind to really impress a jury.

As Steve later said, the attorney was a slick one, all right. He seemed to be doing his job, but there was just something missing from his attitude. When he called Steve, Earl, and me to the stand, in that order, it was the same way. He just sort of washed over us all lightly as if we were dirt which he had to clean from his hands in a hurry.

Honestly, the defendant's lawyer was giving us a better chance to express ourselves. He listened to our answers patiently and with interest. He seemed to treat me very kindly and I couldn't help thinking that he really wanted this trial to come out the way it should. But he had plenty of tricks, gained from years of experience, and right then he pulled one from the bag, as he addressed the jury:

"Ladies and gentlemen, you have heard Mr. Brown testify that he is the rightful owner of this dog. A beautiful hound, we will all agree and one, that I will admit, any hound man would be proud to own. You have heard him say that the dog was tattooed in the right ear and flank, but now the tattoo is gone, removed, he states, by acid."

There was a hum in the courtroom and the Judge toyed with his gavel, but the noise died off with the shifting around of bodies hunting for a softer place on their bench, and the attorney continued:

"You have heard testimony by friends of Mr. Brown, declaring his ownership of this hound. But I must repeat, they are friends and it's not likely that he would have brought with him anyone with contrary opinions on this matter. These witnesses who have testified in Mr. Brown's behalf are, I believe, sincere in their opinions that this dog really is the property of the plaintiff. But isn't it just possible that they could be mistaken and this hound is one that just happens to look like the dog that Mr. Brown claims was stolen from him? Isn't it possible that they have all just made an honest mistake?"

At this, there was a distinctly growled NO from Steve, which caused a ripple of chuckles from the group of hound men, and the old Judge again reached for his gavel, but as before, they quieted down and the lawyer continued:

"After all, it has been several months since the supposed theft took place, but where are the two men he says he caught, especially the one who is supposed to have pointed the finger at my client, Sidney Howser, as the buyer of stolen dogs? They are not here and he says that he can't produce them. Wouldn't you say now that such a coincidence as that is just a little hard to believe? Now maybe Mr. Brown is sincere in his belief that this is the dog that is supposed to have been stolen. Maybe he really thinks so because it actually does look like his dog. Hounds of a particular breed have a way of looking like peas in a pod, in color, size, and conformation. A study of any bench standards will show you this. So right now, ladies and gentlemen, I'm going to ask you all to leave the room for just a few minutes, then you will be called to return to your seats."

Boy, this guy really had everyone's attention now. All eyes were on the jury as they filed out. No sooner had they gone, however than this wise old lawyer motioned towards the back of the room. Then we all saw what he was up to.

The doors opened and in came two men leading five big tri-colored Walkers. They brought them right down front; King was loosened from the table leg and led over to join the pack, his chain now in the hands of the man who had led in only two of the dogs. They milled around, as dogs will when introduced to a stranger, until they had King in the center of the huddle.

Now the jury was recalled. As the jurors took their seats, they all gazed in open-mouthed amazement at that pack of dogs. I had to admit that they sure did look alike, even down to a few ticks here and there, just like King. The attorney took his time, just letting the jury's eyes soak up those peas in a pod. Then finally, he turned to them.

"Ladies and gentlemen, there was but one dog here when you were asked to leave the room, now there are six. Six hounds, ladies and gentlemen, and each one an exact replica of the others. Can any of you pick out the dog that was here before you went out? Can you choose, with absolute certainty, the exact dog?"

There was complete disbelief written on their faces. Puzzled expressions dominated the group as they looked those dogs over. I could see that not one of them was sure which was King.

I wanted to shout, "Can't you tell? That's him, the proud looking one in the middle, the one with the little brown spot on the back of his right front leg." It sure was hard to keep still.

As all eyes in the room rested on them, the jury members tried, but it was just no use. One by one, they looked at the defendant's lawyer and shook their head. As the last one indicated that he didn't know, the defense attorney laughed and motioned the men to take the extras away. Handing King's chain to the bailiff, they led their charges from the room.

I could see his point. Being normally alert and intelligent men and women, he was counting on a perfectly human reaction from them and that's exactly what he got. Strong doubt had been planted firmly in their minds. Without hound knowledge, no one could have told correctly which was the right dog. It was their sincere belief that if they couldn't tell, then it was unlikely that anyone else could tell. I guess it was only natural for them to have that much confidence in their own powers of perception.

It would have done no good for our lawyer to have asked that Uncle Bob be allowed to pick King out. It would have been pointed out that since Mr. Brown and his associates were obviously hound men and had their eyes on that particular dog, it would be most likely that they could tell at once which one he was. Besides, we had been in the room when the others had been brought in. He had covered every trick in that hand. He never did really try to get them convinced that Uncle Bob was actually lying, but only mistaken.

Now that the doubt was planted, he worked fast. Calling the defendant to the stand, he got right on with picturing him as an honest, hardworking farmer, who bred dogs as a hobby because he liked them so much. He stressed the fact that he was also a local man and one whom many of those present had known for a long time. He almost cried when he described the wrong done him by my uncle's charges. Again, he reminded the jury of the fact that the two men who had supposedly stolen the dogs had not been produced. Further still, that our side had no intention of ever producing those two mythical dog thieves.

When the State's Attorney had his turn at old Sid Howser, it was downright sickening. He practically apologized for having to question him. Even the Judge was beginning to look rather strangely at this lawyer's thinly-veiled farce of attempted prosecution. My uncle's attorney was so mad that his face was white.

In fact, the hound men in the crowd were beginning to mutter among themselves and one of the fellows from the American Hound Association said right out loud, "What kind of a prosecution is this?" There was a distinct uttering of opinions from men who had overheard his remark and all in agreement.

The Judge's gavel hit his bench hard and he sternly informed them that he had given his last warning. Right then, nobody, least of all me, knew he was to do that a whole lot sooner than he thought.

Next, they had the defendant's mean-looking boys on the stand. One by one they sat up there and lied through their teeth. The last one really got me. He smirked all over the place and said that he couldn't blame anyone for trying to get that dog, old Rover, he called him. He told how he had worked so hard to train him, just so his Pa could have a really outstanding coon hound. Then he declared, in a loud raspy voice, that nobody from Indiana was going to get away with claiming him.

That did it. Something within me snapped and I just didn't use any sense at all; in fact, I didn't use anything but my mouth. Before I could stop myself, I felt my body jump up and my mouth fly open and heard myself yelling.

"You're a liar, that's my uncle's dog, aren't you, King?" At the sound of his name old King went into action. That little old bailiff ought to have known better than to tie a big dog like him to that weak old desk leg, at least one so high. Recognizing my voice, King was at the end of that chain like a thunderbolt, one loud bawl breaking from him as he moved. The chain jerked tight with a snap and there was nothing strong to stop him.

That weak old desk leg came loose like a piece of kindling wood and King swept towards me. My Lord, it seemed like everything fell in slow motion before my horrified eyes. The desk came down with a crash. The little old bailiff, who was occupying a high stool behind it, gave one loud screech and fell over backwards.

King was on me by that time, trying to lick me in the face, and through the haze in front of my eyes, I just barely realized that the Judge was on his feet, his face as red as a beet, and swelled up like a tromped on toad frog. Through the roaring in my ears, I heard him shouting, "Clear the court, clear the court!" and that's just what I did. Fear lent wings to my feet, as I grabbed up King's chain and shot down the center of that big room, with him racing beside me. Out the big doors we went and headed towards the steps before sanity returned to me with a jolt.

What had I done? Maybe I could undo part of it at least, so quickly turning around, I retraced my steps and once again passed through those double doors, far more scared now that I had taken time to think, than when I had run out of them.

The dust had just barely settled as I stepped into view, with King contentedly by my side. Steve was about half way up the aisle. I couldn't tell by the expression on his face whether he was mad or trying to keep from laughing.

Everybody else just sat there and stared at me and from what Steve told me later, I guess I don't blame them. He said that I was as pale as a ghost so that my freckles stood out like guinea eggs and with my red hair standing straight up, I looked like something that had jumped up and been shot at.

I guess that I stood there, getting stared at through that horrible silence, for about a minute. Then I heard a small chuckle from the section where the hound men were sitting, then another, and all at once, they were roaring with laughter until the tears ran down their cheeks.

I was numb, couldn't move, as Steve took King's chain from me and handed it to the sheriff, who had just walked up. Uncle Bob came up then and said, "Come on, Jody, court is adjourned for today. He didn't look mad, but I was sure that he was and ashamed of me, too. I was, at least, until he put his arm around my shoulders and said, "Seems that I'm not the only one in our family who has a temper."

PART EIGHT

"Are they going to arrest me, Uncle Bob?"

"No, I don't think so, son," he answered kindly, "but I'll tell you what might not be a bad idea."

"What's that?" I asked.

"Well, don't you think that an apology to the Judge is in order? Will you do that?"

My last sight of that man was not a pleasant one to recall, and for an instant after my uncle's suggestion, I had a strong urge to hit the road, in a high lope, straight for Indiana. I knew, though, that it must be done, and that Uncle Bob wouldn't ask me to do something I shouldn't do. So I only nodded and answered, "Sure, Uncle Bob, if you think I should."

"Good boy," was all he said, and telling Steve and Earl to wait, he led the way down the hall to the rear and knocked at the door of the Judge's chambers. A deep voice bade us come in, and as my uncle opened the door, I was right behind him, just as close as I could get and still be able to walk.

"Ah! Mr. Brown," the deep voice said, "I see that you have delivered the culprit to me, well, well, that's fine. It will save me the trouble of having to call in the FBI to help find him."

FBI! CULPRIT! That was the end, I was done for, and I felt myself going fast, my knees were buckling, this was it, the stranger at the bar had done me in.

But as my sight grew dim and the last bit of starch left my legs, a big paw, fastened to my uncle's arm, plucked me from the very door of the Great Beyond and set me directly before the owner of that big voice.

"Your Honor," Uncle Bob drawled, "this is my nephew, Jody Hawkins, and he wants to apologize for all the trouble he caused."

Calling upon my last reserve of nerve, I forced myself to lift my eyes to the Judge's face. It wasn't red any more or swelled up or anything, just sort of stern like and very serious. His keen old eyes studied me through his glasses until I felt like a worm in a high school biology class. Finally, clearing his throat, he spoke to me.

"Well, young man, have you thought about what you did?"

"Yes, sir, Your Honor, sir, and I'm very sorry, sir."

"I see," the Judge said softly. "But if you're so sorry now, why did you do such a thing in the first place?"

I knew that there were tears in my eyes, but I just couldn't help it, and the words came without effort, for they were from the heart and I couldn't help that either. I looked straight into the Judge's eyes and poured out my soul, for they were born that deep inside me. In a voice that grew stronger as I spoke, I began.

"Your Honor, I guess I know why I did it, but I didn't know that I was going to do it until it happened. I didn't think about it any at all, it just happened. It just happened because I know King belongs to Uncle Bob and I love him almost as much as he does. I played with him when he was a little pup. I went with Uncle Bob lots of times when he was training him and saw him finished into a coon dog, a good one. I was with Uncle Bob the night he was stolen, and I saw the worry and sickness in his eyes as we searched and called and waited, then called and waited some more. I felt the heaviness in his heart when he finally gave up and admitted to himself that old King was gone, the victim of a dog thief."

I paused to catch my breath and was comforted by the obvious warmth shining from the old Judge's eyes, so I was encouraged to continue.

"I know that it wasn't the value of King that worried him so much, but because part of him was with King, as he always gave part of himself to every dog that he raised. I knew, too, that he was worried about the kind of treatment he would receive at the hands of someone else. My uncle would never harm any man, and yet, someone had come along and done harm to him. That fellow and his brothers and his father were all still doing harm to him by saying that King was theirs and that they had raised him. They were saying that and I knew better and old King knew better. I guess that's why I did it, Judge, and I'm sorry."

There was a long silence after I had finished, and I just stood there with only a very dim memory of all that I had said. I felt Uncle Bob's big hand on my shoulder, and with his touch, I was prepared for anything the Judge might have to say. When he did, it came out slowly, one word at a time, as if it had to be studied before letting it go.

"I think I understand, Jody, and I forgive you; however, you realize, don't you, that the ownership of this dog will have to be established by the court? We are here for the purpose of protecting aggrieved persons, but the court must have no personal feelings in the matter and must judge solely by the evidence presented."

"Yes, Your Honor," I replied, "I understand."

He turned then to Uncle Bob and said, "Thank you, Mr. Brown, for bringing Jody to see me, I'm glad you did. Now I would suggest that you go to the office of your attorney and formulate your plans for tomorrow. I think that you will find the State's Attorney there, too. Goodbye for now and thank you again for coming to see me."

My uncle shook hands with the Judge and thanked him for being so understanding. Leaving his chambers, we went outside to where Steve and Earl were waiting on the big steps.

"Gonna lock him up, Bob?" Steve asked in a mockingly anxious tone.

"Nope," my uncle answered, "not this time, put him on probation, though, in my care. He has to learn the carpenter trade so that he can build a new desk to replace the one he destroyed."

It really felt good to have them enjoying a laugh at my expense, especially now that I knew my foolish act had been forgiven, so I laughed right along with them. My uncle then told them about having to go to his attorney's office and asked them to wait at the car for him. He didn't tell me not to come, so I trudged right along with him.

It was just across the square, so in about three minutes we were climbing the steps to the office. Seemed that everything that had anything to do with the law around there was up some kind of steps. Maybe that's how they kept it on a high level.

We entered without knocking to find our lawyer, the State's Attorney, and the sheriff in the room. Even I was able to sense the tense atmosphere. The eyes of our young lawyer were shooting sparks and from the harassed look of the State's Attorney, it was apparent that he was being singed by those very sparks.

"Ah, come in, Mr. Brown," our lawyer welcomed us. "This concerns you and I would like your approval of my intentions."

We each took a chair before my uncle answered, "Let's hear them."

"Mr. Brown, would you object if I were to handle your case tomorrow, leaving our HONORABLE FRIEND, THE STATE'S ATTORNEY out of it?"

Uncle Bob's eyes gleamed with interest. "No, sir, I'll say I wouldn't. In fact, I'd feel downright happy about it."

"Good," our attorney exclaimed, "I thought you would feel that way."

"But you can't!" the State's Attorney protested. "I'm in charge of that case, you're there to help me and that's all."

The young lawyer's voice was loud and clear as he answered. "And that, sir, was exactly my understanding before today, but it no longer holds true, not after witnessing your actions up there today." The State's Attorney would have interrupted him at this point, but with eyes blazing, he was on his feet and standing directly over the other man.

"Shut up! I'm not through. What I saw out of you today was the most flagrant violation of justice that has probably ever been administered in that courtroom. By your actions you have denied Mr. Brown the right and impartial representation by a State's Attorney. If you continue in that capacity, there will be no conviction because you want none. You have shown yourself up for the farce you are. A farce and a disgrace to the honorable office of State's Attorney and most of us know why. I suppose that you can stop me, and if you insist, the court will let you continue to handle this case, but if you do, I promise you one thing. If it's the last thing I do as an attorney, I will file disbarring proceedings against you and subpoena every person in that courtroom today as a witness. Before I'm through, even your dog thief political friend won't have anything to do with you."

The State's Attorney turned all the colors of a neon sign and swallowed several times, seemingly unable to speak, and before he did, the sheriff cut in by growling, "And I'll be the first witness against you. You made me sick up there today and I'm telling you that Mr. Brown deserves a better show than that. I've checked on this man and his reputation is above reproach, and that's more than I can say for yours. I've seen enough to convince me that the dog is his and I intend to do all that I can to see that he gets him back. Step out of this case, buddy, or you're through."

The sheriff paused for breath and the object of his wrath waved a hand feebly in the air as he said, "Okay, okay, have it your way, take over tomorrow if you want to, I won't try to stop you.

Our lawyer turned one more disdainful glare on the would-be State's Attorney, as he delivered himself from our presence by slipping quickly out the door. Our lawyer eased himself into a chair with a heavy sigh that spoke more than words. His voice had steadied when he finally broke the silence. "Now, gentlemen, let's see if we can put the pieces together and come up with something to win our case for us tomorrow. Have you any ideas?"

"I'll bet if Little Queen was here she could tell them that King is Uncle Bob's," I burst out, just to ease the tension within me.

The lawyer looked at me in amazement for a few seconds and exclaimed, "From the mouths of babes."

Uncle Bob spoke excitedly, one of the few times in my life that I had heard him do so. "Jody, you did have to shine your light in our eyes after all."

Our lawyer's face was glowing as he said, "That's it, Mr. Brown, that's it."

"I do believe it might work and I think I can have her over here by morning," Uncle Bob said, grinning broadly. "It's sure worth a try."

Man, it looked like I had really come up with something sensible for a change. They started working out their plans at once. The sheriff seemed rather puzzled by it all until they explained just what they had in mind.

"You see, sheriff," the attorney began, "this Queen dog is the running mate of King and he knows her voice as he knows no other. Since they have run together so much, they will break their necks to get to one another when voice is given, either on track or at tree. We can show this guy up for the liar he is by just proving that these two dogs know each other."

"Oh! I see now," the sheriff exclaimed. "If this dog was really raised by Howser, as he claims, then he couldn't possibly know the female's voice and that would leave him without a leg to stand on."

"Exactly," our lawyer replied, "but let's save this as a surprise and don't let it get out. We will throw and hog tie Howser tomorrow before the morning is half over, and finish up this trial in a way that will be remembered for a long time. Now, Mr. Brown, you had better get busy on that call to your friend and get that female started out here, while the sheriff and I get busy on some other details."

"Such as?" Uncle Bob asked.

"Well, for one thing, we have to round up about five other tree dogs for tomorrow and we had better make them all female Walkers, too, if we can find that many. Also, we have to get some wire and posts for a pen and line up a crew to build it. In the morning, when I give the word, how high a fence can King go over?"

There was pride in my uncle's voice as he answered, "Well, he has to take them about fifty inches high back home quite often, and they don't slow him down any."

The attorney nodded his head, "Fine, I figured about that, so we will just make this pen an even six feet. We want him to really put on a show when he goes over, so as to impress the jury with his determination! See what I mean, Mr. Brown?"

"I sure do," he grinned. "Can you get a coon?"

"I'm way ahead of you there," laughed our attorney, "for I've got one myself."

Uncle Bob rose and chuckled, "I had a feeling that you were the right man to handle this case, right from the very start, and now I'm downright certain." Then turning towards the door, he said, "Come on Jody, I want to go call Bill."

We immediately went back to the car and the others were as elated as we were when they heard the plans. As I listened to them talk, the depressing feeling that had been with me ever since the trial started began to leave me. I once more began to daydream of heading down the pike towards home with old King on the seat beside me.

Uncle Bob let us out at the motel and went at once to the office to make his call to Bill. It was only a little past four, so he was pretty sure that he could still catch him at the shop. The rest of us waited on pins and needles for him to come back. We knew, of course, that Bill would agree at once to bring her, but there was always the chance that he just might not be able to.

The big smile on my uncle's face when he returned was all the answer we needed. "He's headed home right now and will be started within the hour," he informed us. With that word, all the men were as excited as I was.

PART NINE

They figured that Bill would arrive about midnight, so we went at once to the little motel restaurant and ordered our supper. While we were eating, the two men from the American Hound Association came in. Spotting us, they came directly to our table; they had some news too, all good.

It seems that some of the hound men from different parts of the country had got together, as hound men will, and had made some discoveries. Some, who had purchased dogs from old Sid Howser, had begun to wonder a little about just what they might or might not have bought. Also, a few who had been the victim of dog thieves during the past year were among those present. As they became acquainted and swapped a few tales back and forth, things began to add up.

To make a long story short, two dogs, purchased from Howser, had already been identified by their rightful owners. Another fellow who had to drive about fifty miles to check on one, had not returned yet, but they were pretty sure that it would prove to be his dog.

Anyway, they had plenty of proof now and were going to hit Howser with new charges just as soon as Uncle Bob's case was cleared. That's why they were there to see him. They offered to throw their evidence into the present case if it was needed.

Thanking them, he said, "Well, boys, I sure do appreciate your offer, and a few hours ago, I would have taken you up on it, things weren't looking too good for us, but now it's different. Thanks to Jody here, I think that we have come up with something that will finish the case pretty quickly tomorrow. It was supposed to be a secret until we spring the surprise in the morning, but I believe you're entitled to know."

When they heard the plan they were as enthusiastic as the rest of us, and just knowing that they thought it would work made us feel even better. They had things to do, so bidding us goodnight, they left. We finished our supper and headed back to the cabins for a quick shower and some sleep before Bill arrived.

I was the first one in bed and hardly remembered hitting the sheets before I was awakened by a light in my eyes and Bill's big voice filling the room. I sat up then and as I finally pried my eyes open, there was Bill grinning down at me while Queen was wiggling all over Uncle Bob. Steve and Earl came into the room then, and for the next hour, the plans for the next day were hashed over and over again.

I found it impossible to stay awake, as much as I wanted to, so the first thing I knew, it was morning. *THE MORNING*! With that thought, I was out of bed and dressed in about two minutes. It was only six o'clock, but Uncle Bob was already gone. Panic that I had been left behind sent me to the door in a bound, but my fears were groundless. He was just out front, in a huddle with the other men.

They all greeted me warmly as I joined them and Bill boomed, "So you're the bird who is responsible for my having to come way out here." But I knew that he was as happy as a lark and wouldn't have missed it for anything. He looked well rested after his trip out, and seemed raring to go. As Uncle Bob looked around at them, he suddenly lost his composure for a minute.

"Boys," he said, "this is a mighty important day for me and I want you to know that whether I get King back or not, I will never forget the way you have helped me."

"Shucks, Bob," Steve answered, slightly flustered, "we haven't done anything special."

"More than you know, Steve, more than you know. It sure gives a man a mighty comfortable feeling to have his good friends with him at a time like this."

Even Uncle Bob seemed slightly embarrassed that such an emotional little speech could come from him, and since nobody else seemed able to say anything right then, I managed to get two words in. "Let's eat."

"Well, now," Bill laughed, there's nothing wrong with that boy's way of thinking—let's go."

It was such a beautiful morning that it was impossible for me to feel any way but optimistic. Though the sun had already started its daily trip across the sky, its heat was as yet no more than very pleasant warmth. With the clear blue of the sky as a promise, and the sweet voices of song birds a reminder, we walked the short distance to the restaurant, secure in nature's assurance that all was well.

Again, the Hound Association men entered shortly after we were seated, and again, they were bearers of good tidings. The man who had gone to look at the dog was back, and it was as they had suspected, his dog. Now they had six very angry men ready to file additional charges on Howser; three who had purchased stolen dogs unknowingly from him, and three others, from whom they were stolen. His goose was cooked. My uncle still wanted them to wait, though, until his case was over. They readily agreed. But with the promise to stand by with their evidence, just in case.

As there was plenty of time before nine o'clock, we all walked back to the cabins and just lounged around awhile. Uncle Bob had tried to get his lawyer on the phone before we left the restaurant, but without success. So, in a little while, he went to the office to try again, this time with better luck.

He had been real busy since daylight, getting everything lined up. He had just come back from arranging for the last Walker female when my uncle called. I guess it took some doing, but he had actually arranged for five females, with their owners to handle them. He had a crew all ready to build the pen. They were not to start until he sent word, which he figured would be around nine-thirty. They were to take only about twenty minutes for the job. It was to be six feet tall and twenty feet square, so old King could have sufficient distance for a running start before he hit that fence.

It was now about eight-thirty, so we all climbed into the cars and headed in the general direction of the Courthouse. The Hound Association men had asked Bill to go with them. They had been told that he was the owner of Big Tom, and they wanted to hear the story from him. So Steve drove Bill's car, taking Earl with him, while I, as usual, rode with Uncle Bob.

Several men were already standing around the foot of the south steps as we pulled up at the old hitching rail to park, so we didn't wait long before heading inside. Bill had to wait at Uncle Bob's car with Queen until he received word to bring her in; she was a surprise that must be kept.

Our young attorney was already busy at his table, but rose when we entered and greeted us with a big smile. We all took the same positions as the day before, my uncle with the lawyer and the rest of us directly back of them, in the front row.

In a few minutes, the State's Attorney came in and took his place at the table, where he sat in sullen silence. Not long after that, Sid Howser and his big old, mean-looking boys entered and seated themselves about the same as us, the old boys in the front row. From the smug grins on their faces, they all but had it wrapped up—so they thought, but I knew better. I could hardly wait for them to get started; this was just about the biggest day of my life.

Howser had been trying to catch the State's Attorney's eye, but with no success. Apparently, he had not yet told him about the change and that he was now at the mercy of an ambitious young lawyer who owed him nothing. He wasn't long in finding out, though, for pretty soon, the Judge came in and after all respects were paid to him, court got underway.

King hadn't been brought in this morning, and surprisingly, nobody seemed to question his absence. Our attorney lit right in the middle with a splash from the very first, and if the Judge wondered why the State's Attorney wasn't running the show, he didn't mention it.

Howser wondered, though, and was beginning to show signs of nervousness as he kept looking hard at his bought man, who always seemed to find something else to fasten his eyes on, while his pasty face grew paler by the minute, if that was possible.

Our attorney called Howser to the stand the very first thing. By the time he was seated, the sheriff came down the aisle with Queen prancing before him. What a picture she made as she marched proudly at the end of that chain—all white, except for the tan head and softly rolling ears and the tan spot at the root of her tail and two black patches on her back. All eyes were on her as she quietly allowed herself to be tied to the railing. She then sat down very daintily and directed her intelligent eyes to those around her. She seemed to realize that she was the center of attention and was actually enjoying it.

Sid Howser was becoming very suspicious. He suspected that

something out of the ordinary was about to take place and he wasn't a bit happy. His suspicions were confirmed and he began to feel the cold sweat of fear trickling down his collar. The barbed questions of that fine young lawyer found his soft spots and dug in.

"Mr. Howser, have you ever hunted coons in Indiana?"

"No, sir, never."

"Now then, if you have never hunted coons in Indiana, have you ever allowed this dog you claim to be yours to be hunted by anyone else in Indiana?"

I think Howser was beginning to get some idea of what was up, but apparently decided that a bluff was his only chance, for he answered in a loud voice.

"Nobody has ever hunted that dog but me and the boys, and we have never hunted in Indiana."

Our attorney smiled and thanked him very graciously and with a light of triumph in his eyes said, "Now, Mr. Howser, take a good look at that little female over there and tell me if you have ever seen her."

Howser had the look of a trapped animal, but he went through the pretense of looking hard at Queen before he answered.

"No, I have never seen that dog before."

"Well, I didn't think that you had, Mr. Howser, for that is an Indiana dog and he has never been in the State of Illinois, and since your dog, I mean the one you claim is yours—"

Howser's lawyer was immediately on his feet with an objection, which the Judge just as quickly overruled, and the questioning continued.

"Now, once again, Mr. Howser, if neither you or the dog in question have ever hunted in Indiana, then your dog could not possibly have seen or become acquainted with this little female, in any way, could he?"

Howser was one flustered man, but he managed to mutter, "No, of course not."

With a broad smile, our attorney said softly, "Thank you, Mr. Howser, you have been a big help; you may step down now."

Sid Howser was a worried man as he left the witness stand and returned to his seat. There was a consultation, very briefly, with his attorney, who seemed to be shaking his head 'no' to whatever Howser had in mind.

Uncle Bob's attorney stood quietly for a minute, until every eye in the courtroom was on him and every person present felt the climax building up. Finally, he turned slowly to face the Judge and then the jury. In a clear voice, ringing with sincerity, he began:

"Your Honor, ladies and gentlemen of the jury, the prosecution is ready to bring this case to a close. In just a few minutes, we will ask you to witness a demonstration, one on which we are willing to risk the entire outcome of the trial."

As he said this, I heard the sound of hammers coming from the courtyard; some way he had given the signal for the pen to be built. He paused, as if listening to the sound himself, then continued:

"We are willing to risk this, ladies and gentlemen, because you will be able to see the evidence with your own eyes. You will be shown undeniable proof as to the correct ownership of this dog. So far, you may be unsure, unsure because you have heard only the sworn testimony of men. Men from both sides of this case, each swearing that the man he represents is the rightful owner. Now we know that one side or the other is telling the truth and that the other side is lying. But which one is telling the truth? That's what you have been brought here to decide, and it's really hard to decide, isn't it?"

Every member of the jury seemed to nod, ever so slightly, at this, but they never took their eyes from him; he had really captured their undivided attention.

"Of course, it is simply because we all know that man can sometimes be completely without scruples. He can be pressured into perjuring himself on the witness stand for many reasons, among these, monetary gain, fear, greed, or just from a desperate effort to save his own hide. Yes, ladies and gentlemen, man with all his frailties, can sometimes be a very unreliable witness. With your awareness of these facts has come the desire to be shown unimpeachable evidence, one way or the other, so that you can arrive at your decision with absolute sincerity."

"All right, ladies and gentlemen, we will relieve you of all men's testimony. We will bring you a witness who finds it's impossible to tell a lie, simply because she does not know how. A witness who has no need for money because she could not spend it if she had it. A witness completely free from all political connections, one who can do no moral wrong. She is incapable of lusting for anything, she only asks for kind treatment, body subsistence and shelter, so that she may be able to live out her full life, serving the purpose for which she was intended. I now give you, ladies and gentlemen, your witness, that little female coon hound, Queen."

A strange quiet hung over the courtroom, as all eyes went to Queen. He let them think for a minute, and then continued:

"Before I take you outside to witness this demonstration, I want to explain a few of the characteristics prevalent in all hounds. I will, of course, in this case, be referring only to coon hounds. This little female belongs to Mr. Brown. She is the running mate of the King dog. She is three years old and he is five, and he has taught her all that she knows about running and treeing coons. From the time she was a puppy, she has been following him around in the woods. She began to help him work on coon tracks when she was six months old. A hound is what is known as an open trailer, in other words, they give voice when on track or at the tree. Hounds that run together learn each other's voice, so that they can tell it from all others, any place, anytime. So King has known this little girl's voice ever since she was six months old. Of course, it has changed some, as she grew older, but it is the voice that has echoed with his, as they unraveled many coon trails, through the hills and in the big river bottoms, during these last two and a half years."

"Hounds that run together learn to depend upon one another for help at times. One may overrun a track and make a loss. If the other one happens to pick up this loss and gives voice, the other will at once quit searching and join its mate, for it knows that the trail is once more up and going. This may happen hundreds of times a year if dogs are hunted a lot and the same holds true for tree. Most hounds bark differently at tree than on track, but they learn each other's tree bark just as well as they do the running voice, and respond to it just as quickly."

"King doesn't know that Queen is here, in fact, he hasn't seen her since last January, and that was nearly six months ago. But he will see and hear her soon. He is in a pen on the east side of the Courthouse. The pen is made of wire, six feet high. Now, this is a foot higher than most dogs can manage to get over without great difficulty. We are, however, counting on his eagerness to get to Queen and are willing to bet that he will get over, somehow, when he hears her barking treed. She will, when we are ready, start barking treed at a coon in a tree on the west side of the building. The dogs won't be able to see each other and neither will know that the other is there."

"Now, to make this a real test and to show that King does know Queen's voice from all others, we are going a little farther. We are going to have five other Walker females brought to the tree, one at a time, and let each of them tree awhile, then Queen will be the sixth. If I predict his reactions correctly, you will see that he shows interest when each of the other five dogs start barking, for he recognizes the tone of their voice as being a tree bark, Yes, he may even show some excitement, but not enough to make an effort to get over that high fence. There will be nothing familiar about the voices of the other dogs, nothing to pull at him with remembrance of past trails, or of her help when the going was rough. There will be nothing about those other voices that has, in the past, been part of him or to set up a wild clamor in his blood. There will, however, be an entirely different reaction from him when this little dog is taken to the tree, so different, in fact, that I won't attempt to describe it, but will wait and let you see for yourself."

He had the jury spellbound; they had hung on every word. He bowed slightly to them as he finished and then turned to face the Judge.

"Now, with the court's permission, I very humbly request that we all go outside to the lawn, south of this building, where our little drama is about ready to unfold. Your Honor, do I have the court's permission?"

The Judge's eyes twinkled, giving the lie to the stern look he had on his face, as he answered, "This is very unusual and I might add, rather presumptuous on the part of the prosecution, as has been this whole presentation here this morning, but the purpose of this court is to render justice, and if such outlandish procedure is deemed necessary, then the court gives its permission. We will all retire to the south lawn as the prosecution has requested."

Our bunch stood aside, out of the press of the crowd, and waited as they filed out, so I had a chance to study their faces and watch the reactions.

The faces of the hound men showed downright excitement, unhidden and tempered with glee. They knew what was coming and were eagerly anticipating the outcome. On Uncle Bob's was a calm glow of composed confidence. Old Sid Howser and his crew showed nothing but hate in the menacing glares they fastened on the State's Attorney. His fear was shining through with every glance of his shifting eyes.

The jury was a study in contrast. The three women had eyes only for little Queen, as she stood, wagging her tail at the passing parade, and the look of friendliness on her face had them purring like a child over a doll as they went by. Some of the men jurors had their feelings pretty well hidden, but if you looked real close, you could see that they, too, felt something; eagerness, doubt, excitement, apprehension? I just couldn't tell for sure, but I knew that I would soon find out.

The Judge was the last one before we fell in at the end of the line, and as he looked down at me, I'll swear that his right eye lid drooped just a fraction in what must have been a wink. At least, I think that's what I saw.

Everyone was in neatly arranged groups by the time we reached the ground outside. Our attorney was making sure that nothing happened to obstruct the jury's view. They were standing in the very middle, so that they could see King in his pen on the east lawn and still have the tree, on the west side, in plain sight.

All in all, it was a very neatly arranged setup, just like the setting for a play, and the main actors were completely unaware of their part in the drama. The Judge had taken his position at the east end of the jury group, and I noticed that he was really very interested in King and that pen. I sure would have given a lot, right then, to have known what that old boy was thinking.

Queen had been taken down a side stairs to the basement, where she couldn't hear the other dogs when they barked, for that might have spoiled everything. Finally deciding that everybody was placed to his satisfaction, our lawyer raised his hand for silence, and a hush fell over the crowd. All present realized that the curtain was about to go up. All traffic on the town square had come to a halt. There were at least two hundred extra eyes fastened on that little play being staged in that courtyard. I'm sure that everyone there felt the undercurrent of breathless excitement. In fact, if I had felt it any stronger, I do believe that I would have fainted, right there before everybody.

"Ladies and gentlemen," he began, "please give me your undivided attention. Absolute quiet is essential, if we are to see this unfold before us in a natural, unrehearsed manner. Your cooperation, ladies and gentlemen, please. Thank you."

With that, he turned and waved his hand toward a man standing by a car at the northwest corner of the courtyard. At this signal, the fellow opened his car door and let out his dog. Chain in hand, he walked briskly with her towards the tree where the coon had been placed. I could see him there, milling around, on the first big limb, about eight feet above the ground. He was a big old fellow and restless, and should draw the dog's attention fast, which he did.

Even before she got to the tree, that little female winded the coon and was instantly at the end of her chain, head up, and singing her song. I looked over at King to see what he was doing, to find that he was listening, prancing a little, and trotting back and forth. He was being tuned in, just about right.

They let her tree about two minutes and then waved her away. The next man then brought up his dog and the same thing was repeated. The third came and went. By the time the fourth was brought up, King had quit his pacing and was just sitting there, facing in their direction and only whining, once in awhile. When the fifth one came to the tree, I hardly heard her, for the excitement racing through me, in anticipation of what was going to happen next.

The main event. The showdown; it was all or nothing, at the next cast of the dice, and the strain was killing me. Last minute flashes of fearful thoughts flew through my mind. What if King had forgotten her voice? What if the fence was so high that he wouldn't even make the try? What if Queen's voice had changed since he last heard her? I was building up a mighty big fright. Then came the touch of a hand on my shoulder. I looked up into Uncle Bob's calm, unruffled face; all my fears vanished as he smiled, and said softly, "Keep your fingers crossed, Jody." He wasn't worried, so why should I be?

Slowly, our attorney turned and surveyed the crowd, sweeping it with his eyes from west to east and then back again. He seemed in no hurry to get on to the climax, but just stood there, letting the tension build up.

Then he turned towards the west side of the Courthouse as if to signal for Queen to be brought out, but stopped his motion, and turned to face the crowd again. Before turning away from them, this time, he raised both hands and made one last motion for silence, a plea in suspense, but he really didn't need to do that. It was so quiet that you could almost hear the grass grow. It seemed that even the pigeons in the tower had stopped their cooing, so deep was the hush that enveloped that crowd.

Only then, did he turn, once more, to the west side of the building, and give his signal to a man standing outside the small door there, who in turn, raised his hand. Slowly, oh, so slowly, the door began to edge open; little by little, it swung back. For an instant, it seemed that nothing was going to appear, then Queen's beautiful head came into view, and she pranced through at the end of a leash, held in the big hand of Bill.

Every eye was on her and being the lady she was, she was aware, and her response was in the proud lift of her head and the gracefully controlled lines of her body, as she danced at the end of her chain.

Slowly, Bill steered her in the right direction. He then did a strange thing, that was at once obvious to us dog men, and I think to most of the crowd, for I saw smiles appear here and there.

He turned in the general direction of the crowd and held up an extra leash. He was showing them his confidence in the outcome. That extra leash was for King, when he came unhampered, in answer to the call of his mate. Slowly, those two, in the center of the stage, drew closer to the point of no return.

Would she wind the coon now? The next step? The next? Yes, now she had it, the hot scent of the coon was in her nose. Up went her head, straight into the air and the lead jerked tight, as she stood on her hind feet, looking directly at that big coon. Her throat swelled, and from her dainty muzzle poured the most beautiful tenor bawl in the world, and as if trying to push it out faster, those melodious chops sounded loud and clear.

Instantly, every eye turned toward the pen holding King, where they beheld a dog transformed. The first bawl brought him to his feet, head up, tail high, and rigidness in every muscle of his body. Every ounce of his sixty pounds was like a coiled spring. Not more than half a dozen chops had come from Queen before he exploded.

One loud, deep bawl rolled from his throat and he was on the wire. Springing high, only to fall back. Again and again, almost hooking those front feet over the top, but not quite enough. He was a dog gone wild, but he had learned something on every try. Again, that bawl broke from him as he wheeled and ran back to the other side of that twenty foot pen, then turned and hurled himself across its width.

Queen was no longer just barking treed. She, too, had come alive like a bolt of lightning at the sound of the first bawl from King, and was answering him, trying to pull Bill's arm from its socket.

As King came across that pen like an express train, I think that everyone there knew he was going to make it. When about five feet from the fence, those powerful muscles bunched and propelled him high into the air, up, up, and his elbows caught over the top; one last kick and he was over, and headed like an arrow in the direction of Queen's clamoring voice.

There was a roar from the crowd, as he dropped to the outside of the wire and Bill, who couldn't see him, knew that he was over and acted accordingly, by releasing his hold on Queen's tugging chain. She was off in a flash. What a show, what a show! The two beautiful Walkers, racing towards each other in wild eagerness. The crowd witnessed the full joy of their meeting, and as one, they understood. They came together, directly in front of us in wild acclaim for one another.

Their soft growling was a continuous purring sound that spoke of lonesome months and unfinished trails, a declaration that from each, a part was gone while they were separated, their mock fighting and chewing on one another and the nuzzling of ears, a promise that it would not happen again.

I realized that my eyes were full of tears, and thought, at first, to hide them, but even as I raised my hand, I was no longer ashamed, but let them be, for there were more wet eyes in that crowd than mine, and them more than thirteen years old, too.

The hound men were beside themselves and were openly declaring their satisfaction that King belonged to my uncle. All was confusion there, for a short time, and I was trying to see everything at once, but that can be a problem when you're just a scrawny little kid, smothered in a crowd of grown-ups.

I did have my eyes on the dogs, though, when Queen took King to the tree. She seemed to have suddenly thought of it, for all at once she broke away from her romping, gave a little bark, and tore out across the lawn towards that tree, with King right behind her. For awhile, there was some beautiful music ringing out over that old town square, as the two of them treed their hearts out. Soon though, Bill went over to them and snapped on their chains. Speaking quietly to curb their excitement, he led them away, but only to a point about fifty feet from the crowd, where he stopped and just stared at us.

His actions spoke louder than words. With legs spread wide and the dogs standing quietly at his side, his dark eyes swept the crowd with a glare of proud defiance, and when they met those of the Judge, you could almost hear him say, *I'll just keep them here with me, until Bob gets back down, there's no doubt now, you know, the trial is over.*

The old Judge's eyes gleamed in understanding as he read Bill's message, loud and clear, for there was just a slight nod of his head toward Bill before he spoke for all to hear, "Court will be resumed inside in exactly five minutes."

I was nearly torn in two by wanting to be two places at once. I wanted to run over to Bill and the dogs, but I just had to hear and see what went on inside, so I compromised. Rushing over to the dogs, I gave their heads a pat, and still caught up with Uncle Bob and the others before they got halfway up the steps.

Everyone was seated and ready before the Judge took his position. It was so quiet, no one stirred, for fear they might miss a single word. The rustle of some papers on the Judge's desk sounded like a trip hammer, and as my eyes caught sight of a little bug marching across the floor, I wanted to shout, "Quit that stomping."

Finally, the Judge cleared his throat, and broke the heavy silence. "The prosecution may proceed."

Our attorney rose and faced the jury, slowly, he addressed them. "Ladies and gentlemen of the jury, I won't insult you by presenting further argument. You have seen and I await your verdict, with absolute confidence that you won't disappoint me. Thank you. The prosecution rests its case."

As he returned to his table, the Judge turned to the other group, and asked, "Has the defense anything to add at this point?"

Sid Howser's lawyer rose, and with all the full dignity of his many years, answered, "The defense has absolutely nothing to add." As he sat down, the look of open contempt that he directed towards Sid Howser was plain for all to see.

The Judge showed no surprise at such a reply, but turned at once to the jury. His instructions were brief.

"Ladies and gentlemen, you have heard and seen the evidence presented here. Your duty is clear. Either to find the defendant, Sidney Howser, not guilty as charged or to find him guilty of knowingly possessing stolen property, aiding and abetting to the crime of dog stealing for personal gain and profit, and of perjury, here on the stand. If that is your decision, your recommendation must be that the dog, claimed by Mr. Brown, be returned to him. You may retire for the purpose of reaching your verdict."

There was a stir among the jury, but no one rose. Then like a ripple disturbing a placid pool of water, they, as one, leaned out, caught the foreman's attention, and nodded their heads. Then, as they all settled back, he stood up, and faced the Judge. Once more, everyone seemed to hold their breath, as they waited for him to speak.

"Your Honor," he began, "we have reached our verdict. We, the jury, find the defendant guilty as charged, and recommend that Mr.

Brown's dog be returned to him at once."

It's a wonder the roof didn't blow off of that courtroom. The hound men all seemed to let out a whoop at once as they began crowding around Uncle Bob to shake his hand. He just stood there quietly, with a happy smile on his face, and thanked them for their congratulations. Finally, during a lull in the noise, we all became aware of the pounding of the Judge's gavel. Immediately, the noise subsided, as we all resumed our seats. The Judge was trying hard to glare at us in a very ferocious manner, but it seemed awfully hard for him to do. His heart just wasn't in it. It took on the right meaning, though, when he turned to the defendant.

"Will Sidney Howser please approach the bench?"

Old man Howser, looking really scared now for the first time, stood and slowly shuffled forward. No hateful scrawl encompassed his face now, only a look of frightened uncertainty. In a deep voice, the Judge addressed him:

"Sidney Howser, you have been found guilty as charged, by a jury of your peers. It is the decision of this court that you are confined to the county jail, where you will remain in the custody of the sheriff of this county until tomorrow morning at ten o'clock; at which time you will be brought back here for sentencing."

Then, turning to the sheriff, he added, "The sheriff will see that Robert Brown's dog is turned over to him at once. Court is adjourned."

The sheriff grinned, as he said to Uncle Bob, "Seems to me that you already have him, from my last sight of that big friend of yours, with his death grip on those chains."

Everybody around us laughed, as the sheriff, too, congratulated him. People were beginning to leave, so Steve, Earl, and I prepared to do the same. Uncle Bob had to go to his lawyer's office with the two men from the American Hound Association.

I guess that I was practically running, because Steve said, "Hold up, Jody, he'll still be there." He was right, of course, but I still couldn't control my legs any longer than it took for us to get outside, for it seemed that I just had to get King's chain in my hand and feel him tugging there, before I could really believe it was over.

Bill knew, as I ran up, for his big, broad face broke into a happy smile, as he held the chain out to me. Honestly, all the men were just as elated as I, only they couldn't show it the way I could. That was one of the few privileges of being just thirteen years old.

After we had all made over the dogs, Steve said, "Well, boys, let's go back to the cabin and wait for Bob before we eat dinner."

Back at the motel, we all relaxed and let the tensions drain out. Me, I felt as if I would never be the same again. The men talked of what would happen to Sid Howser and about the additional charges that were to be filed by the other six men, while I only halfway listened and counted the minutes until Uncle Bob returned, and we started home; seemed to me that we had been over there for a year, at least. Guess I wasn't as grown up as I tried to make myself believe.

Finally, my uncle drove up, and while petting the dogs, tried to answer the many questions we threw at him. In a nutshell, and as near as I can remember, the young attorney was being retained by the other men and the American Hound Association. He assured them that the State's Attorney would file the new charges tomorrow. Uncle Bob would be notified later about just what his expenses toward the trial would be. His attorney had told him that he most definitely was not going to accept anything but expenses. Seems that he had wanted a chance to expose the State's Attorney for a long time and this case had been tailor-made for that purpose. Furthermore, his reputation had been so established by this trial that his career was assured. He had already been approached by members of his party to declare for the office of State's Attorney in the coming election. Since Uncle Bob had actually solved and brought an end to his own dog stealing case, there was no reward for him to pay out, but he gratefully made out a check to the American Hound Association in the amount of one hundred dollars, to help on the expenses of the coming trial, and to partially repay them for the support given him.

My uncle was a humble man and a grateful one. Grateful for all the help and cooperation he had received: from the Hound Association, from the coon hound magazines that carried the story and pictures to their readers, and to all the good people for their individual contributions toward the successful outcome of the trial.

Uncle Bob summed it all up in just a few words, as he said softly,

"Boys, there are some mighty fine people in this old world of ours. It has been my pleasure to get to know a lot of them these last few days. My life and faith in human nature have been enriched by this experience. As of this minute, I'm prouder than ever to be a member of the human race."

The silence that followed lent a respectful approval to his views. Then, once more, my stomach pushed my mouth open, and I heard myself say, "I'm hungry, when are we going to eat lunch?" Everyone seemed in agreement with that, so off to the restaurant for our lunch.

During the meal, my uncle referred once more to the trial as he said thoughtfully, "You know, I feel sorry for those boys of Howser's. They have a mark against their records for lying on the witness stand, and they really didn't have much choice. They wouldn't have dared do anything else, seeing the kind of daddy they had and all. I hope that this will teach them a lesson they won't forget. Maybe such a lesson that it will keep them from doing something real bad later on!" He spoke sadly, for it was obvious that he felt no joy in the discomfort or misfortune of others.

All at once, it seemed that every one of us was impatient to be starting home. As if on signal, and without a word being spoken, our lunch unfinished, we all pushed back from the table and walked out of the restaurant. Quickly rounding up our belongings, we made preparations to leave.

Bill was taking Earl with him and Steve was to ride back with us. By us, of course, I mean Uncle Bob, me, King, and Queen. Steve up front with my uncle and a dog on each side of me in the back.

Sitting proud, heads up, noses to the wind, and ears flapping in the breeze, they were heading home. Back to the river bottoms and hills that they knew. Home to the sanctuary of their kennels, to the care and protection of the man they lived to serve, my Uncle Bob.

Sound of the Horn

High upon the side of the creek bluff, fifty feet above the water's edge, on a narrow ledge at the mouth of a small cave, the old Black and Tan whimpered in pain.

With effort, he slowly gathered his three free legs under him and struggled to a sitting position. Once more the old grey muzzle lifted to the sky, pointed up into the cold driving rain and sent forth that long, lonesome moaning call for help.

Three times the pleading cry of a hound in trouble pealed out and hit the high ridge opposite him in a futile attempt to reach over the top, only to be smothered by the heavy timber.

Reluctant to lie back down on the cold wet rock, he sat unmoving; his gentle eyes, sick with suffering, turned towards the north, searching the fast gathering darkness for sight of that one familiar figure, one who had never failed him and wouldn't now. He knew he would come.

He would have sounded his call once more, but a throat raw from constant use, rebelled, and refused the urgings of his pain-wracked body. Stiff from pain, he settled down on the stone. Slowly, the tired old head drooped, as bowing to the elements and the small confines of the short chain that had become his world in these tortuous hours.

At intervals during the afternoon, he had heard the horn, very faintly, and had sent his call in return. But the ridge of the chimney rock was between them, a bulwark shielding his voice from the aging ears of the one who searched, and for whom he waited.

Halfheartedly, he bit once more at the cruel steel holding his right front foot and then lay still. Head outstretched flat on the stone and eyes closed in patient resignation, he waited for rescue or death.

On the porch of the little cabin at the mouth of East Hollow, the old man stood, peering out into the night. In the yellow glow of a kerosene lantern, his lined old face was wreathed with worry and fatigue. Bone tired, his once powerful shoulders slumped, while his slightly bent old knees quivered in protest against his still standing erect.

As he faced out into pelting rain and the black void that stretched endlessly beyond the feeble circle of the lantern light, he knew what he must do. For himself, no, but for the other, yes. He would ask for help. Stiffly, he entered the house. With shuffling steps, he went to the only modern convenience he allowed himself, the telephone. Without hesitation, he picked up the receiver and gave the operator the number.

It had been one of those days when Bill Goddard had been glad to close the door of his barber shop, and head home. The usual pattern of customers and loafers had not varied as local sportsmen came and went. Hound talk, as usual, was predominant throughout the afternoon and the atmosphere seemed little different from that of any other day. But since noon, Bill had become more and more aware of a tension building within him, a feeling of foreboding, that he seemed unable to explain or shake off.

Since midmorning, leadened skies had given up their rain steadily, easily, and seemingly without effort, as it continued hour after hour. The bleak heavy overcast of a November day had covered the rain-drenched streets and sidewalks with a blanket of gloom. Outside lights began to appear more and more, as man threw his only defense into combat against the hovering darkness, in a desperate attempt to extend his battle lines beyond the perimeter of their feeble glow.

Only an occasional pedestrian scurried along the street, brought out by the necessity of some last-minute errand. And that completed, hurried on, obvious by their haste that their thoughts were of hearth and home, and that man should seek shelter that night.

By four o'clock, the rain that had been falling straight down, took on a decided slant to the southeast. Bill, glancing out the window, knew that a northwest wind was driving against it with the promise of rapidly falling temperatures. By four-thirty, the regular splashing sound on the big front window had taken on an ominous tone of steadily increasing little clicks, and the last customer paused in the open doorway and shuddered at the cold blast that drove at him. Before plunging out, he turned up the collar of his coat as he muttered, "Man! That rain is turning to ice fast."

For a few minutes, Bill stood quietly looking out the window at the emptiness of the big square. Already the large limestone Courthouse in the center was beginning to take on a ghostly glare as its rough surface began to ice up. The parking meters around the hitch rack stood like frozen sentinels guarding a barren waste of empty spaces between white lines, their immediate purpose made even more ridiculous by the solitude about them.

At four forty-five he began putting away his tools with a sigh of relief. The uneasy feeling that had been probing at him all afternoon was even more prevalent now. In the silence of the shop, he was aware of a desire to hurry home, to leave the feeling behind, to lock it up in the shop, where it surely would disappear before another day.

In a little more haste than usual, he closed the door and hurried to his car, finding, as he walked, relief in the fact that ice had not yet begun to form on the street. While the motor warmed up, he scraped away the thin coating covering the windshield and back glass. The car was snug as he climbed in and the wipers soon cleared away any ice that remained.

During the five-minute ride to his home across town, he thought briefly of the hunt he had planned that night and that there would be no need to call Steve. That they could not go was all too apparent. Realization of something else was also on his mind. Whatever it was that had been bothering him that afternoon had not been locked behind in the shop. It was there in the car with him. It perched upon his shoulder and whispered into his ear a message of its presence, but tauntingly withheld the nature of its meaning.

Even as he drove into the garage, he knew that it followed. It walked at his elbow as he entered the bright warmth of the house to the greetings of his wife and daughter. It peered, with him, into his plate as he ate supper. For an instant, he had the foolish feeling that the others must surely know that something strange attended the meal. As he listened to their happy conversation and talk of the day's happenings, he knew that its presence was not known to them, that it must have reason to enter into his world but not into theirs.

Even then, as such thoughts churned through his mind, he was only seconds away from knowing. As he finished his second cup of coffee, the message was on its way, and as his cup touched down upon the table, it arrived. Something about the ringing of the phone was different. He knew, even before his teenage daughter called disappointedly to him, that the call was his.

For a very short period, the thing remained with him as it raced across the floor and hovered close as he listened to the message, and then it was gone. He had the answer; there was no longer any place for the feeling. Certainty of what he must do came instantly, after the first few words.

Exhaustion was evident in the old man's voice on the phone, though he spoke only briefly, wasting no words in apology, for he knew none were needed. "Bill, I need help. Old Tom didn't come in and I'm afraid he may be caught in a trap. I've been searching all day and I'm kinda tuckered."

Bill's words were even fewer in number. "Stay in the house, Josh. Steve and I will be right down."

To his wife, Bess, listening from the doorway, it didn't seem at all strange that he would volunteer the services of Steve without the other's knowledge. That's the way it was with them. And it worked both ways. She remembered another time, two years back, when Steve had done the volunteering for both. That time had been when their close friend Bob Brown had his Walker dog stolen and they had gladly, even eagerly, gone through some rather harrowing experiences that resulted in the bloody capture of the thieves and recovery of King.

Without leaving the phone, Bill immediately called Steve and explained in a few short words, listened to as brief an answer, and then hung up. Worry was in his eyes and in the impassiveness of his rather heavy dark face. As he turned towards her, Bess saw the slight shudder that ran over his powerful body.

"Bess," he said slowly, "that was Josh Harmon. Old Tom is caught out someplace in this weather. We have to go down to the bottoms and help look for him."

As Bill's wife, she didn't have to ask who Old Tom was. She knew, as she knew about all the dogs of her husband's close friends. He was old, about twelve, and she shuddered at the thought of his suffering. She knew that because he suffered, Josh suffered, too.

At once she turned to start the coffee pot and said, "I'll fill your big thermos and make some sandwiches while you get ready. I suppose Steve is bringing his jeep?"

Bill paused on his way out of the kitchen, to look at her admiringly as he shook his head in wonder.

"I'll swear, Bess, you can read my mind. You know more about Steve and me than we do ourselves. Got a half notion not to trade you off after all. Steve will be over in ten minutes."

She smiled as he left the room and she busied herself with the coffee. He was always threatening to trade her for some new dog he had learned about, but he wouldn't do that. Would he? Oh, of course not.

By the time Steve arrived, Bill had changed the batteries in his big light, filled up with fresh carbide, and as an afterthought, put fresh batteries in his small two cell and stuck it in his pocket. A steaming cup of coffee was waiting for Steve when he entered the kitchen. Though his good-natured banter seemed as usual, Bess could see the concern in his blue eyes and sensed his worry from the impatient way he strode about the room. As she surveyed this big blond, rawboned friend of her husband's, she was thankful that they were friends and that Bill would have him by his side all night. She also found time for a thought or two concerning the fact that he was still a bachelor, in his late thirties, and would make some woman a fine husband.

There was no talk between them of what lay ahead. This, too, Bess understood. They wouldn't add to her apprehension by speaking of it in her presence. They would wait until they were out of the house and on their way.

Soon they were ready and as Steve opened the door, Bill kissed her gently and said, "Now, don't worry, honey. It won't take us long to find the old fellow and we'll be right home."

As they climbed into the jeep and stowed their gear, Steve said, "Guess we'd better take the ridge road and come in from the east, huh?"

Bill nodded in agreement as he replied, "Just about have to; Lick Creek is bound to be out all over the bottoms by now and we could never get to Josh's from the west. Sure am glad that he lives this side of Rinkers Creek so that all the high water will be below us."

The road was still without ice as they headed out of town to the north, but the bushes along the side and even the fences were accumulating a heavy covering. The rain came in sheets in front of the headlights, and Bill silently prayed that the old dog, wherever he was, had found shelter. But at the same time, there was an occasional flash of Old Tom's body lying motionless, ice-encrusted, on some hillside, while the elements tried in shame to hide as quickly as possible, the bitter evidence of man's inhumanity towards one who had only lived to serve.

It was an eight-mile drive to the little cabin where their old friend lived. The first six miles threaded their way along the top of the spiny ridge that bore to the northwest. When the blacktop ended at the crest of the ridge, Steve pushed the jeep at top speed, and the drive was mostly in silence as both seemed lost in their own thoughts.

The last two miles were by gravel road, half of which threaded its way downward in hairpin curves that dropped away on the right side to seemingly bottomless pits of blackness. This view was broken only occasionally, as the top branches of a giant hardwood were caught briefly in the glare of the headlights as it pushed up valiantly from its rock-studded bed, in a desperate attempt to reach out of its narrow canyon and meet the rest of the world face-to-face.

All of Steve's driving skill was needed here, as he crept at a snail's pace downward, yard by yard. Soft shoulders pulled at the wheels, while evidence of the rain's destruction became even more prevalent, as more and more ditches appeared across the road. Ditches growing deeper by the minute, as the water pouring down them ate steadily away in its ceaselessly tearing descent.

Not until the hill was safely negotiated and the road leveled off to a narrow ribbon winding its way through a canyon of towering ice- encrusted trees, did Steve relax his grip on the wheel.

With a sigh, he slowly brought the jeep to a stop and leaned back as he said, "You know, I wouldn't want to do that every night."

Bill handed him a cigarette and waited until they both lit up before answering.

"Me neither. But something tells me there will be worse things before this night is over. I've had a funny feeling all day, as if something was going to happen. I really wasn't surprised to get Josh's call. Does that sound silly to you?"

Steve's reply came without surprise. "No, because I've had the same feeling. In fact, it was bothering me plenty just before you called. Sometimes I think we have a second sense about those we feel closest to. And I sure do like that old man. Did you feel that there was something almost uncanny about the relationship between him and Tom? Like maybe they always knew exactly what the other was thinking?"

Bill nodded soberly. "Many times. Such as the way they came together in the first place. I guess we'll never know the truth about that, and I really don't think we are supposed to."

Steve started the jeep moving again as he said, "I guess you didn't let Bob know about this?"

"Heck, no," Bill laughed, "if I had, he would've been right here and he's just too old to be out on a night like this, whether he knows it or not. And besides, Jody would have known, too, even if Bob hadn't told him, and he's too young."

Steve chuckled with amusement that quickly subsided as he spoke soberly, "That's true. There would've been no holding him back or Jody either, and that's a fact. Look how he was always turning up when we were trying to get King back."

Bill nodded in agreement. There was a touch of admiration in his voice as he added, "I'll have to say one thing, though. If he hadn't been along most of the time, things might have turned out different. Bob might have been knifed down there at the bridge; and don't forget, it was Jody who came up with the idea to take Queen over to that trial to prove who really owned King."

"That's right," Steve answered. "For a thirteen-year-old, he sure did some amazing things. But he's still only fifteen. Too young for this night, same as Bob's too old at sixty-five."

Their conversation subsided now as they drew near to the fording of a narrow branch that drained one of the sharp deep valleys. As they crept slowly forward, Bill found time to reflect once more on their talk of Bob and Jody; uncle and nephew, two who were very close to one another. A slight shiver shook him as the roar of the water ahead began to drown out all other sounds. It sure wasn't any night for Bob and Jody to be out in these hills. Things had a way of happening on such a night, as nature flung her full force about, and sometimes, demanded payment.

For a moment, the sodden, narrow road seemed to Steve like an ominous beckoning path of destiny, luring them into an ever-narrowing tunnel, and at the end, was a maelstrom of roaring water, and then nothing beyond.

Stopping a few yards short of the raging stream, they surveyed it briefly before Steve spoke, "Better hit her hard, huh?"

"I believe that would be best. After all, the entire main channel isn't over ten feet wide and the water out over the road can't be over a few inches deep. Can you jump that fast water?"

Steve's answer was to back the jeep slowly for about a hundred feet and propel it forward with his foot to the floor. Going to high as soon as possible, the little vehicle was wide open as they hit the first water, covering the windshield like a waterfall, and completely eliminating everything from their sight. Almost instantly, there was the sensation of being airborne as the wheels left the edge of the main channel, and they were across, into another waterfall and then in the clear. Nothing but a straight easy course lay ahead to Josh's cabin now, as Steve eased up on the throttle and murmured, "Thank God for a jeep on a night like this."

Bill uttered a silent amen as he peered through the rain-splattered windshield for the sight of a light from the cabin. Faintly it appeared through the darkness, not far ahead, and to the right of the road. As they pulled to a stop in front of the snug little house, built so wisely up against the edge of the bluff high above the water line, the light from Josh's lantern gleamed brightly from the porch.

Somewhat apprehensive because he wasn't on the porch to meet them, they quickly dismounted and went to the house. Pushing the door open, they saw, at once, why he hadn't heard them drive up. Strained and white, he sat slumped in his chair. Even in sleep, exhaustion marked his every feature. Thankfully, they observed the dry clothes he wore, and a look about showed them the pile of muddy wet ones in a corner of the room, while a pair of muddy boots sat by the door.

Reluctant to wake him, they stood quietly for a moment, but then looked at one another in agreement. Gently, Bill placed his hand on his shoulder and shook him, ever so slightly, as almost in a whisper, he said, "Josh, wake up! It's Steve and Bill."

Slowly, and with great effort, the old man roused himself. Pity was in both their eyes, as they observed this proof of how he must have driven himself, hour after hour, in his search for Tom. His horn hung from the top of the rocker above his head. They knew of the many blasts that had poured from it today, as he had worked his way laboriously up to one ridge top after another. How he had hoped each time, as he sent out his call through the pouring rain, to hear Tom's in return. They visualized the sick disappointment in his cloudy blue eyes as, hand cupped to old ears, he tried in vain to pick up that familiar voice, and failing to do so, had moved on to another and another, until at last, rain-soaked and chilled to the bone, he could go no further. Then and only then, had he asked for help.

Bill called his name once more before the tired eyes opened. Groaning, he pushed himself up in the chair as he groped for reality. Shaking his head to clear the last traces of slumber, he said, "Oh, howdy, boys. Guess I must have dropped off for awhile. Wait'll I get my boots on and I'll be right with you."

Bill shook his head vigorously. "No, Old Timer. You've done your share of looking; now it's our turn. Just tell us where all you've been and where to go."

Josh's voice was surprisingly deep for an old man. "Thank you, boys. But I'll go, too."

It was obvious that nothing but sheer nerve gave him strength to rise from the chair and walk on wobbly legs toward his boots. The eyes of his friends met in mutual agreement that he must not leave the house. Steve's voice was a little more insistent even than Bill's had been, as he continued to protest.

"Josh, Bill's right, you have to stay in. Tell us where to look, and we'll have him back in no time."

Slowly, Josh bent over and picked up his boots. Then, leaning back against the wall for support, he began feebly to tug them on. Again, his reply was as before, "Sorry, Steve, but I have to go."

Without pause, his gnarled fingers began tightening the laces as his friends looked helplessly at one another. In desperation and with deep regret, Bill tried from another angle. He spoke harshly, in a voice the old man had never heard him use before.

"Now, you listen to us. We came down here to help find Tom, and we'll find him. But we didn't come down to nursemaid an old man. There's nothing but ice and water out there, and you'd be down half the time. You'll just slow us down and make the job a lot harder. You're eighty-four years old and should have a little sense by now, though I'm beginning to doubt it. I'm telling you, Josh, you'd just be in the way, and we don't want you along. That's the way it is."

Surprise had appeared in Steve's eyes at the beginning of Bill's outburst, but as he sensed the pity underneath, and understood what his friend was trying to do, he respected him for it. One look at Josh told him that he knew, too. Boots fully laced now, he stood wavering, with legs braced, as he faced them. Eyes filled with warmth and deep understanding; he slowly shook his head.

"It's no use, Bill. I know what you're trying to do, and I'm grateful, but I have to go. Don't you understand? That's my friend out there, suffering and freezing. He's waiting for me; he knows I'll be there. Do you think I could stay here in the dry, while he's out there? Do you think I could send someone else and not go myself, as long as I have a breath in me? Tom saved my life, you know, the very first time I saw him, and as long as I can drag one foot after another, I have to keep trying to save his."

Deeply moved, Bill and Steve approached him, and each placed a hand on his shoulder. "Okay, Old Timer," Bill said softly, "you can go, and I hope you can forgive us for trying to stop you, but there's just one thing we must consider. Tom might already be dead."

Serenely, the old man shook his head and knowledge beyond their understanding rang in his voice. "No, Bill, he's not dead. He can't be or I would know it. Believe me, it's true. I would know. Now, let's get started."

Silently, his friends stared at each other in awe. Through the mind of both ran the thread of their conversation on the way down. There was something uncanny about the relationship between Josh and Tom.

Through the open door, they could see the impatient Josh, lantern in hand, standing in the yard.

Quickly now, they closed the door and joined him, as Steve said, "Josh, there's no need for you to carry that lantern. Our carbides will give plenty of light for all to walk by, and besides, we have our big lights."

As they stepped back up on the porch to strike the carbides, Josh lifted the lantern up before his face, and said, "Guess I'd better take it anyway. This is all he ever hunted with, and he wouldn't recognize anything else. He has been guided on this lantern all his life, and it's what he's watching for right this minute. I wouldn't want to rob him of the gladness he will feel when he sees it tonight."

Realizing that the old man had reason for every strange thing he did or said, his friends only nodded in agreement. Then Bill asked, "Where do we go?"

"Well," Josh answered, "I've been to the north, to the east, and to the west. Could be I missed him somewhere along there, but I doubt it. So, let's try Coon Hollow up to the forks and then check out Orchard Hollow and Chimney Rock. Seems like he has taken to wandering around all over these hills here lately. Sorta like he was taking a last look at all the places he's hunted over the years. Acts like he knows something I don't.

With Josh setting the pace, they crossed the road, and set a course due south along an old logging road that paralleled the foot of the ridge. From a couple of hundred yards to the right, the voice of Rinkers Creek came clearly. There it tore on in its mad, swollen rush to join Lick Creek three hundred yards further on, where combined, they became the headwaters of Big Rush, to sweep on westward down the big hollow in ever-widening reaches.

The rain was still only about half sleet, but its knife-like edges slashed steadily at their faces. Faces that were soon pulled into the protection of turned-up coat collars as they plodded on due south. Their worry for Josh seemed rather groundless now, as the old man still retained the lead. For a mile, the road had run perfectly level, with little need to search for safe footing. But here the hollow narrowed, as the creek, swollen far beyond its banks, crowded up close towards the foot of the ridge.

At this point, Josh stopped and took the horn from his shoulder. Again and again, it set forth those familiar tones that the old dog had responded to so many times before. It lifted the notes high above the deafening roar of the creek, sent them crashing against the dripping timbered slopes, and on up the hollow in a begging entreaty for an answer. When the last note died away, the men stood in complete silence. Straining to hear, above the maddening turmoil of rushing water, that long bugle call they knew the old dog would give, if he heard, or if he were able. In each man's heart was a prayer, *Answer, Tom, answer*. But as the minutes dragged on, the rain became a little harder, a little colder, and the blackness blacker as they listened in vain.

In the silence that followed, it seemed to Bill and Steve that the gaunt old form of Josh became more slumped, that weariness and worry had at last demanded their toll, and extracted the last drop of energy from him in payment. When he finally spoke, it was as if all hope was gone.

"Boys, he should have heard that. He should have heard it."

As he slowly slung the horn back to his shoulder, it was as if there would be no use to ever take it down again. Feeling the hurt within him, they flinched at the trembling of his hands and at the sickness in his voice. They struggled with him to climb up out of the abyss of hopelessness into which he had fallen and strained to give him strength.

Bill spoke for both. "We're not done yet, Josh. There are a lot of reasons why he might not have heard. If he's too close to the water, there would have been too much noise. He might have been moving around, and you know, a dog doesn't hear his best when he's moving. And maybe he's just too far away."

Josh stood, reeling before them, but as he raised his head, there was a faint glimmer of hope in his eyes. "You know," he said, "maybe he's way up in the Chimney Rock and that does run off at a mighty sharp angle. It might just be that he couldn't have heard. Let's go up to the point and I'll blow again."

Forced by the swollen stream to climb to the side of the ridge, they found the going much slower. No road to follow now and each step must be planned in advance. Bill took over the lead for passage had to be forced through ice-laden brush. A steady crackling sound followed in their wake. Steve, who brought up the rear, kept close behind Josh. Experience had taught him that underneath the leaf mold covering those slopes, flat stones lay loose, ready to slide at the touch of a foot. Even in dry weather, they could be treacherous, and their danger was magnified a hundred times with conditions the way they were.

Occasionally, even with care, one or the other of them would step on a stone, only to have it shoot out and go sliding down the hill. Several times, they saw Josh feel out some particular spot, before putting his weight on it. He was careful enough, but for all his strong will, it became more and more obvious that each step had become a separate ordeal.

The rain's relentless fury had become a way of life, but it was gradually becoming less and less water and more and more ice. All three were soaked through across the shoulders and the front of their legs. Josh seemed lost to all thought. The effort required to place one foot in front of the other in a manner that would keep him from going end over end down the hill was using all the energy he had left.

After a quarter mile of this, Bill paused to lean against a stunted white oak. As he turned to look at Josh, he realized that the old man was definitely on his last legs. How he had ever gotten this far was more than he could understand. From the wrinkled face, pinched red by bits of sleet and cold, the old blue eyes blazed defiantly, as he, too, eased his back against a tree.

He sighed deeply at the pleasant relief of escaping, for the moment, the constant strain of bracing himself against the pull of the sharp downgrade. In spite of himself, his old head drooped, but he jerked it erect almost at once. For an instant, a brief flash of panic was in his eyes. A surge of pity swept over his friends because they had seen and understood.

Josh feared only that he might not have sufficient strength to see the search through to the end, and that the one who trusted him might find that trust misplaced. He was afraid that his slowness might be the cause of not finding him in time. His panic was for the other and not for himself.

Steve moved to the old man's side and lifted the horn from his shoulder, as he said, "You fellows wait here. I'm going to the top of the ridge and do a little blowing."

When Josh would have protested, Bill said, "Let him go, Josh. It's a long way to the top and he's younger than we are anyway. I'm glad to wait here and rest."

The old man's eyes followed Steve as he started to climb. "Steve," he said, "the notes won't be the same, but I guess the tone will. Blow her southeast and listen good, son, listen good."

"Don't worry, Old Timer," Steve called back over his shoulder, "I'll listen as I never listened before."

His friends watched in silence as his light, climbing even higher, weaved in and out among the ghostly silhouettes of shimmering giants. The sleet hissed and sputtered against Josh's old lantern and bounced off to the already-covered ground.

During the fifteen minutes it took him to reach the crest, Steve had only one thought, would the horn bring an answer? If it didn't, then there was no use to keep hoping. If Tom were alive, he would hear the horn.

As he reached the crest, he paused for a minute to ease his quivering legs. Leaning back against a monstrous rock, he breathed deeply. Even for him, the climb had been a tough one. Slowly, he unslung the horn and placed it to his lips. He remembered Josh's way and tried to duplicate it, one long and two shorts. Then the sound of the horn came, beautifully loud and clear, rolling out over the valleys below, slashing through the sleet and ice-imprisoned timber, bouncing off the huge rocks dotting the slope, and softly made its way down the ridge of the Chimney Rock, a half mile to the south. Ever so gently, it floated to the mouth of a small cave where it hovered for awhile and then disappeared.

Only a whisper, faint and fleeting, but it caused a stirring, a flicker of movement in the blackness at the mouth of the cave, a quivering of shadows ever so briefly, and again, all was still. Again and again, the music of the horn crept down over the hilltop and wafted softly down the ridge. A song, breathlessly tantalizing in its promise, and hope was reborn.

Again, a flutter at the cave mouth, that became definite movement as the notes came again and settled gently around the dark bulk lying there.

Slowly, the last flickering sparks of life were fanned anew, as the tired old heart tried valiantly to rally, to pump strength through the half-stiffened body. Little by little, the great old head lifted, weaved weakly from side to side, and briefly, all signs of suffering fled from the gentle old eyes as love was mirrored there. Love for the one who had come, as he had known he would.

As Steve listened to the last notes fade away, he was suddenly aware of the heavy silence. With a start, he realized that the rain and sleet had stopped. One instant it was driving at him and the next it was gone. Not gradually in a slackening off, but all at once, as if a giant faucet had been turned off.

He stood quietly, while an eerie feeling crept over him. With eyes fixed on the solid blackness to the south, he hardly breathed as he waited. Ever so softly, the long moan reached out and found him. Quickly, he once more touched the horn, a question in soft fluted tones, "Tom, is that you?" And as before, the answer came pleadingly, "Yes, but hurry."

Pausing only to fix the exact location in his mind, Steve plunged recklessly down the slope. Unmindful of loose rocks, he merely dropped from tree to tree, as all hunters of the hill country learn to do. Far below, Bill and Josh watched his rapid descent with growing excitement, and anxiously waited for his first words as he hurtled into the light.

Their searching gaze saw the triumph mirrored in his eyes, but his calm voice was tinged with caution. "I'm not sure, fellows, but I did get an answer of some kind. It came from Chimney Rock Hollow, so let's go check it."

Without a word, Josh picked up the lantern and took the lead. For the time being, at least, his weariness seemed cast aside. His companions found time to worry about his apparent unconcern for the dangerous footing, but something willed him on, lifted him lightly over loose stones and dangerous ice, and in twenty minutes saw him safely facing directly into the black void of Chimney Rock. As Bill and Steve pulled up, to stand silently beside him, no words were spoken, for there was nothing to say. Here they would seek the answer.

Slowly, Steve unslung the horn and held it out to Josh. With a prayer in his heart, he accepted it without a word. For a minute he stood gazing at its worn smoothness as he caressed it with trembling hands. He understood why Steve had passed it to him. He and Bill would step aside, for this was something between Tom and himself. Anyone else would be an outsider. If Tom were up there in that blackness somewhere, it was his right to give the old fellow the word that he had been found. And if he wasn't, then it was up to him to admit defeat, to pronounce the search over.

He seemed reluctant to sound the horn, as if afraid of the answer, yet nothing could have kept him from doing so. Slowly, the tired old arms lifted it to his lips. Even then he seemed hesitant, as he searched for perfection in the placing of the mouthpiece against his lips. This had to be just right. There could be no faltering in the promise of the message, no lacking in the sincerity that he had never discontinued the search, that he would have been there sooner if it had been possible, and apology for his frailties and limitations as a human being.

Though both had heard Josh's horn countless times before, neither was able to suppress a prickling of the hairs at the base of their neck when it finally came. For something was different, as if it was all the calls ever sent to Tom all rolled into one. No loud blast thrown in desperation against the ice-bound blackness of uncertainty, but a soft muted sob of entreaty, of words spoken in love, that told of frustration and struggle against obstacles that kept him away. And finally, a begging of forgiveness.

Then it was ended. Just the one long and two shorts. Then silence, while all three held their breath and prayed. As the silence dragged on, they could see the start of the crumbling of his spirit. They knew, that within seconds, would come the end of a man. A wilting from which there could be no recovery, a loss of desire to exist, melting the inner core completely, so as to precede only slightly the collapse of the outer shell of the man.

But when it seemed that there could be no answer, that too much time had passed since the last note died away, it came pleading out of the darkness. One soft low moan, and though they waited with bated breath, there was no more. That his powerful bugle call could be reduced to such a weak sobbing tone told them of the seriousness of his condition and of the hours of suffering he had endured.

Josh expressed the thoughts of all in two words repeated over and over. "Thank God, thank God." Then, as if emerging from a fog, he added, "What has he been through to weaken him so?"

Below and to their right was the fork where the Orchard Hollow and Chimney Rock Creeks met in wild boiling confusion, while straight ahead to the east lay their destination. Tom's voice had come from there.

Again, Josh picked up his lantern and on tottering legs started to lead out, but Bill quickly strode past him as he said, "Let me pick the way, Old Timer, for this slope is a bad one. Lucky for us, though, he's on this side. Be careful where you step."

Long past protesting Bill's taking over the lead, Josh fell in meekly behind, but after a few steps, he said, "You know, I'm afraid I know where he is and what has happened to him. It makes me sick to think about it."

Both Steve and Bill knew instantly what he meant. The little cave up ahead was well known to them also, and the possibility of some trapper setting a trap there was too likely to ignore.

When neither of his friends spoke, Josh continued, "There's been a kid running a trap line across the head of these hollows, Silas Keener's boy, about sixteen, I guess. Saw him up there a week ago and asked him to not set any out in the open. He gave me to understand that he would set them any place he wanted. It's county land and there's no law against trapping on top of the ground, so what could I do?"

His friends could well understand why his voice was full of bitterness. For he spoke for all hound men in Indiana, in disclaiming the law allowing on top of the ground sets. In fact, there just wasn't any law pertaining to that method of trapping. It was just ignored, and until the hound men in the state tried to organize and do something about it, it would remain that way.

Pausing for a minute to let Josh catch up, Bill summed it up in a few words. "There is no protection for a hound in Indiana. Our legislators are always about fifty years behind in their classification of a hound. They won't even bother to find out what they're worth and how wrong they are. Mostly, because too many of them are a bunch of powderpuff desk jockeys who consider such things as hounds and hunting far beneath them. We all know that it's practically impossible to convict a dog thief in this state. In fact, if you do locate a stolen dog, it will be without the aid of the law, for they will give you no assistance; and furthermore, if you do get your dog back, the thief can usually make you pay a feed bill. And the law will see that you do."

His tirade over, Bill again took the lead in their cautious route along the side of the ridge. Josh was stumbling more now, and more than once, Steve had grasped his arm just in time to prevent him from spinning end over end down the ridge to the roaring, rock-strewn creek below. Here and there, a rockslide caused a detour, but for the most part, they held to a straight course. They were traversing a line that should bring them to within just a few feet below the mouth of the cave. As they drew closer with every step, the same thought was in each of their minds. *Was he there? If so, was he still alive?*

Then abruptly, it loomed up out of the darkness. Their carbide lights cast a ghostly glow over the huge rock towering ten feet above them, and were reflected in shimmering shadows that danced over the swirling layers of ice on its front. Ice formed from the steady trickle of water running down its face from the floor of the cave above.

The mouth of the cave was still hidden from their sight by the height of the rock. As Bill started up, he felt the hand of Josh on his shoulder, as he said, "Wait, Bill, let me go up first."

Quickly, Bill stepped aside, slightly ashamed that it had been necessary for Josh to remind him that Tom must see him first, that he must know that his faith in his master had not been misplaced. As Josh pushed past, Bill said softly, "Sorry, Old Timer, I just wasn't thinking."

Silently, they stood looking upward as Josh clawed his way up and around the west side of the rock and onto its table-like top. Weaving like a tree in a storm, he stood upright while he scooped a small flashlight from the side pocket of his old hunting coat. As he flicked it on, his friends knew at once that the search was ended. For he dropped to his knees with a moaning cry, "Poor old fellow, poor Old Tom."

Instantly, Steve started up, but Bill laid a restraining hand on his arm as he said, "Not yet. Wait until Tom recognizes him if he can."

Again, they stood breathlessly waiting for some sign that Tom still lived. Josh's voice was almost incoherent as he called his name over and over, begging him to live. Maybe a minute later would have been too late, but finally, those waiting below heard a low whine and then another and the tone of Josh's voice turned to joy.

Seconds later, they stood beside their old friend and gazed down at a scene that brought tears to their eyes. Josh was on his knees beside the almost lifeless body of Tom. With one hand he held the old fellow's head up out of the water, while vainly trying to remove the large one-and-a-half trap from the hideously swollen right front foot. But the violent trembling of his hand denied him the use of what little strength he had left. With a sobbing cry, he realized that he couldn't even begin to depress the spring.

Looking up at his friends, with tears running unashamedly down his cheeks, and in a voice that told of all the wretched sickness within him, he said, "He didn't deserve this. Surely, God knows he didn't deserve this."

Instantly, Bill was on his knees beside him, as he said, "Easy,

Old Timer, he's not feeling any pain from the trap now. Here, let me get it."

As Josh relinquished his hold, Bill's big right hand grasped the spring of the trap while his left hand held the leg just above. Easily, he depressed the heavy spring, but the jaws had become so imbedded in the swollen flesh that they failed to move. Steve knelt at once and gently pulled them apart. A sharp whimper was all the sign that Tom gave that any feeling at all remained.

The usual shiny blackness of his coat was covered by a white blanket. As he had grown steadily weaker, the fires of life had banked their furnaces, one by one, until all body movement ceased. Without body heat to melt the ice, it had quickly taken over. From the tip of his nose to the end of his tail, he was encrusted with ice. With a look of bewilderment, he seemed to ask, only too plainly, "*Why?*"

For the first time, Josh seemed content to let his friends take over completely. From a body wracked by anguish, worry, old age, and self-condemnation, his voice came plaintively, "Can we save him? Can we save him?"

The actions of his friends were their answer, as they set out to restore some heat to the half-frozen body. Quickly removing his big hunting coat, Bill spread it out on the ground at the side of the cave mouth. Steve then picked up Tom and placed him on it. He then at once removed his coat and his insulated undershirt. This he carefully wrapped around the old dog and placed his coat on top of that. Together, they inserted their hands underneath and slowly began massaging the cold body.

Josh stood quietly by as they worked desperately in their battle against time. How much did they have? Minutes? Seconds, before all life fled? They could only try their best as long as there was any hope left. Little by little, they could feel the ice on his coat melting away. Slowly at first, and then he was only wet, and that was soon absorbed by the undershirt. Excitedly, they realized that heat was definitely returning to his body.

Getting to his feet, Bill jerked off his undershirt, as he said, "Take yours off him and let's get this dry one around him."

As the warmth from Bill's dry shirt snugged about him, Tom looked up at Josh with a soft whine. As the old man dropped to his knees beside him, his pink tongue went out to lick the trembling hand caressing his silvery old head.

Standing silently above them, his friends sadly surveyed this exchange of affection, and then looked at each other with a shake of their heads. Their eyes portrayed identical thoughts. Two grand Old Timers at the end of the trail. It was obvious that Tom would lose his foot. There was just no chance that life would return to it. He had been in the trap too long. Even if he lived, his hunting days were over.

Josh was in bad shape. So bad, in fact, that their most immediate concern was how he would stand the trip back to the cabin. Tom would have to be carried; there was no doubt about that. This they could manage without too much trouble, but Josh would be another problem. For all his age, he was still a big man. With the ridge slick with ice, the two miles would be an ordeal.

Unslinging his big light, Bill turned it on the towering ridge behind them. As the beam cut through the blackness towards the top, great hardwoods seemed to be looking directly down on them. Giant rocks perched with tenuous hold, as if standing on tiptoe, ready to leap down the slope at the first disturbance of the ground about them.

Steve, who had stepped to his side, said softly, "That would be the best way back, but we would never make it to the top with these two."

Bill shook his head in agreement. "Nope, sure can't. Two hundred yards of ice, slate, and loose rock. Josh could never get up that, and we sure can't carry him, for we would all end up down there in the creek."

Behind them, the sound of a grunt and labored breathing drew their attention. Josh, on his knees beside Tom, was trying to lift him off the ground. But his effort was pitifully weak and obviously hopeless. The tragedy in his face was heartrending as he lifted moist eyes to his friends, and said, quavering, "Boys, I can't even get him off the ground. I can't carry my own dog home, when he needs me. I'm sure no good anymore."

Bill's voice, too, was choked with emotion, as he said, "Well now, I'd consider it a downright insult if you were to carry him. As a friend of Tom's, too, I've got a right to do something for him and you're not going to beat me out of that. I'll carry him."

Josh knelt helplessly beside Tom as Steve reclaimed his coat and put it on. Then picking the old dog up in his arms, he waited until Bill slid into his coat, and then relinquished him to the strong arms that cradled him gently against a broad chest. Bill's undershirt was left wrapped around Tom's body.

Steve understood that his task was cut out for him, too. Josh would need help in negotiating those tortuous two miles back to the cabin. If he could make it on his own two feet, they would, indeed, count themselves fortunate.

As Josh climbed groaningly to his feet, Steve quickly slid down the incline beside the cave base. There he turned to brace himself, in case one of the others should come too fast and hurtle off the small table and into the raging stream below. Josh came slowly and easily, and then Bill, flat on his back, with Tom held safely away from contact with the ground.

When Josh feebly picked up his lantern, his friends exchanged glances with a shrug. He didn't have the strength to carry it, but let him try. When he also chose to take the lead, they were also agreeable. Steve would follow close to him, just in case he slipped. Bill, with Old Tom, would bring up the rear.

Silently, the old man led out. He hadn't spoken a word since his outcry at not being able to pick up the body of his four-footed friend. By not speaking, he had admitted to his friends, the acceptance of his weakened condition, and his complete trust in their being able to see them safely through.

Progress was painfully slow. Where the ice covered only the ground, their boots cut gratefully through, but hidden rocks remained a constant menace. At times, it was necessary for Bill to stop completely, as Steve assisted Josh over some particularly hazardous spot. As these waiting periods increased, Bill became aware that the temperature had gone well below freezing and that somewhere along the line, he had been sweating. The damp clammy feeling of his clothes was like a cold compress against his skin.

It was fast becoming more evident that the condition of Josh was worsening. More often now, he had occasion to pause while searching for safe footing, as if reluctant to trust in his own judgment. To see their old friend reduced to such a shambles of the man he once was, brought deep sadness to Bill and Steve. Somehow, they had never thought of him as being old. Now, both realized that, subconsciously, they had taken his great strength for granted, as something that would go on forever. Yesterday, he might have been young, but today, today he was an old man, eighty-four years old, and near the end of his trail.

At the end of the first half mile, when Josh was again pausing to look for a place to step, Bill called a halt. Old Tom's seventy pounds was bearing down considerably by this time. But a chance to rest his aching arms was only half the reason for stopping. A chance to let Josh rest, without calling attention to the fact, was the other.

He shook his head at Steve's offer to relieve him of his burden. Sitting back against the hillside, he let his arms rest on his knees, so that Tom's weight was absorbed without strain. The old fellow was riding quietly, as if he knew that by remaining still, he could lessen the load. His head was up now, and the usual intelligent look was back in his eyes.

As Josh looked back to where Bill sat, stroking the long ears, his eyes held a question, but afraid to put it into words, he said nothing. Bill smiled, as he said happily, "He's doing fine, Josh, he will be his old self again in no time."

Relief shone in the old man's eyes, to be replaced almost at once by worry. "But his foot, Bill?"

"What about his foot?"

"He was in that trap an awfully long time."

Though it made him sick to look at it, Bill gently massaged the leg above the hideously misshapen paw as he said, "Oh, I believe it will mend fast. Now if it had been below freezing, we all know that it wouldn't have taken much over ten minutes in that trap to have made him lose it. But the temperature being what it was, I don't think there is anything to worry about. You'll see, Old Timer. In no time at all, he'll be running these hills as good as ever."

The man of yesterday would have known without asking that there was no chance to save the foot, but the one asking now was as a child. Defeated by time and emotional exhaustion, he trusted his friends to even think for him, and to accept their answers without question.

Steve, heartsick, sat with downcast eyes, unwilling to intrude upon the look of happiness he knew Bill's words had brought to the old man. Time enough for truth later, when Josh was stronger. What was the harm in words that he wanted to hear? Let him dream of the great hound that had split the hills wide open with his bugle cry, as he splashed the creeks dry, and tore like a demon over the ridges with such flashing speed that even the mighty oaks trembled at his passing. Let him dream of the hundreds and hundreds of times that beautiful treeing song had rung out over the hills, in booming tones, that caused hunters for miles around to stop and listen, their own dogs forgotten for the moment, as they said, "Listen, there's Old Tom. He's got another one up." Yes, let him dream. For him, little else remained.

Stirring himself, Steve took out his knife. Selecting a sturdy hickory sapling, he quickly cut and trimmed it to a good-sized walking stick. "Try this, Josh," he said. "Maybe it will ease you a little."

The old Josh would have bristled at such a suggestion, but now he meekly accepted the cane, as he said shakily, "Thanks, Steve. I reckon I can use it."

As before, they let him lead out, slowly, at an agonizing pace. At times, the going was comparatively easy, as more or less level strips, interlaced with small trees, lay in their path. Then the old man's pace quickened, but soon, too soon, the ground was again dropping away from under their feet. The rocky sections, devoid of trees, slowed the old man to an uneasy shuffle.

From below and always to their left, the roar of Rinkers Creek beat a steady tattoo on their ears. A constant reminder that should they slip, it waited hungrily to enfold them in arms of cold, wet, swirling blackness, amid slimy jagged rocks that promised to complete the job that the icy blanket covering the ridge had started.

Unable to relax, for constant need to keep an eye on Josh, Steve, too, was beginning to feel the strain. The old man's pace had become rather erratic. He seemed to call upon some hidden source of reserve every now and then and would suddenly spurt forward several feet beyond the reach of Steve's arms. No word had passed his lips since accepting the walking stick. The need to quickly close the gap between them each time lent strength to the growing conviction in Steve's mind that their old friend hardly realized where he was. That he moved in a semi-conscious state, motivated by desperation and the one compelling thought, in his fatigue-fogged mind, to reach his cabin.

Fretting at the snail's pace they were forced to maintain, Bill shifted the big body of Tom in his arms and looked up, hopefully, at the ridge above. His eyes, searching for any possible escape route to the top, found no change in terrain. They would still have to climb practically straight up; an impossible task under the circumstances.

As the temperature continued to drop, the ice under their feet became harder to break through. Travel along the steep slant of the hillside was becoming more dangerous by the minute. Foot by foot, they ate up the second half mile. As Steve turned to look at him, Bill shook his head. Agreeable, Steve said nothing and continued on in the faltering footsteps of Josh. Nothing to be gained by stopping. They both feared that if their old friend ever came to a stop again, he would never be able to regain his feet.

With the hickory stick in one hand and his old lantern clutched tightly in the other, Josh made about as much time as a terrapin crossing a busy highway. But stoically he plodded on, seemingly unaware of anything but the instinct to continue homeward.

Steve had decided on one thing. Once they reached the old logging road and could get off the side of the ridge, he was going to carry Josh the rest of the way, even if he had to throw him over his shoulder to do it. In another quarter mile they would reach it, but in that last quarter lay some of the most dangerous spots on the ridge.

Apprehensively, he remained intent on staying within reach of Josh, but the old fellow's attitude had him worried. He moved in stumbling silence, not once looking back. And from all appearances, completely oblivious to the fact that Bill and Steve were with him. Even on occasion when Steve's hand had gone out to steady him, he gave no sign that he was aware of Steve's presence.

With half the remaining quarter behind them, Bill decided to risk a short stop. His arms felt like chunks of lead and the need to rest them could not be ignored any longer. Ahead, not more than a hundred yards away, lay a particularly dangerous stretch of solid slate. Though not more than twenty feet across, it was impassable, even in dry weather. They would have to climb up and around it, and with Tom in his arms, it would be rough.

Relieved, Steve saw that Josh obeyed the request to stop, but remained unsteadily on his feet. Together, he and Bill looked down at the rushing waters below. With the varied structure of the ridge, their path had sometimes taken them to within ten feet above it and at other times as high as forty, with always the sheer edge close at hand. Their carbide lights were reflected upon its muddy writhing current as it pounded against huge boulders, leaving creamy suds in its wake, and then tore on relentlessly to crash against the next one below. Though not especially deep, six or seven feet at the most, it had the look of wickedness, capable of sending a man battering against a hundred jagged rocks, or as many as it took until he was reduced to a lifeless mass.

Instinctively, they both dug their heels in a little deeper, as if the incline had suddenly tugged violently at them. And both felt an impelling urge to be away from there. Arms sufficiently rested now, Bill rose to his feet. Old Tom rode high, with head up and eyes fastened intently on the figure of his master. A whine came from his throat as he saw the tottering Josh again take the lead. Then a series of whimpers broke from him, and Bill felt a shiver sweep over the big body.

Startled, Steve looked back, as the sound of Tom's whimpering reached him. A glance at Bill's face told him that he, too, had sensed the connection between Josh and Tom. It seemed impossible to not believe that the old dog feared for something that lay ahead. Instinct, uncanny foresight, almost touching upon the supernatural? *Ridiculous*, he told himself, but as their strange caravan crept onward, foot by foot, through the frozen darkness, he found it not too hard to believe, amid such surroundings.

Ahead, the slated slide loomed up at the edge of their light circle. Ominous, under its coating of ice, it was as if nature, in all her fury, had combined all her efforts into one last attempt to create an obstacle they could not surmount. The wickedness of its descent was accented even more by the sheer drop off at its lip. Straight down to the boiling stream forty feet below.

When it was fully bathed in the glow of their lights, Bill drew to a stop, as he said, "Okay, men, let's rest a minute, while we figure a way around this.

Gratefully, Steve pulled up with a sigh. Even as he was turning around to face Bill, a moaning whimper of terrifying intensity burst from the throat of Old Tom. An unbelievable sight met his eyes.

An amazed Bill was struggling with a wildly-kicking Tom, who was trying his best to dislodge himself from the arms that held him. Again, that shuddering moan broke from him, as his eyes stared with piteous appeal down the trail past Steve.

Suddenly, Steve realized what was happening. Wheeling around in the direction of Josh, a cry of horror burst from his hips. Distracted by Tom for an instant, as his back was turned, he was unaware that their old friend hadn't stopped. Even as he threw himself forward, it was too late. Like a man in a trance, Josh stepped out onto the ice-covered slate. Though everything happened in an instant, he was to relive it many times like a slow-motion picture. Even as the old man's feet flew from under him, his lantern was forming a slow looping arc out over the narrow canyon wall. As it dropped out of sight, Josh, flat on his back, without a sound, shot over the edge behind it.

To Bill, at the rear, it was all like an unbelievable nightmare. One instant, they were all together, with the end of their journey only a short distance away, and the next, chaos. As Josh disappeared, Tom had exploded. Thrashing wildly, as sobbing cries came from his throat, he became impossible to hold. As he tore himself free, with hind legs extended, he hit the ground and propelled himself forward with a limping rush. Vaguely, Bill was aware of the sound of Josh striking the water, just before Tom reached the edge and leapt over after him. And the nightmare was then complete, as Steve tore his coat from his shoulders, knocked his cap backward from his head, and threw himself over after them.

Like a waterfall of bodies cascading down the side of a cliff, one, two, three, and they were gone. Bill was alone and the splashing sounds came back in unison. Stunned by the suddenness of the disaster, he watched in fascination as the walking stick, thrown uphill by Josh when he fell, came sliding down and disappeared over the edge.

Then he was at the edge, with his big light turned on the wild scene below. They were caught for an instant in the glare, and then they were gone, swept out of sight around the curve. But the scene was forever branded on his memory. The body of Josh was being rolled over and over as the current carried him along. Only Old Tom's head was visible, as he swam powerfully after him. And behind, Steve was swimming furiously in a valiant effort to catch them both.

Realizing that there was nothing to be gained by following them into the water, Bill knew that he would be more help on the bank, if he could somehow get below them. Bill struck the slope on a dead run. In desperation, his boots tore at the frozen crust so violently that they broke through with every step, and he was up and around the slide and headed across the point of the ridge. The curve of the creek was a long sweeping one that bore back to the right as it came out into the main hollow. If he could cross the point and get down the other side below the curve before they reached it, he might have a chance.

A trail of shattered ice lay behind him, knocked from the limbs and trunks of small trees that he only halfway tried to detour around. With breath sobbing in his throat, he tore like an express train across the top of the point, in a terrible lonesome race against time, with a prayer on his lips that he wouldn't be too late.

Then he was at the edge of the west slope, and hurtling down. Recklessly, he let himself go freely, with only an occasional slap at a passing tree to slow his descent. The roaring water came up to meet him, as he neared the end of his downward rush. With no cliff to worry about on this side, he slid to a stop at the water's edge, unslung his light, and turned it upstream.

As his frantic eyes followed the beam, a horrible sickness welled up in him. Only huge ugly boulders marred the surface of the swollen stream. With desperate anxiety, he played the light back and forth, searching frantically for some sight of bobbing heads, flailing arms, anything that would prove to be the struggling figures of his friends. But with all his willing that they be there, he still saw nothing.

Turning then, he played the light downstream, but with the same results. Only the writhing, tortured current met his gaze. For a moment, loneliness such as he had never known swept over him; a horrible crushing loneliness, so engulfing as to leave no room for any other thought except defeat, and the terrible feeling that he had failed.

Limp with the sickness of his failure, he stood quietly for a time, head bowed in hopeless acceptance of what had happened. Numbed, he stood there, practically unhearing, his senses dulled by the disaster. He realized later, that he had actually heard the sound a time or two, before realization of its meaning penetrated his numbed brain. But now his head lifted, and a great elation ran over him. There was no denying that which came again to his straining ears.

Head up, every nerve and muscle rigid, he stood, poised like a buck testing the wind, ready to spring off in any direction. Again, it came, the unmistakable sound of Steve's voice calling his name. Like a phantom breeze, it came floating down on the savage current and propelled him like a catapult upstream in the direction of its source.

Furiously, he ran along the side of the ridge just at the water's edge, unmindful of treacherous footing and flailing brush. At the end of fifty yards, he saw them. All three together, pinned against the backside of a huge rock by the pressure of the current. Steve's white-toothed smile flashed briefly, from a face strained and white, as he said, "What kept you?"

The relief was so great it left him weak for a moment as he surveyed the scene. All their heads were above water and visible signs of movement came from both Josh and Tom. Even then, Bill found time to marvel at the connection between those two. He could see Josh's white hand firmly grasping the collar of Tom, while at the same time, the old dog's teeth were clenched tightly on the shoulder of his master's hunting coat. Even near death, their only thoughts were to help each other. Steve, it seemed, was more or less supporting both of them.

Steve's bantering voice snapped him back to reality. "Well, you gonna stand there all night? Get us out of here. This water is beginning to get a mite chilly."

Without replying, Bill searched the slope with his eyes for some means of making their rescue. The boulder that had stopped them lay only about twelve feet out from shore, but between was a deep channel of heavy, fast-moving water. Then above him a few yards, his eyes fell on a possible solution. A slender blackjack tree lay on the ground, a victim of the drought a few years back that had killed so many of that species. Its roots were only shallowly imbedded in the rocky soil.

As he climbed up to look it over, he saw that all the strength he could muster would be needed if he were to do as he planned. About twelve inches at the base and tapering gradually towards the top, the length of about thirty feet would also add to his plan. Quickly, he ripped dead branches away from the trunk. Wasting no time on the large ones, he attacked only those that were within his means. Steve, watching from his icy berth, saw his intentions, and knew that with all his immense strength, Bill would have to call up just a little extra, if he were to succeed.

Silently, he watched, as Bill slid his arms under the butt end, and with thighs and shoulders straining, slowly rose, with it cradled in his arms. At first, with a forward and backward movement, he broke loose any contact the remaining limbs had with the ground. The muscles of his neck swelled as he planted powerful legs firmly and began to move the tree downhill. The almost impossible task was increased by the need to carry the butt upstream to a distance equaling nearly the length of the tree, and at the same time, at an angle that would prevent the top from sliding down behind him.

Gradually, he worked it upstream, foot by foot. Steve's muscles ached as he strained with him, his own discomfort forgotten in the frustration he felt at not being able to help. He could see the sweat streaming down Bill's face, as he threw all his strength into covering those last few feet. From the first, Steve had known what his friend was trying to do. He also realized the narrow margin of safety with this attempt to rescue them.

He was going to let the top rest against the ash growing parallel to their position, while the butt would be thrown in upstream. This would allow the current to carry it down to lodge against the edge of the rock nearest the shore. A mistake in judging the distance necessary for the proper sweep of the tree could have devastating results. If thrown in at too short a distance upstream, it would fall short of reaching the rock and would only be swept back against the bank. But if carried too far upstream, the heavy end would reach those huddled behind the rock with crushing impact.

As Bill paused to look back, a worried frown creased his forehead, as he pondered the correctness of his judgment. A mistake on his part could very well mean injury or death for one or all of his friends.

Not satisfied to leave him with the entire responsibility, Steve called cheerfully, "I'd say that's about right, pard. Let her rip."

For a short time, Bill stood unmoving. Dread of what could happen was mirrored on his face. He found the responsibility a heavy load to bear. But as he watched, Steve moved with his charges, as far back to the left side of the rock as he could. This left a target of approximately four feet of unoccupied space, at which to aim. It didn't go unnoticed, that Steve placed the figures of Josh and Tom next to the rock, with his own broad back between them and the impending danger.

Again, Steve prompted Bill with a motion of his hand, as he called, "Throw her in, boy. Do you think we want to stay in here all night?"

The decision partially taken from him, Bill glanced back, once more, to see that the top was anchored securely behind the small ash. Then, with another anxious look at his friends, he took a deep breath, braced his legs, and with a silent prayer, heaved the heavy end of the log out into the current.

There was an anxious moment, as it wavered between being pushed back to shore or answering the pull of the current. Finally, with agonizing slowness, it began to swing out. Then, as if snatched by a giant hand, it swung around like the pendulum of a great clock and bore down on those huddled behind the rock.

Standing directly at the hub of the sweep, Bill was unable to judge exactly the impending point of impact. For one horrible instant, he was sure that he had guessed wrong, that he had sent certain death down upon his friends. Without breathing, he stood transfixed, as the log picked up speed, and for an instant, blotted out the heads of those in the water. As it swept ever closer to them, it seemed certain that he had failed. With eyes closed, he waited for the sodden squashing sound of the heavy timber smashing into soft yielding flesh.

Then it came, with a solid resounding thump that snatched his eyes open in wonder. With a foot to spare, it had struck short of his friends, and was securely anchored solid behind the big rock. There was a brief shifting of the top as the current pressed it more firmly against the ash, and then it was still. Though the racing water pushed and heaved, as if determined to dislodge it, an excited Bill knew that he had won.

Tossing his light and coat to the ground, he ran as fast as he could. Plunging into the water above the log, he was instantly pressed tightly against it. Unable to reach bottom with his feet, he felt them swept underneath, and only his grip on the tree prevented him from being pulled underneath and on downstream. Disdainful of this small trifle, he pulled himself up, straddled the log, and made his way slowly towards the miserable group in the water.

By this time, Steve had worked all of them around the log's end and as close to the edge of the rock as possible. The body of Old Tom, being the most awkward to handle, was first. A precious minute was lost in the difficult task of getting his clenched teeth to unlock from their grip on the coat of his master. But finally, a flicker of understanding shone in his intelligent eyes, and he relinquished his hold.

With effort, Bill made his way across his precarious perch with the limp body. Laying him down carefully above the water line, he went back again for Josh. He knew his old friend was alive, but more than that seemed doubtful. He was unable to help himself, at all. Steve quickly climbed on to the log and reached the bank, as soon as Bill dragged Josh out of the way.

Now that it was over, Bill allowed a great weakness to take hold of him, as his legs seemed to suddenly give way. Sinking back onto the ground, his chest rose and fell furiously, as he took great gulps of air. Steve, still on his feet, was surprised to see that his hands were cut in a dozen places and that blood dripped from a jagged slash on his cheek. He had not been aware of his injuries until then.

Sadly, he surveyed the limp forms of Josh and Tom. Both still breathed raspingly, but were in an intense state of shock. Bill, strength regained, sat up and looked at the semi-motionless figures stretched beside him. The urgency of the situation brought him to his feet, with the help of Steve's extended hand. "Thanks, pard," Steve drawled, "maybe I can do the same for you some day."

"Not if I can help it," Bill acknowledged with a grin, as he set about retrieving his coat and light. The carbide on his head still burned brightly. One thought, above all others, was in the minds of both; get Josh and Tom back to the warmth of the cabin as soon as possible.

Only one hundred yards of ridge travel remained between them and the logging road. Bending over, Steve scooped up the limp form of Josh, waited briefly as Bill did the same for Tom, and then with fast strides, set out around the ridge. Striking hard, their feet dug in furiously and within a few minutes they reached the road.

With only a mile separating them from the cabin, they wasted no time on conversation. Saving their wind, instead, for as much speed as they could possibly command, in twenty minutes, they reached its pleasant warmth. The clock on the mantel showed the time to be only ten o'clock, a fact that came as a surprise to both. It seemed they had been gone much longer than the actual two hours.

In the light of the lamp that had been left burning, the gaunt, water-soaked figure of Josh looked tragically pale. He lay, unmoving ,on the bed where they had placed him. Quickly, they pulled off his wet clothes and got him under heavy blankets. On his pallet on the floor, Old Tom lay limp and lifeless. Only the faintest movement of his sides gave indication that some life still remained.

Stoking up the fire and throwing on fresh wood, Bill said, "Look around and see if you can't find a bottle someplace. Surely Josh was too smart a man to not have some around for medicine at his age."

In a few minutes, Steve came across the bottle and amply laced the coffee that Bill had ready. Josh's eyes remained closed in his pallid face, as Bill gently raised his head and forced some of the hot liquid between his blue lips. Slowly, just a few drops at a time, waiting for him to swallow the last, before adding more. Little by little, the color crept back into his cheeks, until at last, the heat from within, combined by the warm temperature of the room, met somewhere inside the exhausted old body and he was warm again. With a sigh, he opened his eyes.

For a minute, his gaze rested lingeringly on the faces of his friends, then traveled slowly around the room, caressing every object before going on to the next. When he finally spoke, they could have guessed what his first words would be, "Where's Tom?"

"He's fine, Josh," Bill answered. "A little weak maybe, but he'll be up and around in no time. I'm just fixing him some milk."

Lifting the pan of milk warming on the stove, he knelt beside the inert Tom. Though the old dog's eyes were wide open, he made no move to raise his head. The swollen paw was pushed grotesquely out from under his body, and it was obvious that terrible pain was beginning to take hold of it. The leg was beginning to twitch, and small whimpers came from Tom with every jerk.

Raising his head up carefully, Bill held the pan of milk before him. At first, it seemed that he would ignore it, but then his tongue went out and he slowly lapped up its contents. His coat was dry now and there seemed little they could do, for the present, but let him rest.

Softly, Steve said to Bill, "Are we going to try to take them to town or call a doctor down here?"

More alert now, Josh overheard the question. "Won't do much good to call a doctor, boys, for there's not much time left. But you can if you want to, cause I'm not leaving here."

His words left them with a strange feeling. A day ago, they would have argued, but this night had taught them better. Further strength was added to their convictions when, as Bill went to the phone, Josh said, "Call a vet for Old Tom, too."

Bill nodded soberly. "I was going to do that, Old Timer."

Knowing that Josh's doctor was cantankerous old Doc Heathcock, Bill had expected some kind of an argument when he finally got him on the phone. Bill was pleasantly surprised to receive a quick sympathetic agreement to come at once.

Next, he called Doc Warriner, the vet, and as he had expected, received no complaint. He, too, would be there as soon as possible. A cloud of heavy foreboding hovered over Bill as he walked over to where Steve sat beside the bed. For the first time, he remembered that they, too, were soaked to the skin. Soon their clothes were steaming beside the stove, while they sat wrapped in blankets before the appraising eyes of their old friend.

In contrast to the look of worry on their faces, Josh's was one of calm composure. Softness had eased the lines of strain, as if washed away by a satisfied acceptance of that which lay ahead. No signs of bitterness touched his faded blue eyes. Only an inner light, reflecting the glowing soul of a man who was at peace with himself, secure in the knowledge that he had left no evil behind along life's footpath.

Slowly, he looked from one to the other of his friends before his voice came weakly, "Boys, life must be awfully cold for those without true friends to lean on," and as he eyes went to Tom, "and the winters awfully long for those without someone to love."

When Bill appeared about to answer, he stopped him with a slight motion of his hand. "Let me finish while there's still time. I must lean on you once more. In Bob's safe, at the store, is an envelope containing my last request. Many would not understand, and would think them strange, or the product of a demented mind, but I'm sure that all three of you will understand. One more thing; have the vet make out a death certificate for my friend, Tom."

Steve and Bill bore the look of extreme helplessness, made only too real by an awareness that their old friend spoke from a knowledge of the future that was beyond their comprehension.

Huskily, Bill's voice came out little more than a whisper, "Old Timer, you know that we would do anything you ask us, but maybe it isn't time for last requests. You and Tom will pull out of this. Tomorrow, you'll feel like a different man. But the best thing for you to do now is to get some rest. We'll wake you up when the Doc gets here."

Josh smiled briefly with a slight nod of his head, "Yes, I guess it's time I got some rest, I'm awfully tired."

For a time, he lapsed into silence, with eyes closed. His friends sat unmoving, waiting patiently just in case he cared to continue. He lay so still, so white, that they thought sure he had gone to sleep.

Then he spoke again, in a voice surprisingly strong, "Remember, fellows, I'm a happy man, whose life has been rich for having had friends such as you and a companion like Old Tom. I've had my share of good things and there are no complaints from old Josh."

He paused for an instant and then he added, "Is Tom asleep?"

"Yes, Josh," Bill answered softly, "he's asleep."

Seconds passed before he showed that he had heard, then almost in a whisper, he said, "Good."

Unwilling to disturb him, they sat unmoving, wrapped in their blankets, each lost in his own thoughts. For several minutes, only the crackling of the wood stove invaded the drowsy silence of the warm room. Shadows of flickering flames danced a spirit revue along the wall, while the light from the kerosene lamp seemed to recede within itself.

Just short of the edge of troubled slumber, they were both snapped back to alertness by one word coming clearly from Josh. Without opening his eyes, he called, "Tom."

A whimper came from the old dog at the sound of his name, lifting his tired old head, and with eyes fastened on the figure on the bed, he began to drag himself across the floor. In fascination, they watched his slow progress, as inch by inch, he drew closer to Josh. They ached with the strain of sitting idly by, when their every sense cried out that they should help, but they knew it could not be.

Hardly breathing, they flinched with every scraping sound of his body as he dragged himself along. Josh lay unmoving, as still as death, but he knew when Old Tom reached his side. Slowly, one hand crept out from under the blanket and slid over the side of the bed to rest caressingly on the old dog's raised head. Tom whined as his tongue went out to return the caress in kind.

The two who sat there were unaware that they were trembling, so overwhelmed with the feeling that they should not be there at all, and that they were witnessing something that should be sacredly private.

As the seconds ran on, the strain in each man built up higher and higher. Then the silence was broken briefly by Josh. Hardly audible, his voice came raggedly, "Old Tom. Good Old Tom."

As the old dog whimpered in answer, his head sagged slowly down to the floor and the work-worn hand slid gently away, to hang suspended from the arm that dangled limply over the edge of the bed.

Wild-eyed, Steve and Bill stared at each other wordlessly, while they slowly let their breath out in unison. Visibly shaken, they made no attempt to put into words their mutual impression of what they had seen. The Master of hounds had checked the score card and found only hundreds plus; champions both, and had sent them on to the biggest hunt of all.

Like men rising from a drugged sleep, they both rose and went to their clothes. Unknowing whether they were dry or not, they both dressed in a hurry. With a hand that trembled, Bill dug out a cigarette for each. Not until they were both lit and half-smoked, did either say a word.

Finally, Steve croaked, "Lord, Lord, I don't want to see anything like that again."

Bill busied himself briefly, by adding more wood to the fire, before answering, "Yes, I know, I've been feeling the same way, but do you realize that we have been privileged? We've just witnessed something that most people in the world don't even know exists, and wouldn't believe it anyway."

"Well," Steve answered, "I believe it, even though I don't really understand it. Affection and trust between them, yes. That I can easily understand. But the other gives me ideas that I'm afraid to put into words. I even feel ridiculous thinking such a thing and I'll sure never try to explain it to anybody."

"Nope, me either," Bill said.

For another few minutes both remained quiet, lost in thought.

But then Steve suddenly exclaimed, "Hey, we plumb forgot about the Docs. Do you think that branch has run down yet?"

"Maybe and maybe not," Bill answered, "but we better run up and see.

As both started for the door, Bill halted, as he said, "You go ahead. It just doesn't seem right for somebody not to be with them."

Steve only nodded and continued out the door. Standing on the porch, Bill could follow his headlights all the way to the branch. He was relieved to see that they only hesitated briefly and then swung around and headed back for the cabin.

"Nothing to worry about there," Steve said, as he pulled to a stop, "they can make it easy now."

Returning to the warm interior of the cabin, they each selected a chair and made themselves comfortable. In a little while, Bill spoke drowsily. "You know, I was sorta surprised that Doc Heathcock was so willing to come down here tonight. It was like he might have been expecting such a thing to happen."

Before Steve got around to answering, they were both snapped from their lassitude by the sound of a car drawing up out front. Before either could reach the door, it was opened by a large ruddy-faced man of about sixty-five. "Sorry, boys, that it took me so long," he said, "but it was slow driving."

While he talked, he had removed his coat and hat. Taking them from him, Bill replied, "That's all right, Doc, there wasn't any use to hurry. There was nothing you could do anyway."

Startled, the doctor peered at the figure on the bed, with eyes just becoming used to the dimly-lit room, "You mean—?"

Without finishing the question, he strode quickly to the bed. "Yes," Bill said, "not long after we called. So, you see, you couldn't have gotten here in time after all."

Silently, he made his examination, then gently lifted the dangling arm and placed it across the chest before pulling the blanket over the entire body. From his seat on the side of the bed, he stared intently at the body of Tom that he had been so careful not to disturb. Bewildered, he raised his head to look questioningly at Bill and Steve.

"Yes, Doc, they died together, at the very same instant." Bill paused reflectively, then added, "Does that part seem strange to you?"

Slowly, the Doc shook his head, "Well, no, it really doesn't. Now if it had been anyone else, perhaps it would have. But there was something here that I couldn't put my finger on. It was just sorta—" His words faltered to a stop as if he found an explanation difficult. Then Bill spoke for him.

"No need for you to try to explain, Doc. We know what you mean. We've been around them a lot, but how come you to think such a thing?"

The Doc studied the question for a minute. "Well, I don't really know. Maybe it was when I warned him about climbing the hills after that old dog. He knew his heart was bad, and when I told him that old hound would be the death of him yet, he just smiled and said, 'Now, how could he be the death of me, when he's actually been the very life of me, all these years?' "

The sound of another motor in front of the house sent Steve to the door. As expected, it was the vet, Doc Warriner, a tall serious-faced man of about fifty. During the exchange of greetings, his eyes had fallen on Old Tom and the blanket-covered figure on the bed. Moving slowly, he walked over to stand, silently gazing down. Then, still without a word, he knelt beside Tom and carefully examined him. Satisfied that no life remained, he put away his stethoscope and got to his feet.

Staring intently at the others, he said, "He was an old dog and had a bad heart. His hunting days should have been over a year ago."

Bill nodded, "They both had a bad heart, Doc, and should have quit hunting long ago. And they just did. 10:35, to be exact."

With a motion of his hand, the vet indicated the body under the blanket. "I assume that is Josh. You know, it's quite a shock to come out here expecting to doctor an aged dog, and instead, find both him and his master dead. Don't you think it's about time somebody told me what's going on here?"

Over steaming cups of coffee, the story was told and retold, as both doctors interrupted occasionally to ask questions. When it was finished, not one of them seemed anxious to resume the conversation. The atmosphere of the room held a strange uneasiness, something to be studied awhile before turning thoughts elsewhere.

Doc Heathcock was the first to break the silence, as he set his cup down and ran his hand through his hair in a perplexed manner.

"Well, I must say, that is a very strange tale. Each one of us knows that part of it will never be told because we just don't know enough to tell it. And as plain, simple human mortals, we'll never know."

Reaching for his bag, he extracted a death certificate and proceeded to fill it out without further comment. With this, Bill was reminded of what Josh had requested. Looking at Doc Warriner, he said. "Don't ask me why, Doc, but Josh wanted you to make out a death certificate for Tom, too."

A slight frown wrinkled the vet's brow as he contemplated Bill's words. "I wonder why. It couldn't be on account of insurance because I'm sure that none existed. But if Josh asked that it be done, that's good enough for me."

While he was filling out the form, Bill went to the phone and called his wife. After a short conversation, he returned to the table and spoke to Doc Heathcock, "Steve and I will stay here all night so we will be here when the undertaker comes. Will you make the arrangements?"

Assuring them that he would take care of everything, he gathered up his gear and waited by the door for the vet. Without previous arrangement, it was understood that the sensible thing to do was to drive back together. Gazing solemnly at the two remaining, he said, "Now I'll stop by Hershway's as soon as I get to town, I know that's who he would want. But I think there's something else I'd better do, too. I'll drop by the sheriff's office and explain all this, just to keep the record straight."

Agreeing that his idea was the right thing to do, Bill and Steve followed them outside and stood in the yard until their taillights faded from sight. The night was now clear and sparkling under the millions of stars twinkling above. Steve, standing with head thrown back, said musingly, "That's sure a big, long, old trail for Josh and Tom to set out on, but there's one thing for sure. They won't mind, since they're together."

"No, they sure won't," Bill said softly, as he turned to lead the way back into the house.

Stoking up the fire again, they sat slumped in their chairs for several minutes, before Steve asked, "What about Tom? What are we going to do about Tom?"

"Well, now, I'll tell you what I think. I don't believe we should do a thing until we see what's in Bob's safe. I've got a hunch that Josh had that all figured out. About five we'll call him, he'll be up anyway, and ask him to bring those papers down when he comes. Then we'll see."

In the ensuing silence, as they both half dozed in their chairs, the ticking of Josh's old alarm clock sounded like a gong. Bill was surprised to see that it was still only a little past midnight. It seemed weeks since the phone call from Josh.

Wearily, he got to his feet, and said, "No telling when the undertaker will get here, so we might as well make ourselves comfortable."

Yawning, Steve followed his example of removing his boots, wrapping up in a blanket, and stretching out on the floor beside the stove. Soon the clock was undergoing tough competition from their snores, which continued uninterrupted until the arrival of the undertaker at three o'clock. His entry into the house woke them.

As they forced open sleep-drugged eyes and threw off their blankets, they saw that he was standing above them with a slightly amused look on his face. "Sure am glad to see some life in here. I had begun to think that I had three bodies instead of one."

"The way I feel now," Bill groaned, "you're mighty near right."

Getting sluggishly to their feet, they rinsed their faces in cold water, and prepared to help in the sad task of moving Josh to the ambulance and Tom back to his pallet.

Soon, the job was over and as they watched the ambulance, it was with a terrible, empty feeling. Softly, Steve said, "Well, our old friend has left his cabin for the last time. But he had a lot of happy years here and I think he was ready."

After setting the alarm for five, they again stretched out on the floor. For a few minutes all was quiet again, then Steve said, "Bill, you awake?"

"Sure," Bill replied sleepily. "Why?"

"Do you realize that Josh knew that Tom was going to die, too?"

"What do you think has been keeping me awake? Of course, he did. That's all I've been thinking about. Just can't seem to get it off my mind. But let me give you a little advice, boy. Quit thinking about it and don't try to figure it out."

"Huh!" snorted Steve. "Good advice, but are you gonna quit thinking about it?"

"Shut up, "came the muffled reply. "Go to sleep."

The clanging of the alarm was a rude jolt to their tired bodies and worn nerves. Groggily, they stumbled to their feet. Bill, half awake, fumbled for the clock and knocked it over in the attempt to shut it off.

"Man," he muttered, shaking his head, "what day is it?"

"Don't rightly know, just this minute," Steve answered, "but I do know it's cold in here." Opening the stove door, he was relieved to find a glowing hickory knot. The dried wood he added to the fire quickly ignited, and in a few minutes, was snapping merrily. Soon, heat began to radiate throughout the room.

As soon as he was fully awake, Bill called Bob Brown and gave him the news. Over his friend's indignation at not having been told the night before, he finally delivered the message concerning the papers in the vault. Receiving Bob's quick promise to pick them up and come right down, he hung up and turned to the kitchen cabinet.

"Let's see if Josh had anything to eat around here," he said. "I'm starved."

Soon the room was filled with the smell of frying bacon and eggs. Milk, cereal, peaches, and coffee finished the meal. As they pushed back from the table, the day ahead didn't seem so gloomy.

With still an hour yet remaining until daylight, time seemed to drag heavily. Standing in the middle of the room that had been home to Josh, Bill marveled at the simplicity of it all. Not much more than a bed, stove, table, and chairs made up the old man's meager furnishings. A pitcher pump, for water pumped from a spring above the house, was, outside of the telephone, just about his only splurge towards modernization. Between the few throw rugs scattered here and there, the pine floors gleamed whitely from many scrubbings. One thing was evident: the cleanliness. Even the small curtains at the windows appeared to have been only recently laundered.

As his eyes fell upon their old friend's horn, that they had hastily hung on the back of his rocker the night before, he picked it up and ran his hands over its smooth surface. Steve, watching, noticed the shadows of emotion flicker across his face and said, "How do you reckon that old horn happened to still be hanging on Josh after all he went through?"

"I was sorta thinking about that," Bill answered. "It's a miracle, all right, but maybe it was supposed to be that way. Do you know what I'm thinking?"

Without surprise, Steve answered, "Wouldn't doubt it a bit. I've been thinking about something, too, and I'll bet it's the same thing."

As their eyes met, Bill slowly nodded in agreement. "Okay, that's what we'll do. It may arouse a few comments, but who's to say we're wrong?"

Instead of returning the horn to where it had hung, Bill walked over to his hunting coat and stuffed it into the big side pocket. Steve watched silently.

Opening the door, Bill stepped out onto the porch and Steve followed, leaving the door open. The light from the lamp inside challenged the blanket of ice covering the front yard. Though the wind still carried a bitter chill, they were glad to see that the temperature hadn't fallen much below freezing. Testing the ice with their feet, they saw that it wasn't thick and would soon disappear before the heat of the morning sun, when it climbed the hill and looked down on them.

It had been an hour and a half since their friend Bob had been notified. Now both found themselves glancing, quite frequently, down the road to the east.

"Seems to me," Steve muttered, "that Bob has had plenty of time to be here. Do you think he might have had trouble with the road?"

"No, I don't think so," Bill answered. "He'll bring his old dog wagon and with those tires, plus chains, he'll get here all right. You know how he is. He's probably had an idea or two of his own to take care of before he started."

They knew their friend well. At six forty-five, just as the first signs of daylight began to tinge the ridge tops, the lights of an approaching car could be seen probing their way down the hill to the east. In about five minutes, an old panel drew to a stop in front of the house, and a tall distinguished, gray-haired man climbed from under the wheel. Straight as a pine, he strode purposely around the truck, and with a glint in his eye, came rapidly towards them. Color was high in his lean, tanned cheeks, while a neatly-trimmed, medium-sized mustache seemed to bristle in indignation. And he wasn't alone. From the right side, another tall man stepped out ,who, to their surprise, they recognized as Dale Ringer, a young attorney.

For several minutes, Bill and Steve stood silently, grinning sheepishly under the tongue lashing they knew they would get, while Attorney Ringer waited, with a smile on his face. He knew that this was ritual among friends and something in which an outsider had no part.

Bob finished scathingly, "From now on, I suggest that you let me be the judge as to whether I'm able to be out or not. I was kicking around on nights like last night before you punks quit wearing diapers, and I've forgotten more about that ridge than you'll ever know."

His tirade stopped as quickly as it had begun, and his clear, blue eyes held only warmth for the two who stood uncomfortably before him. "Now," he said softly, "I've got the papers, but first I want to hear the whole story. Don't leave out a thing. I brought Dale along because we may need him before this is through."

Leading the others into the house, he walked slowly over to the body of Old Tom. With bowed head, he stood looking down at him, while the others waited without speaking. Kneeling down, he placed his hand on the grizzled old head, long since grown cold, and said almost reverently, "Sometimes, I had the feeling that he was more than just a dog."

Bill and Steve exchanged glances. He, too, had felt it, though they hadn't known. He was as close to Josh and Tom as they had been, maybe even closer. As his eyes remained fixed on theirs, they nodded in unison; as if that was the sign he waited for, they saw the tension drain out of him and he walked over and seated himself at the table.

As the others took chairs, Bill set out clean cups and filled them from the pot that had been kept hot on the stove. Bob placed a large manila envelope on the table, but made no effort to open it. Instead, he looked questioningly at his friends and waited.

Bill cleared his throat and spoke, "Well, I'll tell you all I can, but there is a part that only Steve knows, so that will have to come from him."

Starting with the uneasy feeling that had bothered him all day, he related every event, calmly and in full detail, excluding what happened to the others from the time they went over the cliff until he saw them again behind the rock. Dale sat in shocked silence, a look of amazement on his face, but merely puffed at his pipe, as he listened to the story.

When Steve finished telling how he swam as fast as he could, trying to catch up with Josh, helpless in the swirling current, and how he saw Old Tom come up to Josh and take his hunting coat in his teeth, while at the same time, the old man's hand had gone out to grasp Tom's collar, the others saw that his eyes were filled with tears.

Emotion choked his voice until the last words were hardly audible. In frustration, he pounded his fist on the table. "It makes me sick to think that maybe I didn't do all I could. If I watched him closer, maybe I could have stopped him from going over. If I could have reached him sooner, in the water, I might have shielded him from some of those big rocks. But I don't know. I just don't know."

Bill looked at Steve with deep concern. "Get such ideas out of your head. My God! You did all you could, and more than most. I tell you it was out of your hands." Pausing briefly, with a faraway look in his eyes, he finished softly, "In fact, I'm almost sure that it was out of any of our hands before it even started."

Bob's voice was a little husky when he spoke. "That's right, Steve. Josh had been living on borrowed time for the last two years. He knew his heart was apt to stop at any time. He told me all about it. I think he just hung on, until Tom was ready to go. He told me once, that he just couldn't go off and leave him."

Visibly moved by what he had heard, Dale rose and went to where Tom lay. For a minute, he stood looking at him. Then bending over, he, too, placed his hand on his head briefly, then straightened up and returned wordlessly to the table.

His dark eyes searched the faces of the others, as he said, "Such a strange tale, but I'm glad, gentlemen, that you called me in to help you. Believe me. I mean it."

That his friends were puzzled as to why an attorney might be needed was evident to Bob, so he hastened to enlighten them. "Boys, we may need him plenty. I know something of what is in the envelope. Josh gave me a hint when he brought it to me two years ago. I took a quick look through it before leaving town. It was as I suspected, so I called Dale to give us his professional opinion of what we are up against."

Removing a sheaf of papers from the envelope, he spread them out on the table. After studying the faces of his friends for a minute, he said, "In a nutshell, Josh has requested that we bury Tom in the cemetery beside him."

Speechless for the moment, they stared at him. Finally, Bill nodded his head and said, "I felt that there would be something sorta like that—but in a cemetery—with other people—can we do it? Is it legal?"

Bob's eyes glinted with determination. "There's no such thing as can we—for we have to. It's just a matter of how much opposition we run into after we do it. Burying him will be simple. The fight will be to keep him there. That's where Dale comes in."

As Bob finished, Dale spoke seriously, "Men, all I can tell you right now is that, as far as I know, the law wouldn't enter into it. I doubt that there is a statute anyplace, covering such a situation. It won't be a matter of legality, but of age-old tradition. Believe me, that will be a harder nut to crack than any law."

Bob nodded in agreement. "I think so, too, Dale. That's a mighty tight knit little group out at that church he belonged to. For the most part, mighty good people, but old shellbacks, every one of them. But Josh foresaw such a possibility and took certain steps ahead of time."

Steve and Bill, highly keyed up with interest, hardly took their eyes from his face as he continued. "Even that may not be enough; it's hard to go against religious beliefs that are so deep set. Threaten something that a person was born to believe in, especially religion, and instant rebellion sets in, so strong that any legal right there might be ceases to exist."

Shuffling the papers, Bob chose one from the pile. "Now here's what he did. A lot is already purchased in Tom's name, right next to Josh's. But Josh just forgot to mention that Tom was a dog. Money has been contributed to the church, each year for the last ten years, in Tom's name. He has receipts here to prove it. And now I can tell you something else. When Josh discovered that he didn't have long to live, he made arrangements, through Dale, to take care of any financial conditions that might arise. Sort of a trust fund, to be used any way we see fit, and of course, keeping Tom buried will come first."

Completely baffled by what they had heard, Bill and Steve were lost in thought as many things churned through their minds. Finally, Steve voiced an obvious question. "I suppose we will dig the grave for Josh. But how will we handle Tom's?"

"Looks to me like it will have to be two operations," Bob answered. "We'll dig Josh's before the funeral, and then after everyone's gone, we'll take care of Tom. There won't be many there anyway and since we will be expected to stay behind and fill the grave, it will work out just right."

"Well," Steve said, "since I'm the carpenter, I guess I had better get busy on a coffin for Old Tom."

"No need, Steve," Bob said, "Josh took care of that, too. According to this paper, if you go out into the woodshed and look in that old bin, you will find one already made."

Steve was out of the door by the time he had finished. Minutes later, they heard him call, "Hey, Bill, come give me a hand. This thing's heavy."

Curious, Bob and Dale waited at the table. Filling his pipe, Bob slowly puffed it to a glow before saying a word. When he was finally satisfied, he removed it from his mouth long enough to say, "Care to guess why a dog's coffin would be so heavy?"

There was no need for Dale to guess. Before he could answer, the back door opened and Bill backed into the room, followed by Steve. Between them swung a rectangular box about four feet long by twenty inches high and the same in width. The reason for its weight was at once apparent. Lead sheeting covered it completely. When the lid was lifted for their inspection, words of awe burst from the entire group. They were looking at an exact replica, in miniature, of a full-sized human coffin, complete even to padding and silk lining.

As they gazed wordlessly, their thoughts were one. They all were wondering how many hours it must have taken to make this beautiful coffin; hours of tenderly administered care to every small detail, until the finished product emerged; a miracle of perfection in protection for Tom, against all things, for all time. Even in death, their old friend had continued to take care of the dog he loved so much.

Finally, Bob broke the silence. "How about fixing Tom up, right now?"

Steve and Bill nodded in unison. Slowly and carefully, they picked him up and placed him in his casket, still in the same position in which he died. Quickly then, the lid was lowered, and the lead seal run into place.

"Well," Bill commented when they were finished, "water will never get into that. It will still be as dry hundreds of years from now, as it is right this minute."

Dale began gathering up the papers that were scattered about the table. "Fellows," he said, "let me take these; I want to check them carefully. Actually, you won't know for awhile whether you'll need me, but I think you will. So, I want to be as fully prepared as possible. Let me know about the funeral arrangements."

As Bob prepared to accompany him back to town, Steve suddenly exclaimed, "Hey, I almost forgot about my coat and cap up there on the bluff. If you're not in too big a hurry, Bill, I'd like to run up and get them."

"Sure, go on up and get them. I'll wash up the dishes while you're gone; besides, it's only eight o'clock."

Slipping into Bill's cap and coat, Steve started for the door, but paused to say, "You know, I don't have any idea where my flashlight is, probably in the creek some place."

As Steve strode purposely across the road towards the ridge, Bill spoke for a few minutes with Bob and Dale. "As far as we know, Josh never had any relatives, so I guess it's up to us to set the date for the funeral."

"Yes," Bob answered. "We'll talk to the undertaker this afternoon. Since this is Friday, I suppose that Sunday afternoon would be okay."

Even as Bob's old panel truck pulled out towards town, Bill noticed that Steve was already out of sight. He had gone straight up over the ridge this time and would probably be back within thirty minutes.

By the time Bill had washed and put away the dishes and made up the bed, Steve was back. Though evidently pleased at having found his big light with the rest of his belongings, his expression was one of perplexity.

For awhile, he busied himself by removing Bill's coat and cap and donning his own. Realizing that something was wrong, Bill finally said, "Well, out with it. What's eating you?'

Looking his friend straight in the face, Steve said in a strained voice. "I kinda hate to mention this because you'll think I've gone off my rocker, but I noticed something mighty strange up there and if you call me a liar, I won't blame you."

"Look, buddy," Bill answered, "after last night I'd believe almost anything, especially if it has anything to do with Josh and Tom."

"Well, okay," Steve said, "but don't say I didn't warn you. First, though, come outside a minute."

When they walked out onto the porch, Steve asked, "Do you see anything that isn't covered with ice?"

Shaking his head, Bill said, "Of course not. Everything's covered."

"Not quite everything," Steve said softly. "The slide's as bare and dry as this floor. There's not a bit of ice on it anywhere."

Bill's eyes widened in amazement. "How about the rest of the ridge? It's a south slope, you know."

"Ice, all ice. Clear up to the slide on both sides. It just stops there, like there was never any on it, sorta like it melted off in shame. I'll tell you, I felt mighty funny up there when I realized what I was looking at."

"Can't blame you," Bill muttered. "Anybody would have. In fact, this cabin has an eerie feeling about it. Let's go to town."

Leaving the box containing Tom's body to be picked up later, they locked the door behind them. For awhile, neither seemed in the mood for talking as the jeep crept up the hill, away from the valley with its frozen loneliness and eerie silence.

Finally, Bill said, "Steve, don't you think we ought to keep still about the slide, with the exception of Bob and Dale, of course?"

"Don't worry. I don't want the men in the white jackets after me."

As they climbed out to the ridge road, they found that early farm traffic had helped to melt the ice and the going became increasingly easier. The sun's modest heat was beginning to take effect, so from all indications, the ground would be bare by noon.

As he pulled to a stop in front of Bill's house, Steve asked, "Gonna open up the shop this morning?"

"Sure," Bill replied, "too much to do to go to bed. Soon as I change clothes and freshen up, I'll be down."

"Okay. I'll drop into the store and find out what arrangements Bob has made, then come over and tell you."

Entering the house, Bill found himself marveling at how so much had happened in the few hours he had been gone. As he prepared for work, he tried his best to answer the many questions that Bess threw at him, but volunteered nothing outside of the basic facts. How could he tell her the whole story so that she would understand? There was no way.

Arriving at the shop only a few minutes later than usual, Bill found the town already abuzz with the news of Josh's death. Customers came to linger, to ask questions, and to listen. The task of having to refrain from going too deep into the subject was proving to be more and more difficult. Any attempt at trying to explain the strangeness that he and Steve had felt, would be to flounder hopelessly under stares of disbelief and questioning looks exchanged by his listeners.

So, it was with relief, that he received Steve's message shortly before noon. Steve had come into the shop only long enough to inform him that Dale had requested their presence in his office that afternoon at two o'clock, including Jody, Bob's fifteen-year-old nephew. Though the last was some source of puzzlement to them, neither cared to speculate before witnesses just why Jody needed to be there.

Calling a part-time barber who sometimes filled in for him, Bill arranged for him to take over and work for him the following day. When he arrived at twelve, Bill left at once for home. Much remained to be done.

A little before two, Steve came past to pick him up. Driving to the front of Bob's hardware store, they parked and went inside to find Bob and a redheaded, blue-eyed youth of fifteen, apparently awaiting their arrival.

The serious look on his usually smiling face was proof enough that the death of Josh and Tom had involved Jody, if in no other way than emotionally. And that was understandable to both Bill and Steve, who greeted him warmly. They knew of the affection Jody had felt for the old man, and of the many, many weekends he had spent in the little cabin with them. They knew that Jody's two-year-old Walker male, Trump, owed his advanced capability as a coon dog to the excellent guidance he received under Old Tom.

Now, as they looked at this nephew of Bob's, they realized how much he was growing to look like his father. The father they had both known so well, but whom Jody had never known. He had been killed in military service when Jody was just a baby. But under the steady hand of his mother, with whatever masculine assistance was needed from her brother, Bob, the boy was showing every indication of becoming a man that any mother would be proud of.

But now, with Jody's new sense of responsibility that was pushing him into manhood a little too soon, they could see some of the confused, not quite understanding, boy showing through.

"Well, Jody," Steve said calmly, "it was bound to happen sometime. They were both very old, you know, and it was just their time to go. They had a full life, and I think Bill will agree with me that they both died peacefully."

"That's right, Jody," Bill hastened to add, "Josh said as much."

The frown on Jody's face deepened. "I know all that, but that's not what bothers me. It's poor Old Tom being in that trap, especially Clem Keener's trap. That's what I can't understand."

Now it was their turn to be puzzled. "Sure, Jody, it was plenty bad for him to suffer the way he did," Bill said, "but what if it *was* the Keener boy's trap? One is just as full of torture as another, no matter who sets them."

"That's not what I mean," Jody said, with a shake of his head, "How come Clem had a trap there at all? He don't trap. Never did. He's too lazy to trap."

"I don't know, Jody," Bill answered, "but if Josh said he set the trap, then he did."

"Yes, I know that," Jody replied, "but I still can't figure why he would ever set a trap in the first place and I won't be satisfied until I do."

Standing there, listening to the boy's firm voice, accompanied by the fire of determination flashing in his eyes, they had no doubt but what he would. They had previously seen, on more than one occasion, how stubbornly he stuck to an idea until he was either proven right or wrong. And they were reminded that he was usually more right than wrong.

Having had a last-minute talk with the clerk in charge of the store, Bob came from the back, and said, "Well, it's five minutes until two. Let's go."

Dale's office was just across the big square, and by cutting through the courtyard, they could halve the distance. Walking slowly, they reached the stairs to his office as the clock struck two. The sound of their treading feet brought Dale smilingly to the door. "Right on time, fellows," and rather jestingly to Jody, he said, "Have any trouble getting out of school, Jody?"

"No, sir," Jody answered. "Guess you fixed everything up just right when you told the principal that it was important. I'm here, although I can't figure out why."

"Well, you'll find out real soon now," Dale said, as he directed them to chairs and took a seat behind his desk.

The papers that Bob had turned over to him that morning lay in assorted piles, but it was not to these that he first turned. Instead, opening a drawer, he pulled out a single sheet, studied it briefly, and then placed it on the table before him.

His dark eyes shone with satisfaction, as he looked intently at Jody for several seconds. Then, as if pleased with what he saw, he again picked up the single sheet of paper. Glancing at it once more, he then directed his words at the boy.

"Jody, this paper has to do with something that Josh came to see me about over a year ago. He told me of your friendship and what it meant to both him and Tom. He talked of how much you enjoyed visiting them down at the cabin and how you were always saying you were going to have one just like it someday."

As he paused to scrutinize the paper again, Jody squirmed a bit uneasily. He couldn't imagine what the paper had to do with him. He was both eager and apprehensive, as he waited for Dale to continue. His older friends, though, seemed to have some idea, for brief smiles were beginning to flicker across their faces.

So, bracing himself, he waited for Dale's next words. "Jody," he began again, "Josh knew that the end would come at any time and he wanted to make sure of this before it was too late. For a year now, you have been the owner of Josh's cabin and the forty acres that go with it. It's yours, lock, stock, and barrel, without any encumbrances and tax free. Here's the deed and abstract. Keep them in a safe place."

Overwhelmed by what he had just heard, Jody sat immobilized, as his mind whirled. With fumbling fingers, he managed to grasp the papers, and though he looked at them, he saw nothing. The words were merely a blur before eyes wracked by dizziness.

Brought back to earth by the congratulations of his friends, he made no effort to hide the happiness reflected on his face. That little farm, all his. It was too much for just a kid, he wasn't deserving, and it must be a mistake. But as his eyes cleared, he saw that it wasn't a mistake. It said right there on the paper, Jody Hawkins.

Soberly, he let his mind go back to many little things that Josh had said, all seemingly unimportant at the time. But now, as he put them all together, they added up to an answer. The answer was there in his hands.

He knew now, Josh had recognized in him, a kindred spirit. The unrestrained love he had felt for the little home in the valley had not gone unnoticed by the old man. He had felt that there would be little change in atmosphere if it were to pass into Jody's hands. And that was important, very important to him. Jody would feel about it as he had. An unfeeling stranger would be in violation of all it had meant to him. It had to be the boy he had come to love as his own. It had to be Jody; one who understood.

Vaguely, Jody was aware that the others had gone on to other business, but he was still content to swim in the pool of deep thought about everything that had just happened. One thing that Josh had said to him, on more than one occasion, kept coming back repeatedly. The same words each time, as if he wanted to impress them upon the boy's mind so deep that he remembered those words now.

The deep voice of his old friend had been unusually soft, as he stood there in the deepening twilight and looked north, up the valley, to where the hills and bottom merged into a mysterious shadow of engulfing solitude.

"Jody," he had said dreamingly, "it would be a shame to change any of this. Old Tom and I might want to come back for a visit sometime, and wouldn't it be awful if it had changed so that we couldn't recognize it?"

Boy that he was, Jody still knew that the old man saw from eyes that were different from most. He knew nothing of the loneliness that would have weighed so heavily upon the average person or felt the pressure of the silence that would have pounded at their ear drums. Instead, to him, there was only a soft blanket of quiet. Where the thoughts of an old man and his dog would have opportunity to reach out, one for the other, and by mutual union, become a blending of one.

And lonely? He could never have become lonely with Tom by his side. Was that the reason for the semi-hidden meaning so often injected into Josh's conversation? Why he seemed to take for granted that he and Tom would end their lives together? That neither could exist without the other? That the merging had become so complete, that the passing of either would leave the other as but half of a whole, and thus, bring about the impossibility of survival.

Like a drowning person, Jody felt himself pulled from the whirlpool of thoughts by the sound of his uncle's voice. "Jody," Bob was saying, "snap out of it. What's the matter, son?"

Looking around the table, he realized that the others were staring at him.

"Oh, I'm sorry, Uncle Bob. Guess I was thinking," he responded groggily. "What were you saying?"

Bob, with strong affection for this only child of his youngest sister, said, "I only suggested that maybe you would like to go home and give the good news to your mother."

"Oh, sure, Uncle Bob, I would like to, if it's all right."

To his questioning look, Dale answered, "Sure, Jody. Go ahead. We've taken care of your business anyway. There's plenty of time for the few remaining legal details."

Shouting goodbye as he floated to the door, the sound of his rattling down the steps came back to them, as youth pushed him to hurry. In the silence following his rather noisy departure, Bill and Steve exchanged glances with Bob. Where had the boy been, so lost in thought? Shaking their heads, each refused to speculate.

As Dale went through the papers, group by group, it was definitely apparent that Josh had been preparing for the inevitable for a long time. The carefully-laid plans seemed to leave no stone unturned for combatting any crisis that might arise. There seemed to be little left to do now, but wait for the outcome of Tom's burial. They had no doubt that there would be repercussions. But until then, they could only remain inside their defenses, awaiting the point of attack before drawing up their plans of battle.

Time for the funeral had been set for two o'clock Sunday. The services were to be held at the funeral home, which would have sufficient capacity for the few who would attend. The grave for Josh would be dug on Saturday, and then, immediately following the departure of the last one to leave the church yard, Tom would be taken care of. Josh had even left a drawing of how the double headstone was to be prepared. With the adjournment of their meeting, Bob agreed to see that his instructions were carried out at the local monument shop.

Saturday dawned clear and bright. It was with relief that they found the ground unfrozen and the digging comparatively easy. By mid-morning, the job was near completion. Steve tossed aside his shovel and pulled himself up over the edge of the hole, as he said, "Let's take a break and look around a little. There's something I'm curious about anyway."

"What's that?" Bill asked, as he eased himself into a sitting position and lit a cigarette.

"Well," Steve answered, "the kind of records they keep here, for one thing. You noticed that Josh's lots were carefully marked off, and only recently, at that. Maybe as late as yesterday, and yet, we've seen no one. I've got a feeling that someone had more than usual interest in seeing that we chose the right plot."

As he strode towards the church, fifty yards to the east, the others rose to follow. With Jody at his heels, he soon reached the door, and as he expected, found it unlocked. "Look around, Jody," he said, "see if you can find some kind of record book; there must be one here someplace."

It wasn't difficult. In a drawer of the desk, located in a tiny cubicle of an office in the right front corner of the building, they found what they sought. A common ledger with the words, "Cemetery Records" printed on the front. By the time Bob and Bill entered the building,

Steve was turning towards them, with the book open in his hands.

"It's here, all right,' he said, in answer to their questioning look, "but what do you make of this?"

Reading the lines indicated by his pointing finger, they were as puzzled as he was. By plot numbers 142 and 143 they found the names of Josh and Tom Harmon listed as purchasers, but with one difference. While Josh's name was written clearly in ink, the name Tom Harmon was written in pencil, and rather dimly, at that.

Bill's eyes gleamed, as he spoke through clenched teeth. "Now if I was a guessing man, I'd say there's a reason for that little difference and a mighty important one, at that."

"No doubt about it," Bob said, "somebody knows about Tom."

Jody glanced from one to the other, excitedly waiting for a chance to speak. "Do you think they intend to erase Tom's name and act like it never was there in the first place?"

"That's just about what it looks like, Jody," his uncle answered. "So, I think we should change our plans a little."

"Sure," Steve added. "Might as well bury Old Tom at the same time we do Josh. Maybe we can flush him out right from the start."

"Suits me," Bill growled, as he headed for the door. "Let's get busy, since we have another grave to dig today."

By noon, the job was finished and the fly up to protect the openings. After putting their tools in the back of the panel truck, they paused to take a look at the surrounding country. The church and the cemetery were located on one of the highest points for miles around. To the west ran looping chains of hills, like giant chocolate drops arranged in a semi-circle, from north to south, as far as the eye could see. Three miles to the west lay the valley where Josh's cabin stood.

For a few, they gazed wordlessly in that direction. Jody, with the impetuosity of youth, and somewhat disturbed by the brooding silence of the men, felt impelled to speak.

"Is that where the cabin is?" he asked, as he indicated with pointing finger.

"That's right, son," his uncle answered.

"Well, then," Jody continued, "Josh and Tom can look right down on it; I mean if—if they could. Or I mean they're not far from home, and—well—oh! I don't know what I mean."

As the boy stammered to a halt, in flustered confusion, Bill placed a big arm around his shoulders, as he said softly, "That's okay, Jody. We know what you mean, all right; you have just said what we've all been thinking."

Abruptly then, he turned away from the west, back in the direction of the truck, as he said, "We had better get going if we're going to be at the funeral home by one o'clock."

Within minutes, they were on their way back to town. They had agreed that some of them would stay in attendance with Josh's body at all times. And then would act as pallbearers. Even Jody was being allowed to serve in this capacity out of respect for his deep friendship for the old man.

Throughout the afternoon, Jody stayed beside his old friend. The others took turns; they would stay the night, while Jody would not. As the small circle of friends trickled through to pay their respects throughout the afternoon, the picture was one of quiet composure. But sometime along about dark, there was a marked difference in the reaction of the occasional visitor who stepped up to take a last look at Josh.

The same bewildered look was on all their faces as they turned away, disturbed by what they had seen, but reluctant to ask with their eyes. They would have been no more enlightened had they seen the broad, dark-visaged man, who had earlier stood gazing quietly down into the casket for a full minute, before leaning over and placing what he held beside the old man's body. Neither would they have understood the meaning of his words, as he said softly, "Here, Old Timer, just in case you need to call him."

At the insistence of his mother, Jody appeared only briefly at the funeral home on Sunday morning, so as not to break his regular habit of attending both Sunday school and church. But he had little thought for the words from the pulpit that morning. Instead, he found it impossible to dwell upon anything except the task he knew his uncle and Bill were performing at that very time. They had gone down to the cabin to load Tom's body into the panel truck, where it would remain until after Josh's burial.

Boy-like, Jody wondered if he should feel guilty because of certain other thoughts that eventually began to probe at him, until he gave up any attempt to concentrate on the minister's words. Maybe a person shouldn't be thinking such things in church, but try as he might, he was unable to do otherwise. The one nagging thought that Old Tom's trapping had been deliberate kept returning, regardless of how many times he tried to shrug it off. Too, he couldn't help but wonder if the one who had performed the deed was sitting in church that very minute, pretending to believe in the word of God. In Jody's mind, such a person could never do more than pretend.

Youth that he was, he knew that there were those who could sit in pious meditation during the services, and immediately following, callously poison their neighbor's dog. And just as guilty, to his young mind, were those who could sit serenely undisturbed by certain sounds from the city dog pound, that often wafted in through open doors and windows during Sunday services; the cries of the homesick, the frightened, and the lonely.

Jody knew that there were those who cringed in shame for that portion of the human race who could sanction such treatment, while yet others remained unmoved, because of a complete lack of compassion for the rest of God's creatures. Then there were those who chose not to hear unpleasant things, when nothing could be done to correct the situation.

So deep was Jody in his thoughts, that he wasn't aware of the end of the service, until his mother's voice reminded him. As he rose to follow her out, one predominant thought remained. Someway, somehow, he intended to find out the truth of why Old Tom found a trap where he shouldn't have.

At one o'clock, his Uncle Bob and Aunt Min came by to take him and his mother to the funeral. They were joined at the entrance by Bill and his wife. A few minutes later, Steve entered, accompanied by two other men, thus rounding out the complement of pallbearers.

As the ladies presented themselves at the casket, there was a noticeable start from each, at the sight of the horn resting beside Josh. Though their husbands immediately became the focus of questioning stares, they voiced no words. Maybe later, if they decided there was a chance of an answer, they would ask. Maybe.

The service was short, and within forty-five minutes, the hearse, followed by a small caravan of eight cars, was winding its way north along the hill road to the little country cemetery. The truck containing the body of Old Tom had been left at the edge of the church yard that morning. Jody noticed many curious glances cast toward the truck as the procession wound its way back to the graveside. Quite audible, too, were the many exclamations from the crowd, as they first became aware that there were two graves, instead of one.

While the brief services were being conducted, Jody noticed the Keener boy standing off a small distance from the crowd. The tall, lean, elderly man beside him must be, he guessed, his father. Cold, black eyes gazed unemotionally at the scene, out of a face like a hatchet. Boy that he was, Jody sensed, rather than saw, the unfriendliness in the man. The face of his son bore a sneer of contempt as he met Jody's eyes. He, at once, felt instant dislike course through him. What had brought them to the funeral? Certainly not friendship for Josh. What then? Curiosity? Just because they were members of the same church? Jody could find no logical answer for the questions he was asking himself. But he knew one thing, he would be suspicious of any reason they might have had for attending.

Minutes after the last words of the preacher had died away and even as the small crowd was still drifting back towards the parking area, Bill and Steve headed toward the truck. Since only two were needed to carry the small lead-covered box, Jody and his uncle remained beside the grave.

Idly watching the two approach the rear of the vehicle, Jody's attention was drawn by a movement from the Keener boy. His puzzled eyes had seen the furtive gouge of the boy's elbow into his father's ribs and the leering grin as he did so. The face of the father remained impassive. Only eyes glittering with intensity showed that he, too, had interest in the errand of the two men.

As the two reached the truck, Bill at once opened the rear doors. For several seconds, both he and Steve stood rigidly transfixed. Then they whirled around to expose faces gone suddenly white. Realizing that something had gone wrong, Bob and Jody immediately crossed over to join them.

Jody had once previously seen Bill wracked by savage anger, on a bloody night two years before, when a captured dog thief had tried to cut Bob with a switchblade knife. But it had not been like this. So intense was the anger within him that Jody was awed by the great trembling that was shaking the powerful body of his friend. A wildness blazed in his eyes. Eyes that normally held only warmth now gleamed with icy bleakness of frozen fire. Without speaking, he merely indicated the back of the truck with a motion of his hand.

One glance inside caused Jody's breathing to catch in his throat. Only a horrible emptiness met his shocked eyes. Old Tom was gone. Instantly, the furtive actions of the Keener youth flashed through his mind. Looking quickly in their direction, he was just in time to catch a leering sneer from the boy from over his shoulder, as he started to follow the stiff-necked figure of his father in the direction of their car.

Never one to hesitate over a decision once made, Jody exclaimed, "It's the Keeners." Then in the next breath, even as he spurted in their direction, "You, Clem. Hold up."

The others, even Bill in his anger, found time to marvel at the suddenness with which Jody acted, and the turmoil that erupted within seconds, as he bore down on the startled Clem.

Like a red-headed tornado, he swept across the church yard. And his purpose was not lost on the other youth. Frantically, he looked about for some avenue of escape, looked up desperately at the elder Keener, then as if deciding that help from that direction would be inadequate, he bolted away down the hill toward the woods.

With the speed of youth, he ran swiftly, blindly, and in fear-stricken desperation to escape that blazing nemesis bearing down on him, but he never had a chance. Reaching the high wire fence bordering the west side of the yard, he was able to wildly claw his way halfway to the top, before disaster struck.

Like a catapult, Jody launched his body from a nearby knoll and his arms went around the waist of Clem as they collided. Dragged down from the fence by Jody's weight, Clem fell on him as they both struck the ground. As a cornered rat will fight, so did young

Keener. Outweighing Jody by a good twenty pounds, he was able to keep him down for a minute. To the others, running towards them, it looked as if maybe their red-headed protégé had finally tackled more than he could handle.

But the fury coursing through his slender body lent strength to wiry muscle. Like a small volcano, he erupted from beneath Clem's heavier body with its flailing arms and legs. Bursting to his feet, he turned quickly and again launched himself at the partly upright Clem.

The savageness of the attack seemed to instill unbridled fear in young Keener. His pitiful whines of fright came clearly to those who were fast approaching. Through the confusion, his words poured out in hysterical repetition, as he cried over and over, "Let me alone. I didn't do nothing."

As Jody got to his feet, he dragged the wildly kicking Clem up with him and began shaking him viciously. With a savageness in his voice never before heard by his friends, he demanded over and over, "Where's Old Tom? Where's Old Tom?"

Even as the cringing hulk of Clem pointed and whimpered, "Down there in the woods by the spring," disaster struck Jody without warning. Too busy to notice Silas Keener striding up, he was unprepared for the hard blow delivered by Silas to the side of his head. Bowled over and sent rolling by the blow and the stars that exploded before his eyes, he was somewhat, for the moment, out of touch with reality.

But through all his haziness, he was aware of a terrible roaring coming from someplace near. As his eyes struggled to focus on the scene beside him, a cold chill swept him, as he recognized the awesome deadliness in that voice. Shouts of other men came through the fog enveloping him. Then his eyes slowly cleared to a sight he was to remember for a long time.

The expression on Bill's face stood out the most from the melee above him and would remain with him the longest. Never would he have believed that the regular good-natured face of his friend could have ever been so transformed. Cold, savage jungle wildness was in every feature. He was a man gone berserk.

The body of the elder Keener, gripped in Bill's big hands by an arm and a thigh, was being held at arm's length over his head. Squeals of protest poured from his throat as he looked with horror-stricken eyes at the ground that was about to come rushing at him with bone-crushing impact.

Steve and Bob's demands that he put him down fell on unhearing ears. It was as if he hardly recognized them. He kept turning away from their crowding bodies and reaching hands, in an apparent effort to find an opening through which to slam the writhing Silas to the ground. Big men though they were, both felt the futility of their efforts, as their hands slipped from those mighty arms holding Keener aloft.

Aware of the impending disaster, Jody struggled to his feet. Groggily, he wavered into the pushing, whirling group. Gripping the front of Bill's coat, he began tugging as hard as he could, while his voice came high and imploring, "Bill, Bill, don't do it. Put him down. Josh wouldn't want you to hurt him. Bill, Bill, listen to me! Josh wouldn't want you to hurt anybody."

What the heavier, demanding voices of the others had been unable to do, the piercing entreaty of the boy somehow managed to accomplish. As if coming out of a trance, the wildness in Bill's face slowly faded away, and the great rigid muscles of his arms and shoulders began to relax. Almost in surprise, he blinked his eyes at the limp, dangling body of Keener that he still held overhead, and then gently lowered him to the ground.

For an instant, he stood staring down at the lanky form, then stepped back, shaking his head, and brushing his hand over his eyes, as if to rid himself of something unfamiliar and unwanted. Slowly, he raised his head and gazed blankly at his friends. Little by little, realization of what he had nearly done became apparent and a terrible shuddering shook his body. Like waves, they shook him from head to foot. Legs as mighty as young oaks suddenly became too weak to hold him erect, and he sank limply onto the ground. Still without speaking, he dropped his head into his hands as the trembling continued to wash over him.

Emotionally exhausted themselves, now that it was over, his friends stood silently by, waiting for him to return to the man they knew. In the meantime, Keener, who had remained motionless until then, like a rabbit that had been removed from a trap and laid aside, playing possum until a chance to run presents itself, opened his eyes and glanced furtively about him. Seeing that no one was even bothering to look at him, he abruptly bolted to his feet and ran shakily up the hill towards his car.

The others paid no attention to his departure. Not until he felt safe at a distance of a hundred feet or so, did he stop to call back in a voice still wildly hysterical, "You'll pay for this, every one of you. You won't get by with burying that mangy hound there either. I'll take you to court."

It seemed that he might have more to say, but the voice of Clem, urging departure from a yet safer point farther up the hill, seemed to change his mind, and he turned away with fast strides toward his car. To Jody, watching after them, it didn't seem so strange that Silas, when reaching Clem's side, delivered to the boy a stinging slap to the head, then continued on, while his son ran, whimpering, after him.

But the others hadn't even bothered to look up. Bill still sat unspeaking, as Steve and Bob seated themselves, one on either side of him. Patiently, Jody dropped to the ground in front of the little group, and for once, remained silent.

As the minutes sped by and Bill still hadn't moved from his bowed position, Steve and Bob exchanged worried glances. Facing them, Jody took all this in with much concern. Why didn't they say something to Bill? Tell him it was all right; say anything, just to break the brooding silence. Well, if they couldn't, he could.

Rising to his knees, just an arm's length in front of Bill, he moved as if to touch him, but withdrew his hand as both Steve and Bob shook their heads. For a moment longer, he silently held his position, but the strain was a telling one. Still much too young to have learned extended patience, Jody could stand it no longer.

Looking directly at the bowed head of his friend, he drawled, "You know something, Bill? You're purt near as good a fighter as I am."

Slowly, the dark head of Bill lifted until he was looking directly into the smiling blue eyes of his young, freckle-faced friend. Darkness in his eyes softened and turned warm, finally crinkling around the edges, as a full-grown grin broke through.

Reaching out a big ham-like hand to ruffle the boy's hair, he chuckled, and said, "Well, now, that's quite a compliment and I'm right pleased you think so, but I kinda doubt I'm that good. These red-headed people sorta have the edge, somehow, when it comes to fight'n."

With the tension broken and Bill, once more, his old self, they proceeded to finish the grim task to which they were committed. While Steve and Bill went down to the spring to recover the body and casket of Old Tom, Jody and his uncle busied themselves with the filling of Josh's grave. In a few minutes, the two returned with the small casket still intact, and after placing it gently in the remaining grave, at once began the job of covering the casket.

In an hour they were done, and none too soon. Heavy clouds were rolling up in the west and a cold moist bite to the wind gave indications that snow was eminent. Even as the last of their tools were stowed into the back of Bob's truck, the first flakes began drifting down. Big, fat, and moist, they settled silently, each to be covered at once by another, until it seemed to Jody that they must be actually crowding one another in eagerness to cover the two ugly mounds of red clay. *What could be more appropriate*, he thought, *than a mantle of white for those two lying there?*

One more little job remained to be done: filling in the proper lines in the cemetery record book. Listed merely as Josh Harmon and Tom Harmon, the simplicity of their entry gave little indication of the storm that was to follow. Or the court trial that was to shake customary procedure to the core, and to cause many to take a second look at what had long been accepted as right and wrong, and wonder if there really was any answer.

Steve, having ridden out with one of the other pallbearers, elected to drive Bob's truck back to town, while Bill and Jody rode back with Bob. There was little conversation en route, other than occasional remarks of speculation that immediate reprisal by Keener could be expected, and that their plans should be laid accordingly. Within Jody rested one persistent decision; somehow, someway, he would have the truth from young Keener.

Evidence that they were in for a fight was not long in coming. On Monday, Silas Keener filed his charges. Bob, Steve, and Bill were notified by Dale before noon of that day. Gathering in his office immediately after lunch, the legality of answering the charges was dispensed with, and the specific charges discussed.

The Prosecuting Attorney had boiled it down to one simple charge. They had willfully and knowingly desecrated a country cemetery by burying a dog there. He would ask that conviction of the defendants result in fine and jail sentence, plus the automatic removal of Tom's body. All in all, it appeared to be a rather grim penalty in case they should lose. There was nothing concerning Bill's attack on Silas.

But when Dale informed them that the Prosecutor had agreed to drop the charges, providing they voluntarily removed Old Tom's body from the cemetery, they were unanimous in their decision to continue. Bill, apparently, voiced the opinions of all when he said, "If we were to give up now, we would not have been worthy of the friendship of this fine old man."

"Or of Old Tom either," Steve added, looking to Bob for agreement, and receiving a nod of his head in answer.

Dale's eyes shown with the prospects of the battle ahead.

"Good," he said, "I thought that's what you'd say. Now, it may be a tough one, but I think we can win. The Prosecutor has promised us an early date when court reconvenes. Maybe we can get it set for the first week in February. Meanwhile, I'll explore every legal angle. I'm just sure that there is no law on the books that says you can't bury a dog in a cemetery along with people. It's probably one of those things long taken for granted as something that would never be done. I'll bet my shingle that no one ever thought there would be a need for such a law. But," he added with a chuckle, "I'll bet it won't be long before some are forthcoming after this. Yes and some cemetery by-laws rewritten, too. But by then, our job will be done. So long, boys. See you next week."

There was little for any of them to do but depend upon Dale to prepare his case. When they met again on the following Monday, he did indeed inform them that no such law existed, but warned them again, that fixed ideas and rigid beliefs could be just as formidable an opponent, and that the changing of age-old convictions was not easy. But with honesty and reason on their side, there was a good chance that the curtain might be lifted, just this once.

Through questioning several members of the little church, he was convinced that, as a whole, the congregation wasn't too opposed, but were reluctant to go against the decision of Keener and two or three others who seemed to be running the show. Apparently, they hadn't even bothered to ask for authorization from the membership, but had taken it upon themselves to oppose Tom's burial. Too, it was evident that some fire of resentment had been kindled by their high-handed manner, among the other members.

The solution to their victory, Dale figured, lay in finding a way to fan those flames into a fire of open rebellion. It seemed obvious that Keener and the others held the purse strings, and by that means, had always managed to bend the others to their will. How strong those strings were remained to be seen, but to win, they must see that they were broken.

As the weeks passed, Jody still brooded about Clem Keener's trap and how it came to be there. Though constantly watching for a chance to catch him in town, he had not seen him since the day at the cemetery. He remained determined as ever, however, to get the truth from Clem before the trial.

Soon after the first of January, Dale informed them that since only two criminal cases were on the docket for the first week in February when court reconvened, the trial was set for Monday of the second week.

Jody never even considered attending school on that Monday morning, but went straight to his uncle's hardware store, and as he expected, found Bill and Steve there before him. Exchanging smiles, the men nodded to each other, but made no mention of his playing hooky. His appearance was accepted as a matter of fact.

From his position by the big front window of the store, Jody could see that many people were already converging upon the Courthouse, though the time was only eight-thirty. The novelty of the trial had apparently created extensive interest.

Though he grew a bit apprehensive about finding a seat, Jody decided to wait and accompany the others, since he was likely to be a little less conspicuous in a group. The last thing he wanted was to be spotted by the truant officer.

Within a few minutes, however, the others decided to go on up and take their seats in the defendants' chairs, so he walked up to the courtroom with them. They, at once, joined Dale at the defendants' table. Jody found room to squeeze in on the end of one bench beside a couple of big men whom he recognized as local coon hunters. His questing glance about the room convinced him that nearly half the crowd was known to him as hound owners of one kind or another.

Across the aisle, nearly all the seats were filled with a compact group of stern-faced, somber-dressed men and women, that he guessed correctly were members of the little church. As Jody watched, the Prosecuting Attorney crossed over to the table occupied by Bill, Steve, Bob, and their attorney. In his hand, he carried a sheet of paper that appeared to be a list of names. After studying it for several minutes, there was a nod of agreement among them and it was then returned to the Prosecutor. The selection of the jury had been dispensed with that easily. Apparently, all were known and approved by the defendants.

By nine-thirty, the jury was seated, and court got underway. Bill, Steve, and Bob, of course, pleaded not guilty, and with a bored expression, the Prosecutor prepared to present his case. He spent exactly twenty minutes in doing so. His demands were brief and to the point. That the body of one Tom Harmon, a dog, be removed from the place of interment in the little cemetery. Also, that the ones responsible for the burial be made to suffer the extreme penalty allowable by law.

Though there were four plaintiffs, only Silas Keener was called to the stand by the Prosecuting Attorney. Seemingly, he had been selected as spokesman for the group. Even his questioning of Silas was brief. It soon became obvious, that in his opinion, the whole thing was a waste of time. Something to be disposed of by a few formalities and the verdict a foregone conclusion: guilty. This became more evident to Dale when neither defendant was questioned.

A slight frown wrinkled the Prosecutor's brow when Dale declined to cross examine Silas Kenner. If the reason had become a slight source of worry to him, it was not enough to dampen his arrogance. With a small bow and a flourish of his hand, he turned the floor over to the Defense Attorney. The wintry smile on his face gave mute indication that he considered regular procedure but a mockery of necessity.

The young Defense Attorney ran appraising eyes over the seven men and five women sitting in judgment on the case. He knew that, for the moment, they felt ill used. The Prosecutor's comment for the whole thing had gotten home to them.

As they moved uncomfortably on the hard seats of the jury box, their deepest thoughts were easy to read. How had such a trivial matter ever reached the circuit court in the first place? Why was their time being wasted on something that should have been settled so much simpler?

Slowly and gracefully, he rose and faced the jury. Speaking softly, with a note of apology in his voice, he said, "Rest easy, ladies and gentlemen. Make yourselves comfortable, this may take awhile."

As they surveyed this big rugged, dark-haired young man with the engaging smile, the exuberance of his youth would not be denied. In spite of their irritation of only moments before, their set faces relaxed and returned the generosity of his smile.

The hard seats had, all at once, become more comfortable, a little softer. They were not interested in what he had to say. His assured manner, tempered with courtesy, had won their respect. And they were suddenly aware that he was far from done. Knowing that they were his, at least for the moment, Dale lost no time in getting on with his defense.

Turning then, to look directly at the Prosecutor, he said, "My honorable opponent is in fine form today. His sarcasm has saturated the air until one must consider the need to open a window."

The Prosecutor acknowledged these frank remarks briefly with a wry smile and a small flap of his hand. Interest had, however, been kindled in his eyes. This boy would bear watching.

Speaking in a strong, firm voice that reached every corner of the room, the Defense Attorney addressed the court. "Your Honor, ladies and gentlemen of the jury, the purpose of this court is to render justice for all that might have need of its sanctions, and not for just a privileged few. If we were to do as the Prosecuting Attorney asks, and tear Tom Harmon's body from its grave, where it lies beside that of his best friend, then justice would not have prevailed here today. If we were to cast it into some roadside ditch, as he had also suggested, then the last wish of a dying man would have been ignored."

Pausing for a moment, to let his words sink in, he ran his eyes over the crowd of silent spectators, letting them feel the fire of his intensity, and then, once more, turned back to the jury.

"Ladies and gentlemen, this is not a case of charity or an argument over small footage in a potter's field. Tom Harmon paid for the ground in which he is buried. When Robert Brown, William Goddard, and Steve Rainer placed the casket containing his body into the grave, they did so knowing that very ground belonged to him and no other."

There was a gasp of indignation from the four complaining witnesses, but he burned them quiet with his eyes, and continued, "He not only paid for his burial plot, but made regular contributions to the church as well; the church supposedly represented by the aggrieved parties, when, in fact, they represent only themselves."

His voice, vibrant with emotion, seemed to lift all present up and pull them to him. Unmoving, they waited silently for his next words. "Aggrieved parties," he laughed scornfully, "not as far as the true aspects of this case are concerned. Aggrieved only to the extent that someone has dared to enter into the warped confines of their dark, narrow little world and refused to bow to their will. Aggrieved because the halos with which they enshrouded themselves have at last been lifted from their heads, laying bare before the world the true, cruel, cold, and selfish character cringing underneath."

The air of the courtroom had suddenly become electrified, and many heads were turned to stare at the tense, white, drawn faces of the plaintiffs. With a sweeping motion of his hand in their direction, he continued, "There they sit, ladies and gentlemen, in all their puritanical dignity. From all appearances, as wronged as an outraged virgin. When in fact, they are more like vultures, sitting beside the road, waiting to pick clean the bones of a rabbit that has been struck down by a car."

Surprised by the Defense Attorney's attack upon the plaintiffs, the Prosecutor had sat unmoving. But now he burst to his feet, his face purple with indignation.

"Objection, Your Honor," his voice rang out. "The plaintiffs are not on trial here. What he has just said is irrelevant, unwarranted, and can have no bearing upon the case. I request that it be stricken from the records and that the Defense Attorney be ruled out of order."

The big, rangy body of Dale Ringer whirled, with whiplike grace, to face the Judge. "On the contrary, Your Honor, it has everything to do with the case."

The keen, blue eyes of the little gray-haired old Judge flashed behind his spectacles, as he stared intently at him. "In what way, may I ask? Will you explain to the court the justification of such an attack upon the plaintiffs and show reason why I should not do as the Prosecuting Attorney asks?"

With a dignity far beyond his twenty-five years, he answered softly, "Your Honor, the whole basis of these charges brought before the court is that the sanctity of a church cemetery has been violated. I hope to prove these charges false. And that nothing has been violated except the determined refusal of a few people to believe that anything on this earth has a right to decent treatment, with the exception of them."

All eyes, even the Judge's, went to the four complaining witnesses, three men and one woman. The mode of their dress was as much alike as the pinched mouths look on their gaunt faces. Faces aged with time and constant rebellion against anything they didn't understand, stuck atop scrawny necks that protruded from still yet scrawnier bodies. Clothed in black, perched on the edge of their seats as if ready to take instant flight, they did, in fact, seem to lend truth to the description of the Defense Attorney. Like a bunch of vultures.

For a moment, the Judge seemed lost in thought, his face a serious study of conflicting emotions. Finally, after calm deliberation, he cleared his throat and began:

"The subject of this trial is unique, so much so, that I doubt if another just like it ever appeared before a court of law. Due to this fact and that unusual procedure can be expected, the request to rule you out of order is denied, though the remarks of the Defense Attorney will be stricken. However, unless your education in common law procedure has been neglected, and I doubt that it has, you must be aware of the proper conduct expected of you by this court. I would suggest that the Defense Attorney govern himself accordingly."

Though apparently taken to task for his attack upon the plaintiff group, the young attorney smiled at the Judge, as he answered, "Thank you, Your Honor. I'll remember."

Dale Ringer was satisfied. He knew that he had been treading on thin ice, but he had made his point. The jury had been made aware of the possibility of personal prejudice on the part of the plaintiffs, a slight shifting aside from the religious angle. So far, so good.

Bowing slightly in the direction of the jury, he said, "Ladies and gentlemen, I beg your indulgence for just a minute. Would you be so kind as to look carefully at the slide I am about to show you?"

Quickly setting up a screen, he turned to the Bailiff and asked politely, "May I have the lights off, please?"

As his request was quickly granted, the gloom of a bleak February day lent little light to the inside of the room and the color slide stood out in bold relief before the court. Stark raw reality was before them; a plain double, red granite headstone, encompassing the nearer end of two red clay mounds, side by side, in the frozen ground of a windswept cemetery.

Clean cut simple block letters carried Josh Harmon's message from the grave. On the left side they read: TOM HARMON—Born December 5, 1948–Died November 30, 1960—Age 12 years. And on the right side: JOSH HARMON—Born December 5, 1876–Died November 30, 1960—Age 84 years; and in the middle, a hand clasping a dog's paw, while underneath was one line, "Friends To The Last."

As he stood silently, letting the minutes drag on, as all present sat with eyes glued to the vivid picture, he knew that the time had come. Tom Harmon must be brought into focus as something of flesh and blood. The time of the name had passed, now must come the living image. The jury must feel him, hear him, and sense his presence right in that very room.

Requesting the lights turned on, his first glance at the jury showed that emotion had been aroused. To keep it there, he plunged straight ahead, risking the rapids, but sure of his footing.

Softly, caressingly, his voice sought them out, probed for their response, and found it willing. "Ladies and gentlemen, is it so strange that a man would want his dog buried beside him? One who gave generously and unselfishly of his love and devotion, so that an old man's last remaining years might be a little less lonely?

As you hear the story of Tom Harmon, you will begin to see, as I do, that these two seemed destined to come together, to share a life of mutual understanding and love for one another."

Dale paused for a moment. With eyes lowered to the floor, he stood as if in deep thought, then raised his head and continued, "Josh never referred to Tom as his dog, but as his friend. He had other friends, but Tom had only one. But to this one he gave his all, his powerful body, his big heart, his keen intelligence, and his completely trusting faith. To all this, Josh responded in kind. He used to say, "Old Tom has never lied to me or found fault with what I did. He doesn't care if I'm poor or rich, famous or unknown. I can trust him, for he is my friend."

Again, he paused, as his eyes swept over the jury. They were intent, waiting for more, and he had more to give. In a stronger voice now, he addressed the jury, "Josh Harmon had reason to appreciate a true friend. He came to this county fifteen years ago, a broken and bitter man. Fresh out of prison, after serving ten years for a crime he didn't commit. His car was involved in a vicious hit and run accident and a man was left to die. He was unable to prove that he was home alone that night. He was convicted and sentenced to twenty years. For ten years, he died a little bit each day. His young wife divorced him and married his partner. Then, as a result of an accident in which his ex-wife and former partner were killed, his innocence was proven. Before the woman died, she admitted that the partner was driving the car the night of the accident. Josh was released."

The Prosecuting Attorney, who had been growing more impatient by the minute, rose to his feet and in a disdainful voice said, "Your Honor, I fail to see the necessity of listening to the story of a man's life, or that it can in any way have any bearing on the case. We are here to judge an act of sacrilege committed by the defendants. I suggest that we get on with the trial."

The Judge's words came rapidly. "The Prosecuting Attorney is reminded that I'm fully aware of the purpose of this trial. Whether an act of sacrilege has been committed has not yet been decided. I would deem it advisable for you to refrain from assuming the duties of judge and jury and stick solely to your position, that of Prosecuting Attorney.

For an instant, the Prosecutor stared at the Judge and seemed on the verge of speaking. But then, red of face, he muttered an apology and sat down.

Turning then, to speak to Dale, the Judge said, "The court has previously acknowledged that unusual procedure seems to be expected. It will be condoned just as long as it doesn't touch on the ridiculous. Please see that it doesn't."

"Thank you, Your Honor," he answered. "This has all been a necessary part of proving that Josh and Tom must remain buried side by side. It could appear ridiculous only to those who are without love of compassion for other living things."

Facing the jury again, he took up the story of Josh at the point of interruption. "He was able to salvage a little from what was left of the business that had been stolen from him and the state paid retribution of a few thousand dollars. Broken in spirit and body, he looked for a place to be alone, a place to give his wounded soul a chance to heal. He found it in the little place he bought at the mouth of Big East Hollow. For three years, no one hardly knew him. He came to town to buy provisions, paid in cash, and went his own way, asking for no friendship and receiving none."

Scornfully, he looked directly at the four plaintiffs, as he drove barbed words at them. "For three years he lived there, right in the community with our complaining witnesses, without recognition. Every Sunday, many members of the church passed right by his house, and not once did anyone stop and invite him to attend the service."

Abruptly, he stopped his delivery and changed tactics. Politely, he addressed the court. "Your Honor, I would like to recall Silas Keener to the stand."

As his name was called, Keener rose and approached the bench. After being reminded that he was still under oath, he quickly perched on the edge of his chair. In cold defiance, he glared at the Defense Attorney.

"Will you state your name again, please?"

"Silas Keener," came the answer in raspy nasal tone.

"Mr. Keener, will you please tell the court why no one in your church ever invited Josh Harmon to attend the services during the first three years he lived among you?"

In a voice full of indignation, Keener answered, "How could I be expected to know?"

Leaning slightly forward so as to look him directly in the eyes, Dale said, "Isn't it true that you threatened to withdraw your financial support if any member of the church approached him? And you relented only when Josh made it known that he wished to make regular sizeable contributions? Just answer yes or no, Mr. Keener."

For a moment, Keener's reluctance was obvious to all. Then he answered harshly, "Yes, I ordered them not to."

"Why, Mr. Keener? Why did you order them not to?"

"He wasn't the right kind of a person to have in our church. He was a jail bird."

"But, Mr. Keener, his innocence was proven. He never should have been in jail in the first place."

"Ha! That's what you say. Once a jail bird, always a jail bird, to my way of thinking."

Smiling, Attorney Ringer said, "Thank you, Mr. Keener, that will be all." Then turning to the Prosecutor, he added, "Your witness."

Quickly approaching the witness, the Prosecuting Attorney asked, "Mr. Keener, will you tell the court how long you have been a member of the church?"

"I've been a member for fifty-five years. I joined when I was ten years old."

Nodding slightly, as if at a foregone conclusion, the Prosecutor said, "Isn't it true, Mr. Keener that you have only the best interest of your church at heart? And that you have always been generous with your financial contributions?"

Keener's shoe button eyes glittered, "Yes, that's true. I always do what's best for my church and my money has been its main support. My father before me did only what was best for the church and his money supported it then."

Keener's voice was becoming louder, as he continued, "The Keeners, more than anybody else, have always known what was best for the church and that's the way it's gotta be. We support it because our way is the right way and that's what the rest have to do or—"

There was now a wildness to his tone that brought alarm to the eyes of the Prosecuting Attorney. Quickly, he cut Keener's tirade. "Thank you, Mr. Keener. That will be all."

When, even then, Keener would have continued, the Prosecutor grasped him by the arm and steered him back to his seat.

No sooner was the chair vacant, than Dale requested that the woman member of the plaintiff group be called to the stand. As he surveyed her sitting stiffly erect, he had a fleeting thought that all she needed to complete the picture was a broom. But no trace of his thoughts was in his voice as he addressed her.

"Will you tell the court your name, please?'

"Thelma Stringer," came the words with machine-gun rapidity.

"Miss or Mrs.?" At this question, a ripple of amusement swept the room and the witness grew a little more rigid.

"Miss," she fairly hissed, and again, chuckles were heard throughout the crowd.

With a supreme effort, Dale smothered a smile and continued,

"Now, Miss Stringer, will you please tell the court the exact nature of your duties in connection with the church?"

"I am the financial secretary."

"In other words, all collections and contributions must pass through your hands, to be recorded and deposited."

"Yes, that's right."

"Good. Now, Miss Stringer, will you please examine these documents and tell the court what they are?"

Her scrawny hand, looking more like a claw, had hardly grasped the papers before she snapped, "These are receipts for money received by the church."

"Now, will you please state whose signature appears on each one?"

With a jerk of her head, she answered, "Mine, of course."

"Fine, now, Miss Stringer, there are twenty different receipts there. Will you examine them and then tell the court to whom they are made out and for how much?"

Quickly, she divided the papers into two piles and studied them for a moment before she answered. "There are ten made out to Josh Harmon for the amount of one hundred dollars each and ten made out to Tom Harmon for the amount of one hundred dollars each."

"Thank you. Those receipts cover a period of ten years; one from Tom and one from Josh for each of those ten years. Now, Miss Stringer, did you ever protest any of these contributions?"

"No! Of course not!"

"In other words, you were glad to receive the money in the name of the church?"

"That's right. How else could a church survive?"

"Of course, Miss Stringer, monetary contributions are indeed a necessity. However, isn't it a bit strange that you so gladly accepted Tom Harmon's money, yet deny him a small piece of ground in the church cemetery?"

Defiantly, she glared at the Defense Attorney. "When I accepted the money, I didn't know that Tom Harmon was a dog."

"But, Miss Stringer, weren't you curious, since Tom Harmon never appeared at the services. Didn't you ever wonder who or what he was?"

"I did ask once, and Mr. Harmon said that he was just a friend of his who wanted to contribute."

"But didn't you think it very strange that he would contribute money, and yet, never attend?"

"I asked about that, too. Mr. Harmon said that it was because Tom Harmon's work kept him out late on Saturday nights and he needed to sleep late on Sundays."

A roar of laughter burst from the crowd, and even the Prosecutor seemed to smother a smile. Attorney Ringer waited until all was quiet again and then produced two more slips of paper.

"Miss Stringer, here are two receipts for burial plots in the church cemetery, made out to Josh and Tom Harmon for two hundred dollars each and signed by you. Look at them and tell me if that's true.

She hardly glanced at them before answering. "Yes, that's what they are."

"Now tell me, Miss Stringer, was there any difference between the money contributed in Tom Harmon's name and that of any other?"

"Well," she stammered, "of course not."

"Obviously not," Dale said dryly. "But there is a difference now that Tom Harmon is dead and can no longer contribute."

Her thin face reflected the fury within her, and her voice was shrill as she cried, "I didn't know he was a dog, I tell you. I didn't know he was a dog."

Dale waited for her to calm down a little before he added softly, "Just two more questions, Miss Stringer. Would it have made any difference, at the time, if you had known that those one hundred-dollar donations were made in the name of a dog? And are you prepared to see that the church gives up the twelve hundred dollars in Tom Harmon's name if the court decides that he cannot remain buried there?"

For the first time, her loss of composure was complete. Her thin hands closed spasmodically over the arms of her chair as her eyes shifted to the tense, stern-faced figures of her brothers in complaint. At last, the answer drained from her tight lips, as her voice came plaintively, and without its former snap. "I don't know. I don't know."

Almost apologetically, Attorney Ringer said, "Thank you, Miss Stringer, that will be all." Then to the Prosecutor, he said, "Your witness."

For a full minute, his eyes rested upon the uncomfortable woman before saying, "No questions."

Permitting the witness to step down, Dale stood looking at the two remaining members of the plaintiff group. Shifting uncomfortably under his scrutiny, they stared back with unwinking eyes.

Then turning abruptly away from them, he addressed the court. "Ladies and gentlemen, it's time we learned more about Tom Harmon. You have heard the defendants, Bill Goddard, Bob Brown, and Steve Rainer testify that they buried one Tom Harmon according to the last request of his friend, Josh Harmon. You have also heard them plead not guilty to the charge of desecrating a church cemetery. Let's now hear the story of Josh and Tom Harmon from those who knew them best. I wish to call Steve Rainer to the stand."

Steve's big rawboned figure had a commanding appearance as he strode to the stand. Keen blue eyes looked out of a rugged, tanned and smiling face, from under a thatch of blond curly hair. That most present knew and approved of him was apparent from the smiles that followed him.

Formalities over, he sat patiently, waiting the Defense Attorney's questions. "Steve, will you tell the court how long you knew Josh Harmon?"

The voice of the witness was pleasingly firm. "I knew Josh for about ten years."

"How did you get to meet him? Was it connected in any way with your trade as a carpenter? Apparently, he was a hard man to get to know, so just how did you manage to break through the wall he had built around himself?"

Steve smiled broadly before answering. "Well, sir, it wasn't hard at all. It had nothing to do with my trade. I'm a coon hunter, same as Josh was, and one day, as I was passing his house, I noticed this fine-looking Black and Tan in the yard. So, I just stopped, and we started talking hounds. That's all there was to it. I guess we were friends from that time on."

"Now, Steve, according to the date on the headstone, Josh and Tom died on the same day. Also, they were born on the same day of the same month. However, Josh was eighty-four years old and Tom was twelve. Do those dates have any special significance to you?"

Steve nodded soberly before answering. "Yes, sir, they do. It means that they were what could be called exactly the same age, right to the day." At this statement, there were small exclamations throughout the room.

"In what way do you mean?"

"Well, of course, there's no doubt that they died on the same day, and in fact, at the same second. But even Josh didn't know exactly the day Tom was born. They first came together when Tom was four months old. Josh knew that because Tom was shedding his puppy teeth. So, since that would have been December, Josh just guessed at the day, and then gave him the same date as his, December 5. And since science says that one year in a dog's life equals seven in a human's life, that would have made them both eighty-four years old to the day."

As the Defense Attorney paused for a moment to look at the faces in the courtroom, he could easily read the strong interest reflected there. And even more, Steve's incredible statements had established what he had hoped for, an awareness of the unusual; the coming together of two living things in a way that left no doubt that they seemed destined to do so. He knew that he must keep that realization foremost in their minds. Not only keep it there, but make it grow, until no other thought remained except that they belonged together, even in death.

"Steve, would you tell the court just how Josh and Tom came together?"

"Yes, sir. It was sometime around the first of April 1948, about nine o'clock in the morning. Josh had been to the back of his place to clean out a spring. He didn't know that Abe Sutter's bull was on a rampage and had broken through onto his farm. The bull came up on Josh just as he reached the gate to his barn lot and knocked him up against the gate before he even knew he was there. The bull had pulled back to smash him good, when all at once, Josh received some unexpected help."

As Steve looked directly at the jury, they sat rigid, their intense concentration a silent plea for him to continue. Without removing his eyes from them, he slowly complied. "Josh said he never knew where he came from, he hadn't been there a minute before. But just when the bull was ready to hit him the second time, there was the pup. From out of nowhere, this scrawny little, wobbly-legged, four months old Black and Tan pup was suddenly standing between Josh and the bull. With his little hackles raised and puppy teeth bared, he bawled his puppy bawl right in the bull's face. The bull was so surprised that he backed up a couple of steps and this gave Josh time to scoop up the pup and sail over the gate."

Steve's eyes were shining as he paused for a moment to catch his breath. You could have heard a pin drop in the courtroom as they waited to hear the rest. He didn't keep them waiting long.

"This pup had saved his life and Josh had found his first real friend since moving to this county. Josh never found out where he came from, though he spent weeks trying to do so. No one had ever seen him before. It was just as if he had suddenly appeared out of thin air, right when Josh needed him the most. It didn't seem possible that such a well-blooded pup would be without an owner, but there didn't seem to be any other answer. Josh was absolutely unable to trace him beyond the spot where he first appeared, his barn gate. So, he named him Tom and they became inseparable."

There was complete silence in the courtroom for several minutes after Steve came to a halt. The presence of Tom Harmon had impregnated the very air about them. Many present were sure that, in the middle of the floor at the front of the room they saw, for just an instant, a wobbly-legged Black and Tan hound pup, snarling defiance at any and all enemies of the one man in the world to whom he belonged.

And there were those who swore that the eyes of the four

complaining witnesses were also fastened upon the spot in the middle of the floor. And their faces turned white as reality and uncertainty faded to a merging of one and defied separation.

When Dale released Steve to the Prosecutor for cross examination, he came forward with a look of disdain on his face. With a leer in the direction of the jury, he turned to Steve, and asked scornfully, "Mr. Rainer, have I interpreted your word correctly in assuming that you have attempted to inject something of the supernatural into the relationship between this man and his dog?"

Steve's eyes drilled directly into those of the Prosecutor, and no one present doubted the sincerity of his word, as he answered in ringing tones. "You, sir, have injected the word supernatural, not I, and by doing so, have lent truth to what you say I imply."

A brief flurry of laughter rippled across the room. The Prosecutor's face was livid as he turned to the Judge. "Your Honor, I move that the defendant's words be stricken from the record."

The Judge nodded and turned to the clerk. "Please strike the words of the defendant."

After warning Steve to reply to the questions with only a yes or no, the Judge sat back and waited for the Prosecutor to continue. For a moment, he appeared uncertain as to whether it would be advisable to continue probing Steve, but he decided to continue.

"Mr. Rainer, will you tell the court whether or not you informed the church officials that you intended to bury a dog in their cemetery?"

"No, sir. We didn't think it necessary."

"Oh! I see. By any chance did you deem it inadvisable because you knew they would object?"

"We expected some opposition, yes. But that was not the real reason."

"Ah! So, you admit knowledge of the fact that you were committing something that defied all conventions and would not have been allowed to happen in their cemetery, had they known. What other reason could there have possibly been for your secrecy?"

Steve's eyes blazed. "We had all the reason we needed, and we weren't secretive about it. There were two graves for all to see.

That should have been evidence enough that there were to be two burials."

"Mr. Rainer, you didn't answer my question. What made you think you had the right to do such a thing?"

Steve's answer came with force. "I'll give you our right. You speak of conventions, not law. There is no law against what we did. And conventions, sir, are but mode of practice as accepted by most people and are subject to change with the times and the workings of men's minds. We broke nothing but a convention and who can say how it will be accepted? Not you. Not I. If it is accepted, then we have broken nothing. You called it their cemetery. That's true. But Old Tom was buried in his own lot. Not theirs. Not anybody's, but his. That, sir, was our reason."

A glance at the jury told the Prosecutor that they were moved by Steve's words, and recklessly, he attempted to bring them back. Scornfully, he lashed out. "Mr. Rainer, you have said repeatedly that this dog purchased his own lot. Now, don't you think such a statement is a bit ridiculous?"

"No, sir," Steve replied with emphasis. He was elated, for this was a line of questioning he had hoped for. The fact that the Prosecutor was following it was complete indication of his lack of knowledge concerning the subject. His previous disdain had apparently resulted in neglect of research, because he thought it unnecessary.

"Well, now," the Prosecutor continued with sarcasm, "will you tell the court just how this dog obtained his purchasing power? Perhaps he was a farmer. Or maybe he worked at one of the factories here in town. Which was it, Mr. Rainer?"

"Neither of those. Old Tom was a coon dog and caught many dollars' worth of fur for Josh each winter. Besides that, he trained one young dog each year, from the time he was two years old. He trained ten young dogs in all and the owner of each dog paid one hundred dollars. Josh kept an itemized account of Tom's earnings, that and the hundreds of dollars from the sale of fur that he caught. That, sir, was the money he turned over to the church in Tom's name and that's how the lot was purchased."

As Steve's words died away, a chuckle swept over the room of spectators, and a few smiles flashed among the faces of the jury members. They were obviously enjoying the Prosecutor's discomfort. He had been bested. He should have never questioned this witness.

Somewhat flustered and red of face, he muttered, "No more questions."

As Steve returned to his seat, the Defense Attorney rose and said, "I wish to call Bill Goddard to the stand."

After being sworn in and his name and occupation attested to, his attorney said, "Bill, will you tell the court, in your own words, exactly what happened on the night of November 30th of last year?"

In a deep voice, Bill began the story. Beginning with the premonition he had during the day, right on through the complete evening of dramatic events. He finished with a vivid description of the last moments of Josh and Tom. His relating of Steve's plunge over the cliff after those two caused many admiring glances to be cast his way.

A solemn hush lay over the room after he had finished, and a subdued atmosphere prevailed. More than one pair of moist eyes could be seen among the spectators, as well as the jury. A careful observation of this by the Prosecutor convinced him that an attack on Bill's story would do little but arouse antagonism for the state's case among members of the jury. Quickly, he declined to question.

The fact that Dale had chosen fearlessly to put all three defendants on the stand had made a definite impression on both Judge and jury. For when Bob was also called and complied with the request to explain Josh's financial preparation for Tom's care after death, little doubt remained as to his absolute belief in the honesty of the case. His last question to Bob was only further proof.

"Bob, with respect to the charges made against you and your friends, would you still do the same again, if it was to do over?"

With dignity and deep concern, Bob answered slowly, "Yes, sir. I know that I can speak for the others when I say that we most certainly would, and without hesitation."

With that, he was offered to the Prosecuting Attorney, who

again declined to question. There was absolutely nothing in Bob's testimony to attack. The trial was running against him and he knew it. Awareness of his miscalculation of the intensity with which Dale would prepare and present his case had caught up with him. He had left too many loose ends. He desperately sought a way to tie them up before the whole case slipped away from him. But in the depths of his desperation, he saw the Defense Attorney all but hand it to him on a platter.

For a short time, Dale was lost in deliberation of his next move. Then deciding to gamble, he called his next witness, Ike Ponder, a somber-faced, but rather pleasant looking, elderly member of the plaintiff group. Within minutes after placing him on the stand, he knew he had made a mistake. The look of exuberance on the Prosecutor's face was easy to diagnose.

Knowing Ike Ponder to be an easy-going man and one who was well liked in the community, he had hoped for a partially friendly witness from the plaintiff group. He was that and more. So much so, that Dale reeled under the feeling that he had asked for a drink and someone had turned on the hose.

Ike's voice held no bitterness, but expressed deep sorrow for both Josh and Tom, and for the defendants because of the situation they now found themselves in. Two questions and Dale realized that to continue further would only compound his mistake. In dread of what was to come, he reluctantly turned Ponder over to the Prosecutor. The Prosecutor eagerly and with considerable skill, proceeded to make the most of the advantage handed him by the Defense Attorney.

In soft tones that blended with the atmosphere of friendliness surrounding the witness, he encouraged him to tell, in his own words, his reasons for being opposed to Tom's burial in its present location. One by one, Ponder presented his reasons, logically and sensibly, in a quiet voice completely without rancor. His very manner of respect for the plaintiffs' cause was doing far more towards nailing down the state's case than all the bitter rantings of Silas Keener and Thelma Stringer. With sinking heart, Dale knew that he was in trouble.

It was with a sigh of relief that he heard the Judge announce the noon recess, following Ike's dismissal from the stand. With a minimum of conversation, he, Steve, Bill, and Bob, with Jody bringing up the rear, retired to a nearby restaurant to have their lunch. When the serving was completed, he began to discuss the way things were going.

"Well, boys, I sure goofed by putting Ponder on the stand. I guess it's only fair to tell you, that right now, we stand a good chance of losing."

Bill clapped a hand to his shoulder, and said, "Don't blame yourself. I would have done the same thing. In fact, I wondered earlier why you didn't call him. None of us would have thought of it backfiring that way."

"That's right, Dale," Steve interposed, "I still don't think we'll lose, but if we do, I want you to know that we think no one could have handled our case better. If we had it to do over again, I would still want you to represent us, and don't you forget it."

Nodding his head, Bob added, "Don't ask me why, but for some reason I feel that we won't lose, even as bad as things look right now. You warned us that breaking an age-old convention might be harder than any legal status, so we understand why Ponder's words had such an effect upon the jury. If we lose, we lose, but I still think that something will break for us yet."

Jody, who had been eating and listening, took time between mouthfuls to inject a question. "If those church members attending this trial was to decide that Old Tom didn't have to be moved, do you think they could kill Keener's charges?"

Dale managed a wry smile. "I suppose they could, Jody, but dropping the charges would have to be strictly between them and Keener. If they decided they wanted the charges dropped, they might browbeat him into withdrawing them. But I'm afraid that's just wishful thinking. After all, he does hold the purse strings, and it's not likely that they would go against him."

"I know most of those people," Bob said. "They are good, honest, and sincerely religious folks. We know that it didn't set too well with them when Keener took matters into his own hands. But they would have to be really convinced that he was wrong before they would do anything. I'm afraid that Dale is right, Jody."

"If they only knew what I know," Dale muttered to himself.

Instantly, the others snapped alert. "What's that?" Steve asked.

"Nothing I can explain now," Dale answered, with a shake of his head.

Bursting with questions, the others would have liked to pursue the subject further, but from the expression on his face, they knew there was no use. But within minutes they were to forget all about it as Jody, true to character, exploded from their midst.

Facing the window, he was the only one at the table who commanded an unobstructed view of the sidewalk. Suddenly, without warning, he burst to his feet. "There goes Clem Keener," he cried. "I aim to have a little talk with him."

While the others stared in amazement, he was out of the door in a flash. As the door slowly closed, they could hear him shout, "Hey, Clem, I want to talk to you." And then the sound of running feet fading away.

By the time the others reached the door, neither boy was in sight. Obviously, Clem had taken to his heels down a side alley, with a red-headed nemesis in pursuit. Worriedly, the others half started in that direction, but gave it up at once, with the realization that they probably couldn't find them anyway. With a glance at his watch, Dale said, "Boys, it's almost time for court to start."

"Boy!" Bill mused, as they walked toward the Courthouse, "That kid sure is a little wildcat, but one of these days, he's going to bite off more than he can chew."

"Well, he hasn't yet," Steve chuckled.

"No, but there's always a first time," Bob said, with a shake of his head. "But he's just like a bulldog when he gets some idea in his head and there's no quit to him. Like now, he's convinced that there's something about Clem's trap on Old Tom's foot that might help us. And right now, I'll bet he's well on the way to finding out if he's right or wrong."

Pausing at the top of the Courthouse steps, they took one last look in the direction the chase had gone but saw nothing, so they continued inside to take their place at the defendants' table. The trial, once more, got underway. Dale continued where he had left off.

As he let his eyes drift over the members of the jury, he found that the majority met him with a friendly gaze, but here and there, it seemed to be an extended expression of sympathy. Strangely enough, he found that left him with an uneasy feeling. Young as he was, he realized that it could mean that they were in complete disagreement with him, that their minds were already made up, and that they were only feeling sympathetic for his lost cause.

Shaking off a slight feeling of foreboding, he forced a smile, and courteously addressed them. "Ladies and gentlemen, I beg your indulgence once more. I have one more slide to show you."

As the lights were again turned off, the picture of the cemetery entrance appeared on the screen. Looping high from the large stone posts guarding the gate was a metal arch with three short words emblazoned directly over the center, "REST WITH FRIENDS."

It was these words to which he directed their attention. "Ladies and gentlemen, please notice those three simple little words and think what they mean." Leaving the picture on while he talked, he continued, "Rest with friends, ladies and gentlemen; three little words, but with so much meaning. Is that not an open invitation to the tired, the weary, and the lonely to seek comfort in death, by knowing they are lying beside those they have known, trusted, and loved while here on earth? Can you see anything in the meaning that says humans only?"

As Dale snapped off the projector, the lights were at once turned on to reveal him lost in thought, as he contemplated a single sheet of paper he held in his hand. As the silence mounted, the impatience of the Prosecuting Attorney made him think that the Defense Attorney was finished.

But as the Prosecuting Attorney half rose from his seat, Dale lifted his head and said softly, "Not just yet, if you please."

Glaring in anger, the Prosecutor appealed to the Judge. "Your Honor, would the court please instruct the Defense Attorney to continue or else end this farce at once?"

Dale turned to the Judge at once and apologized. "I'm sorry, Your Honor." Receiving a small nod of acceptance from the bench, he again addressed the jury, "Ladies and gentlemen, we have just heard the Prosecuting Attorney refer to this trial as a farce. I'm forced to accept that as an ill-considered remark. We are here to bring justice before the people. And you, ladies and gentlemen of the jury, are the people. Josh Harmon asked no more than that when he prepared a message for you, written several months before his death. With your permission, I would like to read it." Not a sound was heard as he proceeded to bring them Josh's message from the grave.

* * *

Josh's Plea to the Jury

Ladies and gentlemen, I write this completely without shame. To have known the one for whom I plead makes such a feeling impossible. I, Josh Harmon, who has groveled to no man, now do so, as I prostrate myself at your feet in begging entreaty. Please allow Tom, my dog, my friend, to remain by my side.

If, in the past, pride of ownership of this dog has bordered on the brink of vanity, a natural indulgence in human weakness, it has long ago become overshadowed by humble gratefulness that I, of all the earth's peoples, should have been selected by one greater than I to be recipient of his devotion.

He was propelled into my life at an exact instant when, but for his appearance, I most certainly would have met death from the attack of an enraged bull. Then, at the age of four months, he offered his life for mine and has been prepared to do so ever since.

His body has felt the fangs of the copperhead that were intended for my flesh. His jaws have ripped asunder a rabid fox, as I lay helpless on the ground, when every instinct within him must surely have cried out; do not touch this creature of death. But for him, ladies and gentlemen, I would have died many times. He lived only to serve me and asked nothing other than being allowed to do so.

He was more than just my dog. He was my solace, my comfort, my companion. His coming saw the end of my solitude, brushed away the cobwebs from a mind bruised from human abuse, and cast light into the dark corners of my existence.

He was my self-appointed protector. At the slightest sign of illness or injury to me, he was instantly at my side. His eyes full of luminous sympathy, searching my face for signs of pain; his worried whimpering telling me that he wanted to take the pain from me upon himself, so that I would not suffer.

I do not know what conditions have brought about the necessity of having this read to you, other than that death has come to both of us. But I do know that up to and including his last breath, Tom's thoughts were of me. And that every last ounce of his remaining strength had been directed towards helping make things easier for me, as I approached that last unsurmountable obstacle. Can I do less for him?

Deep silence hovered over the courtroom after he was finished. While the spell lasted, Josh Harmon's presence was prevalent throughout the room. And for the time being, none there would have denied his plea. Here and there could be seen a pair of moist eyes, especially among the lady members of the jury.

* * *

Though reluctant to break the silence, Dale knew that he must strike while the iron was hot. As the fire of intensity in his eyes probed for response among the jury members, he plunged, at once, into his summation. "We have been told that there are no dogs in Heaven. Who knows this to be true? If Heaven is a place of eternal happiness, as described, then why should there not be dogs in Heaven, for those who found them such a necessary part of their life while here on earth?"

"I cannot believe, I will not believe, that God would have given us these noble animals, capable of returning affection and love for the human of their choice in life, and then deny us that companionship in Heaven. These animals that have lived to serve man since the beginning of time, and deliberately chose to lay down their lives numerous times for the one they called master."

"No, ladies and gentlemen, I cannot agree with the age-old concept that there are no dogs in Heaven. When I leave this earth and enter those gates, I expect to be met by my Old Shep, of my boyhood days, whose wagging tail and eyes full of ecstatic welcome will say, 'Welcome, Master, I've been waiting here by the gate a long time, but I knew you'd come.' Yes, ladies and gentlemen, he'll be there. I will see him because I want to, because he will be a necessary part of my Heaven."

"Ladies and gentlemen, Josh Harmon believed this. Do not tear his dog from his side. Leave him where he lies, so that they may make the trip together. Thank you."

As his last words died away, a muted sound floated into the room. To Bill, it was a call from beyond, and he felt the prickling of hairs on the back of his neck. Startled, Steve and Bob turned to stare incredulously at each other. Again, in soft pleading tones, it came to them, as if from far away, and then gradually faded until there was nothing but a memory. Among the crowd, one could see faces suddenly gone white, while others wondered if they had heard it at all. Silas Keener's face was a study of fear, while at his side, Thelma Stringer sagged, on the verge of fainting.

"God!" Bill whispered, "I don't believe what I just heard."

"You'd better believe it, buddy, for that was a horn, all right," Steve said in a strained voice. "A long and two shorts," he finished in an awestricken whisper.

The sound came no more, though many strained to hear. Now a mutter swept the room, as neighbor turned to neighbor, to verify what they thought they had heard.

"Must be a trick of Dale's," Bob whispered.

Though all three looked closely at the figure of the Defense Attorney, there was nothing about the impassiveness of his face to give them any clue. There had been many coon hunters attending the trial throughout the day, and it was possible that Dale had arranged for one of them to sound the horn, on a given signal. But as they looked around at those they knew, they could think of no one they had seen earlier that was not still present. But it was impossible to be sure. Most certainly, they told themselves, there must be an answer, but they could only guess. As before, on the night when Josh and Tom had died, there was that strange feeling of something uncanny about those two.

Quietly, Dale retired from the floor as the Prosecuting Attorney rose quickly and strode vigorously forward to take his place before the jury. As he faced them, the words of sarcasm about to spring from his lips died before they were spoken. One searching look at their faces, and he knew that the spell cast by the Defense Attorney still hovered over them. Any type of insulting attack would definitely be detrimental to his summation.

Forcing a smile to his normally arrogant face, he began to address them in a soft voice, fairly dripping with sympathy for the defendants, Josh and Old Tom. The candor of this about face was not lost on Dale. He realized, with sinking heart, that by his very own actions, he had prepared the jury to find the Prosecuting Attorney's suggestions acceptable.

From the seriousness with which they followed his every word, the Prosecutor knew that he had chosen the right weapon, and he used it with considerable skill. In a tone of regret, he continued to explain why a dog just couldn't be buried in the cemetery with humans. With words for a brush, he painted a vivid picture of what could be expected in the future if Tom were allowed to remain. In their mind's eye, he asked them to see graveyards torn asunder, as more and more stones over the graves of dogs appeared among those of their loved ones. To foresee the time when there would no longer be room for humans, because the plots were already filled with dogs.

Keeping his eyes on the members of the jury, Dale couldn't be sure how they felt. The fact that they were following every word with deep concentration didn't necessarily mean that they were buying what was being said. But yet, he admitted to himself, the gentleman was very good at appearing to be interested only in presenting facts; facts that would, indeed, make sense to most people.

Intently listening to the Prosecutor, he didn't notice the disturbance at the door of the courtroom until Bill's whisper caused him to look. A bareheaded, scratched-faced Jody stood just inside, and in his right hand was gripped the arm of Clem Keener. From the condition of their torn clothes and Clem's bruised face, it was obvious what had happened. And from all indications, Jody had emerged the victor.

By now, everyone had become aware of their entrance and were turning to see. The Prosecutor's delivery came to an angry halt at the interruption. Catching Dale's eye, Jody beckoned him forward. Retaining their seats, Bill, Steve, and Bob waited in breathless anticipation of what was happening.

They didn't have long to wait. After a couple of minutes, Dale came back down the aisle, followed by the two boys. Showing them to a seat near the front of the room, he turned to the Judge, whose stern look of disapproval was accented by the tone of his voice as he said, "Will the Defense Attorney please explain the meaning of this interruption?"

"Yes, sir, Your Honor. I have just received new evidence that I believe to be vital to this case. With the court's permission, I would like to present it."

Appraising the two battered boys, the Judge then looked piercingly at Dale. "Well," he intoned, "I must say, the longer this trial goes on, the more the unusual is compounded. However, if you're sure this evidence should be heard, then the court has no objections."

Then turning to the Prosecuting Attorney, who was standing quietly and red-faced, he asked, "Does the state have any objections to this procedure?"

Though he was obviously displeased, only by branding his whole soft approach as an out and out farce could he refuse. "No, Your Honor," he answered stiffly, "the state has no objections."

A bit unsteady, Clem got to his feet and slowly started towards the front of the room. Those who looked sharp could have seen Jody whisper a few words to him before he rose. Not once did Clem look towards his father, although the elder Keener was trying to catch his attention with glaring eyes.

As he reached the witness chair and was seated, Bill expressed his opinion to his friends during the swearing in. "You know what I think, fellows? Jody has beat some truth out of that boy and made him agree to tell it on the stand."

"Looks like he'd be too scared of his dad to tell anything that would get him into trouble," Steve said.

"Well," Bob chuckled, "we all know that he's scared to death of him, but right now, he's more scared of Jody."

Noticing that Dale was ready to start questioning Clem, they fell silent, so as to not miss a word. Clem was casting furtive eyes around the room, and appeared ready to bolt out of his chair, but Dale nailed him with his eyes, as he asked the first question.

"Will you tell the court your name, please?"

"Clem Keener," came the answer in plaintive tones.

"Thank you, Clem," Dale said politely. "Now will you state your relationship with the plaintiff, Silas Keener?"

After one quick glance in Silas's direction, he answered meekly, "He's my pa."

"Now, Clem," Dale continued, "on last November 30th, Josh Harmon's Black and Tan coon hound, Tom, was found in a trap, more dead than alive. Would you please tell the court to whom that trap belonged?"

"It was mine."

"Good. Now, Clem, are you in the habit of setting traps?"

"No, never did before."

"I see. Since this trap that caught Old Tom was a new one, maybe you had just started to take up trapping to make a little extra money?"

"No, sir. I don't like to trap. Besides, I only had six traps."

"Were they all new, Clem, just like the one that caught Tom?"

"Yes, sir. We bought them all at the same time."

"Clem," Dale's voice probed softly, "you say that you don't like to trap, yet you bought six traps. Why?"

"Pa made me."

"Oh, I see. Were you setting the traps for any special animal?"

The boy's answer was hardly audible, and Dale was forced to

ask him to speak louder. "Yes. He made me set them to catch a dog."

Dale's questions were being put to Clem in a friendly manner. And now that he had learned the Defense Attorney wasn't going to eat him alive, his answers came more readily.

"Did you set the traps to catch any certain dog, Clem?"

"Yes, sir. I was supposed to try and catch Mr. Harmon's old hound."

There was a series of gasps from the side of the room that was, for the most part, filled with members of the little church to which the plaintiffs belonged. At once, angry stares showered upon Keener like a barrage of arrows.

Dale's eyes gleamed with elation. This was better than he had dared hope for. "Now, Clem, I want you to tell the court, in your own words, just why your pa made you set traps for Mr. Harmon's Old Tom. Just take your time and tell it your own way."

By now, young Keener seemed warmed up to his subject, to the point of eagerness. It was not lost on the others that the look towards his father was now full of defiance instead of fear. Apparently, all was not well between those two.

In a voice that gained strength as he went on, Clem began, "Well, in the first place, Pa knew all along that Tom Harmon was a dog, though he didn't tell the others. Just kept it to himself. He said that if a man was crazy enough to give money to the church in the name of a dog, then let him. He almost told the others, though, when Mr. Harmon purchased the lot, but at the last minute, decided not to. He said they would just take the old fool's money, if he wanted to give it away, but he would see that the dog was never buried there."

At this point, Dale interrupted briefly. "Is that the reason why Tom Harmon's name was entered in the ledger of lot sales in pencil instead of ink like the others?"

"Yes, sir. That was part of his plan. He waited as long as he dared, but one day he said, "The time has come to do away with that dog. They are both old enough to die and are liable to go at any time.""

As Clem hesitated briefly to collect his thoughts, Dale felt a pang of remorse. He felt no enjoyment from pitting son against father, but it was just possible that the younger Keener would emerge the better boy for it.

Clem's eyes found Dale's, indicating that he was ready to continue. A brief nod gave him the go ahead. "Pa spent several days scouting the hills around Mr. Harmon's place, trying to learn the habits of Old Tom. At first, he aimed to shoot him and hide the body. If there was no body to bury, that would solve the problem. But he was afraid to take a chance on being seen around there when the dog disappeared. So, when he saw the dog visit that little cave two or three times, he got the idea about the traps. That was so far from Mr. Harmon's house that he figured he'd never find him. And later on, after the dog had finally died, he would slip down there and hide what was left there."

The strain of such a long testimony was irritating the patience of the Prosecuting Attorney almost to the point of exploding. Several times, he seemed on the verge of doing so, but so intently was the jury hanging onto every word from Clem that he dared not interrupt.

This time, Clem's voice nearly broke, as he said falteringly, "Pa even said that if the shock of the old dog's disappearance was to finish off the old man, why so much the better. They'd be rid of both of them at the same time and the church would be several hundred dollars better off."

As these words fell upon the ears of the shocked listeners, an angry murmur swept the group of church members. Silas Keener blanched and seemed to shrink within himself, as he felt the other plaintiffs draw away from him as far as their seats would permit. Under the hostile attention, Keener appeared to wilt before their very eyes, and no man was ever more alone with his guilt.

Obviously saddened by the necessary course of events, Dale hastened to draw to a close. Kindly, he said to Clem, "Just one more thing and then you can be excused. I will try to sum up the whole story in just a few words, and you just answer yes or no as to whether I'm right or wrong. Do you understand?"

Clem nodded. "Yes, sir. I understand."

"Fine," Dale answered. "Now, here it is. Your father had full knowledge of the fact that Tom was a dog. But at the same time, he had expressed his intentions of never allowing the dog to be buried there. Because of the advanced age of Mr. Harmon and his dog, he knew little more money would be forthcoming, so he decided to do away with the dog and hide the body. He forced you to trap for the dog until he was caught. He intended that Tom would be left to suffer for days in the trap until he finally died. He also expressed his opinion that if Mr. Harmon happened to die from the shock of losing his dog, it would be of little consequence. Am I right or wrong, Clem?"

With eyes downcast, Clem answered huskily, "Yes, sir. That's the way it was."

A white-faced Prosecuting Attorney declined to cross examine. As the Judge sympathetically excused Clem, Dale became aware of confusion behind him. Turning around, he observed Ike Ponder cross over to the group of church members, and bend over to converse with those on the end of the row. After a few words, he straightened up and beckoned for Dale to join them. Receiving a nod of permission from the Judge, he walked over to the group.

In a minute, he turned to the Judge, and said, "Your Honor, would the court please allow a ten-minute recess?"

"Under the circumstances," the Judge remarked dryly, "I don't see any reason why not. Court is recessed for ten minutes."

Instantly, the whole group rose and followed Dale to a side room. Only Ike Ponder paused long enough to motion Keener and the other two plaintiffs to join them. The Prosecutor sat sullenly, a look of stupor on his face, while the whole room buzzed with speculation. The suspense was short lived. In less than ten minutes they were back, and quietly took their seats.

Only Silas Keener returned to the seat he had formerly occupied. The other two, along with Ponder, had chosen to sit with the others of the church. For a few minutes longer, the crowd was kept waiting while Dale stepped up to the Judge and whispered something to him. Listening quietly until he was finished, the Judge nodded his head. Dale then stepped back to the floor.

"Your Honor," he asked, "may Ike Ponder approach the bench?"

"He may," the Judge answered, and then added, "Ike Ponder will approach the bench."

Slowly, Ike walked to the front of the room and stood looking up at the Judge. Not a sound came from the spectators, and an air of breathless excitement hung over the room, as they waited for him to speak.

"Your Honor," he began, "I have been selected as spokesman for the majority of our church members. This knowledge of Silas Keener's doings is as new to us as it is to you, and we are just as shocked as anyone else. By his actions he has created a wrong that dwarfs, by comparison, the charges against the defendants. Our church may possibly survive without the Keener money, but could not if we were to sanction this unholy deed; a deed that has cast a shadow over our church and wrapped the cemetery in a cloud of gloom. The purpose of this trial has ceased to be important. We, the church, with the approval of the plaintiffs, hereby submit a request that the charges against William Goddard, Robert Brown, and Steve Rainer be dismissed. We also request that it be entered into the records of this court, as it will be into the records of the church, that the body of Tom Harmon is hereby granted full sanctity for all time. Thank you."

For a few minutes, pandemonium reigned, as congratulations showered upon the defendants. Turning around in his seat, Bill reached a big hand back to ruffle Jody's hair, a big grin splitting his face wide open.

"You little red-headed devil," he said huskily. "You did it again."

Jody, though obviously pleased at the praise, was still somewhat flustered. "Oh, shucks, Bill," he said happily. "It wasn't much. Besides, I wanted to beat up old Clem anyway."

As Bill gave him another admiring glance, the sound of the Judge's pounding gavel brought his head around to the front. As they grinned at each other, they realized that some semblance of order had been restored, so they turned their attention to the front. All eyes were on the Judge as he concentrated on a paper he was reading. Finally, he raised his eyes and motioned to the Defense Attorney.

Facing the church group with a smile, Dale said, "Ladies and gentlemen, before His Honor formally discharges this case, I have something to tell you. By your decision to allow Old Tom to remain where he is, you have done your church a far greater service than you know. Josh Harmon was not the nearly penniless man you may have thought. When he salvaged his business, after getting out of prison, he invested it in sound securities. His wants were simple, so he never had reason to touch it. That investment has now grown to the amount of forty-seven thousand and three hundred dollars, which I am now prepared to turn over to you."

As the group expressed open-mouthed amazement, he smiled broadly at them again, and continued, "If you had decided otherwise here today, then the money would have gone elsewhere, as he had directed. He was too proud to offer the money as a bribe. Your acceptance had to come from your hearts or not at all. But I believe, ladies and gentlemen, that he had implicit faith in your understanding. I'm happy that you proved him right. Thank you."

While they waited for him to close the trial, the Judge seemed to be collecting himself. Removing his glasses, he took out his handkerchief and wiped them thoroughly, before finally returning them to his face. For another minute, his keen blue eyes scrutinized the room, as if to impress upon his memory the faces of everyone present.

Then, clearing his throat, he began to speak, "Everyone here in this room can assure himself that he has the unique distinction of having witnessed a trial, that in all probability, is unparalleled in the annals of court history. Justice has strange ways of asserting itself at times, when the right answer seems almost too elusive for us, as mere humans, to grasp. It is sometimes thrust upon us when we are in a most indecisive state of mind. When this happens, we would do well to be humbly grateful for a higher power that recognizes our frailties and limitations. And thus, delivers us from that which is beyond our comprehension. Who among us is to say that such a thing did not happen here today?"

As his last solemn words hung in the air, not a man or woman there would have disagreed with him. For the time being, all felt a bit smaller, as they recognized the reminder that man, in all his arrogance is, in truth, a puny thing, and but a speck on the map of life.

Leaving them to contemplate their lowliness, the Judge then turned to those upon which the burden of the trial had fallen. First, he thanked the two Attorneys for a job well done and commended them on their attitude throughout the trial.

Then, with a smile, he spoke to the jury, "Ladies and gentlemen, I want to commend you also on the attentive manner with which you attended this hearing. And to assure you that I am as happy as any of you that you were relieved of the need to arrive at a decision in this case."

Broad grins sweeping the faces of the jury members clearly showed that he had not underestimated their relief at having the matter taken out of their hands. Briefly then, the Judge looked out over the room. Then picking up his gavel, raised it high, as he finally spoke the words all had been waiting for. "Case dismissed."

As the gavel came crashing down to emphasize those two important words, the room became one large mass of confusion.

Since most of the crowd was pushing toward the doors, Bill, Steve, and Bob, along with Dale, who had rejoined them, sat quietly where they were. Caught up in the mood of their victory, they were content for awhile just to bask in its pleasant glow. As the throng thinned out rapidly, two lonesome figures still retained their seats. Although only one row and a few feet apart, they seemed completely oblivious to each other. Sitting stiffly erect, with blank eyes and drawn features, facing straight ahead, Silas and Clem were pitifully alone in their solitude.

As Dale's glance fell upon them, his eyes softened with sorrow. Regret that the instrument of his victory had served as a pry pole between father and son. Silas Keener had the look of a beaten man; one who had, at last, paused to take a good look at himself and didn't like what he saw. Sick at heart, Dale felt that he must make at least one effort to bring the two back together.

Crossing over to where Clem was seated, he sat down beside him. In a low voice, he said, "Clem, you did right today and what's more, I think your father knows it and will agree. But it has hit him rather hard and he feels very much alone right now. Clem, he needs you beside him as never before. Won't you go over to him?"

Slowly, Clem turned to look at his father. Little by little, the look of defiance left his face, to be replaced by one of sorrowful affection, as he realized that his elder had suddenly grown old within just the last hour. With eyes on the verge of tears, he whispered a husky thanks to Dale, and rose to go to Silas. Standing beside where he sat, still unmoving, Clem stood looking down at a gaunt, drawn face and bony shoulders. Slowly, his hand went out to rest on his father's left shoulder.

"Pa," he said softly, "let's go home."

Raising his head, Silas looked long into the face of his son, whom he had suddenly begun to see for the first time. "Sure, son, I guess we'd best be getting home, at that." Assisting him to rise, Clem threw Dale one grateful glance before grasping Silas by the arm to guide him slowly down the aisle and out of the room.

Silently, Bill, with the others, followed their progress with their eyes until they disappeared through the big doors. "Well," Bill said, "there's a boy who has grown up today."

"No doubt about it," Steve added, "And all for the best, too. I predict there will be more harmony between those two from now on."

Rising to make their own departure, they all shook Dale's hand and thanked him for a job well done, and then quickly left the building. Going down the broad front steps, each of them suddenly remembered with dismay Jody's torn and dirtied clothes. What would his mother say?

But to anyone who might have noticed, a small grin soon crept to his freckled face. He knew he could fairly swamp her with his talk of the trial, until she would forget the torn clothes in exasperation at trying to understand this son of hers. This red-headed, grinning, freckled-faced replica of his father, who could always get around her with his fast talk, a hug, and a kiss until she gave up all thought of reprimanding him and succumbed to his enthusiasm.

If by any chance, you should ever pass by the little country cemetery overlooking the bottoms of Big Rush, you might see a red-headed youth and three adult friends, with heads bared, standing in respectful silence, as they gaze at an unusual red headstone. And if you care to take a closer look, you may wonder at the strange picture that stands out so vividly; that of a human hand grasping the front paw of a dog. Were you to let your curiosity get the better of you and timidly ask its meaning of those four standing there, you would probably be met with courteous evasiveness. When you have departed, it will be with the knowledge that you learned nothing.

But if you're the type who desires to pursue the subject further, and are headed south into town, it's quite possible that you may have your curiosity appeased. Stop at the very first service station you come to or drive on to the square and drop in among the loafers in the courtyard. They all know the story and will relish again the telling, as they have a hundred times before.

As you listen, you will begin to realize why the four you saw at the cemetery might be reluctant to talk. And as you listen further, you may even begin to wonder just how much more there is to the story that only those four know.

Especially, if the teller happens to mention that not many coon hunters will hunt the area around Big East Hollow anymore, and you ask why. Then if he's really wound up right and completely lost in the narrative, you may hear the strangest part of all. How occasional reports from those who did hunt there, at first relate some strange goings on. How the heavy tree barking of a big hound would sometimes break out atop a high ridge, and the light of an old kerosene lantern could be seen as it flickered its way toward the sound of the treeing hound. And how sometimes the one who heard had made his way quickly up in the direction of the lantern's destination, only to have the light disappear and the dog grow silent, as he drew close. Or how at other times, when the great treeing voice would roll out over the hills, and no lantern was seen, there would, instead, come the far off sound of a horn, one long and two shorts, and the tree hound would be heard no more.

As you drive on your way, you may shrug your shoulders and try to console yourself with the knowledge that most tales start from nothing and grow into something all out of proportion to the truth. But then you may have a second thought about the part he told last:

How the three men and the red-headed boy spend weekends in the little cabin at the end of the hollow and continue to hunt that country as before. And especially the very last part will be hard to forget; when he explained that to ask those four if they had ever heard the dog and seen the lantern, was to be met with a strange look and an unanswered question. Yes, you, too, may wonder.

Code of Honor

Through the gloomy mist of an early September morning, the uneven whine of the German bomber's motors came clearly. Minutes later, ugly eggs of destruction poured from the gaping hole in its belly and tons of English soil erupted skyward, as they struck harmlessly in the open field to our north. Then, climbing high to avoid the ever-increasing flack, it headed back towards the Channel and home. As its sound faded into the distance, and then was gone altogether, quiet again reigned over the ancient countryside.

Though we watched without taking cover, we were prepared to do so if necessary. We had known of the plane's approach. Without benefit of man-made detection, we had, nevertheless, received an unimpeachable warning many minutes before our ears had picked up the sound of the motors.

Satisfied that the bombs had done nothing more than tear vast craters in the otherwise unmarked expanse of a beautiful bluegrass field, I turned back to the saddle room of the stable area where I had pitched my gear. As I entered, my eyes sought the darkest corner, for there, under my cot, I knew I would find our warning system. Two eyes glowed as I knelt to console, and a heavy tail thumped in response to the hand I placed upon the craggy head.

Several minutes passed, before our personal radar allowed himself to be talked out from under the cot. What fear he still retained fled quickly under the friendly hands and words of praise from those who stopped by to express their thanks and admiration.

Whether he came with the place or had just decided that we needed him, we never knew. But from the time we moved onto the old estate and set up headquarters, he was with us. Just a big old spotted mongrel dog, but one who was to win a place in our hearts and memory for all time. Time after time, he was to warn us of approaching enemy planes, and not once was he wrong. Our dependence on him was absolute. We had no doubt that he would remain with us as long as we were in England. But suddenly, one morning he was gone, disappearing in the night without a word, and in truth, we were hurt by his abrupt departure.

Almost as children, we accused him of being ungrateful. His going was, for a time, beyond our comprehension. We had always treated him kindly, fed him well, and never once gave him an unkind word. How then, could this dog who had become so much a part of us, throw our hospitality back into our faces so rudely, so completely, as to leave us shocked by his sudden decision to sever relations?

For some reason, I could not shake the thought that it must have been the result of a misunderstanding. The more I thought about this, the more I became convinced that I had hit upon the answer. I and the sergeant, who shared the room with me, went over every little thing that had happened in his life while he was with us. Finally, after much sifting of facts, we found the answer, and in doing so, were ashamed.

We had let him down very badly, and in all our human stupidity, had not realized that we were doing so. And, too, as we reviewed, we realized that there had been signs of his feelings. Feelings that we had been too blind to see and reproach in his eyes that we had chosen to ignore. Further proof of this became evident a few days later. Some of the boys reported seeing him in the town close by and stated that he had ignored their attempts to be friendly. Quickly, I made a trip to town myself. I was convinced that he would never snub me. After all, I was the one who made sure he was fed and allowed him to sleep under my cot.

After about an hour of walking and searching, I found him browsing on a street corner. Calling his name, I knelt down and placed my hand on his head. For a minute, he stood quietly, allowing my hand to rest there, but with never a sign of friendliness. Not once did his tail wag in recognition, as I talked to him, trying to convince him that we wanted him back, but those eyes told me that he knew. The reproach I saw there, as he looked directly into my face, was too obvious to miss. And I saw that I was not forgiven and never would be. Slowly, without removing those accusing eyes from mine, he backed away from under my hand, turned, and walked off.

I was dismissed, definitely and thoroughly. Though I saw him occasionally after that, I never approached him again. There were times, I knew, when he was aware of my presence close by, but he never let on. He was through with us, once and for all, and as we went over the reason, again and again, we could find no means of excusing ourselves. We knew that he was justified in disowning us.

The reason, so simple, once we realized it, left us with nothing but disgust at our ignorance. We could have blamed the little fireplace that we always kept burning. Or we could have laid all the blame on the large buckeye tree that grew directly above the chimney. But that would have eased our conscience none at all, for the fault was ours alone.

We were aware, from his actions at the approach of an enemy plane; he at some time or another had been in the immediate target area of German bombers, and maybe on many occasions, for all we knew. To him, the high-pitched sound of their engines meant only one thing, death and flaming destruction from the skies, amid thunderous explosions.

His ears would pick up their sound long before we could hear a thing, and he would begin to whine as he looked towards the direction from which they were coming. He would run about the room, looking up at first one of us, then the other, as if trying to tell us individually that hell was on its way. That was always the routine he went through before he hunted the darkest corner, where he could crawl under something and remain deathly silent until well after the bombing was over.

He had a favorite spot before the little fireplace where he liked to lie. For weeks, he snoozed there in peace and quiet, and then came the nerve-shattering ordeals that we dismissed too lightly. All went well, until the buckeyes, in their large green hulls, began to fall down the chimney to lodge in the ever-burning fireplace. There they would lie, getting bigger and bigger by the minute, as they became swollen by the heat. Then with a loud explosion, they would burst, sending ashes flying all over the room.

Though we laughed the first time it happened to Oscar, lying there in comfortable sleep, it was a terrifying experience. We should have realized that. To be so rudely awakened by the report and hot flying ashes meant, to him, only one thing at that instant, bombs. Maybe it was the laughter, the first time or two, that he resented. Or maybe it was just the fact that we were there and allowed the ordeal to continue. Maybe, to his canine mind, we, the human gods of his world, were supposed to remedy the situation, instead of letting it go on and on until, at last, he could stand no more. Or maybe, he was just too proud to accept lodging and subsistence from someone who had so little regard for his suffering.

Later, we were to realize that he gave us a chance, time and time again, to show him what happened to him was important to us. We remembered, after he was gone, the looks of reproach after each buckeye explosion, and interpreted them too late as a plea to do something about the situation. Yes, too late, we realized that he had asked us for help, over and over, and we had denied him.

We could have let the fire go out, we could have climbed up and knocked the buckeyes from the limbs that hung over the chimney, or in most cases, we could have picked them from the fire before they exploded. But instead of doing even one of those things, we did nothing, and for that reason, became failures in the eyes of a dog.

How often, down through the years, as first this dog and then another, for a brief span of time, becomes an important part of our lives, do we fail to live up to our part of the bargain? Made without verbal confirmation, still, it is an agreement between man and dog. When he looks to you with trust, and indicates his willingness to serve you, your part of the bargain is assured with the first acceptance of all he has to offer.

Who among us has ever begun to probe the canine mind? Who can say for sure how deep his thoughts are? We know he has great intelligence, unquestionable courage, devotion to the point of laying down his life, if need be, and the will to serve unrewarded, if for no other reason than he be allowed to stand beside the one human he has chosen, from all others, to be his master.

Who, then, can knowingly deny that maybe the dog, too, has a standard into which we must fit? Who can be sure that, within the canine mind, a code of honor does not exist, binding the pact between dog and master? If that could possibly be true, then one could safely say that it is broken far more times by the master than by the dog. In any case, there is no doubt, that if our dog in England had such a code, it was we that broke it and not him.

By way of comparison, the following true incident is offered as food for thought. One that was to again find me looking into a pair of reproachful eyes, only this time, those of a man. And if there was any difference between the accusations I saw there and that which burned in the eyes of the dog, then it would have taken a much smarter man than I to detect it. And again, the reproach was justified, for through no fault of mine, I had once more been tried and found wanting.

While serving as company supply sergeant in North Africa, a group of Italian prisoners was attached to us for work and signal training. The one I drew, for help in supply, was a tall, handsome man, gentle and obedient to the point of offering absolute servitude, if I had been so inclined as to accept it. As my daily contacts with this man extended into many weeks, I was to realize that his mind was subnormal. How, I marveled, could this fellow, so incapable of a single hostile or rebellious thought, have ever served as a combat soldier, as, in fact, he had?

As an example of just what kind of a simple soul he was, he told me that he had been a corporal, or he guessed he was, for he had been in charge of five mules. As his unit was pounded tighter and tighter into the Tunisian pocket, that was to eventually see their capitulation, he realized that the end was near. So he sold the mules' feed to the Arabs. Then, since he no longer had feed for the mules, he sold them to the Arabs, too.

He was completely honest and trustworthy. I allowed him to spend hours alone daily among the various supplies, and never did he misplace my trust. As I handled PX rations, too, there was always candy, chewing gum, cigarettes, soap, etc. available for the taking. He never took as much as a single stick of gum. He was that honest. I'm sure that he knew it would have made him a big man among the other prisoners, to have suddenly turned up among them with an assortment of those items. I'm also sure he was fully aware that the other prisoners considered him below them in status, but he never weakened.

That was the kind of a man he was, and to show my appreciation, I made things easy for him. His every action indicated that he was happy with the setup, too. When he reported for work every morning, he would enter briskly, come to attention, rake off a snappy salute, and with a big white-toothed smile, say, "Good morning, Sergeant, now we are together."

I can honestly say that never would I have let this man down intentionally. But at the time I was head over heels in work. We had just gone under a new T.B.A. The company was cut to a smaller, more compact unit, which meant turning in equipment, drawing new and different items of warfare, training on new weapons, and a million other things that kept me going day and night, until my mind was in a constant whirl. This was the excuse I offered myself, to ease my conscience. When I found out what I had done, or I should say, hadn't done, I never really bought that excuse, any more than he did, when I tried to explain to him why.

Anyway, that's why, when one morning he didn't report for work, I never thought too much about it. The stockade was under the jurisdiction of a regiment across the road from us. The commander had overall control of the prisoners, so I just took for granted that he had been temporarily reassigned. I was somewhat concerned as the days sped into weeks and he never came back, but not enough to investigate the reason.

Then I received the news of what had happened. I was sick with disgust at my lassitude concerning his absenteeism. I'm sure that I could have done something about what happened. Even if I hadn't been able to help him, the fact that I had tried would have been sufficient to his simple reasoning. But I didn't try, because I didn't know. I was too busy to make even a small attempt to find out.

The story was short. He had been accused of stealing G.I. equipment and of selling it to the Arabs. Other prisoners had testified as to his guilt. He was convicted and sentenced to several weeks of hard labor. When I learned who his accusers were, I knew who had really stolen the equipment. The prisoner who served as our barber and his little group of followers were, no doubt, the guilty ones. They had been involved in minor infractions before, that were known only to a few of us, but we had said nothing.

The barber was a skinny, undersized, weasel-faced, conniving little rat who was the leader of a few more prisoners of the same ilk. He had been steadily accumulating money, from some source or another, ever since he had been with us. In fact, I had grudgingly allowed him to hide a large roll of franc notes in my supply tent one time, to enable him to avoid detection during an inspection of the prisoners.

When I accused him of framing Baudini, my prisoner, he just gave a smug little smile and a shrug of his shoulders. He didn't care that I knew the truth. It was too late and there was nothing that I could do to him. Baudini had served his sentence by that time. I did, however, bar the barber and his clique from my supply tent. That really caused them no worry because they were in solid with somebody bigger than a supply sergeant.

Within an hour after I was told, I visited the regimental area in search for Baudini. I found him outside the theater tent, where he was lounging with some more prisoners. I greeted him warmly and extended my hand. He accepted neither, but only stared at me, in silence. I faltered, guilt sweeping over me. Then I asked him to step away from the group so that I could talk to him privately, but he only shook his head. As his eyes bored into mine, I was once again back in England, kneeling on the sidewalk, as I looked into the eyes of a big mongrel dog, and saw only reproach. There was no difference. The look was the same in the eyes of this man as with the dog; I knew him to be justified.

I tried to tell him that I had not known, that I knew him to be innocent, but still, he remained silent. Only his accusing eyes spoke, and I understood the meaning that left me defenseless, alone with my guilt. Desperately, I offered to go to the regimental commander and explain his innocence. Again this brought only another shake of his head. The message in his eyes said that it was too late. I pleaded with him to come back to work for me, and again, the head shake of refusal. Then abruptly, as had the dog, he dismissed me, as if I didn't exist, by turning away, leaving me staring at his back.

Defeated, I walked slowly back to my company, flogged by guilt at every step. This simple soldier, whose mind I had considered inferior, had, without saying a word, placed me among the small people of the world. Those burning eyes, so full of reproach, had extended to me the same message as those of the dog. "I kept my part of the bargain. Why didn't you?"

That similarity, of feelings and thought, between man and dog, has not been one to entirely forget. As it returns to me occasionally, down through the years, I still have but one question to ask myself: *"Why didn't I?"*

Out There Someplace

Mud, cold, freezing rain, wet clothing, and empty bellies soon became a way of life for Allied troops occupying North Africa during that dark and uncertain winter of 1942. Misery was their constant companion and warmth their only desire. All dreamed of escape, but few recognized it when it appeared. But occasionally, there were those who did.

As if in shame, the Lord of Darkness slowly spread his mantle, and for awhile, the sordid rain-soaked ugliness of North Africa was hidden from the eyes of man. The pup tents, like Chinese sampans floating on a sea of mud, crouched; cringing anew with each deluging onslaught. The perimeter of their defenses, pitiful little drainage ditches, were now rivers in retreat, as if finding the pond in the company street too formidable to encounter.

Men inside the puny canvas, wrapped in sodden blankets, felt wet fingers crawling beneath their backs. They cursed again the engineering genius who had selected the site for the camp.

Inside the supply tent, candlelight dodged fearfully, as the flap was thrown back, and the dripping, rain-coated figure of Conway pushed inside. Hayden, leaning back against a packing crate, looked up from his magazine. Why, he thought bitterly, do they all have to come in here to drip off, right where I throw my bedroll? But then he was ashamed, for where else in that godforsaken camp could a man stand upright out of the rain?

"For God's sake, close the door. Do you want some German fighter to spot us?" Conway snorted. "Don't worry; there'll be no German planes up tonight. In fact, they ain't never gonna come looking for us again. Don't need to. Got it straight from Axis Sally. They're just gonna sit and let us drown, and that's what we're gonna do, sure as the devil."

Removing his coat, Conway threw it across a box beside the door. His shoes made little squishing sounds, as he walked over and took a seat on an upended packing crate. For awhile, he sat in silence, grazing morosely down at his feet. "It's the mud, the durned, filthy, stinky mud."

Hayden's voice came mockingly, "So it's mud? Surely, you've seen this stuff before, like in your Indiana cornfields, for instance, when you're coon hunting?" Conway studied his shoes in utter dejection. "Sure, I've walked in plenty of mud, but it's different, not like this stuff."

"How the devil could mud be different? Mud's mud."

"No, you don't understand. Indiana mud, same as all the mud in our country, is clean. It's clean because it's young."

"Clean mud? Young mud? Conway, you're talking like a nut."

Conway persisted stubbornly. "Yes, it's clean. Compared to this stuff, it's absolutely pure, because man only started disturbing it such a short time ago. It's young, because it was so recently still virgin soil."

"And that makes it different?"

"Sure! Now take this stuff." He grimaced as he lifted a foot and viewed the brown glob hanging to the sole. "It's old, with five thousand years of man's filth mixed with it. It's dirty from the decayed bodies of a million people and animals, from camel dung and donkey urine, and from ancient diseases and plagues."

Hayden was silent, digesting the meaning, disgusted with what it implied.

Conway wasn't finished. "You know what I keep thinking? That some of them old plague germs may still be alive, just crawling around in this stuff, waiting for a chance to find a crack in our hides; so they can get inside and give us some disease so old that our medics never even heard of it."

For awhile, both were silent. Muted sounds from outside penetrated the tent's wet walls. A miserable guard splashing by, the soul stirring chant of jackals in the distance, and above all, the constantly maddening drumming of the rain against the canvas overhead.

Conway still sat, looking at his extended shoe, eyes glued in fascination on the mud that still clung to the shoe. Angrily, Hayden shook his head. "Durn you, Conway, you depress me. Here I am, practically frozen to death, and all you can do is sit around and talk about young mud and thousand-year-old germs. My God, all I can do is think about getting warm again."

Conway still stared at the muddy shoe. "You know, that may be part of some old Arab chief hanging right there on my shoes. Boy! I sure hope he died healthy."

"Now I know you're crazy. How could he have died healthy?"

"Well, you might get shot just when you're in the pink of condition. That way, you would die healthy."

Hayden was not convinced. "You might be healthy before you were shot, but you would sure be mighty unhealthy after it happened, so you still die unhealthy."

Conway was about to become interested in the shoe again. Hayden's voice snapped out sharply. "Conway, how would you like to sleep in here tonight? You can use Jonesy's bedroll."

"Man, you've got yourself a buddy. Sure will be a relief not to have water running under me all night."

Conway was already spreading out the designated bedroll on the other side of the tent. "Hope old Jonesy knows how I appreciate this. Say, does he really have pneumonia?"

"I'm not sure. Maybe. Anyway, it's a wonder all of us haven't got it. Do you know we have sixty men in the field hospital, right now? Lucky that nobody but poor old Jackson has died. I told my wife to send me a bottle of Vicks and some cold tablets, so I can doctor myself."

Hayden's bedding was spread now and both were silent, as they stripped to their long johns, sliding down into the inviting confines of snug, even if damp, blankets. Hayden lay unmoving, hoping to warm that part of his clammy blankets by unbroken contact. "I'll tell you one thing I've found out. When a guy's wet enough and cold enough and hungry enough, there are plenty of things to think about instead of home and his wife."

"My God, what's that?"

"Warmth, dry blankets, and a belly full of C-rations. Never thought I would see the day when I would say it, but right now, I can't even remember what my wife looks like."

"Hayden?"

"Yes, Conway."

"Did you hear Sergeant Golden singing last night?"

"Yeah, sure did make me feel awful."

"You know, it sure was strange the way the rain stopped all at once, and then started again, as soon as he got the last note out."

"I thought so, too. Sorta like it had to wait until he was through."

"Hayden?"

"Yeah, Conway?"

"Did you feel kinda like crying?"

"Not only felt like it."

"God, me, too."

Drowsily, each fell silent, shifting about slightly, in a vain attempt to find a softer spot on the dirt floor. From the box supporting the field desk came a slight rustling, only a whisper, but Hayden smiled into the darkness at the familiar sound. The kangaroo mouse was moving her young again.

"Hayden, you asleep?"

"No, and I'm not apt to be, if you keep yapping all night."

Conway didn't seem to notice the slight irritation in Hayden's voice. "How would you like to hear a good coon chase right now?"

Hayden seemed less sleepy as he answered, "Of course, I would, but there's no chance of that here."

For awhile, Conway didn't answer, as if brooding over the impossibility of such a thing. "Well, no, I guess not, but Vic said he saw what looked like a red fox cross in front of his jeep the other night, and some of these Frenchmen might have some fox hounds."

"Probably a jackal."

"No, he said it wasn't a jackal."

Memory of past pleasure from nights spent with the hounds was reflected in Hayden's voice, as he said wistfully, "Sure would like to hear a pack running right now. Wouldn't care whether they treed or not, just so I could hear them run."

Conway, now fully awake, also spoke with thoughts of past hunts. "Say, what kind of mouths would you like to hear out there right now?"

Hayden's reply came slowly, as if giving much thought to his selection. " Well, first, I'd want an honest to God, real bugle mouth, just like old Slim used to have, and one that opened that way even when he was running. Then, of course, I'd throw in a keen chop, and then I think a clear bell mouth would add something."

Conway studied on Hayden's choice for awhile. "Yeah, now that sure would be nice to hear, but I think I'd like three more in there. Of course, a short bawl, a heavy chop, and high screamer, probably a female. You know, the kind that really sounds like she's running to catch when she makes a jump."

For a short time, Hayden dwelled upon the pleasure that listening to such a pack would bring, and momentarily, he was standing on a familiar ridge, listening to the music rolling up from the creek bottom below, and wondering who would be the first to tree. Suddenly, the sharp challenge of the guard on post number one snapped him out of his lassitude. The return to reality was a definite shock.

Almost angrily, he said, "What's the use of thinking of such a thing? You know it can't happen here. Besides, the French wouldn't be able to keep hounds. The durn Arabs would steal and eat them. Now shut up, so I can get some sleep."

Again, all was quiet for a few minutes. Hayden, in spite of his denunciation of their previous speculation, dwelled drowsily on the topic of their conversation, as warmth crept slowly over him.

Conway's voice came as if from far away. "Cain't never tell. They might have some hounds with all these jackals around. They might follow them on horseback so the Arabs couldn't get them. It sure would be nice to hear. Boy, it sure would."

His last words drifted out softly, as if he, too, had found the warmth too inviting to continue. Only half-hearing Conway's voice, Hayden was dimly aware of the steady beating of the rain on the canvas above. He vaguely tried to remember what it was like in dry weather, and gave up in resignation, accepting the feeling that it had been raining all of his life.

It seemed to come from far away, but faded quickly, and he thought that he had been mistaken. But then again, closer, more distinct, and now, there was no doubt. Out there some place, within hearing, hounds were running. It couldn't be ... he was dreaming ... but then he could hear Conway's snoring from the other side of the tent. Breathing deeply, with intense excitement, he pushed backward in the bedroll, and sat up. Now he could pick them out, one, two, three, four, five, six—the same size pack they had dreamed up. It was incredible ... and too good to keep.

Still he hesitated, savoring the intimacy he felt with the pack, reveling in the elation brought on by a strange feeling that he, alone, of all the peoples of the world, was hearing that beautiful music drifting across those rain-swept plains.

But only for a moment, for this was something that must be shared. "Conway! Hey, Conway! Wake up!"

Conway's snores bubbled to a stop, seconds passed, and then he answered, "What's the matter? What the heck did you wake me up for?"

Hayden's voice tremored with anticipation of the excitement his news would arouse in Conway. "Listen! Do you hear anything?"

"Sure, I hear the durn neverending rain. What the devil is the matter with you?"

"NO! NO! Besides the rain, what do you hear?"

Conway answered quickly, a slight harshness creeping into his tones. "You crazy or something? Don't hear nothin' but the rain. That's all there is to hear. Won't ever hear anything but rain again. It was raining before I was born, I was born in rain, and it has been raining all my life, and I'll be buried in the rain. Ain't ever gonna be anything to hear again, but rain ... rain ... rain."

Hayden was beginning to feel a bit frantic. Conway was on the verge of going back to sleep. "Conway, listen! Don't you hear those hounds?"

In the shocked silence that followed his announcement, he could hear them clearly and steadily, running hard to the southwest.

"Hounds? Hayden, boy, you've been over here too long."

The frantic feeling within Hayden grew. He had to hear them; he just had to. "Yes, hounds! You're not listening. My God, can't you hear them?"

"Hayden ..."

"Shut up, and listen. There are six of them, just like we talked about. There! Hear that bugle, the bell? There ... There's the keen chop ... and ... and the screamer. Hear her? Hear her?"

It seemed he could almost hear Conway straining his ears through the darkness. "I ... I ... think ... "It seems like I ... YES! I DO! I DO! I hear them now. I hear 'em, sure enough. Listen, there's the short bawl ... and ... and the course chop ... HEY! There's the screamer again. Man, they sure are running. Boy, Hayden, ain't that sumthin' to hear."

"Sure is, sure is," Hayden spoke softly, not wanting to drown out any of the musical pleasure.

Minutes passed while both remained silent, selfishly hoarding each precious sound coming to their hungry ears. For both, the war, with all its misery, was non-existent, as they waited eagerly in anticipation of the next hound note to drift in to them from out of that vast area of desolation.

"How do you figure they can run that track so steadily, with all that water on the ground?" Conway asked, hardly breathing the words.

"They're not tracking, just running the scent; it's that hot. Now, they're beginning to circle to the east. Boy! Listen to that bugle mouth."

"Yeah," Conway breathed again, "sure would like to have a dog with a mouth like that."

"Me, too. What do you think they're running? Hey! They're turning north now."

"Sure are. It's running like a grey fox. Reckon that's what it is?"

Hayden continued to listen for awhile before answering, picking out the hounds, one by one, voice by voice. "Cain't be grey fox. They're only found in North America. Listen! The screamer sure got the jump on them that time."

"She sure did, but the bell is with her now, and there comes the high chopper. Man, talk about a matched pack. Reckon they're running a jackal?"

"Don't think so. They stay in packs. Must be a red fox, after all." Again, Hayden fell silent, straining to hear each cherished note. Only the excited breathing of both broke the stillness within the tent.

Moments later, Hayden whispered, "Turning west now."

"I thought so, too," Conway muttered just as quietly. "Running in a circle, sure enough."

Again, only silence prevailed, as each felt joy unto himself, and dared not interrupt with needless conversation. Time without beginning and without end; only luxury to be measured in depth … and how deep is a man … a lonely man?

"Ah," Hayden said softly, "there they go, turning south."

Conway's words were hardly audible as he answered, "Yes, sir, they sure are. Reckon they'll hole it?"

"Don't know, but we'll soon find out."

The silence of the next five minutes was broken only once, when Hayden said, "They're almost around to where they hit him."

Again, for minutes, only the slight rustling of the kangaroo mouse could be heard within the tent. Finally, Hayden spoke disappointedly, "Well, I guess that's it. Don't hear a thing now. Do you?"

A minute passed before Conway said sadly, "Nope, not a thing, not a thing." Strangely, neither seemed inclined to continue the discussion, each lapsing into his own private world of languor.

Only once more was the silence broken, as Hayden whispered in awed tones, "Maybe we can hear them again tomorrow night."

Conway didn't answer. Only low snores could be heard coming from his side of the tent.

The sentry, on post number one, shifted miserably, as more water trickled down his back, and he thought enviously of those inside the tents. Boys, hardly out of their teens, tossed fitfully, attempting, even in sleep, to find one remaining dry spot, as the far too thin canvas slowly lost its battle with the elements. Jackals cackled dismally in the distance, while they tried desperately to dream of home, young wives, and of children they had never seen. And in moments of complete dejection, came to believe that their misery was to be without end. But for a few, a very few, there were to be periods of respite and escape, though only briefly; for those with ears to hear.

Alfred, in his Army uniform in 1942.

Adolph—France—1944

How do you write about a dog you knew nearly twenty years ago, and then for only a brief time? What is one-two-hundredth of a beagle? That's how much of him I owned. In terms of tissue and bone, I suppose it would be nearly nonexistent. However, if the measure was of guts, devotion, brains, and faithfulness, then it would have been a pretty good-sized chunk.

I first made his acquaintance in the summer of 1944, soon after the invasion of Southern France. My outfit, a Signal Company, had just made camp alongside a thicket, when the Mess Sergeant, Vic Lockridge, from Kennard, Indiana, heard the voice of a hound in trouble. No Hoosier coon hunter could let a plea like that go unchecked. In a few minutes, Vic found him, wired to a small tree by his hind leg. Seconds later, he was free and a permanent member of our Company.

It's hard to say who adopted who, but there was never any doubt in that little fellow's mind that he belonged to us, and us to him. We named him Adolph; why, I don't know, for we hated that name, and loved that little dog. But he didn't seem to mind and came running and wiggling with happiness whenever his name was called.

Now, after so long a time, it's hard to recapture just what he meant to us. It would be impossible to express our true feelings, for part of them were the result of the environment in which we struggled, and are now long gone; lost and faded with the return to the peaceful life here at home and the passing years.

I'm sure, though, that he brought something of home to all of us. Here was a friend in a strange land, one who spoke the same language as the dog we left behind, one free from the hatred engulfing the millions locked in combat. But to the hound men among us, he meant more than that.

He was a bright, dewy meadow on a summer morn, when he first discovered that he liked to run a rabbit; a hilltop in the dead of night, when he learned the joy of joining the men around the fire, as the voices of the hounds floated up from the valley where they drove hard after a big red fox; he was us being proud of our first efforts to train a tree dog, when the men at the barber shop said, "Bring the kid along tonight. He catches more fur than any of us. Let's see that dog of his work."

He was a powerfully-built little dog, with beautiful conformation, and a mouth to put many big hounds to shame. He had an extra deep bawl for a beagle, and a fine musical chop. He ran rabbits, fox, and deer, and wasn't particular which, for he handled one as easy as the other.

Though he recognized Vic as his real master, he readily responded to the rest of us in a way that made you feel he was trying his best to give each man his 200th part of devotion.

As the Seventh Army rolled pell-mell through Southern France and on into Germany, Adolph accompanied us all the way, riding in or on any vehicle available. The confusion of war being what it is, there were times that he became separated from us as we moved on, but sooner or later, he caught up.

When it was discovered he was missing, every truck driver making a trip to the rear was constantly on the lookout. Usually, within two or three days, one of them would spot him trudging along, those short little legs carrying him as fast as possible in the direction he knew we had gone.

It was always a proud driver that brought him into camp after one of those times. When the little fellow would jump gleefully from the truck, the word would spread like wildfire through the camp that Adolph was back. Other duties were forgotten as the men converged on him, each to get his part of a tail wag, or a lick on the hand, or maybe just a chance to bask in the friendly glow of his intelligent eyes.

There were times, however, when no driver was able to locate him along the back trail, and he would just turn up on his own; how, we never knew. We often accused him of hitchhiking with strangers, but he would never admit it. That's one secret he kept.

There was the time he left the convoy in Southern France when we made a short stop. He just couldn't stay motionless for very long, so off he hopped, and soon had a track going along a ridge above the road. When the convoy started up suddenly, as convoys do, there was nothing to do but leave him. We traveled thirty miles without a stop, and all mourned his loss, for we knew that we would never see him again.

But we should have known better. In about four days, he came trotting into camp, leg weary and footsore, but none the worse for wear. How he found us was beyond our comprehension. There were thousands of vehicles traveling those roads day and night, and tens of thousands of GIs. But he wanted only us, and kept going until he found us.

Thanksgiving Day found us in Epinal, France. There was a big snow on the ground. I was staying in an old board shack and Vic was holed up in an old stable about a quarter of a mile away. Things were kind of bogged down, so we decided to take Adolph to the woods. We should have known that the snow was too deep for him, but I guess we were desperate for hound music. Finally, after watching him plow through the stuff for about an hour without hitting a thing, we became ashamed of ourselves, and picked him up and carried him into the stable, where he stayed with Vic.

Two days later, Vic sent one of his KPs to tell me Adolph had pneumonia and a request for a bottle of Vic's Salve. He was going to try and steam him out, for he was sure to die before morning. That was one time when a big cooking pot served a good purpose. Vic dumped Vic's Salve into a pan of boiling water, and placed both the pan and Adolph under the big pot together. He had the help of one of his cooks, a fellow by the name of Begien. Begien now has an animal hospital somewhere in Ohio.

While the whole company waited and worried, those two heated water and steamed away all night long. By morning, the word went out that Adolph would live. For the rest of the winter, Vic was very careful about exposing him to inclement weather of any kind.

By early spring of 1945, we were in Germany and the end of the war not far away. I found time to get to the woods with him just once more, when we stopped for a few days in a vast territory of thickets.

For one whole afternoon, I had him all to myself and that beautiful mouth was singing to me most of the time.

Soon after we started out, we saw a herd of about twenty deer in a clearing a couple hundred yards away. Adolph must have scented them, because I doubt he could have seen them from his place so close to the ground. He just threw up his head and lined out. In minutes, he had them scattered and running.

He drove deer past me all afternoon, sometimes two at a time. Though I had my rifle, of course, I never fired a shot. The does were with fawn, the weather was too warm to keep the meat, and besides, I didn't have it in me to kill anything as unafraid of me as they were. Sometimes they ran within fifty feet of me. They would roll their big eyes at me as they trotted past, but wouldn't increase their pace at all. I say trotted, because that's as fast as Adolph pushed them.

They were a strange type of deer, long-bodied and short legged, not nearly so graceful looking as our White Tails. I never saw a set of antlers, though I'm sure some of them were bucks.

I never got to go out with him again. The war was over not long after that. We were always moving here and there, getting ready to go home. In the meantime, Vic was transferred to another company, while Adolph stayed with us. We had a new First Sergeant and were then transferred to the Third Army just in time to catch General Patton's no dog order. All dogs were to be disposed of.

This new First Sergeant soon found out how the company felt about Adolph and didn't push too much. In fact, we thought it was settled that the order would be ignored. However, all he was waiting for was the right chance to make it look as if he had no choice.

I wish this story had a happy ending. I wish I could say that one of us brought him home with us, as we longed to do, but it would not be the truth. I never cared for that First Sergeant and hadn't judged him wrong. On the first possible flimsy excuse, he acted.

One of his drinking buddies came in one night, soused to the gills, and stepped on poor Adolph, who was sleeping across the threshold of the building in which he was staying. The guy said he was bitten; I always doubted it. Before any of us knew it, the First Sergeant hauled out his forty-five and killed him.

Such was the reward granted that great little dog that had gone through so much just to stay with us, and who asked nothing more than a chance to lick your hand, or to look at you with affection, in exchange for a kind word.

Alfred, in North Africa during WW II.

The Golden Crucifix

Probably every GI who spent time in the combat zone during WW II experienced at least one incident that made him fully aware of that one great Higher Power. During the spring of 1945, two Sergeants from Salem, Indiana, Alfred Boling and Arthur McKillip, witnessed such an incident.

While the once mighty empire of the Third German Reich was crumbling under the overpowering onslaught of the Allied war machine rolling over her borders, the unit of the two men occupied the small Bavarian village of Tauberbishofscheim.

As the troops fanned out in search of empty buildings in which to throw their gear, the majority found quarters in a large four-story apartment house. Making their way to the top floor, in quest of an empty room, the Sergeants became more and more aware of considerable damage from shell fire to the top section of the building. Pushing open the door to a small room, they stared in amazement at a scene that would forever remain etched in their memory.

The interior of the room was in shambles. Six inches of plaster, broken lathes, and other debris covered the floor. They could see the blue sky through a four-foot-wide gaping hole in the ceiling, indicating a direct shell hit. That anything could remain unshattered under the terrible impact of such destruction was unbelievable. But yet, there it was.

Along the right wall, amid all the destruction, stood a fragile glass-fronted, spindle-legged bookcase, about five feet tall. On its shelves, no books, but instead, surgical instruments laid out in neat order. Incredible as it was that the thin glass of the case had not been broken, it was the object on top that held their gaze.

For the time being, the war and the millions of men locked in a death struggle had suddenly become nonexistent. Before them was proof of God's all-powerful protection of that which is entrusted into His care, and evidence that in comparison to man, with all his destructive force, he is, in fact, a puny thing.

On top of the fragile bookcase was a beautiful golden crucifix, enclosed in the thinnest of glass, as if in all its awe-inspiring splendor, it had encompassed the bookcase with an invisible mantle of protection. Slowly, they made their way over to that side of the room, where they stood, lost in admiration of the glory with which it seemed to shine. Fully twenty inches tall, yet they dared not touch it, for fear the flimsy glass would shatter in their hands.

During the two days they remained quartered in the building, others in the Company came to see and to marvel, but none to ask why. Veterans of three years of overseas duty, they had long since learned to accept some things as beyond human comprehension, and were quite willing to leave it at that. When the outfit pulled out, many came to have a last look. They left it where they found it, but they would not forget.

Lonely Vigil

A gusty fall wind rattled the windows in the old brick house, and the lonesome little boy inside shivered and drew closer to the stove. No sudden start of hopeful anticipation, this time. No pitiful little rush toward the door, that would have stopped even as it began, with the realization that it wasn't the sound he waited to hear. No scratch of tiny claws to tell him that his prayers had been answered, that she still lived, that Trixie had come home.

In the hour that had passed since he refused to accompany his family in the usual Saturday night pilgrimage to the town square, he had learned to distinguish one sound from another. The dark night and the old house talked, and he listened.

The thud of a walnut from the tree south of the house, the brushing of the sugar maple's leaves against the front porch, the squeak of a mouse somewhere in the attic, wind sighing dismally under the eaves, loose mortar trickling down inside the ancient boarded-up fireplace. Sounds to be heard, filed away, and from then on, ignored.

A kerosene lamp cast its yellow glow over the center of the room. The dark corners crouched with cavernous mouths. Huge beasts of prey, silently stalking that dejected little figure, slumped in his chair by the stove.

Again, as he had many times during the hour, he picked up the lamp and went to the door. Pulling the door open, he held his light high, peering out into the darkness, as he called softly, "Trixie, Trixie!" Nothing, only the howl of the wind and the sound of another walnut plopping into the yard. Each fruitless trip had seen his thin little shoulders slump just a little bit more and the sickness in his eyes grow a little deeper. Eyes red and swollen, the well of tears had long since run dry.

Returning the lamp to the table, he turned it up a little higher.

He watched for a moment to make sure that it didn't smoke, and then returned to his post by the stove. Who knew all his thoughts as he waited, or the great weight of despair engulfing his young mind as he kept his lonely vigil? Even he could not be expected to remember.

It's certain that he found within himself reason to blame the person responsible, his mother. She had a good reason, she always did, and he couldn't question that. Her word was law, the good law. But even with that acceptance, his grief was no less. A horrible crushing grief, brought on by something he couldn't understand.

The verdict had been rendered that afternoon. Trixie must go. Without benefit of defense, the trial was over. The vague explanation handed down with the sentence from the adult world, caused him only bewilderment.

Trixie had signed her own death warrant. By being a dog, she had created a problem. She was going to have pups, a situation with which the young mother of three very small children felt unable to cope. Already overburdened with the care of her own young, any additional mouths to feed were more than she could face.

Her decision made, she acted quickly, before she could weaken. The boy, standing to the side of all this, saw and heard, but comprehended little.

Reality had not yet set in, even as his mother stopped a farmer on his way home and bargained. He sat on the high bank above the road, with his arm around his little fox terrier. He saw the half dollar change hands, still without complete understanding.

As if it were happening to someone else, through a dense cloud of hazy uneasiness, he saw the deal completed, and heard the farmer say he would throw her in a sinkhole. Then and only then, did the true knowledge of what was happening hit him with its full impact. His dog was to be killed.

Even as his mother's hands reached up to lift Trixie from his side, he reacted violently, hysterically. Too late, he tried to clamp the small body against him, only to have her pulled from his grasp, crying, "No! No! Mommy, no!" He held on as best he could, but felt his strength too puny, the dominance of his mother too great, as in wild confusion, he saw his dog handed to the farmer.

Through a flood of tears, he saw her placed in the front of the spring wagon between the farmer's feet, saw her securely tied, and there was nothing he could do.

He would have followed, but his mother held him back. Later, he was to understand how it must have been for her. It must have made her sick to hear his terrible sobbing, and the hurt she experienced as she tried to take him in her arms and he jerked away.

An hour later, she went to him in the woodshed, his place of refuge. She bent over him, as he sat huddled in the corner, face down on drawn-up knees, hiding like a wounded animal, alone in his grief. Then, as if from far away, her voice came to him, reached through the blanket of despair, until at last, he became aware of what she was saying, "All those tears for such a little dog! All right, honey, I'll see what can be done about getting Trixie back."

Much happiness must have glowed in his eyes, as he raised his head and felt the fog slip away. Taking his hand, she led him from the shed. She cautioned that it might be too late, but realized that he was unable to even consider such a possibility.

Together, they waited in the front yard. Side by side, watching for someone, anyone, who might be coming up the hill, headed out of town to the north. Three passed within the hour, but weren't going far enough, then came a fourth, with a heavy team and wagon. He would travel slow, but would carry the message: *Turn the dog loose—Let her come home.*

Again she cautioned, two hours had passed, the farmer would have reached home long ago. It might be too late. But her words went unheard. He sat with his back to the old maple tree. He faced to the north, eyes glued to the crest of the hill from which she would come, down that dusty road, and into his arms. The shadows fell, one by one, and became joined together in complete darkness, and he kept his post. Not until the hill faded entirely from his sight did he allow himself to be talked into the house. Beyond that, he would not go.

Dull-eyed, supper untouched, he watched his younger brother and sister prepare to accompany his parents to town, and would not be a part of their planning. When his mother would have insisted, she saw again the rebellion in him, the rising hysteria in his eyes, and heeded his pleas that he must wait for Trixie. So, they went without him, and he waited alone.

At first, he was hopeful with each passing moment, sure that the next sound would bring her scratching at the door. Now that he was alone in the big old house, the eerie silence weighed heavily upon him. He was aware that time must be measured in minutes—minutes between life and death for his dog.

The fright that had been probing at him for so long would no longer be denied. It had been so long; too much time had passed since he had seen her loaded into the spring wagon. Surely, she would have come home by now, if she were coming.

So it was, that monsters crouched in the corners, and the mouse peering from beneath the old cupboard, saw him bowed by hopeless resignation and the acceptance of tragedy. They saw the heaving of his shoulders, heard the terrible dry sobbing, and were sorry. Finally, emotionally exhausted to the point of illness, he slept. To dream that he and his little dog were on one of their daily lion and bear hunts in the back field. His pop gun at ready, he approached cautiously towards the lion his dog had brought to bay. Side by side, they advanced, one step at a time. Reaching shooting range, he stopped. Trixie stood stiff legged, bristles up and fangs bared, as he slowly raised his gun and fired.

The lion roared defiance and prepared to spring. He had forgotten to load his gun; the cork was still in his pocket. Sensing the beast's intentions, Trixie snarled and met it halfway. Locked jaw to jaw, they rolled on the ground in mortal combat. The din of their savage battle filled the air. His gun was fully loaded now. He danced around, looking for an opening, a chance to drive the cork home into some vital spot in the lion.

But he didn't have to shoot. Trixie did it all by herself. Her deadly jaws, closing on its throat, had done their work. With one last ear-splitting roar, the lion died. Of course, it didn't really have a chance against such a terrible fighter as his dog.

She fought with all she had, not with just her mouth alone, but with her feet, as well. He could see the great long tears in the yellow hide of the lion, where her hind claws had raked it. Above the sound of battle, he had heard those claws ripping away. He heard that scratching sound, above all else.

Slowly and with effort, he roused from the stupor of his dream. It was so hard to get awake, but groggily, he fought to do so. Something tugged at him and kept pushing, when he would have given up, until the cobwebs of slumber were at last brushed aside.

Trixie was still raking the lion with her hind feet. He could still hear the scratching. But that couldn't be—that was a dream—now, he was awake. There it was again, scratch, scratch.

Electrified, he suddenly snapped wide awake. That sound—it could only be—it had to be! In a flash, he was at the door. Throwing it open, he stared wild-eyed out into the night, and knew a joy almost too great for his small body. Into the center of the lamp's soft glow hurtled a little spotted, four-legged bundle of wriggling happiness.

With a cry of ecstasy, he dropped to his knees and gathered her to him; who knows what conversation, what words passed between them? What adult really understands that special language reserved solely for a boy and his dog?

When the family returned from town, they found him asleep in the rocking chair, the little dog snug in his arms. He was awakened by the chatter of his smaller brother and sister. He heard their talk of what he had missed, the ice cream cone and the maple sugar candy, and was not impressed. Serenely, he scorned their childish prattle and looked down upon them from his lofty plain of happiness, and realized he was one apart. A boy complete, for his dog had come home.

*Alfred and son, Max, with one
of Alfred's coon dogs.*

When Fate Steps In

It is inevitable that a man who follows the hounds for many years will come to realize that fate often plays a hand in such a subtle manner as to actually go unrecognized, until the incident suddenly becomes compounded.

With the awareness of just how little we sometimes have to say about the future, comes humility, and it is intensified as we finally admit that when it happened, we were but bystanders. And gloriously so, if by coincidence, one outstanding moment in the life of a dog of years gone by, is to return to bear fruit long after that dog is dead.

It is so often said that history repeats itself. In what respect does this apply to everything, in general? I can't say. I only know it was true in the story I am about to tell.

One night this past winter, my hunting buddy of many years almost lost his fine big Walker male in a large ditch filled by a bulldoze pile. The dog's margin of safety between life and death was so narrow, it hardly tipped the scale in his favor. If not for the presence of Old Lady, a little Black and Tan female, the balance would have certainly gone the other way.

It is there where fate was compounded, and the part she played in saving Spot's life was the bearing of the fruit. If not for the loyalty and intelligence of another dog, twenty years ago, Spot would have died under that bulldozer, and no one would have ever known what happened.

It all began in the fall of 1945. Fresh out of the Army and eager to get back to coon hunting, I had commented to my friend Harry, if I had a car, I would buy a coon dog. Harry was a fox hunter at the time. He replied that he had a car, so go get the dog, and we would hunt.

The next day, I purchased a big red and white hound on trial. He was ¾ hound and ¼ bull. We hunted him that night and I bought him. He was all the owner said he was. We hunted him alone that winter, but the next fall, I bought a six-month-old grade Black and Tan female to run with him.

This little female started the first coon she ever smelled ahead of Ring, and ran it with him until it grounded. Though not exactly a natural, she had treed several coons by the time she was a year old. It was easy to see she had what it took to make a great coon dog; as she later proved, by any man's standard.

One night, while hunting Ring and Fanny in the Turkey Point area, they struck a hot track and faded dead away. Though we kept walking in the direction they had gone, still, we heard nothing. The ground was only slightly hilly, so we should have been able to hear them.

Then, from only about a hundred yards away, came Old Ring's tree bark. Then silence. After awhile, two or three more tree barks. We waited. It wasn't like him to act that way, and where was Fanny? Then that big red dog came right into the lantern light. Turning back to the woods, it was obvious he wanted us to follow him.

As we started walking, he went well ahead, sending back a bark or two, every once in awhile. The timber was heavy, and we lost him more than once, but he would soon call us on. Finally, he moved no further. We came upon him standing by a large brush pile. He looked at us as if to say, I've done my part, now you can do yours. We were extremely puzzled, and realized that he knew something we didn't. It had to do with Fan. We thought we could hear her, very faintly, but decided it was just imagination. Then, quite by accident, we found the answer.

While milling around in confusion, I had ended up on top of the brush pile. I stood, straining to hear some sound of Fan. It seemed that we could hear her way off in the distance. Again, we assumed it was our imagination. We all know that if we listen long and hard enough for a certain dog, that we begin to hear it.

It took a little while for me to realize what was happening. Then, all at once, it was clear. A tremor was coming from beneath my feet. Somewhere beneath the pile, something was moving.

Quickly, we dropped to our knees and probed beneath it, and to our surprise, found that the brush pile covered a sinkhole. Fan was in the sinkhole; about five feet down, but over a shelf that prevented her from jumping out. By stretching full length, I managed to reach her collar and was able to drag her up, over, and out. She could never have gotten out by herself.

But for Old Ring, she would have died in that hole. She would have disappeared as completely as if the ground had swallowed her; as indeed, it would have. At less than one year old, she would have ceased to be, but instead, lived to be thirteen.

Fan raised three small litters during her lifetime. When she was two, I bred her to Old Ring. A little young, but she had been treeing her own coon for more than a year, and Ring was getting old. At less than a month old, seven of the pups grew stiff and died, within a matter of hours. I took the remaining one, a strong red male, to the house, and raised him by hand that winter.

He hasn't much to do with the story, except to substantiate the quality that Old Fan passed on to her pups. He lived to prove wrong those who say there is no such thing as a straight coon dog. He ran rabbits and gray fox until he was over two years old. He didn't seem interested in coons, at all. However, he treed his first coon at two and a half. Though he still tapped a gray fox, once in awhile, the first winter after he started treeing, he quit rabbits immediately. After he had a little fur in his teeth that winter, he cared only for coon. From then on, as long as he lived, he was absolutely straight. If he as much as grunted, it was a coon. He never treed a possum in his life, and he never treed in the ground. If all men were as honest as that old Red Hound? I buried him in my backyard at twelve years of age.

It seems he may have had considerable influence on this chain of events, after all. He was the one who taught Old Lady the finer points of unraveling a coon track, thus enabling her to be there as a coon dog that night. She was the only survivor of Fan's last litter. I had sold Fan to my friend Harry when she was three.

As on that night twenty years before, Harry stood, straining his ears, or I should say ear, because he has only one good ear, and he can't tell directions of sound. He was alone in a difficult situation.

The dogs had faded quickly after making a hot strike.

After walking for what seemed to be an endless amount of time, he was suddenly elated to hear Lady's tree bark. Then it ceased for awhile, only to be continued again within a few minutes. Finally, by trial and error, he reached the spot where she stood beside a long ditch filled with bulldozed logs and brush.

He quickly reasoned that since Spot could not be seen or heard, that he must be under the brush pile. But where? Lady finally showed him, by partially entering a hole, then backing out to stand, looking up at him. As he lay flat and edged into the hole, he could see that she had been in and out several times. This explained why she had seemed to quit barking at times during the search.

As he studied the situation, Lady stood at the entrance and whined continuously. With his flashlight, he finally located Spot about six feet down, wedged beneath an eight-inch log. He lay flat on the bottom with the log wedged tightly across his back. The situation indicated that he had crawled under and become fast in a manner that prevented him from backing out. He had struggled until completely exhausted and had given up by the time Harry reached him.

By practically hanging straight down, Harry could reach Spot, but could in no way exert enough strength to pull him from under the log. He received no help from the dog, who lay limp, a quivering mass, resigned to death. Spot weighed around 70 pounds, one half as much as Harry. It soon became obvious that since Spot wouldn't help himself, then Harry would have to cut the log in two. That meant leaving him there in the hole, while he drove six miles home to get a saw. When Old Lady saw him back out of the hole without Spot, she protested loud and clear. But there was nothing else to do.

When he started back to the car, she refused to go, but instead, stood beside the hole, barking. He made the trip as quickly as possible. As he walked back through the woods, he could hear her barking. When he reached them, he patted her on the head, and then slid back into the hole. It was a painfully slow process, suspended the way he was, but the little handsaw gradually ate its way through.

Finally, after many short rests, the job was done, and the ends of the logs pushed from Spot's back. But still, he refused to move. He had tried too many times before, and still believed it was hopeless. Harry tried to lift him, but was too exhausted himself, and had too little room. There seemed to be only one solution.

Backing out, he stood erect, while Old Lady barked her disappointment. Then he started away, while calling to her. But she refused to come. So, snapping a chain on her, Harry forced her to come with him, though she protested every step. She just plain wasn't going to leave Spot in that hole. About fifty yards away, he stopped.

In his judgment, that was about the right distance for Spot to still hear Old Lady, but also be aware that she was no longer at his side. Ten or fifteen minutes passed, and he had about decided that this wasn't going to work; then Lady went wild and Spot lunged out of the darkness. So what could have been a very bad night, ended happily.

If an old Red Tennessee coon hound hadn't come back and taken us to a trapped little Black and Tan female that night long ago, then another female would not have been there this winter to save this fine big Walker.

This wasn't written for those who believe the so-called experts who say that a dog can't reason. No man can make me believe that. How can you follow hounds for forty years and not know better?

This story was written for those who may recall a similar event, and perhaps, encourage them to relate the event through this magazine. It should make good reading. How about it?

Alfred and Stella, in Washington DC in 1941.

No Time for Sorrow

All afternoon, the cars had low-geared down the winding hill into the narrow canyon, dragged across the three sharp cuts that had, for years, defied all efforts at bridging, and then pulled slowly out into the broad valley below the fork of the creeks.

As, one by one, they drew to a stop beside the others parked there and disgorged their howling occupants, the man, standing quietly aside watching all this, was filled with a slight feeling of disgust mingled with sadness. The spoilers had found Big East Hollow and nothing would ever be the same again.

And still, they came because of the ballyhoo of local politicians extolling the greatness of their foresight and genius, making possible the soon to be lake and recreation area. Each new car only added to the clamor and confusion.

Mothers screeched at wild-eyed kids, running blindly through immense patches of cocklebur and sticktights. As one after another of the racing tikes gradually collected enough burs and sticktights, they slowed to a spraddle-legged halt, where they stood in utter dejection, and screamed for Mommy at the top of their voices.

Men, in immaculate sport clothes, looked worriedly at dust, fast collecting on sleek new cars. They picked their way gingerly across the gravel road to the edge of the field, where the great politicians preened and strutted in unrestrained pride of their generosity in letting the common people view them in all their glory.

As the dust cloud grew steadily, more and more flashing arcs could be seen, as throwaway cans landed in the clean bean field, and bottles collected in the roadside ditch.

Mothers were fast becoming disenchanted, as pushing sweat-soaked hair back from dust-streaked faces, they tried in vain to separate their darlings from the vast collection of burs that each now possessed, only to eventually give up and stuff them back into cars, stickers and all, as fast as they could round them up.

As the human circus milled about under the disapproving faces of the towering slopes, the man wondered just how much of the rare natural beauty the crowd really saw. How many had actually looked up at the glorious blue of the October sky or had caught their breath, in awe, at the splendor of the frost-tinted foliage of the hardwoods, reaching high above them on all sides?

Then, as if almost on signal, the exodus began. People unused to the outdoors grew slightly panicky as they felt the sudden chill penetrating the valley. The sun was dropping without warning behind the western rim. Car doors slammed, tires spun, and the dust rose even higher, as the stalwarts fled from their brief sojourn into the wilds, back to the comforts of civilization.

As the humming motors and crying voices of kids faded rapidly into the distance, the politicians, for the moment, seemed stunned at so quickly finding themselves alone. There was the man, of course, but since he had refused to worship at their shrine, he was probably too dumb to appreciate them anyway.

They looked about disdainfully at the beautiful valley that they had so recently been raving about. Then they climbed quickly back into their cars and were soon only a painful memory to the man, who felt peace returning to him with every foot of distance that grew between them.

It was good to be alone; to enjoy again, as a thousand times before, the soul-soothing isolation that was so much a part of this particular section of the county. Solitude could, he knew, have adverse effects, depending upon the individual. Some found it frightening, engulfing, a sea in which to drown; while others such as he, immersed in its silence, knew only contentment.

Slowly, his eyes swept across the valley to the north line of timber that reared abruptly from the edge of a cornfield. Ah! What memories! Far to the east lay Ringers Creek, flowing toward the hills bordering the state highway. Then it began its descent, gathering water from never-failing springs, seven in all, as it came to meet the lesser Lick Creek at the forks, thus making the proposed lake possible.

As he followed the creek with his eyes, every foot of its length brought back memories of the past. There, just beyond the low water bridge, was the slate bluff, the location of an event that was to be the source of much ribbing from his wife.

It was there that young Fan, after being soaked from stem to stern in a bottle of fox-proofing liquid, chose to tree a gray fox in the base of a hollow beech. He reeled, with a shudder, the times that fox-hunting friends came to ask just what it was he put on his coon hound to make it tree foxes.

And over there to the left, where the big drainage ditch crossed the bottom, was where young King lost interest in chasing cattle when a big herd of whitefaces converged upon men and dogs and ran them clear out of the pasture and into the creek.

Along the lane paralleling the creek, the big sycamore still stood. He remembered well the night that Big Red, as a young dog, treed a coon there, when it was raining so hard that he could hardly stand to look up to shoot it out.

But it was from the south fork, better known as Coon Hollow, that memories came to engulf him in overwhelming numbers. Nostalgia clutched at him with powerful fingers. His gaze slowly swept its boundaries to where it ended in a smaller joining at the creeks of Chimney Rock and Orchard Hollow.

It was there, at the junction where the old sawmill used to be, that he, as a teenager, had learned a valuable lesson in woodcraft from an old veteran coon hunter. After days of pouring rain, he had been taught how to build a fire, by using strips of bark torn from a Shellbark Hickory, and the dead branches still hanging from the tree that had not yet touched the ground. The amazement he had felt as the fire blazed in defiance of the weather was again fresh in his mind. It was a lesson he used many times.

He had named the hollow, as a boy, and it had stuck. Only a mile long and a quarter wide, yet it had almost been his private hunting grounds for many years, because of its ruggedness and the unyielding fierceness of the surrounding hills. Even when coons were scarce, they could still be found there, simply because the average hunter found the terrain too formidable.

Over on the left, Lick Creek clawed a tortuous route along the foot of the ridge. It was there where he had looked on in disgust at the summer slaughter of a female coon with a litter of kittens. He was never ashamed of the lie he told that night. His young dog had treed and he had gone to him alone and found a young coon in the tree. He had returned to the others and reported that his dog had nothing.

Across the bottom, at the foot of the west ridge, was where he had learned that it is possible for a coon to lose its scent. Standing at the bottom of the slope over which Ring and Fan had taken a coon, he waited for them to come back into hearing. When he finally heard them driving in hard from the west, he also heard the coon coming down the hill straight at him. He stood quietly until it was only a few feet away, then, thinking to make it climb, he had crashed onto a brush pile and yelled at the top of his lungs.

As the dogs reached his spot only minutes later, he waited for the tree bark. But none came. He stared in disbelief as the dogs searched high and low for some trace of the coon. It was as if it never existed. They never opened again and something else had been added to his education.

Then back behind him, the hill dissecting the west ridge came to a point. This was where the last stand of virgin timber still stood. Red had treed a big boar coon up a giant red oak so tall that it took three high-powered shells from a .12 gauge to bring him out, and then with plenty of fight still in him.

And over there by the corn crib, that same night, was where they had returned to find that the truck wouldn't unlock. The temperature hovering at twenty, and it was around three o'clock in the morning. They were eight miles from home, so he picked up a stick to knock out a glass, when Red treed again on top of the ridge. By the time they had gotten that coon and returned to the truck, he was able to think more calmly. He found a hole in the fire wall, through which he was able to poke a stick and turn the door handle, thus saving the price of a glass.

The memories seemed endless, and he shook his head to throw them off. All those memories of the times he had walked those bottoms, first as a boy, then as a man. It did no good to live in the past. All things changed, and usually for the best. The project about to submerge all those bottoms would be for the betterment of the county.

As he walked back to his car, he knew that he wouldn't change it, if he could. A beautiful lake would soon be there to furnish pleasure for hundreds, instead of just a few. A hundred years' water supply for the county seat would be impounded, thus warding off the ever-summer fear of drought. And wildlife would, in fact, flourish more abundantly in the area after the lake was formed. Coon would have a paradise, even if they would be a lot harder to tree. And deer would abound in the surrounding hills, instead of just the few that were there now.

As he climbed into his old car, he sat still for a few minutes. He looked dreamily all around him. In all honesty, he knew he must admit the brief resentment he had felt was based upon what he considered an invasion of privacy. And he had no right. He owned not one inch of the ground around him, and yet, in a moment of weakness, he had allowed himself the luxury of feeling that it all belonged to him.

As he put the key into the switch and turned on the ignition, he looked once more at the towering bluff above him and broke into a chuckle. Durned if those hills didn't grow a little every year. They were, indeed, a lot higher now than when he was a boy, first seeing the splendor in their magnitude. But that's absurd, he reflected with a grin, hills don't grow. It must just be that the bottoms are getting deeper.

But as he drove off, he realized that he was really looking forward to the change with eagerness. He would, he knew, be a part of anything involving those beloved hills, and there would be no time for sorrow.

Army portrait of Alfred.

Reprieve for Napoleon

With Nora and the kids gone for the weekend, Ben Stayley was in no hurry to finish the Saturday evening chores. He could take it easy and still get an early start coon hunting. Being quite content to dawdle, it was only natural that he had forgotten to throw hay down to the pony. And it was just as natural, that as he squeezed the last drop of milk from Bessie, he remembered.

With a sigh, he set the full pail to the side and climbed up the ladder to the loft. But here the tempo quickened, as he started over towards a broken bale. Perched directly above it, on a sill, was a small, red ball of feathers. Dottie's bantam rooster glared at him through hostile, beady eyes. The rooster was his sworn enemy, or at least, it had always seemed that way to him. He hated that bird with a vengeance and he was certain the feeling was mutual. How else could he explain the number of times that rooster had gone out of its way just to cause him trouble?

Just last week, the rooster happened to be directly above where he had set the milk pail, and he chose that particular moment to crow and flap his wings. Chaff rained down into the bucket. He knew beyond a doubt, that durned bird had marched around until he found the exact spot to jump up and down and fan his wings, in order to send as much chaff down as possible into his bucket of milk. No one could tell him this was just an accident. No, sir! And the crowing was but a cry of mockery.

Now about that crowing, there was something he could really hate him for! He never waited until dawn, like any sensible rooster; not that bird. He sounded off night after night at ten, two, and four. There was something positively uncanny, he reflected with a shudder, about how that feathered devil knew what mornings he had a chance to sleep late. No wasted crowing in the barn on those mornings at daylight! No, boy!

244 :: Come Into My World

Ben had imagined, many times, how the rooster crept stealthily up to the house until he was directly beneath Ben's bedroom window. Always his window; never any other. Oh, that little monster knew what he was doing!

Once there, he just knew how the rascal paused for a minute, with a chuckle, with his head cocked sideways, as he cast a reflective eye up at the window. He was contemplating with glee the sudden start he would give old Ben, when he flew up there and started screeching at the top of his lungs.

Now, as Ben approached the bale of hay, some of his thoughts must have become apparent to his adversary. For what happened next only convinced Ben more than ever that danged varmint could read his mind. As he grabbed the pitchfork and started to draw back to take a swipe at the devil, the rooster rose with a squawk; and instead of flying to the side, as any other rooster would have done, it came straight at him.

The point of impact during the attack, as Ben called it, came at the height of his back-swing and with devastating results. Caught off balance, Ben fell flat on his back, when the feathered bombshell exploded in his face.

As he hit the loft floor with a rafter-shaking thud, the fork flew from his hands, arched to the ground below, and landed tines first, directly into the bucket of milk. Climbing shakily to his feet and finding the bird nowhere in sight, he cast an angry eye below. There, to his dismay, stood the fork with the handle still quivering, as the ground around it soaked up the milk spurting from the holes in the side of the bucket where two tines protruded.

That did it! That ... did ... it! That bird had to go. It was either him or the rooster. Quickly, he climbed down to salvage what milk he could, by pouring it into the sow and pigs. Then, he ruefully remembered that he still hadn't fed the pony. He went back up to the loft and completed that chore.

Eager, now that his mind was made up to settle with the rooster, once and for all, he finished at the barn and headed for the house. The shotgun would do it, and he would tell Dottie that a fox had eaten him.

The rooster was nowhere in sight. He experienced a feeling of heady exhilaration at the thought that, at last, the rooster realized it had gone too far. Some second sense had, no doubt, warned it that his wrath, now fully aroused, was a terrible thing. He was sure it was hiding out in deathly fear.

As he entered the backyard, there was slight twinge of guilt when he realized he had left the back door open. With a shrug, he dismissed such laxity as being of no consequence. The November day was warm and the flies were all gone, so what was the harm in leaving the door open?

Glowing with satisfaction at his unconscious rebellion against female tyranny, he approached the back door. But for some reason, a sense of urgency made him hurry. With extreme effort, he managed to control himself. As the rooster bobbed and weaved on the table top, Ben moved further to the left, in an attempt to send the bird fleeing out the door.

Still the bird refused to be maneuvered into something he didn't understand. Within seconds, whatever sanity the man still possessed, snapped. In desperation, holding his shotgun in his right hand, he grabbed the heavy leather cushion from his easy chair, and hurled it viciously at the bobbing foe with his left hand. Because Ben was right handed, the heavy cushion not only missed the rooster, but ended up going through the glass of Nora's pride and joy, the picture window.

As the shattered window flew in all directions, and the bird went straight up in the air, Ben managed to dodge just a might, and it was enough. He had told Nora a hundred times to stop waxing the floor under the throw rugs, but she had done it again. As the rug shot out from under him, his arms milled violently in an attempt to maintain his balance. But anyone who has fought a rug on a waxed floor knows just how hopeless it all is. With the cocked shotgun waving furiously at arm's length, he started over backwards. At some time during the descent, the gun flew from his hand, and as he hit with a crash, there was an ear-splitting roar, as the gun discharged upon impact with the floor.

Stunned, he lay unmoving for a moment, as the plaster dust slowly filled the air. Then, little by little, he began to comprehend, as his eyes gradually came into focus. Aware of a ringing in his ears, his mind groped for an answer. And then he remembered the sound of the gun discharge.

Lifting himself to one elbow, he began to survey the shambles of the room. There, next to the sidewall, lay the remains of the gun. The rooster seemed long gone. With a groan, he rolled over, and on hands and knees crawled over to where to gun lay. He was not surprised at what he found.

The gun had been reduced to little more than a pile of junk. Not only was the barrel split, but the breech now lay in pieces. Numbly, he poked at the wreckage with his finger. The barrel had been plugged up. But how? He was always careful of such things. Wait a minute! Nora had said something about her nephews having it out in the yard before she caught them. He hadn't paid too much attention at the time, but now it was all too clear. She hadn't caught them soon enough. No telling what the little monsters had crammed down the barrel!

Slowly, his realization of his narrow escape caught up with him, leaving him weak and shaking. If he … if he hadn't … if it hadn't been for the rooster provoking him into grabbing the gun … and if it hadn't flown from his hand when he fell …

Basking in pride of his sudden male dominance, he quickened his step toward the kitchen. He wasn't prepared for what he saw. Right smack dab in the middle of the table, amid all the partially-filled dishes that he had neglected to clear away after lunch, stood the rooster. And he had been busy. All over the milk-soaked tablecloth were big, black, sticky tracks, which obviously had come from the bird walking through the blackberry jelly dish and then back and forth across the table to clean his feet.

Intent upon eating, as he stood knee-deep in a bowl of baked beans, he was unaware of Ben's presence. Ben gave way to an ear-splitting roar. From then on, things happened so fast that Ben was never quite sure in just what sequence they had occurred. But when it was over, he was practically a broken man.

At his rude interruption, the rooster first straightened up to his full height and met him, glare for glare. He was not to be driven from that delicious food so easily. But from somewhere within his chicken head must have come a warning. This was not the man he had bested so many times before.

There was, in fact, a bit of insanity in those eyes burning at him. Battle-wise veteran that he was, discretion seemed the better part of valor. So, being a believer in the old axiom that he who decides to run away may live to fight another day, he left the table like a jet plane from a catapult.

A shudder swept over Ben, as the horror of what might have been came in overwhelming waves. He would have taken the gun hunting that night. And in all probability, he would have had a coon to shoot out. Thoughts of the result, had the gun been snugged down against his cheek when it went off, were too terrible to think about.

He did, in fact, he thought as he climbed shakily to his feet, owe his very life to the rooster. On stiffening knees that threatened to buckle, he began to survey the damage. Front window broken, pole lamp broken, glass all over the floor, holes in the plaster, gun busted, half the china closet cleaned out, clock busted, glass and food all over the kitchen, milk bucket punctured, milk lost, and all because of a three-pound package of dynamite.

It just didn't seem possible that something so small could create so much destruction in such a short period of time. It must be some kind of record. A record! Why, of course! And probably a world one at that! Who else could boast of a rooster who could wreck so many things within a few minutes, and still have time left to save his owner's life? Why nobody, that's who.

Pride was rapidly replacing all anger at the little bird, but then Ben suddenly started with alarm. What about the rooster? Maybe the shotgun had wounded the bird and he had wandered off to die in agony of his wounds. Quickly, he bolted out the front door to stand looking wildly about in the front yard. But as eagerly as his frantic eyes searched, he saw no sign of his feathered savior. Carefully, he sought signs of blood on the ground, but found none of that either. Sick with remorse, he slumped down on the front steps and dug gloomily for his old pipe. He was a man completely without pride in himself, as he puffed sadly away.

That poor innocent little chicken had probably become so scared that it had run off to the hollow someplace, where it would be easy bait for a fox. My Lord, what had he done? The poor little guy. It was all his fault. Well, he would see about that, right now. He was halfway into the house to get his gun, when he realized he had none. Well, he would go down to the hollow and search for him anyway.

As he anxiously started around the corner of the house, the sweetest music he had ever heard fell on his ears. There, atop the corn crib, strutting back and forth like a drum major, was Napoleon. He had named him after he decided he was a celebrity. Little and mighty, that was him alright. As the barnyard rang with the sounds of Napoleon's crowing, Ben stood watching. "What a rooster! What ... a ... rooster!!" He exclaimed out loud, "Crow you little record holder, crow!"

On sudden thought, he again entered the house, to emerge, minutes later, with his camera. A world record holder should be photographed for posterity. Advancing as close as possible, without frightening him off, he quickly snapped several pictures. There was just one thing, though, Nora must never see the finished photos.

Remembering the cleanup job at the house, he turned away reluctantly from the wondrous sight, and worked fast and furiously. In an hour, with the help of a shovel, mop, and broom he was practically done. With the tablecloth in to soak, he surveyed the broken window. It was only 4:30. If he hurried, he could still get to the building supply house before they closed, and he could purchase a new glass. Since Nora wouldn't be back until Monday afternoon, he would have plenty of time to repair the window.

On Monday morning, he would hide the broken gun in the woods, go to town, and purchase another one. He'd just tell her he had traded. He could replace the broken clock and lamp at the same time. He would explain them as coming home presents for her. And, oh, yes, a new milk bucket. He'd say the old one had started to leak.

As he walked to the car, he also remembered he had to get some patching plaster and paint for the front room. As he motored toward town, Nora's name buzzed in his mind. Then with dismay, he realized why. He still hadn't figured out an explanation for the missing china and her grandmother's bowl.

But then, growing bolder as most husbands do, finding

themselves free, for a time, of their better halves—he dismissed the thought with a shrug. So what, who did she think she was, pushing him around that way? Well, it was about time she found out who was the boss of that family! He'd just straighten her out on a few things, that's all. And besides … well … he'd … well; Monday was a long way off, anyway.

Alfred, in Washington DC in 1941.

Old Buck

I could see the answer written on Pa's face, as he walked slowly back to the wagon where I sat perched on the seat. I knew, without asking; there had been no loan. He walked with the fluid grace of the tall mountain man, but he looked older than his thirty-six years. For the first time, I noticed the sprinkling of gray in his dark hair and the lines of worry etching his bronzed face.

"No luck, Danny," he sighed, as he leaned back against the wagon. "Seems like April 10, 1904 is just a bad time to borrow money, especially for someone who just moved here."

We had moved to Indiana from Tennessee the fall before. Bad luck had dogged us ever since we moved. No sooner had we arrived, than the cow was poisoned on snakeroot and died. Then we discovered that the hay rake and mowing machine were nothing but a pile of junk. Replacing the cow and machinery had just about depleted our small amount of cash. With spring planting just around the corner, Pa was hard put for seed money.

Reluctantly, he pushed away from the wagon and turned to look at Old Buck, my hound, who sat in the wagon at my feet. The sadness in his dark eyes became instant cause for panic. Unconsciously, I tightened my grip on Buck's collar. I was afraid of what he was thinking. Vividly, I recalled a scene from a few weeks ago. A man had tried to buy Buck, when he saw the evidence of Buck's ability, in the number of coon hides we had stretched.

Buck was a medium-sized, brindle-covered hound of the Plott breed; we had brought him with us from Tennessee. I could still hear old Sam Pruitt's deep voice as he picked him out of the litter and handed him to me, "Danny, it's high time you had a hound of your own. This one is the gamest of the lot. Treat him right, hunt him hard, and he will make a dog to be proud of."

I was ten then and now Buck was five. He had been my companion ever since he was big enough to follow me around. I wished now that I hadn't begged so hard for Pa to let me bring him to town.

It just wasn't safe to let him get into a fight with another dog. Though not quarrelsome, he was always ready to meet one halfway. He was weaned on bobcats, wild boar, and bear; he just naturally fought to kill. Once aroused, he was a wild savage and usually ended a dog fight quickly. But I had promised to keep him in the wagon, so Pa consented.

Now, as Pa stood there looking at us, I dreaded for him to speak. We had to plant to live and Buck was all we had to sell. I had a sick feeling in my stomach, and as if Old Buck could tell, he started licking my face. The look in Pa's eyes was just as sick as my stomach, as he cleared his throat and said, "Danny."

I waited for more, but that was all he could get out. He just stood there swallowing, as I said, "Yes, Pa?" His words came slowly and with effort. "Danny, you know how important it is for us to get seed." Again he stopped, and I knew that he would rather take a whipping than to say more.

I was numb, sick in body and soul, as I answered, "Yes, Pa, I know." I knew, too, that a fifteen-year-old boy was supposed to face things like a man. Pa's only concern was his responsibility to his family, Ma and me.

His hand went out to stroke Buck's long soft head and ears. "You know, Danny, that I don't want to sell him. I don't want to do this to you, but I'm at the end of my rope. He is the only thing of value that we can spare. We have to keep the cow and horses, you understand that, and if we don't plant this spring, we don't eat next winter. If the farm was clear, we could borrow on that. But with the back taxes against it, we can't even do that. Now, son, can you think of any other solution? If you can, I'll be glad to listen."

I could only shake my head numbly, as I fought back the tears, for it would hurt him worse to see that. "No, Pa," I finally answered, "I guess there is nothing else to do." I could say no more, for my voice was beginning to give me away.

Buck's battles were written on his beautiful head in scars. That long one on his flank, from the tusk of a wild boar; we had almost lost him that time. The smaller ones on his ears and nose were from the claws and fangs of many bobcats.

And the big one, across the top and down the side of his head; that one meant the most, and as Pa's finger traced from top to bottom, his eyes grew misty. I knew that he was thinking about how it got there, how it happened to be on Buck, instead of him, and how he might have been in his grave if it wasn't for Buck.

I could still see it, as my mind went back two years. Pa, with his back to a ledge, an old sow bear reared up in front of him, and his rifle ten feet away, where that old sow had knocked it. My blood still ran cold at the memory of the sound of her terrible savage growling, almost a bawl. As she started to lean forward with front legs extended, her mouth a vast, dripping cavern of red and white, and Pa yelling, "Run, Danny, run!"

Then, from out of nowhere, a hurtling brindle bundle of savage fury, as his wild squalling battle cry peeled out all over the valley. He hit that bear like a snarling rocket. He caught her high and her arms went out as if to hug the dog. She might as well have tried to capture a tornado. Buck was too smart to hold on. Before she could grab him, he cut loose and hit the ground, then was at her flank, but not before one of those vicious front feet raked down hard across the dog's head.

Still, as the blood gushed out, he was at her flank, and she had had enough. Up a big pine she went, with Buck leaping high, trying to drag her down. But by this time, Pa had him by the collar. Turning him over to me, he quickly retrieved the rifle, and brought the bear tumbling out of the tree. We rushed Old Buck home, so we could fix him up, leaving the bear where she fell until the next day.

Yes, I knew that was what Pa was thinking about, as he focused on Buck and what needed to happen in order to feed his family next winter. As Pa and I remained silent, Buck's intelligent eyes went from first one to the other. He could sense the tension within us. I'm sure he could tell it concerned him, for he whimpered, just a little, as his nose went out to nudge Pa's hand.

Almost with a look of guilt, Pa jerked his hand back. Then, as if steeling himself for the unpleasant job ahead, his voice came harshly, as he turned abruptly away and climbed into the wagon. "Well, that fellow who wanted to buy him was the blacksmith here. His shop is just down at the end of the street, so let's get it over with."

I couldn't answer, as he poked Old John into a trot, as if he must hurry before he changed his mind. All I could do, as we clopped along, was to keep running my hand over Old Buck, trying to soak up some of the feel of him for future remembering.

In a few minutes, we drew up in front of the blacksmith shop. I sat where I was, holding Old Buck, while Pa jumped out and went inside. Soon he was back, with a big smiling-faced, blond-headed fellow in tow.

There was no such thing as coming right to the point in a transaction like that. First, there had to be the small talk, age, experience, health, temperament, and the relating of some of Buck's catches. Price was the last thing to be mentioned in a deal involving something as close to a man as his dog.

When the man casually asked what it would take to buy a dog like that, Pa just as casually replied, that any man lucky enough to own a once-in-a-lifetime hound like Buck would be plumb crazy to sell him. The blacksmith's voice was both courteous and soft as he answered, "Yes, I'll agree, either crazy or dead broke."

There was no gloating in the man's voice, just a sincere note of sympathy. And though Pa's face blanched, his reply was firm and steady. "Yes, it would be one of the two, all right. There just couldn't be any other reason for selling a dog like that."

The man's sharp eyes had told him, of course, the real answer. As he took in the patched harness on Old John, our worn jeans, and the meager little box of groceries in the back of the wagon, the look of sympathy on his face grew deeper. He seemed reluctant to pursue the subject further, until Pa got to feeling a little more like it. There was respect for Pa in that big man. Respect for Pa and for what he had to do. It gave me considerable satisfaction, at least, to know that Buck would go to a kindly man.

Neither had spoken a word for at least a minute; the blacksmith out of respect for Pa's pain, and Pa, because he had to get the pain under control before he could do a decent job of bargaining. I sat there, withering away by the second, literally drying up, like a cucumber on a squashed vine, as cold inside as the letters on a tombstone. I hoped they would never break the silence.

Suddenly, the silence was broken, but not by them. A big, ugly mongrel dog appeared around the corner of the blacksmith shop, and right behind him, a man equal in appearance. The dog spotted Buck right off and stopped, stiff-legged. Snarling viciously and with hackles raised, he fixed his hot, glazed eyes on Old Buck, just like a pointer at a squatting quail.

Instantly, I took a firmer grip of Buck's collar. He had recognized the challenge, and I felt the quiver of eagerness for combat run through him, as he rumbled deeply in his throat. The man, as big as the blacksmith, had a three-days' growth of heavy, black beard through which glared a pair of mean, pig-like eyes.

"Well, Colter," he bellowed, "about to buy another dog for old Sugar here to practice on?" He then went into a braying laughter.

The blacksmith's voice held an edge like the steel of his anvil. "Crandle, whether or not I buy another dog is no concern of yours. But I'll tell you this. If that killer of yours ever jumps another dog of mine, without reason, I'll kill him with my own bare hands. Now take him and move on."

The laughter died on Crandle's lips, but his ugly face retained a sneer, as he said, "Ok, Colter, guess you can't take a joke. But if you ever get one that you want to lay a little money on, just let me know." That parting shot came from over his shoulder, for he was already moving off towards the center of town.

The big dog turned once more to snarl at Buck, and I felt him quiver again. I guess a dog can feel insulted the same as people. I thought of what the man had called his dog—Sugar. What a name for a brute like that. He must have weighed at least seventy pounds, a good fifteen more than Buck. He stood all of twenty-seven inches at the shoulder, while Buck was only twenty-four. His ugly head, too, bore scars of many battles, and it would have been hard to guess his breeding. Bull terrier was there, for sure, and maybe a trace of hound and shepherd.

Colter watched their retreating figures for a moment, and then said, "Now, there goes a real mean pair. He takes that dog with him everywhere he goes. He's just hoping for a chance to sic him onto some poor animal that doesn't have a chance. Somebody will shoot him one of these days, but until then, there's no telling how many more dogs he will kill or cripple. Why, he has torn the life out of three just this month."

Pa waited a short time after Colter had finished before saying anything. Then, all he said was, "Well, now, I don't figure that any man who owns Old Buck here would ever have cause to worry about anything like that." Colter's expression was a question in itself, but he didn't ask for an explanation, and Pa didn't offer any.

I knew they were going to get at that bargaining in real earnest now, as each waited for the other to begin. But once again, an alien sound thrust itself upon us—the high, angry voice of a girl. Her words came to us clearly, down the wide expanse of that dusty street. "You keep that dog away from mine, you, you dirty brute, you." A glance told us what was happening. Bellowing with laughter, Crandle and his big dog had cornered a girl of about fifteen, who had a tall, slender Russian Wolf Hound on a leash. She was trying to keep herself between the two dogs as she backed away.

Colter exploded angrily, "He's gone too far this time. That's Elmer Keller's daughter, with her expensive Wolf Hound. It's just a yearling and won't have a chance. That big devil will cut those long slim legs clean in two and then finish him off. Let's get down there."

"Get in the wagon," Pa cried, as he yanked Old John around and laid the whip on him. Colter caught the rear end as it snapped past him and vaulted in. We only had about fifty yards to go, and with Old John running like a scared rabbit, we were there in seconds.

Pa pulled Old John to a plunging stop in a swirl of dust, and for a second, I found time to wonder what was holding that creaky old spring wagon together. But no time for thinking, after that. Colter hit the ground running, and plunged straight into the middle between Crandle and his dog and the girl and hers. "Crandle," he roared, "catch up your dog, now!"

A mask of hate swept over Crandle's face, and his eyes gleamed at having his fun interrupted. "Not on your life," he snarled. "Old

Sugar is going to get some meat today. Get out of my way, Colter."
Then he made a big mistake. He suddenly shot his hands out against
Colter's chest and shoved. For a large man, that blacksmith sure
could move fast.

His powerful hands grasped both of Crandle's wrists, as he threw
himself backwards, pulling Crandle down towards him as he fell.
He lit on his back, with his knees pulled in tight against his chest.
Using Crandle's forward momentum as leverage, and still retaining
his grip on the wrists, he planted his feet in his opponent's stomach,
and shot his powerful legs straight upward. Crandle's big body was
propelled up and over, in a looping arch, and he came to rest, with a
bone-jarring plop, on his back, in the dusty street.

Quick as a flash, Colter was on his feet, and in a bound, reached
Crandle's still inert figure. Bending over him, he grabbed the front
of his overalls and jerked him to his feet. Crandle seemed dazed,
as the blacksmith's tense voice said again, "Call him off! It's your
last chance."

But Crandle was beyond reasoning. Sheer insanity was in his
cry, as he yelled, "No!" and then wildly, "Get him, Sugar!" And
Sugar was ready. As he lunged forward, the girl screamed, and the
young trembling Wolf Hound jerked the leash from her grasp, as he
dashed under our wagon in a desperate effort to escape.

But the noise and lunging dog had scared Old John. As the pup
came out the other side, he reared and jumped a full length ahead
and a little to the left. This partly blocked the pup's escape route, so
that for an instant, he stood motionless, confused and shaken. Then
he whirled to face the raging Sugar, who came charging around the
wagon. His breeding had told him to go down fighting. I was barely
conscious of the girl's figure flashing past and knew her efforts
would be futile. Then Pa's voice, loud and clear, "Turn Buck loose,
Danny; send him in."

I didn't hesitate. For the last minute, anyway, it had been like
holding onto a fused bomb. He had recognized Crandle's dog for
what he was, a killer, and he hated him, instinctively. As I turned
loose of his collar, I said only what he wanted to hear. "Go get him,
Buck." We had never sent him in on a dog before, just big game in
the mountains, but it meant the same, and he did not question, just

exploded.

Whenever he attacked something large, it was always the same. That wild squall pealed from his throat like a death knell, as he launched himself from the wagon directly into Sugar's path. And he, recognizing that challenge for what it was, pulled up short, and for an instant, they faced each other across five feet of ground. But Buck never let him get set. It wasn't his way, and in the bat of an eye, he was on him.

From experience gained in battles with animals many times his size, Buck knew better than to try matching pound for pound. He had learned from every fight. The tricks stored in his scarred old head were many. With a rush, he feinted for Sugar's throat as the big dog went up to meet him, jaw to jaw. Buck started the beginning of the end. Dropping instantly into a crouch, his jaws closed around the big dog's left front leg, as he hurled himself straight under Sugar's belly, jerking the leg with him as he went. Sugar collapsed on his back, with a thud, but not before we all heard the sharp crack of that leg bone.

Buck had turned loose, as Sugar went flying. Checking his forward rush, he wheeled and sounded that wild battle cry, once more. The big dog had just regained his three good feet, when Buck hit the right front leg, and it was the same all over again.

Sugar was still on his back, when Buck whirled to start his third charge. Even those who had never seen him fight knew that it would be the last one, that it would be the throat, that the fight would be over in seconds.

In the instant that it took Buck to get set for his attack, a strange, pleading cry fell on our ears. Crandle's voice coming pitifully, "No! No! Please, no!" Then Pa's ringing command, "Hold off, Buck." And Buck held, muscles still ridged and trembling with eagerness, but rock still. Then Pa's voice again, "Catch him up, Danny."

Quickly, I leapt from the wagon and snapped the leash on Buck's collar. Crandle was at the side of his dog, talking to him, keeping him from struggling. Sugar was whimpering terribly, but Crandle's hands and voice seemed to be taking some of the pain away. Soon, Sugar lay still, just trusting his master to take care of him.

There was love between those two vicious characters. The display between them was a strange thing to see. Gathering him up in his arms, Crandle rose to his feet. As the tears ran unashamed down his dirty cheeks, he turned to Pa, and said, "Thank you, mister, I'll never forget what you did. I can fix his legs so that they will heal good enough to get around on, but he will never fight again. It's all my fault, and I have learned my lesson. I made him mean, and I made him fight, but that's all over. Thank you, again, for Old Sugar here." And with that, the crowd of spectators silently cleared a path for him. He walked slowly away, carrying the big dog in his arms.

By that time, men were crowding around Old Buck and me. It seemed that none of them had seen a Plott hound before. That wasn't strange, because his breed had been guarded jealously by southern mountain men for generations.

Then my attention was taken by a flurry of skirts, as the girl pushed through the crowd. Rushing right up to Old Buck, she knelt down and planted a kiss right on the top of his head. Crooning, she thanked him over and over, as she pressed her cheek against him, and her tears mingled with the softness of his long ears.

Finally, she stood up and turned to me. Before I could dodge away, she grabbed me by my shoulders and kissed me right square on the mouth. I was so startled, that I jerked back. As I did, there was a burst of laughter from the men surrounding us. But as she stood there, with her blue eyes wet with tears, and thanked me the same as she had Buck, I knew I hadn't minded that kiss too much, after all.

About that time, a portly, gray-haired man came up to us. "Oh Daddy," she cried, "did you see?"

"Yes, dear," he replied, "I saw, and we are in their debt." He stuck out his hand to me, "That's quite a dog you have there, young fellow, better hang onto him."

I dropped my hand to Buck's head, as I answered, "Yes, sir, he's quite a dog, and I would like to hold onto him if I could." His eyes looked steadily into mine, as he asked, "*If* you could, why can't you?" I hesitated a minute, just hating to put it into words, as if just saying it would make it so. Softly, his voice prompted me. "Why, son? Why can't you keep him?" I had to say those words, as much as I hated to. "Well, sir, it's planting time and we are sorta up against it, so I guess we will have to sell him."

His hand went out to rest on my shoulder, "You think a lot of him, don't you, son?"

"Yes, sir, and so does Pa. Old Buck here has saved his life more than once when he was hunting bear." His hand squeezed my shoulder, as he spoke with just a trace of emotion in his voice, "Well, now, maybe things have changed for the better."

I waited breathlessly for his next words. "You see, son, that pup is a valuable animal. There aren't many like him in the whole United States. He would have been dead, if not for your dog here. Now, the way I see it, that most certainly should be worth the price of the dog."

Reaching into his pocket, he took out his wallet and extracted a new, crisp bill. As he held it out, my eyes bugged, because I had never seen a one hundred dollar bill before. I backed away, almost scared, as I said, "Oh, no, sir, you had better talk to my pa."

He smiled as he turned to Pa, who had stood silently by as he talked to me. "Mr. Clemins, it looks like you will have to do me the honor of accepting this. Please believe me, I don't want it any other way. I'm getting off too cheap, at that."

Pa smiled, too, but his voice was serious, as he spoke, "Thank you, Mr. Keller, but it just wouldn't seem right for one old mangy hound to earn so much for less than a minute's work, and for doing something he enjoyed, at that. No, sir, that just wouldn't be right, at all, but I will let him earn half that amount. That way, maybe he won't get to feeling so important and swell-headed."

The man that Pa had called Keller looked solemnly at him for a moment. He had recognized the finality in his voice. Without saying another word, he took out his wallet again, replaced the hundred, and pulled from it another, just as new, but it said fifty.

Slowly, Pa's hand went out to grasp it, this newfound wealth, and try as he might, he was unable to keep a slight tremor from his hand. Only *he* knew what that fifty dollars meant to us. His eyes went to the other's face as he said, ever so softly, "Thank you, Mr. Keller, I'll remember this for the rest of my life."

"On the contrary, sir," the man replied, "it is I who will never forget, and must thank you. A compassionate man is a gentleman, and you proved to be such a man when you let Crandle's dog live. That was a fine thing you did there, Mr. Clemins, and I will be honored to have you visit my place of business. Drop in whenever there is something I can do for you."

"Thank you, I will," Pa answered quietly. Their hands met, and then, Mr. Keller put his arms around his daughter, and they and the Wolf Hound pup walked away. But as she looked back and smiled at me, I had an idea that I was going to like that family, too.

Colter came up to us then, with a big grin splitting his face wide open, as he said, "Yes, sir, a man would have to be crazy or dead broke to sell a dog like that, and I don't guess you're either one."

Pa smiled happily, as he answered, "No, I reckon not."

They had a little talk and the blacksmith went back to his shop a happy man. Pa promised to write to Sam Pruitt and ask him to find a young Plott female, unrelated to Buck, and ship it to Ben Colter. That way, they could be sure of some little Plotts running around now and then.

I stayed in the wagon, petting Old Buck, while Pa bought his seed. After he was through doing that, we both went to pick out something real nice to take home to Ma. When we did, finally, head Old John out that dirt road towards home, I kept wishing Pa would tickle him just a little with the whip. I was sure anxious to see the joy in Ma's eyes, when she saw her new dress and bonnet, and heard all the good news. I was dying to tell her that it was going to be all right living here in Indiana, after all, that the people were no different than the friends we left behind in Tennessee.

I did break into my daydreaming once to ask, "Pa, how come you and Mr. Keller knew each other?"

He chuckled, and said, "Well, you see, Danny, he was the banker I went to see about the loan."

Alfred, with his dog, Red.

Come Into My World

U gly clouds of yellow dust bounced along in the wake of the high-powered, sleek convertible. The man seated in the passenger seat realized that the speedometer was resting on 80. He knew that was no speed for an Alabama back road. Then it happened, as the big car rounded a long curve, three little raggedy, barefoot figures, followed by a scraggly, flop-eared mongrel puppy, popped out of the woods and trotted across.

The faces of both men turned to horror. The driver instantly realized there was no time for brakes. His shoulders tensed, as lightning-fast reflexes took command. Powerful hands gripped the wheel; the vehicle swerved wide to the left. To Ed Weaver, the passenger, the edge of the forest hurtling towards them seemed like an ominous wall of death. But then, as low-hanging pine branches gouged deep furrows in the side of the car, they were past.

The dirt-smudged faces of the children, two girls and a boy, loomed large, like a blown-up still life, as they looked up at Ed as he shot by, only inches away. For a second, the overwhelming relief of the kids being safe blotted out everything else. Then he allowed himself to hear—to hear the scream of the oldest girl, then he knew the pup hadn't made it.

Even then, as he remembered the sickening thud beneath the wheels, the thought came. *My God, the poor little creature didn't have time to even cry out, in protest of this high-powered metal monster invading his slow, easygoing world.*

Then came the anger, not slow and kindling, but bomb-bursting anger, that must have satisfaction—that must lash out. As he turned to the one beside him, and drew in his breath to speak, he suddenly remembered the conversation with Lauri, Johnny's wife, a few days before.

Lauri's words were clear and fresh in his mind, "Ed, I can't take it anymore. I'm leaving him. If I'm to retain my sanity, there's nothing else to do. He's changed, Ed. Changed so much that I don't even know him anymore. He's not John Cathoway, whom I married. He's Link Battle— tough, woman-scorning private eye. He has made too many movies, played the part too long, and now, the character has taken over. There's just not room for a wife. I've tried, Ed. You know, I've tried."

He knew, all right! No wife could have tried harder. He saw it coming, the strain on Lauri's face, that never seemed to go away. The cold cynicism in Johnny's every remark and his constantly growing lack of warmth. One by one, his friends had been frozen out, until only Lauri and he remained.

He had tried to tell himself that it was the ten percent, as Johnny's agent, that held him. True, it had made him financially independent, but deep down, he knew there was another reason. He loved Johnny, just as Lauri did. They had been together from the start of Johnny's career, and he would stay to help pick up the pieces.

There was no trying to talk her out of it this time, as he waited for her to pack. She had cried silently on the way to the airport, and he knew there was nothing he could say to help. But he would remember her beautiful, haunted eyes, as she turned and said to him, just before boarding the plane, "Oh, Ed, if he would only come into my world, once in awhile."

Ed remembered, too, the tightening of Johnny's jaw as he had broken the news, and his bitter anger directed at Lauri for leaving him. Wordlessly, he had watched, as Johnny quickly threw a few things into a bag and locked the doors. Still no words passed between them, as he climbed in and the car shot away. Now, three days later, here they were on a godforsaken back country road that was going nowhere.

"Aren't you going to stop?" Ed asked bitingly.

"Why should I? We missed the kids," Johnny answered coldly.

"My God! You killed their dog."

"So."

"Doesn't that mean anything to you at all?"

"Should it?"

"It should, if you have any human decency left in you, at all. Do you realize how much that pup might mean to those kids?"

"It was just a mongrel. They can get a dozen more tomorrow."

"You really don't know, do you? It is impossible for you to understand just how much love children like that, who have nothing, can feel for a little bundle of fur that is all theirs. Possibly the only thing in the world they can call their own."

"You nuts or something?"

"Not anymore. I thought there was something worth saving in you, but now, I know better. You don't have an ounce of compassion left in you, Johnny. And without that, you're just a shell, nothing but a shell.

At Ed's bitter words, Johnny's face whitened, but he remained silent.

"Stop the car!"

"Why?"

"Because I want out. I'm done, Johnny. I don't want to know a person like you!"

For an instant, the foot on the accelerator seemed to bear down harder, but then gradually let up. A hundred yards down the road, the car came to a stop. Johnny's hard eyes were fixed straight ahead, as Ed opened the door and got out. Reaching into the back for his bag, he saw the taut set of the shoulders, the unrelaxed hands gripping the steering wheel, and shook his head sadly.

He stood without moving, as the car roared off. Until the car was out of sight, he remained where he was, just watching. For a full minute, he stood there with eyes fixed on the point where the car had faded away.

Then, heaving a sigh, he looked around. A stump at the edge of the woods caught his attention. Slowly, he walked over, set his bag down, and removed his coat. Carefully, he folded it and laid it across the bag before seating himself on the stump.

Now, as the turmoil inside began to subside, he had time to think. He was miles from nowhere. He had no idea how far it was to the nearest town. But then, did it matter? His whole life had just changed. A light had gone out, and for awhile, he would grope alone through the darkness.

He sat silently, allowing the solitude to engulf him, until the realization came, for the first time in many months, he was completely relaxed. Slowly, he became aware of the life around him. Birds of all kinds singing in the pines, while overhead, a chicken hawk soared in majestic circles. Occasionally, its screaming cry came floating down to him, and a shiver ran over his body at the sheer wildness of the sound.

Down the road a few yards, a cottontail crept to the edge of the trees and then scurried back to cover, as the hawk's cry came again. A slight rustling in the woods caused him to turn around slowly. Finally, as his eyes grew accustomed to the gloom, he saw a large chicken snake slithering, ever so carefully, in the direction of the cottontail. *What a life the rabbit had*, he thought. The snake wouldn't follow him out into the hot sun, but out there, the hawk waited. He now understood the rabbit's dilemma.

He was reluctant to move, to frighten nature's children back into hiding, but he had something to do. Regretfully, he rose and gathered his coat and bag. It must be about two miles back to where they had hit the dog, and there still remained the task of locating the children. Surely, they wouldn't have been too far from home. But he must find them. He couldn't rest until he did.

Little puffs of dust rose with every step, as he walked slowly, but steadily, back down the road. Shimmering heat waves bathed the way ahead and no signs of life were evident, as the distance stretched out before him. How desolate must be the lives of those who lived here.

He had covered about a mile before he heard it. At first, he let the sound build, without pausing to turn around. But finally, it became necessary to check, to see if what he thought was true.

No emotion showed on his face, as he turned slowly and saw it was true. The same cloud of dust followed, but this time, the speed was not nearly so great. He stood waiting and hoping, but afraid to believe it was true.

As the car drew to a stop, they stared silently at each other. Both unyielding at first, but there was communication. They had been together too long for there not to be. Finally, Johnny broke the silence.

"Okay."

Without a word, Ed stowed his bag in the back seat and climbed in. They rode in silence for awhile, then Johnny asked," How much further?"

"About a mile, I guess."

There was no denying the spot. The ugly dark pool of dried blood was too obvious. But the pup had been removed. Carefully, he steered the car to the side of the road, turned off the motor, and removed the key. Silently, they walked to the spot where the pup had been struck. As Johnny looked down at the blood, Ed noticed a slight quiver run over his jaw. Ed's hope flickered a little higher.

They both saw the path at the same time. Just a brief little strip of bare ground, winding inward through the thicket, with small barefoot tracks. In answer to Ed's pointing motion, Johnny nodded, and led the way. About fifty yards up the path, the small footprints led around a curve, and up ahead, they saw the shack—tar-papered and desolate.

However, their eyes remained riveted to the scene before them. Neither of them were likely to forget this moment. Three small figures stood, looking down at a little wooden box, sitting on the ground beside a mound of dirt.

With a lump in his throat, Ed realized that a funeral, of sorts, was evidently in progress. Slowly, they approached within a few feet of the children, whose eyes remained downcast, and then they knew why.

The boy, who Ed had guessed to be about five, was speaking. As he listened to the soft childish voice, coldness swept over him. Transfixed, they both stood rooted to the spot, as they listened.

The boy's words came without bitterness and implied a faith that knew no doubt. "God, this here's Fluffy. He was runned over by a car that wuz goin too fast for his little legs. Somebody wuz in a bigger hurry than he wuz, God. That's how it happened. Don't be mad at him who done it, God, cause he must have had to git some place awful fast and couldn't help it. We know you will take good care of Fluffy, God, cause he wuz a good little dog. He didn't git to live long, but he wuz good to us while he did. I hope you won't hold it against him cause he chased butterflies. He never did catch or hurt'em or anything. It just seemed like he had to do it. Guess he just didn't know any better, God, so please forgive him. Amen."

A slight, muffled choking sound came from Johnny. Ed raised his eyes to see the strained look on Johnny's face. The children, too, had heard and looked at them, for the first time. Wisdom, far beyond his five years, shown in the boy's face, and they saw that he knew.

As his little tear-streaked face lifted to theirs, he said," We'uns is having a funeral. Fluffy would be glad you come to his bury'n."

As his eyes took in the few dusty, wilted daisies covering the top of the little wooden box, and the lost look in the tiny pathetic faces, his throat constricted. Ed couldn't speak.

But not Johnny. He dropped to his knees, and slowly and tenderly, gathered the children to him.

"That was a beautiful sermon," he said in a choked voice, "the most beautiful I've ever heard."

As they looked intently into Johnny's face, as only the innocent can, the boy said, "Don't feel bad cause you kilt him, Mister. Fluffy knows you couldn't help it."

And then, as an afterthought, "Do you think God heard me and will take good care of Fluffy? I ain't much for words."

Johnny was obviously deeply touched. There was a slight tremble to his voice, as he said, "He heard them, all right, He sure enough heard them."

The youngest girl, her clear blue eyes wide with confusion, looked up at Johnny, and said, "Fluffy's dead?"

He tried to answer, but his dry throat failed him momentarily. The oldest girl, her eyes shining with unshed tears, said softly, "Did you get where you wuz go'in in time, Mister?"

Though they searched her face for sarcasm, they could find

none. The question had been asked in all innocence. She believed that anything wrong was the result of an accidental happening.

Johnny blinked, as he gazed into her small upturned face. Gently, he placed his hand upon her soft blond hair. The words he whispered were for her alone, but Ed heard, and the flame of hope burned even higher.

"Yes, honey, I got there, but when I did, I didn't like what I found. I didn't like it at all. So, I came back."

As she nodded, Ed had the uneasy feeling of being the child and the child the adult. And from the look on Johnny's face, he knew that some similar thought must have crossed his mind.

Johnny's next words were those that Ed had wished for. "Now, will you take me to your house? I want to talk to your parents."

The boy answered, "Yes, sir. But first we have to bury Fluffy."

"Of course," Johnny answered. "Can I help?"

All three little heads nodded at once. Then, while Johnny placed the little box carefully in the hole, the boy picked up the shovel. Then, the ritual began. As the boy placed the first shovel full in the hole, he passed it to the oldest girl. She followed the boy's lead, shoveled dirt into the hole, and then passed the shovel to the smallest girl. Johnny was next, and then the routine started over. Soon, the grave was filled and the daisies strewn on top of the mound.

When the task was completed, the children led the way to the house. A gaunt, tired-looking woman of about thirty came out to wait on the small porch. Though the dress she wore was patched, it was clean. The group halted just short of the porch.

As she stared unemotionally at them, the boy was the first to speak, "Mama, they come to Fluffy's bury'n."

She nodded, as her dark eyes rested upon them. "You the ones that ran down their pup?"

Johnny's eyes widened. "Yes, but how did you know?"

"They described you," she answered in a dull voice.

Then Johnny was speaking. Ed was amazed by his humble tone. "Yes, Ma'am, I'm the one, and I'm terribly sorry. I'd like to make amends."

"No need," she replied tonelessly. "They've learned to accept things as they are. They'll get over it."

The woman was completely without spirit. Johnny tried another tack. "Ma'am, may I speak to your husband?"

"He ain't here. Works at the sawmill down at Linton. Don't get home but once a week."

"But," he pleaded, "I want to do something. I'd like to get the kids another pup."

For the first time, her eyes softened a little. She looked at her children tenderly, and then replied, "Guess you can, if you want. They have never had much, and they did set quite a store by that pup."

Apparently, that ended the conversation as far as she was concerned, because she abruptly turned and entered the house. For a few seconds, Johnny stood, staring at the door. Then, shaking his head, he knelt again with the children.

"We have to go now," he said softly, "but we'll be back. Would you like to have another puppy?

The boy studied his words for a moment, and then turned to the oldest girl. "Do you think it would be all right with Fluffy?" he asked in a tiny voice.

A slight frown wrinkled her small brow, and then she nodded. "Yes, Jimmy. I think Fluffy would like that. We could take him out to the grave every day, and that way, Fluffy wouldn't mind at all."

Ed wasn't really surprised when Johnny kissed each of the little solemn faces. There was a glimmer of wetness behind his eyes, as he walked back down the path, but Ed pretended not to notice.

In the car, Johnny sat without speaking for several minutes. He needed to think things out, to completely clear his head before proceeding.

"Ed, I'm going to adopt that family."

The day before, Ed would have found such a thing unbelievable, but not now. Not after the last hour.

"How do you mean?" He tried to speak casually, but it was difficult, with all the elation running through his mind.

"I'm not sure yet, but there'll be a way. But first, we're going after that pup."

"What about the adoption?" Ed asked. "They may be too proud to accept charity."

"I know," Johnny answered, "but we'll figure out a way. Lauri will know what to do."

At his mention of her name, there an immediate and uncomfortable silence. Ed waited.

"Ed," Johnny said, "do you know where she is?"

He felt the glow start at his toes and work up until it covered his whole body. It was a good feeling. Yesterday, Johnny wouldn't have asked that, would have been too proud. But now ...

"Sure, I know."

"Will you tell me?"

Ed couldn't resist waiting, to make Johnny suffer a little more. But he knew what he would say. Again, Lauri's last words flashed through his mind. He knew now that Johnny was ready—ready to enter her world.

"Sure, Johnny, I'll tell you where she is."

Say a Prayer for Old True

Now that it's all over, I realize that I never did really know the kid, at least not until that Saturday morning, when he failed to show up for work. He had a way with dogs, and was better than most men around my kennels, and it wasn't like him not to let me know.

Even as I reached for the phone to call his home, it practically went off in my hand. Something told me that it had to do with the kid, and Griff's first words proved me right.

"Kel," he said quickly, "Johnny's here at the shop waiting for Teak Johnson."

Irritated, because he was in town, instead of at work, I snapped, "Well, what about it?"

Griff sounded incredulous. "You mean, you don't know why?"

I wasn't in any mood for riddles. "Griff, what are you driving at?"

His next words carved a hollow in the pit of my stomach. "You don't know that Teak killed Old True yesterday?"

Mixed emotions raced through me. Instant anger at Teak, quickly followed by sorrow for Johnny. Poor fatherless boy, with nothing in the world to call his own but that old hound, and now he had lost him.

It was a moment before I could speak. When I did, I guess it was to convince myself, as well as Griff. "How do you know he's waiting for Teak? Besides, he's too timid to try anything, and what could a scrawny, fifteen-year-old boy do against a two-hundred-pounder like Teak Johnson?"

Griff spoke flatly, "Listen, Kel, that may be the kid *you* know, but it's not the one sitting here in my barber shop right now. He didn't say that's why he's here, but we all know. Everybody knows that Teak comes in for a store-bought shave every Saturday morning at exactly ten o'clock."

I must have sounded pretty dense to Griff, as I still insisted, "But that still doesn't mean he's waiting for Teak. I tell you, the kid is too gentle to hit anybody."

His next words raised the hair on the nape of my neck, as he exploded. "My God, Kel, don't you understand? Johnny hasn't spoken to a soul since he came in. He's just sitting back there in the corner, real quiet like, and not taking his eyes from that door." He paused for an instant, before continuing, and when he did, I slammed the receiver back on the hook, even while his words still hung in the air. "Kel, don't worry about Johnny trying to slug Johnson. He has a gun under his coat."

The wall clock in the kitchen said 9:35, as I tore through on my way to the pickup in back of the house. I still found it hard to see the kid in the kind of role Griff had described, as I floor-boarded that old heap, and went bouncing down the lane. Eight miles of rough road to town, but somehow, I had to get there before Teak.

Chased by a cloud of dust, I bounced from one ballast stone to another, as I gave the old truck all it had. A thousand trips over it had left little need for concentrated driving. My mind went back to the time three years before, when I had first seen the kid.

"Well, now, son," I had said, "I have been thinking of hiring somebody to help around the kennel, but I'm afraid you're a might small. Some of those dogs weigh almost as much as you."

His eyes never left my face, as he replied, "Yes, sir, I know, for I've looked them over, but it doesn't take size and strength to handle a dog, just understanding."

Even as I had to admit the wisdom of his words, my head shook in refusal. That sprite, trying to handle that pen full of spirited Walkers, was out of the question. "I'm sorry, lad, but I just couldn't take a chance on you getting hurt. They just don't trust strangers."

Without a flicker of emotion on his lean, dark little face, he turned and strode towards the pen. I was too late when I finally realized his intentions, but he wouldn't have stopped anyway. He was out to prove something, and he did, in a way that sent cold sweat trickling down between my shoulder blades. He opened the gate and stepped inside.

Ten hounds that allowed no stranger in their pen, came roaring, and he was in the middle. But before I reached the gate, I stopped. There was no need to hurry. In amazement, I stood transfixed, staring at a scene I had never expected to see. Those big spotted devils slid to a halt around him and then went mute. Not a hackle was raised, as boy and dogs just stood there and looked at each other.

I don't know what he said. I could hear the tone of his voice coming softly, and then they were on him. Fawningly crowding against one another to get closer, to lick him in the face, to rub against him, and to nibble his hands. Tender hands that brought whimpers of delight from their throats, as he stroked their heads. I had raised every one of those hounds, yet when he walked among them, every dog in that pen was ready to call him master, and follow him home.

But not until I told him the job was his, to work after school and on Saturdays, did he say why he wanted to work. His father had died the week before, leaving his mother with the responsibility of grubbing out a meager living on their small farm, and the care of him and a smaller sister. He waited to tell me until after he got the job, simply because he had wanted sympathy to play no part in it.

This, then, was the boy I had come to look upon almost as my own. This boy, sitting cold-eyed and tight-lipped in the corner of the barber shop, waiting for the killer of his dog. I had seen this boy cry over wire cuts on the dogs, even as his hands tenderly administered aid. He attended every whelping and went around with pain in his eyes for a week if a pup was lost. Could this be the boy that Griff's fear-touched voice had described? It didn't seem possible.

It was a little easier to understand Teak's shooting of Old True, for that could have been pure spite. True had come from my place. I had given him to Johnny only a few months after he started to work for me. He was retired and had the run of the place for the few remaining years left to him. But from the very first, he hung at the boy's heels every minute he was around. And finally, that wasn't enough, so he started following him home, and that did it. I don't know which was happier, Johnny or True, but from then on, they were inseparable.

Soon after that, Johnny incurred the wrath of Teak Johnson, when he refused to breed the old dog to one of Teak's females. He had calmly told him that the blood of Old True flowed in most of my pack, and could be had, for a price, at my kennel.

It wasn't that Teak couldn't afford the price of a good stud, for he could, and then some. But that's just the kind of a guy he was, the kind that enjoyed taking advantage of someone. And Johnny had set him back on his heels, when he refused to be taken in. I had never cared for his kind—the big blustery, red-faced, loud-talking, gentleman-farmer type, but I didn't think that even he would stoop so low as to get back at the boy the way he had.

As I crossed the low water bridge, a glance at my watch told me that the time was nine-fifty, and with two miles yet to go, I knew I would make it. But I assumed too much, for the left rear tire had ideas of its own. It blew, within a hundred yards of the bridge. Frantically, I fought against time as I changed it, but with sinking heart, I knew that valuable minutes had been lost.

I would never reach Griff's shop by ten o'clock. Nevertheless, I tried, but as I rounded the southwest corner of the square, a cold vacuum engulfed me. Teak Johnson's big Cadillac was parked directly in front of the shop.

My guess was that Teak couldn't have been there more than three or four minutes, but that might have been long enough; it was all according to what the boy had in mind. Recklessly, I whipped the truck into the curb beside Teak's car, and hurled myself across the sidewalk and through the door of the shop.

The quietness hit me like a battering ram, and I pulled up short. No one had noticed my entrance, for all eyes were glued to the small figure of the boy who was speaking to Teak, who stood before him, and whose size seemed to fill the middle of the room. Apparently, he had not had a chance to even sit down, before Johnny called him.

Though the boy's voice was the ultimate of politeness, it seemed only the more deadly for it. "Mr. Johnson," he was saying, "why did you shoot my dog?'

Though his hands hung at his sides and no gun was in evidence, there was something about the boy that was making Teak mighty uneasy. His feet shuffled nervously, as he threw a questioning glance around the room to the half a dozen of us there. If he had previously entertained any thoughts that he had friends in that room, they were immediately dispelled. Only cold blank stares met his muddy-colored eyes, as he searched our faces one by one.

Somewhat flustered, he turned back to Johnny, who stood quietly waiting, his dark eyes drilling into Teak's red face. Even though it should have been obvious to Teak that he stood alone, the ingrained feeling of self-importance would just not let him believe. We all were waiting breathlessly, in eager anticipation of one of the great Teak Johnson's witty remarks.

"Well, now, kid," he bellowed, "I thought I was doing you both a favor by putting him out of his misery."

It was as if he had never spoken, for without a change of emotion, Johnny repeated the question. "Mr. Johnson, why did you kill my dog?"

Johnson was puzzled. His loud voice and bullying manner had no effect upon the boy. "I told you that he needed killing," he said loudly, with a mean edge to his voice. "You ought to be thankful."

Again, Johnny ignored his answer. "Did he harm anything at your place, Mr. Johnson? Did he cause any damage? Did he act mean towards you or anyone in your family?"

Teak stood, speechless and red-faced, staring down at Johnny, as if finding it impossible to believe that this elf of a boy could actually stand there, completely undaunted by his threatening manner.

Again, Teak shifted his feet nervously and glanced about the room. Johnny waited until he again faced him, and then said softly, "Mr. Johnson, True wasn't but twelve years old. He might have lived several years yet. He was a good old dog and was only crossing your pasture on his way home from trailing a late-running coon. Mr. Johnson, Old True enjoyed living and wasn't ready to die. Why did you kill him, Mr. Johnson?"

Teak had never experienced such a situation. He could, by this time, beyond doubt, sense the hostility in the room. His eyes blazed at the focal point of his misery, Johnny's slight figure standing there in front of him. In rage, he threw caution to the wind, as he spoke harshly. "I'll tell you why I killed your mangy old hound. He was on my property and I didn't like it. That's all the reason I needed."

As he finished his explanation, he threw out a big hand to the side of the boy's head, knocking him to one side. As he brushed past, he snarled, "Now, get out of my way. I have to get a shave."

There was an instant growl from every man present, and I was halfway to Teak, who was starting to hang up his hat, when a chill went over the room. Johnny had dodged the main force of the blow, so he only staggered a little, and regained his balance in an instant. There was just a slight movement of his hand and an old Army model .45 appeared in his fist. He was speaking, even as he pulled back the hammer.

Teak's face went white at the sight of the gun, but became panic-stricken as the boy's words came out cold, flat, and deadly. "Don't bother to hang up your hat, Mr. Johnson, you and I are going to take a little ride."

Teak, for all his size, was reduced to a blubbering bowl of jelly. Fascinated, he stared in apparent disbelief, and a shiver ran over him, as the boy repeated his demands. "Walk out the door, Mr. Johnson, and get into your car. There's something that needs taking care of."

As Teak took one faltering step towards the door, he looked wildly around in a silent plea for assistance, and I decided that it had gone far enough. Striding towards Johnny, I held out my hand. "All right, kid, that's enough, give me the gun."

His voice was courteous, but his black eyes held no warmth, as he said, "Stay back, Mr. Taylor, this is something that has to be done. You know this gun has a hair trigger and if anyone grabs me, it will go off anyway, so it will be best if everybody stands clear."

He was right, for he had shown me the gun several times before, when I had visited his home. It had belonged to his dad and he had seemed proud of it for that reason. At the time, he had indicated that he had never fired it, and had no intention of doing so. But I recalled, with great alarm, that all it took was a flick of the finger to release the hammer.

"He's right, men," I cried hoarsely. "All it takes is a touch to drop that hammer, so don't try anything."

Only the sound of heavy breathing could be heard in the room, as we stared at the big gun dwarfing the small hand that held it. The tips of those big, ugly slugs glinted dully as they peeped from the cylinder chambers on either side. Somewhere back in my mind, another thought about that gun kept probing at me, but it just didn't seem to break through. Something that I believed would prove to be important, if I could just recall, but the thought just wouldn't come.

Sweat was trickling down Teak's face, as he sought for some avenue of escape. Then, in desperation, he made one more feeble attempt at bluffing. "See here, kid, I've had just about enough of this. Put that gun down."

As he made a halfhearted motion with his hand toward the .45 held unwaveringly in the small hand of the boy, there was a slight shifting of the barrel and the big bore was staring him directly in the eyes. Teak gave a gasp, as his hand froze in midair.

Johnny's voice had the touch of ice. "Let's go, Mr. Johnson, we've fooled around long enough."

There was the look of hopeless resignation on Johnson's pale, dripping face, as he threw a last beseeching look around the room, and started toward the door. I had to try again, although there was the strange feeling that I could never get through to him, that I was talking to a complete stranger, a cold, deadly stranger, who would not be swayed from his purpose.

"Johnny," I pleaded, "don't do this. Don't ruin your life this way; Teak's not worth it. Think of your mother and sister."

There was a slight wavering of the barrel at these words, but it steadied immediately. "Mr. Taylor, I like you, for you have been mighty good to me, and I'm sorry to go against you," he said, without taking his eyes from Teak's cringing bulk. "But this is something that has to be done. Besides, I owe it to Old True. Mom will understand, for she loved him, too."

With those words, he dismissed me, as if I had never existed. With a motion of the gun barrel, he herded Teak toward the door. Just short of the door, Teak balked for a moment, and looked wildly about from terror-stricken eyes.

"Are you going to let him do this?" he cried hoarsely. "My God! You can't. Do something. Do something."

But even as he pleaded, the hopelessness of the situation was reflected in his voice. Right then, there was nothing we could do. With a hair-trigger .45 held cocked in the fist of a kid strung up as tight as a fiddle string, whatever we might be able to do would have to wait.

For Johnny's sake, if not for Teak's, this had to be stopped before it was too late. Grasping at straws, I called to him, "Where are you taking him, kid?"

"Out to my place, Mr. Taylor," he replied, without taking his eyes from Johnson's broad back.

As they moved out the door, I had time to whisper to Griff to get hold of the sheriff. Following them out, I said, "I'm going with you, Johnny."

For an instant, he hesitated, sweeping me with those dark eyes before replying. "Suit yourself, Mr. Taylor. You sit in the front with Mr. Johnson. I'll sit in the back."

Shaking like a leaf, Teak fumbled with the keys, making several attempts before getting them into the lock. He was seemingly beyond speech, and his skin crawling, as the big bore of that gun remained pointed directly between his shoulder blades.

Teak killed the motor twice, before he finally got it started. As we pulled off the square and took the highway north, I looked back at Johnny, trying to catch his eye, to start a conversation, to do anything that would maybe change his mind. But those burning black eyes drilled through me as if I wasn't even there, as if he didn't see me at all.

I noticed two things, though, when I looked around. One, that he had lowered the hammer on that old gun, and two, three cars were pulling away from the curb in front of the shop. And a glance over my shoulder a couple of minutes later, showed me that we had company. The sheriff's car wasn't visible, but I didn't know whether that was good or bad. Right then, I wasn't too sure of anything or anybody.

Johnny's farm lay about six miles out of town and joined Teak's large acreage on the south. They were both only about two miles east of me, as the crow flies, but a good five miles by road. There was one big difference, though, Teak had inherited his, while Johnny's parents had grubbed theirs out of sassafras and persimmon thickets with their hands. They had looked every inch of their tillable ground straight in the face and knew how it came to be.

Teak was driving slowly, but in complete silence. Even then, I noticed that on a couple of occasions, he had gotten off on the shoulder. As much as I disliked him, I couldn't help but feel sorry that he was suffering such an ordeal. He was like a man walking his last mile.

Another glance at the rear view mirror told me that three cars were still with us, but a couple of hundred yards behind. They were being cautious and all for the best. Spook the boy now, and no telling what he might do.

Soon we came abreast of Johnny's south boundary, and I saw that the fence rows were clean and the wire drawn tight. The work of a man with pride showed in every post and staple.

"Turn in at the gate and follow the lane to the right, Mr. Johnson," the boy directed, breaking his silence for the first time since leaving town. Teak moved jerkily, like a mechanical man, acting only on command from that soft voice coming from the rear seat. A hundred yards from the gate, the lane drew close to the foot of a long sloping hill. Here, Johnny tersely called a halt, and quickly climbed out on Teak's side. Keeping his face towards us, he backed up a few steps, well out of reach, but always keeping that gun centered directly on Teak.

When he spoke, it seemed that I could detect a slight change. Still those same cold, flat tones, but now, a slight tremor had crept in. I realized, with further fright, that he was strung up to the point of breaking. Johnson, meanwhile, kept hanging onto the steering wheel, even after he was ordered out.

"Mr. Johnson," he said, "you won't change anything by hanging in that car. It's something that has to be done and on top of the hill is where it has to be."

Teak blanched even more, as the last few words rose on a high note. Slowly, he pulled his hands from the wheel and opened the door. As if in a trance, he turned sideways and placed his feet on the ground. At first, it seemed that his legs would be unable to support him, but after the second attempt, he stood erect, and with dragging feet, started slowly up the hill.

Johnny kept a safe distance, a little behind and to our left. Once more, I tried to talk to him, but the bleakness in his eyes cut my words off in midair, shattered them like a clay pigeon, so they fell useless and silent to the ground between us. Up until then, I had never lost hope that someway, somehow, I would be able to stop him, before it was too late. But now, for the first time, serious doubts were beginning to creep in. Just a wrong move, maybe even one word, might set him off. I had to wait for just the right chance: there would be only one.

For the last few minutes, I had been vaguely aware of the sound of car motors, but hadn't bothered to look around. But with the closing of doors, I turned to see eight men milling around at the foot of the hill. With faces white and drawn, they gazed up at us in awestricken disbelief.

If Johnny heard their arrival, he gave no indication, for locked in his present world of hate, there might not have been room for anything other than Teak Johnson and that driving force that was propelling him headlong toward the deed he felt he must perform.

We were near the crest, when I turned to see the others trailing, not over fifty feet behind. Wordlessly, they moved in our direction, as if pulled by a string, one that couldn't be seen, but was yet too strong to break. Determined expressions were beginning to form on some of their faces, now that some of the shock had worn off, and I knew that they, too, were ready to take almost any chance to end the nightmare.

As I was looking back, I heard a loud gasp from Teak, and his moaning cry of, "Oh, God! No!" I jerked my head around in time to see him collapse, loosely, grotesquely, like a half-filled bag of potatoes. For an instant, I thought I was going to be sick.

Just over the crest, where the hill leveled off, it waited. Beckoning with its emptiness, its mouth gaped wide in gruesome welcome from its position there beside that ugly mound of red clay. Footsteps and exclamations from behind told me that the others had seen it, too. Words of sympathy were also now breaking from the group, as they viewed Teak's sagging body and bloodless face.

Quickly, Johnny mounted the pile of dirt and motioned the rest of us to stand about fifteen feet to his front. There was only the grave between. For a full minute, he just stood there, looking across at us. The bore of that .45 looked big enough for me to crawl into. Again, I wracked my brain for whatever it was that had been bothering me about that gun, but it was no use.

I was unable to suppress the feeling of horror that swept over me, as I viewed that ugly hole in the ground, a full-sized legal grave. The boy must have worked all night. Even then, it would have been impossible for just one slender boy to accomplish, unless motivated by some strange feeling that gave him strength.

Johnny's eyes bore a look of desperation, as they gleamed at us from across that six-foot hole. My skin crawled every time I looked at it. And though I tried not to, my eyes returned to it again and again, in horrified fascination of all it implied.

Teak, still on his knees at the end, seemed unable to tear his gaze from it, as shudder after shudder shook his body. Man's emotions are capable of reversion, within an instant, and without explanation to self or others. And so it was with this group facing the boy. Such a short time before, they had been with him, their feelings of contempt for Teak definitely obvious, as they gloried in the way he was exposed for the kind of person he was, and by the hand of a kid.

But this was different, and had gone much farther than they had ever expected. The reduction of Johnson to the cringing hulk he had become was now a thing of revulsion. No man can enjoy for long the sight of another laying bare before the world, a core of craven fear. Inner shame of one's self for having witnessed that must find a source of anger, an outward direction for hate. Man fears that in all of his brotherhood of men, each is capable of crawling into the deepest depths of shame.

The attitude of the small group around me was becoming more menacing by the minute, and I knew that just one word could cause a rush on the boy, regardless of the consequences. I still found it impossible to believe that he would fire on the rest of us, but he was in no condition to test. Even if he didn't, there would be plenty of time for him to turn the gun on Teak. But I knew that I must wait.

The fact that he had driven himself to the point of exhaustion, both mentally and physically, was definitely obvious. Try as he might, he could not hold back the slight tremor in the hand holding the .45. And it was more than the weight that caused it, I was sure. A constant battle must have been going on within him from the very first. Slowly, but surely, he was being torn asunder, as his true self struggled valiantly to regain control, and to eliminate the character he had become.

For awhile, his eyes rested on Johnson, and I was sure, that for an instant, a flash of pity was reflected there, but if so, it was fleeting. They were cold and chilling again when he turned back to us, but his voice belied the stoical expression. It seemed vibrant and forced, as he spoke rapidly, as if in desperation to get the job finished before he himself should weaken.

Johnson seemed incapable of getting to his feet on his own. In fact, he acted like a man who didn't even know where he was. "Mr. Taylor," the boy's voice broke the silence, "will you and Griff help Mr. Johnson to his feet, please."

It was a command, not a question. Griff growled, as he glared across at him. "You'll get no help from me, you cold-hearted little whelp. He's a broken man now. What more do you want?"

There was an instant chorus of agreement from the others and a small surge forward that halted at the ominous click, as Johnny pulled back that big hammer and turned the gun again directly upon poor old Teak.

I believe they would have gone, even then, if it hadn't been for the explosion in my numbed brain. BROKEN! That was it. Now, I remembered. The firing pin had been broken the day he had shown it to me; just the end, but enough to prevent it from reaching the cap. I hadn't mentioned it, nor had he. If he knew it, he made no mention of getting it fixed. He had only said that he had no intention of ever shooting it.

It was a gamble, but one I had to take. There seemed to be no other way. If it was still broken and he knew it, then the boy's true character had been in control all the time. Within minutes, I knew I would have the answer.

But as uncertain as it was, I felt as if a great load had been lifted from me, and I was swept with a beautiful feeling of relief. Touching Griff on the arm I said, "Come on, Griff, let's help him up."

He recoiled from my touch as if from a lighted match, and angrily struck my hand aside, as he rasped, "What's the matter with you, Kel, have you gone crazy, too?"

Good old Griff. My hand stung where he had struck me, but I only thought more of him. I wouldn't have had him be any other way. Quickly, I whispered, "It's all right, Griff. Everything's gonna be all right. I can't explain now, but trust me, and do it my way. You'll see, soon, that I'm right."

Angry, questioning glares met me from the others, as they waited on Griff's decision. Slowly, the anger left his face, and with it, went the tension of the group, as a small sigh escaped them. But his voice was still brittle, as he said, "Okay, but you had better be right."

"I am, don't worry," I replied. But was I? Maybe I was counting too much on the flimsy possibility of a broken firing pin. But then, that wasn't really all I'd put my trust in. There was the boy I'd known, the one I had to believe was still the stronger of the two characters. I prayed silently that I was right.

Johnny seemed a bit confused by our actions, for he could only guess at what they meant. It was obvious that he felt the need to gather himself together a bit before proceeding. Finally, he again repeated his command of minutes before, "Please get Mr. Johnson to his feet."

Without a word, Griff started walking towards Teak, and I immediately followed. A glance at the boy's gun showed me that he had again lowered the hammer. Was it because he didn't trust himself to leave it cocked? I hoped not.

"Couldn't you get hold of the sheriff?" I asked Griff softly, as I came up beside him.

"He wasn't in," he whispered, "but I left word for him to get out here pronto if he got back in time. And it looks like he didn't," he finished darkly.

Reaching Teak's side, we bent to take an arm each, but to our surprise, he climbed to his feet unaided. From somewhere within, he had scrounged up a little something that resembled nerve. His eyes darted here and there like a cornered animal, looking for some avenue of escape. He appeared ready to bolt, at any second, and I didn't trust my judgment of that firing pin enough to allow that to happen. Any sudden action could trigger the boy into instant retaliation, and there was still too much chance that the gun might not be broken.

My hand tightened on his arm, as I felt a ripple run through him. Quietly, I said to him, "Take it easy, Teak, there's nothing going to happen. Just play along with his game a little while longer."

He turned to stare me directly in the face and his bloodshot eyes bore a wild expression. I wouldn't have believed that so much of a change could have taken place in a man in such a short time. He in no way bore any resemblance to the arrogant, bluffing person he had been earlier that morning.

The baffled expression he wore was of one who doesn't know who or what he can trust. Again, I urged, "Come on, Teak, let's humor him just a little while longer, for I think it's about over."

He still hadn't spoken, when Johnny's voice interrupted. "Mr. Johnson, will you come up here to this clump of bushes, please."

Again, it was more command than question, and as he spoke, he was walking sideways towards a small clump of buckbrush some twenty feet beyond the grave, but all the time, keeping the gun trained on Teak.

Intense curiosity kept everyone quiet, as Teak walked slowly, stiff-legged, towards the spot designated. He looked neither to the left nor right, as he approached the bushes, but kept his eyes focused in hypnotic fascination upon them, as if there was nothing else in the world to see.

Johnny had eased himself around until he was standing at the edge of the undergrowth, but at the same time, keeping all of us under that old equalizer that must surely have been getting mighty heavy by then. As Johnson came up to him, the boy did something that left us all flabbergasted. From his pocket, he pulled a pair of new white canvas gloves.

Holding them out to Teak, he said, "Mr. Johnson, put these on, please."

Mechanically, Teak's hand went out to grasp them, and having done so, stood looking at them bewilderedly, as if he had never before seen a pair of gloves. His fogged mind was really confused now, but not much more than the reeling brains of the rest of us.

Again, Johnny prodded him. "Put them on, Mr. Johnson, for we can't proceed until you do."

Like a child obeying, Johnson pulled on one, then the other. Immediately, Johnny pulled the brush apart, exposing a small pine box. There was no doubt in my mind what that box contained.

"Mr. Johnson." That same cold voice was back again. "Old True is in that box. I want you to pick it up and put it down into the grave."

The fact that he hadn't already been shot dead must have been surprising to Teak. Enough so, that by then, he must have begun to have some hope, for I noticed the back of his neck beginning to turn red, as anger struggled to overcome his fear.

But without a word, he bent to do the boy's bidding, only to be halted, as Johnny spoke again. "You understand that it was necessary for you to wear gloves before you touched that box, don't you, Mr. Johnson? You know, of course, that it's because your hands are not fit to touch Old True's coffin?"

Johnson stared at him in slack-jawed amazement. I believe that he comprehended, but he was slow to answer. Johnny's voice cracked out like a whiplash. "Do you understand that, Mr. Johnson? Do you?"

As the muzzle of the gun lifted to the height of his eyes, the red in Teak's eyes quickly faded, and he blanched as he nodded. Johnny seemed satisfied, for he motioned again towards the box, and stepped back, as Teak picked it up, and with a few steps, set it down at the edge of the grave. Turning then, he slid down inside, reached up for the box, and dragged it off over the edge, and left it resting in the middle of the hole.

Then, as if awaiting further commands, he stood, looking pathetically up at us. He was apparently past asking for help, so without a glance at the boy, I stepped to the edge of the grave and held out my hand. I don't know whether I expected a protest from the boy or not, but none came.

Teak's face bore the look of a man who had just been reprieved from death row. That he had been in the grave and out again, and was still unharmed, was slowly getting through to him with significant impact. Hope was further kindled, as he took in the sympathetic attitude of the rest of us. All at once, he was a man reborn. Almost his old arrogant self, he pulled the gloves from his hands, and threw them viciously to the ground.

Johnny stood starkly alone, and for a minute, his forlorn little figure, outlined against the drab hillside, brought a lump to my throat. I thought of an old saying, "He that has so little to love may only love that more." How true here, with this boy and his dog.

A few scrubby trees stood in the background, cold, naked and bare; their abundant foliage torn from their limbs by an early freeze, leaving exposed the deficiencies of their imperfections, the weakness of structure, the shocking thinness of the unclothed. *How well*, I thought, *did trees compare with man?*

I never was quite sure why, all at once, everyone took for granted that it was all over. But we did, even Teak. That's why the boy's next words hit us like a stroke of lightning and we were spiked to the ground where we stood.

Above the short exclamations bursting from the crowd, his voice rang sharp and clear. "Gentlemen, please stand where you are. I am not finished."

As all stared in open-mouthed stupidity, he continued, "I'm sorry that you other men had to be a part of this, but it was not my doing, for you came uninvited. So, since you are here, please don't interfere, until I'm finished with Mr. Johnson."

That was no fifteen-year-old kid talking. I had an eerie feeling that he had somehow borrowed five years from the future, and had added them to his age, just for a long enough time to get this ordeal over. Then, completely ignoring the rest of us, he said to Teak, "Mr. Johnson, step over to the end of the grave and kneel down facing it."

Sharp protests broke from the crowd, as we, along with Teak, reeled from the blow. Teak started numbly and shook his head like a poleaxed steer. CLICK! The sound of that big hammer was like an explosion and the recovery of Johnson was too incomplete to withstand its meaning.

Instantly, the regained arrogance was gone, and he was, again, the crumbled shell, even worse than before, because for awhile, there had been hope. In complete subjection, he did as he was directed. Without a will or thought of his own, he knelt at the edge of the grave, and with bowed head, awaited the inevitable.

A sinking sensation, that went clear to my boots, left me weak and shaking. And as Johnny stepped up to the rear of Teak, Griff echoed my thoughts, as he exclaimed, "My God! An execution!"

A roar of angry words went up from every throat, and as one, they surged forward. I was sick with the knowledge that I had guessed wrong, and the burden of guilt must rest entirely upon my shoulders. Its weight was staggering, as I bolted with the rest.

And as quickly, we were halted in midstride, as the kid's movement struck us dumb, and the meaning of what he was saying somehow penetrated the density of our passions.

Without even glancing in our direction, he bent to hold a small sheet of paper before the kneeling Johnson, as he said, "Say a prayer for Old True, Mr. Johnson, and then you can go."

It took some time for Teak's numbed mind to grasp the meaning of what he had just heard. Realization was slow in coming. He raised his head to look up at the boy in the manner of a frightened puppy, still fearful that the club, in the hand holding it, will again descend. Finally, acceptance of his deliverance was accented by complete concentration on the paper in his hand, as in a tremulous voice, he began to read the prayer.

Amazed looks were exchanged among members of the group, as the words fell upon our ears. The texture of its contents shook our badly addled thoughts. Though in the beginning, it touched upon the good dog that True had been and asked that he be accepted in dog Heaven; for the most part, it was a plea for Teak himself.

There before us, kneeling at the edge of the grave, Teak Johnson asked that he be forgiven. He prayed that he be granted the strength to change his ways, and that he be lifted out of his narrow self and set on the right path to brotherhood, without losing sight of one most important goal, learning how to become a friend to man.

Complete silence hovered over the hillside after he finished. Teak remained in a kneeling position, with head still bowed, as if turning over in his mind the words he had just said, and from all indications, finding it hard to believe that they had come from him. But, how human it is, to underestimate the power of prayer.

It was Johnny who made the first move as he stepped back from Teak with a sigh. "You can go now, Mr. Johnson, I've done what had to be done. I owed it to Old True. I'm ready now to be turned over to the sheriff; I see that he has just driven up."

None of the rest of us had noticed his arrival, but a quick look showed that he was already climbing rapidly toward us. Our attention was, once more, drawn to Johnny. Lowering the hammer on the old .45, he tossed it to the ground, as he said, "It won't fire anyway."

Elation ran through me, as the others gasped in unison. I hadn't been wrong after all; he was still the same boy I had known. Older, perhaps, in a way that enabled him to be hard when necessary, but underneath, still the same kind, shy lad I had taken to my heart three years before.

Teak was still slowly climbing to his feet, as his mind groped for reality. Once more, a terrible, wracking shudder shook his big body and then he was still. Silently, he stood, staring at the boy, as the pallor faded and the normal red of his complexion returned. For a full minute, those two didn't remove their eyes from one another. The rest of us didn't exist; their world consisted only of themselves and the few feet of ground between.

A glance down the hill showed me that the sheriff was about halfway up and would reach us in about three or four minutes. A lot could be done in that short time, a lot that could make the difference between ruining a boy's life and saving it. But knowing the nature of Teak Johnson, I feared for the worst. He alone would make the decision, and I had little doubt what it would be.

Finally, Teak spoke, his voice the same arrogant bluster as always. "Did you say that gun won't shoot?'

"Yes, sir, that's right. The firing pin has been broken for years." By the way his voice trembled, I saw that he was near to breaking. Nothing but iron will had enabled him to play the character he had assumed, and now with the reversion to his actual self complete, the dam of self-control had little left to support it.

As he answered Teak, his eyes had gone to the sheriff's rapidly approaching figure and he added, "I'll admit everything to the sheriff when you turn me over to him, Mr. Johnson, for I know I'll have to pay."

A glance over his shoulder told Teak that he had but a minute to make up his mind. Looking back piercingly at Johnny's ramrod stiff little figure, trying so hard to be brave, he made his decision.

Scooping up the .45 from the ground, he snarled, "Still trying to tell me what to do are you, you little brat? Well, you've run this show long enough, now, it's my turn. So just keep your trap shut and let me do the talking," and turning to the rest of us, he added, "and that includes you guys, too."

There was no denying his tone; he meant every word he said, maybe more than he had ever meant anything in his life.

Seconds later, Roy Andrews, the sheriff, topped the rise and stopped. For a minute he said nothing, as he took in the scene with serious eyes. Johnson was the first to break the silence.

"Well, sheriff, just in time to help with the burying."

Teak's words must have taken Roy back a bit, for from the look on his face, it was obvious that he had come expecting trouble. Sternly, his eyes drilled into Teak's florid face, as he said, "What's this about the kid here threatening you with a gun?"

Teak looked incredulous at the sheriff and roared with laughter. "Threatening me with a gun? That squirt? Me? Sheriff, you must be joking."

Wave after wave of relief washed over me, now that I knew Teak's decision. A glance at the others led me to believe that they felt the same way. Suspicion flashed in Roy's eyes, as he looked sharply at the rest of us, and finally centered on Griff.

"You, Griff," he barked, "called me in a panic!"

Flushing, Griff looked at Johnson, read the message, and then, with downcast eyes replied, "I'm sorry, sheriff, I misunderstood."

"That's right, sheriff," Teak bellowed, "old Griff here just got excited when he saw the kid show the gun to me and jumped at conclusions, when all the time, he was just trying to sell it to me."

"Sell it to you?" Roy echoed, in obvious disbelief.

"Yeah," Teak answered with a laugh, "and a broken gun, at that. Can you imagine a punk kid trying to get the best of Teak Johnson in a gun deal?"

Roy managed a bleak smile. "No, I can't imagine anyone getting the best of you in any kind of a deal, Teak. But why are all of you out here?"

Immediately, all the bluster was gone, as Teak answered softly, "It's my doing, Roy. I'm ashamed to tell you that I shot the kid's dog yesterday, and I thought the least I could do was to help bury him. The others only tagged along. Just nosey, I guess."

Roy wasn't any fool and his eyes rested on Griff. That a barber would leave his shop unattended on Saturday, of all days, just to tag along to see a dog buried was incredible. If a bunch of men were ever called out and out liars by a man's eyes, it was us. He wasn't at all satisfied with the explanation he had received. He was a good sheriff and believed in the law to the letter, but he also had his share of common horse sense, and knew that it should be applied, sometimes, for the best of all concerned.

"I see, I see," he muttered, as his features softened somewhat. Then he turned to Johnny.

Poor kid, I thought, as I took in that forlorn little figure, still stiffly erect, but held so only by the last shattered remnants of self-control. I knew that he wouldn't lie if Roy asked him for the truth, and I'm sure that Roy knew that, too. All at once, he turned abruptly away, and with a curt warning to Griff to be more sure of the facts next time, strode rapidly back down the hill to his car.

It seemed that everyone was shuffling around and trying to talk at once. They hadn't made up their minds yet just how they would feel about the boy from then on. With everything happening so suddenly, they were still confused. It would take some thinking on.

But there was no doubt in my mind, as I walked over to him and said, "Better be there as soon as possible after school Monday. We'll have a lot of work to do on account of missing today."

Though I was trying to bluff, I made a poor job of it, and he saw right through me. A tremulous smile broke over his dark poker face and his eyes shone with unshed tears, as he answered softly, "Thank you, Mr. Taylor, I'll be there."

He needed to be alone, to find solace in the comforting healing of privacy. So turning quickly away, I said to the others, "Come on, boys, let's get out of here and let the kid get on with his work."

Sensing the reason for my remarks, they turned, and without a word, started following me down the hill, all that is, but Teak. For a minute, he stood staring at the gun he still held, and then with a frown, he threw it contemptuously to the ground. Looking fiercely at Johnny, he growled, "Let that be a lesson to you about ever trying to cheat Teak Johnson, boy. The next time, I might get mad."

As Teak quickly joined us, he left Johnny staring after him, perplexed. It must have been awfully hard for him to comprehend that this was the same man he had escorted earlier in the day.

Teak was still as much on trial as was the kid, so it was a rather silent group that slowly made its way back toward the cars. About halfway down, something impelled me to stop and look around.

When I did, a choking sensation brought me to a sudden stop, and in spite of myself, I felt tears brushing at my eyelids. The others, noticing my actions, stopped, too, and turned to look. Sympathy twisted my insides into knots, as I beheld that pitiful heartrending scene above me at the top of the hill.

I turned in time to see him spill one shovel full of dirt into the hole. The others had witnessed his reaction to the sound of the first clods clattering against the box. The box that was to hold, for all time, the body of his dog. How final it must have sounded to him. How utterly final.

They were in time to see the casting away of the shovel, as he dropped to his knees at the edge of the grave and buried his face in his hands. His frail little shoulders shook with sobs. Deep, soul-wrenching sobs from within, that tore painfully at his entire insides, and left little but the shell of a boy with their passing.

Minutes went by, and still, there was no let up. He was being consumed by his grief and there was nothing we could do. But there was one who would try. The half-sick silence engulfing us was broken by a low moan from Teak, and he started back up the hill.

After a few minutes, he stopped and turned to fasten his eyes on me. His face was that of a stricken man, but his voice was determined as he said, "Taylor, I want to tell you now, don't try to force one of your cull pups off on him. I'm going to see that he has only the best, and that will be the pick of the litter from Ike and Sue."

Right then and there, I knew that I would never again feel harshly towards Teak Johnson. I knew what he meant. Ike and Sue were the leaders of his pack and top dogs in any man's country. Right then, he could call my dogs culls; it was all right with me.

I only nodded my understanding, and we watched, silently, as he climbed the rest of the way up. If Johnny heard him approach his side, he never looked up and the heaving of his shoulders continued. It seemed he was powerless to stop.

Then Teak did something that endeared him to all of us. Suddenly dropping to his knees, he put one big arm around those jerking little shoulders and drew them close to him. Slowly, the sobbing subsided, and when Johnny, at last, raised his tear-streaked face to Teak's strained one, I knew it was time for the rest of us to leave. To stay longer would be an invasion of privacy and one we had no right to make.

I guess the feeling was mutual, for we all turned away at the same time and continued to the cars. Griff expressed the thoughts of all of us, I guess, when he said, "Boy, I wouldn't want to go through anything like that again, but a lot of good has come out of it, after all."

Aye, I thought, a lot of good.

Blaze of Glory

"Right on the heels of Old Big'un, as he headed straight across the bottom towards the river. That coon knowed that death was sure enough a grabbin' at his tail. Bent sure wuz runnin' ... head up ... ears back ..."

And then it had happened like a bomb, and the shame of it still wrenched at his insides, like a grappling hook. He hadn't seen her walk up, didn't know she was there, until she screeched:

"RUN! DID YOU SAY, RUN? THAT DOG, RUN!! Why, Seth Piddle, the last time that dog ever got out of a slow shuffle was four years ago, when Ruthie's banty rooster chased him under the house."

As Seth gaped, in profound shock, that confound woman got purt near hysterical from laughing so hard. Got so weak, she couldn't stand up. Collapsed right there on the floor, all quivery like, and kept right on laughing.

And, of course, since such laughter is contagious, they just all naturally got in on it, until Seth had the only dry eyes there. But not for long. Humiliation and anger at Marthy's betrayal did for him what laughter had done for the others. He was ruined for all time, but worst of all, was the injustice to Old Bent. Others meeting him in the doorway, as they came to see what was so funny, noticed the tears in his eyes, and wondered how a man could laugh until he cried and still look haunted.

The frustrating thing now, the morning after, was the way Marthy was goin' about the house, just as if nothing had happened. Acting just as innocent as a lamb, she was. Didn't do him no good to sulk either, he had decided. If she noticed his surly mood, there was no sign.

Seated on the back steps, he slowly tamped tobacco into his old pipe. The sound of her humming came clearly through the open door. Suddenly, her cheerful tune was just too much, like rubbing salt into an open wound. Rising as quickly as seventy years and creaking knees would allow, he strode towards the back lot. In the shade of the wild cherry tree, he stopped, looking down with affection at the motionless figure that lay there. The least he could do was to apologize to Old Bent.

Bent's response to his master's presence was dynamic. One eye opened slightly and a quiver rippled the end of his tail, as he greeted Seth with spontaneous affection. The old man's seamed face beamed with pride.

"There, there now, old fellow, calm down," he said soothingly. "Don't carry on so. Just take it easy. You need your rest, so don't get so excited. She's not gonna get away with it, I'll promise you that. Just you relax now and leave everything to me."

Satisfied that the old dog had finally relaxed, Seth patted the big gray head of the old saddle-back, and quietly tiptoed away. "That's good," he muttered to himself. "The old boy is just plain smart. He's alayin' there athinkin' and plannin' for when we can make Marthy eat her words."

The thought of making Marthy eat even one word that she had said was wonderful to think about, but as to her eating several, well, that was almost too much to contemplate. The pleasure of such speculation brought a crafty grin, and Marthy, watching through the kitchen window, frowned apprehensively, and wondered.

Now that she thought about it, maybe she had made it just a little too strong the night before, but then, it wasn't something she had planned. It had just happened. The thought of that fat Old Bent getting into a run was just too much. Even now, a chuckle bubbled up, at the merest recollection.

But that crafty grin on Seth's face had her worried. Fifty years' man and wife, had taught her the meaning of such a look. He was up to something. Well, she had learned something else, too. The best defense was a strong offense. Take the bull by the horns, right off, before he could get set.

As Seth stomped into the kitchen, a scowl had replaced the grin, but she was ready and waiting. Hands on hips, feet braced, steel-rimmed spectacles pushed down onto the bridge of her nose, and all one hundred pounds of her sizzling with indignation, she pounced upon the poor, defenseless, and unsuspecting Seth.

"Well, I sure wish I was a hound, tied up at that box out there. Maybe I would get some attention around here."

Seth, taken back momentarily by her outburst, rallied quickly. "Are you right sure now, Marthy? Would you really like to be that dog out there? Ain't you afraid that if you was, somebody would come along and poke fun at you, and make you a laughingstock?"

Marthy paused, the sharpness of her tongue tempered, somewhat now, by regret. But then the old fool hadn't oughta lied like that. And she couldn't give in now, not after fifty years of never losing a battle. "It's your own fault for telling such lies. You know it was all of five or six years ago, that Bent caught that coon. And besides, he was in a trap, to boot."

"Warn't neither," Seth howled. "Besides, he'd done pulled out."

"Yeah," Marthy added, "and apullin' six feet of fence rail behind him."

"Well, maybe I did exaggerate a mite, but that didn't give you no call to carry on so. Besides, Old Bent's got feelings."

"FEELINGS!" Her voice was rising again. "I'll say he's got feelings, and all in that big old belly. That's the only part of him that's still alive, and you know it. I know it's alive cause it's always growling."

"That ain't so, and I don't know it. He's got to eat and he's plenty alive. He's just building up strength for this winter. He knows there's no use to thresh around out there when the season's not in. He's just smart, that's all, and is saving hisself for when it counts."

Marthy's hands flew up in exasperation. "Saving himself, is he? Well, in that case, when he does cut loose, it really oughta be a humdinger; cause he's been saving himself just about all of his life."

At mention of the word 'life,' Marthy's eyes began to gleam strangely. An alarmed Seth gasped at what she might be thinking.

His mouth opened once or twice, as desperately he tried to inject some words, any words, into the conversation, in order to erase that possible thought from her mind.

But he was too slow. "Say," she asked, "just how old is he, anyway? Ain't he about old enough to …?"

"MARTHY!"

His tone was so pleading and fear-stricken that, in spite of herself, she was pricked momentarily by a twinge of conscience. "Well, all right," she grumbled, "I guess we can just wait for nature to take its course. And that won't be too long, either, if he keeps alaying out there like that. The honeysuckle vine is gonna climb all over him and choke him to death, anyhow."

"Marthy, you quit talking like that and lower your voice. Do you want him to hear you?"

"Hear me! Ye gods! He ain't heard nothing but the rattle of that feed pan for nigh onto twenty years."

"He ain't that old, and you know it," Seth screeched. "He can hear plenty good. It's just that he's too sensible to waste time on foolish sounds."

Marthy squinted and nodded her head approvingly. "Well, now, you've got a point there, for if there's anything that ain't foolish to him, it's food. And he can sure enough hear that feed pan a long ways off. Oh, well, there's always the honeysuckle vine."

A wild-eyed Seth stared foolishly at her, then bolted from the house. Again, she felt a brief twinge of conscience, but it faded quickly. A few minutes later, she laughed softly, as she glanced out of the kitchen window. Seth was industriously cleaning away the honeysuckle from a large area around Bent's box.

As the late summer days wore on, things returned to normal. Marthy was relieved that Seth had, apparently, forgotten all about it. But as September faded into October and the nights began to grow more crisp, there was the slightest indication of a change.

Occasionally, she had caught Seth, with Old Bent in tow, taking walks around the yard. Lately, they had become more frequent, and, at times, he could be heard urging the old dog into a trot. Also, it had become obvious that Seth did not pass up the slightest chance to inject the old dog into their conversation.

Caution, born of long experience, bade her to tread softly. He really had her worried now, for the reason behind his actions still remained elusive. Convinced, finally, that he was trying to bait her into some kind of argument over the dog, she remained more determined than ever to avoid the entire subject.

It was now Seth's time to be worried. Things that ordinarily were enough to set her off, now seemed to make no impression at all. Impatience seemed to be pushing at him, as his insistence on bringing up the subject of the dog became more pronounced daily. Bragging didn't get a rise out of her anymore, and as October rapidly faded, his actions began to border upon desperation. He was completely beside himself, when he saw Marthy out at old Bent's box with some cornbread.

This was too much. She had to be sick. But on second thought, maybe it was something else. Maybe she had … no, that couldn't be possible, but then maybe … why, yes … that had to be it … Marthy had turned over a new leaf. And after all those years. She was ashamed of insulting Old Bent. It was like a miracle come true. Well, bless her old naggin' heart.

In that case, Seth could forgive, too, and felt that so could Old Bent, given a little time and some more of that cornbread. Sympathy for her attempts to bring about a reconciliation with the old dog became overwhelming, when he saw her giving him fresh water, and even stooping to pet the old fellow.

It was time to let Marthy know that her attempts to make amends had not gone unnoticed. He was all set to tell her right then and there, but became so choked up at the unbelievable sight of her scratching Bent's ears, that before he could regain his composure, she had entered the house.

The change in Marthy was something to be thought on for awhile. Why she was downright human, after all! Bless her old soul again. But the task of convincing Old Bent would take a lot of doing. The old dog seemed inclined to disbelieve, for after about twenty minutes of serious lecture, he groaned miserably and rolled over on his other side.

So while Marthy busily cleaned and waxed the kitchen floor, Seth kept after him to find just a little bit of forgiveness in his heart for a repentant Marthy. But as the snores began to rise steadily, Seth shook his head in discouragement. It wasn't going to be easy. Poor old fellow must have really been cut to the bone. Maybe he would forgive, for he was proud. Then, what? Marthy was proud, too. Almost as proud as Old Bent. She would go just so far towards a reconciliation and no further.

Sudden fear clutched at him. In the face of Bent's scorn, she might change back to her old self. A chill ran over him at the thought of such a horrible possibility. Well, he couldn't let that happen. Maybe Bent was just playing hard to get. In that case, then he would just hurry things along.

For once, he was insistent in his attempt to get the old dog up on his feet. Finally, after considerable lifting, the job was done, and Bent stood alone. Still half asleep, but reelingly erect. Hardening himself to the pleading look in the half-opened eyes, Seth snapped on the leash and pointed him towards the house.

The more he thought about his plan, the better he liked it. If Marthy saw that the old dog had come to her, she would just naturally be overjoyed. Man, would she be happily surprised. Impatiently, he hurried Bent into a faster, if reluctant, walk.

Anticipation of the warm and loving reunion about to take place, sent shivers of delight up his spine. Urging Bent into a faster gait, the back porch was soon reached, and with a small boost, Bent was upon it and headed towards the door. As if to prolong the agony of awaited joy, Seth paused a moment to look affectionately down at Old Bent, who stood with head down and sides heaving.

"Why, you old rascal," he said softly, "you're plum shy about the whole thing."

Old Bent quivered in answer, and plopped down with a thud. Slightly irritated, Seth hoisted him to his feet. But with his hand on the knob, he paused again, and came to an instant decision. He would send Bent in alone. The reunion was apt to be tearful and kinda mushy like, so those two ought to be alone at a time like that. Quickly opening the door, he pushed a protesting Bent inside and pulled it to, stepping to the side, as he did so.

Breathlessly, he waited for Marthy's cry of joy. One minute passed ... then two. Ah! He could hear the tap of her heels now, coming through the living room towards the kitchen. The anticipation was killing him, as eagerly he listened for her happy exclamation.

Would she never see him? Seth clearly visualized the tender and touching scene about to unfold. A shy and hesitant Bent, standing there with adoration shining in his eyes, as he waited for acceptance. Surely she must see him now, poor old fellow, how hard it must be for him to wait. Ah!! There! She ... she ...

Seth was to say later, that on that day he lost his hair; that it just plain raised up and flew off his head. Her screech was a wonder of magnificent volume. Unofficial records of females reaching high C fell by the wayside, as her voice rose higher and higher, until, as Seth described it later, "She must've run right offen the scale."

On quaking knees, he moved to the door and peered inside. Marthy had all the appearance of a wild woman. With face contorted, hands outstretched like eagle claws, and staggering steps, she was advancing with terrible determination towards a most definite spot on the kitchen floor.

Seth stood, in shocked disbelief. Where was all the love and affection that she was supposed to show? Something had sure gone wrong. Then he saw, and went cold with horror. The floor still shone with a fresh coat of wet wax, while in the middle, stretched out and sleeping soundly, lay Old Bent. She was almost to the old dog, but missed one stride, to snatch the rolling pin from the cabinet, as she went by.

Now, Seth wasn't necessarily a brave man, especially when it came to facing up to a well-armed Marthy. But that was his dog alayin' there, at death's door, and there was no time for thinking. Flinging the door wide, he hit the fresh-waxed floor in what might have been a dramatic charge to the rescue, if a pair of number tens hadn't suddenly seemed to have a mind of their own.

First, the right, and then the left, took off for the ceiling, like a pair of flushed quail, while the rest of poor Seth headed for the floor. When the dishes quit rattling, he lay stretched out, full length, beside the still prostrate form of Old Bent, who snored blissfully on.

Startled by his violent entrance, Marthy halted. Her eyes bulged with the desire to tear them both to shreds. A badly-shaken Seth looked up at the trembling woman, and knew that he must rise or expire there on the floor. Quickly, before she could regain the use of her tongue, he scrambled to his feet, and snatched the dangling rolling pin from her hand. From a fall that would have ordinarily kept him grunting about the house for weeks, he emerged, not only unscratched, but a mighty and daring warrior.

Marthy still sputtered, open-mouthed, at the change in him. She could only stare, in silent amazement. Seth was ready to do battle. His faded, blue eyes shone with furious light, as he planted himself firmly between her and the sleeping dog. Waving the rolling pin wildly, he faced her staunchly, as his words poured out with reckless abandon.

"NO, YOU DON'T, WOMAN! You ain't about to touch a hair of this dog while I'm alive."

Again, he didn't like the look in her eyes at the mention of the word alive. Her next words supported his convictions. "Well, now, we can fix that in a hurry. You first, then."

Briefly, his great burning courage all but flickered out, but regaining the iron hard composure that he always knew he had, he plunged, once more, to the attack.

"You just plain ain't got no appreciation, woman, no appreciation at all. You wuz plum set on doing Old Bent in, when all the time, he thought he wuz doin' you a favor."

"FAVOR! FAVOR!" she raged. "Since when, is ruining a fresh-waxed floor, some kind of favor? The only kind of favor that old crow bait can do me is to disappear from the face of the earth."

Little tacky sounds came from beneath Seth's feet, as he hopped around in the fresh wax. "Crow bait, is he? Well, I'll tell you, he just come up here to show you that he don't hold no grudges. His big old heart wuz just plain full of forgiveness, cause he knowed how hard you had been tryin' to make up."

Seth paused, took a deep breath, and continued, "Marthy, you're a cold-hearted woman. He, most likely, won't ever forgive you now. You've flung his friendship back into his face, and he won't ever forget. He's proud, Old Bent is."

Martha spewed and sputtered in wrath, in effort to get her words out. "Forgive me! Hurt him! Proud! Proud! He ain't got enough life to be proud. Look at him! You telling me, he ain't dead? He ain't heard a thing that's gone on here."

Seth raised his hand in what was supposed to be a command to stop, but her tirade flowed on. "Now, get it out of here, before IT gets stuck fast to that wax, and you have to bury a piece of floor with it."

Seth's anger fled, before the horror of her implication. "Now you've done it, for sure," he said, shaking his head sadly. "I know he won't ever forgive you now."

Frustration lent pitch to his voice, as he thundered, "AND DON'T CALL BENT AN IT, MARTHY, THAT THERE'S A COON DOG …"

Something within her seemed to snap. All her determination of past weeks to avoid this particular subject vanished. And the trap that had gone unsprung all this time, despite Seth's crafty baiting, at last, had its victim.

PART TWO

Harshly and mockingly, her voice rang out. "COON DOG! Why, I could come just as near to catching a coon, as that old piece of lard!"

She knew instantly, by the flash of triumph in Seth's eyes, that she had made a mistake. "Well, now," he chortled, "so you are just as good a coon dog as Old Bent!"

Briefly, panic swept her and, for once, she fluttered for an answer. But quickly regaining control, she snapped, "I didn't say I *was* a coon dog. And don't you dare call me one, Seth Piddle."

Seth was completely beside himself. After all these years, he finally had her on the defensive. "All the same thing, Marthy. All the same thing."

"It's not nary such a thing. All I said was, that I could come just as near to catching a …"

As she came to a halt, a gasp of dismay escaped her. The germ of an idea was beginning to break through, and it was not pleasant to contemplate. Oh, darn him, for being able to make her so mad.

He added the finishing touches to her sentence. "A coon just as easy as Old Bent. So that's the same as saying you're a dog."

"DON'T YOU DARE CALL ME A DOG!!"

Seth literally hopped up and down with joy. He never thought the day would come when he would have the upper hand. It was the chance of a lifetime. But with all his eager anticipation, discretion still seemed the better part of valor. Marthy was proud, too. Almost as proud as Old Bent. There was a limit on just how far she could be pushed, and as he noticed her eyes beginning to dart here and there about the kitchen, he decided to back off a little.

"Well, of course, I know you're not really a dog, Marthy," he said in sympathetic tones, "cause a dog's got feelings."

Even he was dismayed at how these words sounded, and there was no doubt of his mistake when her screech rose up to scorch the ceiling, and the blue birds on the wallpaper sought cover beneath the leaves of the twigs on which they were sitting.

"I'll say it again. That fugitive from a graveyard cain't feel nothin.' Cain't feel nothing cause it's plum stone dead, and dead things don't feel. It's been dead for years, only it just ain't buried."

As she stopped to get her second wind, Seth, from force of habit, edged toward the back door. But upon the very threshold of flight, from some inner recess of his gaunt old frame, came one last ounce of courage. Nothing was more important than to see Marthy eat those words. If he never lived another day, it would be worth it.

But he faltered too long and Marthy struck again. He was totally unnerved by her complete change of tactics. From a wild, raging woman, she had suddenly turned into a soft and sympathetic female. He found the change in her absolutely uncanny.

With luminous eyes, she slowly walked over to him, and gently laid her hand upon his trembling shoulder. Smiling sadly up into his panic-stricken eyes, she murmured, "It's all right, Seth, dear. I understand now."

He wanted to back away from the touch of her hand, but his knees had suddenly become too weak to function. He tried twice to speak, before he was able to croak, "Under … understand what, Marthy?"

Her small hand patted his arm tenderly, before she answered. "Why, what it is about Old Bent that has worried me so much. And you've known all along, you poor dear, but chose to carry your burden alone. Of course, you just couldn't bring yourself to do it. Well, dear, you don't have to worry anymore. I'll do it for you."

Stark, raw terror stalked him as he stared, with dismay, into her upturned face. "D … d … do … wha … what, Marthy?'

He quivered, like a thoroughbred at the post, as she patted him again, before answering. "Why, bury him, dear. It must be done, cause he's dead, you know."

Seth could only gape foolishly under the impact of her words. Reeling helplessly, his mouth opened and shut like a beached salmon, but his confused brain refused to function. Then, she literally, ripped him asunder.

Gazing apprehensively at the still prostrate form of Old Bent, she all but whispered, "I'll tell you … it's downright scary."

Seth gulped. "What's … what's … scary … Marthy?"

"Why the fact that IT'S dead, but still eats. Why IT even gets upon ITS feet and moves around sometimes."

For Seth, it was all a terrible nightmare, as she continued, "Lord, it's downright awful. I'll go dig the grave, while you carry IT out. Then you can leave, so's you won't have to see."

Quickly, she moved towards the door, decisiveness in her every action. But by her very movement, the spell was broken, and Seth was no longer immobilized. Dismay fled before anger, as he planted himself in the doorway. His formidable appearance forbade her to take another step. The wildness in his eyes was a terrible thing to see; he became a raging lion.

Now, it was Marthy's time to quake. My goodness! What had she done? He was a man gone berserk. Loudly, he roared, "HOLD UP THERE, WOMAN. DON'T TAKE A NARY OTHER STEP!"

And she held, poised, but steady. Her temporary indecision was cue enough for Seth, and his newfound courage burned higher. It was a strange and thrilling position in which he found himself. Exhilarated by this new feeling, he plunged ahead.

"It's high time we settled this thing, for once and all, Marthy. You've done insulted Old Bent for the last time. There he lays, so hurt that he cain't even raise up his head. You sure had oughta be ashamed of yourself."

Marthy was not one to remain on the defensive for long. Fairly sizzling with indignation, her voice held all of its old snap. "HURT, IS HE! That cain't be, cause dead things don't feel no hurt; NOW GET IT OUT OF HERE."

Seth swelled up to what he thought must be size enough to purt near fill the whole kitchen. Grabbing his hat from his head, he slammed it to the floor. "I've told you for the last time, don't call Bent IT. That there's a ..."

Her laugh rang out scornfully. "A coon dog! BALONEY!! And I've told you, for the last time, that he ain't no more a coon dog than ..."

In her anger, caution had taken to its heels. Again, she had unwittingly nibbled at the trap. With the sweet taste of victory so close, Seth closed in fast.

"THERE! You said it again; that you're a better coon dog than Bent. All right, by gum, let's see you prove it!"

Marthy could only stare, aghast at what he had implied. Finally, she stammered, "Prove ... prove it. Wha ... what do you mean ... prove it?"

Seth's whole being reeked of extreme joy. "Why, it's plain simple, Marthy. Old Bent has done gone and challenged you to a hunt. Then we'll just see who can tree a coon."

Surely, it was all a bad dream, she told herself. It must be. But as she staggered to a nearby chair, his next words convinced her that he was serious. "Yes, sireee, that's the only way to do it; a three-hour hunt, UKC rules. That way, it will be all fair and square. I'll carry the score card."

Her mind reeled under the realization of what she had let herself in for. There just didn't seem to be any face-saving way out. Though she knew but little about night hunt procedure, one thing was all too clear. Seth must not be allowed to carry the score card. Already, her fertile mind was beginning to work on the germ of an idea, but much depended upon somebody else acting as judge.

Her small foot lifted and came down with a thud. "Okay! It's a deal, but on three conditions."

Seth was reckless in his newfound happiness. "All right, Marthy, just name 'em."

"Well, first, I get to pick the night."

Seth nodded his head in complete approval.

"Then, Charley will be the judge."

Instantly, Seth's face became set with his howling expression. "Charley! Now, how would I know if it was fair, if he judged? He's always been jealous of Old Bent. No, Marthy. He might cheat."

She was indignant. "HE might cheat! Well, you're crazy, if you think I'd trust you to carry that card. It's Charley or no hunt."

He hesitated but a few seconds. He couldn't let anything spoil his game now. "Oh, all right," he grumbled. "But I'll be watching him every minute."

"Uh huh," she snorted. "And unless I miss my guess, Old Bent will be right there watching you watch him. So I guess between the two of you, you can keep him straight."

"Now, you look here, Marthy!"

She was not about to be drawn into another argument. "Now, the third thing is this. If I win, you have to promise to quit bragging about IT; no more lies."

Even in all of his eagerness to obtain her full agreement, he could not surpress a shudder at her apparent determination. But her winning was just too ridiculous to even imagine, and he had to get this settled before she changed her mind.

"Lying!" he exclaimed. "Who's been lying? And quit calling IT an IT." Now she even had him doing it. Durn her, anyway.

"Marthy smirked and nodded her head sagely. "Well, I'm glad to see that you finally agree with me."

Even as a sharp retort teetered on Seth's lips, she snapped, "Well, is it a deal?"

Seth nodded sullenly. "Yes, but it sure is a stupid thing to have to promise not to tell lies. As if I ever would lie about Old Bent."

There was much to be done. Marthy had selected the following Saturday night, four days hence, for the big hunt. This was her choice. Just wouldn't want to go too long, with what she had in mind for Seth on her conscience, she told herself, smiling in anticipation.

It was a puzzled, but not too surprised Charley who appeared at the house on Wednesday afternoon. A longtime friendship had prepared him for almost anything. Marthy greeted him warmly. With Seth away at the general store, this was the chance she had waited for.

Charley went right to the point. "I've just seen Seth, Marthy. What in the tarnation is that old coot up to this time?"

A broad smile spread over his face, as she unfolded her plan. "Marthy, this will be the chance of a lifetime, and for his own good, too. But let's make it two, just to be safe. You know, Old Bent did get in on a few coons when he was younger, with other dogs."

After a hearty laugh between them, Charley went over some of the finer points of the rules. Seth would be quick to take advantage of every minor infraction, they knew. If this was to be a thorough squelching, then nothing must be overlooked.

Final plans made, Charley turned to leave, then stopped. Looking quizzically at Marthy, he asked, "Now, what is the one thing that will rouse Old Bent, besides food?'

Marthy's face split from ear-to-ear. "Why, Carrie Wells' old tomcat. That's one thing that will get him on his feet besides that feed pan."

Charley grinned and nodded his head. "Well, it won't hurt to copper our bets, just a little. See you Saturday night, Marthy."

PART THREE

Seth spent much of his time with Old Bent. The once a day drag around the house had now been increased to three. A liquid vitamin bottle had suddenly appeared, and its contents liberally added to the daily ration, along with a frequent dish of chopped liver. When Marthy caught sight of Seth attempting to spray Bent's nostrils with an atomizer, her loud laughter could no longer be contained.

The hunt appeared to be a well-kept secret, which was, most definitely, to Marthy's liking. The whole thing was just too ridiculous. Since it was, of course, understood that Marthy would have to go through the farce dependent upon eyes alone, her purchase of the most powerful electric lantern she could find brought no more than a grunt from Seth. He had polished the globe on his old lantern a half dozen times, and had laid in a good supply of batteries.

On Saturday, Seth reckoned as how Old Bent wouldn't be exercised that day, due to the danger of him becoming overtrained. A full hour before dark, he started donning his hunting clothes. Slowly and elaborately, he attended to his dress, checking each item thoroughly, as if to satisfy himself that it would hold up through the grueling hours ahead. Had he been a little less attentive to his gear, and more observant of things down toward the spring hollow, he might have noticed a shadowy figure pause at the dogwood tree above the spring, before it flitted ahead down the branch, to stop again at the scrub walnut to the right of the forks.

Then he really would have been puzzled, as the figure swung a gunny sack from its shoulders, and unmindful of the growling and hissing that came from it, stuffed it into the end of a hollow log some several yards to the left of the branch.

Not until Charley walked into the backyard, did Marthy calmly pull on a pair of galoshes, slide into a pair of Seth's overalls, cut off considerably, wrap a scarf about her head, pull on an old windbreaker, pick up her lantern, and announce that she was ready.

Seth stood waiting impatiently, but Old Bent seemed much more calm than his master; too calm for Seth, who began a furtive attempt to poke him to his feet, as the undeniable sound of snores arose from the prostrate form.

Charley still found it all a bit unreal, as he surveyed the contestants. Seth, tall and lanky, towered over the pint-sized Marthy, like a pine over a scrub cedar. But as her sharp eyes blinked from behind the steel-rimmed spectacles, and the knot of gray hair on the back of her head bobbed up and down with each quick movement, he was reminded that dynamite caps were small packages, too.

With grave formality, he proceeded to fill out the score cards. A little apologetic, he said to Marthy, "Now, here, where it says dog's name ... I'll have to put Marthy."

Her only answer was a loud snort, but something resembling a choking sound came from suspiciously near the spot where Seth was standing. With Charley leading, the trio left the yard, heading toward the upper end of the spring hollow. Within a few minutes, Charley stopped, took out his watch, and announced that time had started; rather shyly notifying Marthy that she didn't have to call herself until after three minutes had passed. But, upon turning to Seth, he burst in a loud laugh. Old Bent still dangled from the end of the leash. He had forgotten to turn him loose.

A fumbling Seth quickly unsnapped the leash, as he snarled, "What's so goldarned funny? I didn't have him loose because I didn't want no edge a'tall. That there dog is charged up like a dynamo, and I want Marthy to have an even break."

Old Bent did break away, almost immediately, to a distance of six or seven feet, where he found a pile of leaves to his liking, and at once, flopped down. A startled Seth stared, shut his eyes, turned his head away, opened them, and looked back again. It wasn't a bad dream, the old dog was still there, curled up, with eyes shut.

By this time, Charley and Marthy were reduced to blubbering hulks. Finally, too weak from laughing to get to his feet, Charley just lay flat on his back, gasping. Marthy had all but collapsed, but had managed to remain on her knees.

Yanking a protesting Bent to his feet, Seth glared at the others and asked, "Well, is this a hunt or a laughing party?"

Slowly, Charley staggered to his feet, mumbling, "I don't know,

Seth. I just don't know."

Seth led the way. Old Bent was actually trotting in an effort to keep up, but still fell steadily behind, as Seth, if anything, increased his pace. At the near edge of the branch, Seth pulled up and turned to his companions.

Pointing indignantly at Marthy, he said, "Judge, how about scratching her for not hunting? She's not been outta the lantern light yet. Don't see Old Bent around here, he's out there aknockin' these hollows dry, trying to scare up a coon track.

Charley nodded dryly. "Yeah, that he is; only he thinks you've got one in your hip pocket. Turn around, Seth."

As he whirled, Seth swallowed a good-sized chunk of pride. There was a yip, as one of his feet tromped the toes of Bent's right front foot. Finally, after much pounding on the back, Seth's coughing subsided. Still a little green around the gills, but otherwise undaunted, he declared, "Well, I swear, he's got a bigger heart than I thought. He's just aholdin' hisself back, so's to give Marthy a head start."

Charley only shook his head silently. Then, with Marthy's best interests in mind, started walking down the branch. Seth had decided to ignore the presence of Old Bent at his heels. He had taken only a few steps, however, when Marthy's voice stopped him.

"Now you two, just hold up a danged minute. It's time we got one thing straight. What's this about the Judge having the right to scratch one of the contestants?'

"I'm sorry, Marthy, if I failed to explain that to you," Charley quickly answered. "That's one of the penalties. If certain rules are broken, then the one that breaks them gets scratched."

Marthy's hundred pounds seemed to double in size. "Oh, they do, do they? Well, let me tell you something, Charley Riggs. If you as much as lay a hand on me, you'll think you tangled with a buzz saw. If there's any scratching to be done, I'll do it. And you'd better believe that."

A dumbfounded Charley looked around for an assist in explanation from Seth, but that gentleman was already twenty feet away and still backing up. But as he patiently explained, her feathers slowly became unruffled, and the hunt resumed.

Clearly remembering her conversation with Charley on Wednesday, Marthy stepped out briskly. Crossing the branch, she started down the other side, carefully scanning the ground as she went. Suddenly, she stopped, playing her light on the ground at her feet. Then she announced calmly, "Strike me."

Instantly, Seth set up a howl. "Whata ya mean, strike me? There ain't no 'me' on that score card."

Glad for the darkness in which to hide his gleeful smile, Charley said, "It's all right, Seth. She means strike Marthy. Okay, Marthy. You're struck for 100 points."

She hadn't stopped to argue, but was already several yards down the branch. Seth was still standing flabbergasted, but rallying quickly, he loudly exclaimed, "By gum, she's a durn silent trailer! Scratch her, Judge, for not opening on track!"

"Now, Seth," Charley protested, "don't you think that's going a little too far?"

Having heard, Marthy called out, "It's all right, Judge. I'll open on track. Anything to keep that old coot's mouth shut."

Then, as good as her word, a high-pitched and quavering yoo-yoo-yoo came floating back to them, topped off with, "I've struck a coon track; I've struck a coon track." Then for good measure, "A half-grown female coon track; yoo-yoo-yoo."

Seth just couldn't believe his ears—tried to speak, but could only say, "You … you … cain't," but since nobody was listening, gave it up, and crossed over to where he had seen her looking at the ground.

A heavy lead weight seemed to have suddenly lodged in the pit of his stomach. There, clearly outlined in the mud beside the branch, was full a set of fresh coon tracks, just about half-grown. Old Bent stood on the opposite bank, droopily blinking across at him. Excitedly, the old man called him over and pointed with trembling finger.

Bent slowly sniffed the designated spot, wiggled the end of his tail a little, and grunted. Then, with Seth standing prayerfully by, he walked back and forth along the bank, but seemed unable to become interested in any place except where the tracks showed. Finally, he looked sadly up at Seth, then sat down, and gazed mournfully down at them.

From a hundred yards down the branch, Marthy's soulful yoo-yoo-yoo came beautifully loud and clear. In Charley's opinion, Seth was dangerously near the explosion point, so he said, "Go ahead and encourage him, Seth. We will forget that part of the rules tonight." Seth tried, tried real hard, but Old Bent just sat and refused to budge, as he held those four tracks on point, as if daring them to get up and walk away. Then Seth heard a haunting and fear-laden sound. Marthy's yoo-yoo-yoo had changed, too.

"Yah-yah-yah ... I'm treed ... Tree me ... I mean, Marthy ... Tree Marthy ... Yah-yah ..."

Charley checked the time and remarked that it was 8:20. "Wanna wait the five minutes, Seth?" he asked.

"Might as well go on in," Seth growled. "Taint likely she'll leave the tree. Besides, Old Bent don't think she's got a coon anyway. Probably a possum."

Marthy was treeing solidly, in what to Charley, seemed a mighty cheerful voice. He couldn't resist saying, "Sure got a good tree mouth, hasn't she, Seth?'

Seth glared at him for several steps before he said, "Listen, boy, that woman's got plenty of mouth, ain't no doubt about that. Oughta have, by gum. She's had a hundred years of practice, and I've got the scars to prove it."

As they drew closer, they could see her light bouncing up and down, all over the tree. A little further, and they saw that she was literally dancing a jig around the tree. Walking into the circle of her light, Charley caught a wink from under her scarf, and caught himself just in time to keep from laughing. Seth was right at his heels, but Bent didn't seem to have followed them.

Seth stood spellbound, gazing at a half-grown coon, clinging to the top fork of a large dogwood. Charley rudely snapped him out of his trance, by saying, "Well, Seth, I'd say that's sure enough a coon. Wouldn't you?"

"I don't know if it is or not," the old man snarled. "It's mighty light colored and that tail looks awfully slick to me."

"Well, now," Charley said dryly, "in that case, maybe you better climb up and take a closer look. Then you can check to see if it's a female or not, too."

Seth's grunt contained a thousand words better left unsaid. Marthy had quit treeing and was just standing there, with a look of triumph on her face.

As Charley brought the score card up to date, Seth walked back down to the branch. He was obviously worried about old Bent's absence. Turning to Charley, he said, "Old Bent must be working on a cold one. He never was one to open much at first."

Then looking disgustedly in Marthy's direction, he added, "Pop ups, like this one here, don't interest him none a'tall. He wants the tough ones, he does."

Marthy's cackling laughter was like a file upon his nerves. "Yes, sir, Charley," she exclaimed, "he likes' em so tough, that right now, he's a setting down there, trying to make them tracks turn into a treed coon. That old dog's got a heart like a lion, he has."

Seth glared daggers at her, then said, "All right, Judge, she opened more than three times, so mark her struck."

"Now, wait a minute," Charley began, but Marthy cut in quickly, "Sure, go ahead and strike me, Charley. I smell one ahead down the branch there, anyway."

Immediately, she started off, and soon, her yoo-yoo-yoo came winging back to them. Seth stood crestfallen and open-mouthed, staring after her. Even Charley felt a twinge of conscience at his pathetic expression. "Want me to wait here while you go look for your dog?" he asked sympathetically.

Seth snorted disdainfully. "Look for him? Man, how in the world would I go about looking for a dog that's hunting like he is? I'll just ease back up the branch a bit, so's I can hear him if he's way off runnin' someplace. Sure cain't hear nothin' with all that catawallin' down there."

Charley waited until Seth's light bobbed out of sight around the bend, then went quickly to the big log and jerked out the sack. With one eye out for Seth's light, he untied the mouth, and dumped the snarling, growling contents upon the ground. A big striped, puffed-up tomcat lit all spraddled out, hissed once or twice, and was gone like a streak. And none too soon, for Seth's light had reappeared.

With a start, Charley realized that he had forgotten Marthy completely. An ear cocked now in her direction, showed that she was treed solid. A stunned Seth, too, had heard, as he drew abreast of Charley, with Bent at his heels.

Charley clucked sympathetically. "Well, Seth, looks like she's got another pop up. Just don't seem possible, does it?"

Seth seemed to find conversation a difficult task, but finally managed to mutter, "Not with her, son. Not with her. Impossible with a human, but not with her."

Picking up his lantern, Charley started down the branch to a treeing Marthy. He hadn't missed the relief reflected in Seth's eyes, that no questions had been asked about Old Bent. With each step, he expected to reap results from the gunny sack contribution, but had just about given it up as a miss, when the air was suddenly electrified by Bent's heavy bawl.

Turning, he beheld a man and dog transformed. Bent actually resembled a hound, as he trotted around with tail up and nose to the ground. Seth was so elated that his hopping about was obviously interfering with the old dog's attempts to get the track straightened out. In a couple of minutes, however, Bent lined up in a trot, straight away from the branch. An excited Seth stood, spellbound, quietly listening.

Without a word, Charley struck Bent as first, on a separate strike. His estimation of time passed since Marthy treed would not be challenged. Bent's race was of short duration. At about a hundred yards from the starting point, he suddenly started saying, "Come and get it."

"Tree, Bent! Tree, Bent!" Seth yelled, in wild acclaim. And as Charley made the entry, the old man did a war dance around his lantern.

But Charley needed to check Marthy first, so he found it necessary to be a little crafty. "I'll bet you don't have to run to that old dog, do you, Seth?'

A proud Seth answered emphatically, "I'll say, you don't. Why he'd stay at that tree until he starved. Man! When he trees, he stays treed."

"Well, good," Charley exclaimed, "we can go check Marthy first, then."

"But ... but ..." a flustered Seth protested.

Charley paid no heed. From the grumbling behind him, he knew that Seth was following. Marthy's tree music was like hammer blows to a jaded Seth. His confusion was only compounded by her injection of, "Yah ... yah ... I've treed a half-grown male coon ... a half-grown coon ... Yah-yah ..."

They found her dancing beneath a scrub walnut, while in the top hung a half-grown coon. Seth was reduced to a muttering wreck. A quick appraisal by Charley indicated that the old man was not looking too well. That greenish color, he was sure, was not caused by something he had eaten.

As Charley scored the tree, Seth jabbered softly, "I see it, but I don't believe it. Just cain't believe it."

Putting away the score card, Charley said, "Come on, let's go to Old Bent."

There was no keeping up with the old man. His talk of Bent's beautiful tree music floated back to them continually, as they managed to stay within a hundred feet of his flying heels.

Bent was steadily chopping away, as they approached the bottom of the small ridge upon which he was treed. Charley and Marthy were still several yards behind, when Seth camped beneath the tree and turned on his big light.

His groan was an awful thing to hear. Inwardly, both his companions felt a pang of shame, fleeting perhaps, but shame, nonetheless. The first words of the old man, though, once they reached the tree, eased the feeling of shame considerably.

With great bravado, Seth called out, "Well, there he is, kinda small, but Old Bent's got him solid. Look at that scrawny little old ringed tail."

As Charley fumbled for his flashlight, Seth quickly admonished, "Hey, better not turn your light on. It's too bright and he looks like he might jump. I don't want Old Bent to get his jaws on one while the season's not in. He'd crush 'm like an egg shell."

Charley gazed up, as solemn as an owl. "Yep, there he is, all right. Sure has got a mighty scrawny tail, ain't he?

"Uh huh," agreed Seth. "Well, some has, and some ain't. Must be a ground coon. Well, mark him down, and let's go hit another one."

Picking up his lantern, Seth began walking away. Charley just stood and watched him, while Marthy, hand over mouth, shook and trembled like the leaves on a Quaking Aspen. After a few steps, the old man stopped and hesitantly looked around. His eyes beseechingly pleaded with Charley to plus that tree and follow.

Instead, Charley walked around the tree and turned on his light. Seth said not a word as the light played squarely upon 'his coon' for several minutes.

For awhile, Charley never moved or spoke. Finally, in an awed voice, he said, "Well, Old Timer, I've judged a many a hunt, and I thought I'd seen just about everything that could happen, but I sure don't know how to score this one."

"W ... what ... you ... mean, Charley?" the old man stammered.

"Why, how to mark down a half and half deal like this," Charley answered in an anguished tone. "I know it's a coon on the back end, cause you said so ..."

He paused, shaking his head sadly at Seth. "Now, I know you ain't gonna believe this, cause it sounds plum scandalous, but ... but ... that there tail end coon is a front end cat."

Marthy literally came apart. The effort of holding in her laughter had taken its toll. Plopping flat on the ground, she laughed, until she was nothing more than a blubbering bowl of jelly. Charley found it impossible to refrain from joining her, until he, too, was reduced to a near stage of helplessness.

Seth stood, ashen-faced, under the impact of their laughter. His eyes, full of pain, went to Old Bent and then back to them. And then, again, rested upon the old dog, who still sat beneath the tree, looking proudly up into its branches.

Slowly, the old man crumbled, as inch by inch, his stiff old knees folded, until, at last, he rested on the ground beside Old Bent. As Charley began to realize what was happening, laughter died unborn, in a throat suddenly gone too dry to laugh. A glance at Marthy told him that she, too, no longer found the situation humorous, as the sheen of unshed tears glimmered behind her glasses.

Waves of remorse washed over them, and a hush fell over the scene beneath the tree. In that soul-shattering moment, as an old man's pain-drenched words were torn from him one by one, by need of confession, they understood.

Not for himself had he lied, but for Old Bent to be the dog he never was. To Seth, their laughter was not for him, but instead, every taunt of ridicule, a vicious shaft driven deeply into the heart of Old Bent, and he and he alone was responsible.

Tears ran unashamedly down the old man's face, as he took the grizzled head of Bent between his hands. Tenderly, he caressed the long silky ears, as the old dog's tongue flicked out to touch his wrinkled cheek. Time stood still beneath the tree, and a half moon shone over those two alone, because, for awhile, Charley and Marthy didn't exist. The world was small, no larger than a few square feet beneath the tree; there was no one else.

In silence, his companions listened, and in the end, doubted not that the old dog understood.

"It's all right, old fellow," he said softly. "It's all right. It's me they're laughing at, not you. You ain't done nothing to be laughed at about, nothing a'tall. It's my lying that put you in this spot, and I had no right, no right a'tall. You ain't never lied to anybody in your life. And I'm proud that you can still tree a house cat at your age, downright proud."

As Charley stood humbly silent, two things happened at once. Old Bent whined and touched a moist tongue to Seth's leathery cheek, as Marthy, with a smothered cry, flew to his side. Crying unashamedly, she fell upon her knees, and threw her arms around him. Charley turned and walked away. He was unwanted, unneeded, and unseen.

Seated patiently upon a stump, several yards up the branch, he waited in deep reflection. His heart sang with the unexpected turn of events. He had always suspected that the constant, and sometimes seemingly bitter, battle between them was only surface deep; he had never really known, until now.

Lost in thought, he hadn't noticed their approach until they stood beside him. With pleasant surprise, he saw that Marthy held Old Bent firmly on leash. Her other hand was tucked neatly beneath Seth's arm. At his astounded expression, they smiled at each other, with such understanding that Charley knew at once that the problem of Old Bent was forever behind them—washed clean, in those few heartrending minutes beneath the tree.

"Hunt's over, Charley," Marthy announced calmly. "We've decided to call it a draw. And I reckon that ain't all ..." she paused, looking questioningly at Seth, who grinned and nodded. "We have decided to retire, as of now, all three of us. We've treed our last coon."

Charley nodded silently in agreement, as he surveyed the three standing there in mutual affection. Marthy's hand rested lightly upon Old Bent's head, while Seth beamed approval upon both. Surely, Charley thought, she must have told him the truth of how the hunt was rigged. But they didn't say, and he would never ask.

Reminded then, that he still had two coons to untie, he said, "Well, I'll say one thing, all three of you sure signed off in a blaze of glory. I'm glad that everything turned out so well; I'll just go on home from here. Oh, say, Marthy, maybe you had better take this score card ... for, you know ... just in case ..."

Grinning mischievously, she accepted the card with a nod. "Sorta like insurance, you mean?"

Seth watched these proceedings with sober face, then said, "Won't need it no way, cause my lying days are done."

As Charley stood, watching the three of them pulling up the hill towards their house, a pleasant lassitude settled upon him. He had no doubt that he had heard the last great tales of Bent's exploits. But with some apprehension, he knew, too, that for a man of Seth's nature, there must be some outlet, or else, he'd explode. Such worry, though, was quickly dispelled, as the old man's conversation drifted back down the hill to him.

"Marthy," the old man was saying, "do you realize how fast and how big our potatoes growed this year? Why, if they growed just one mite bigger, we would've had to rent the field next door."

Town on Trial

Thoughts of the author at the time of this article's submission to the Time Capsule:

Having been a conservationist all my life, and a lover of the outdoors, I can't help but wonder, how much of nature's bounty that we enjoy today, will still be available fifty years from now?

Will our hills still be covered with timber, and will thousands of acres still be open to most for hunting privileges? And will there still be game to hunt? For that matter, will citizens still be allowed firearms in their possession? Even now, every year, bills are introduced in Congress by wild-eyed fanatics, demanding that all firearms be taken from the people of this country. One can't help but be suspicious of their reasons for demanding the removal of a right granted to all of us by the Constitution of this great country.

Will one be able to catch sight of the white flag of the Whitetail deer, as it flashes away, as is such a common sight today? Will cottontail rabbits still romp in the city yards, and will the sight of an opossum crossing the city street be something unheard of? Will the tracks of raccoon be plentiful, even along the banks of the streams that run through town, as they are today?

Will one still be able to enjoy the sport that so many of us love today; the running of hounds at night in quest of the raccoon? Or will there be any need for the larger type of hound we breed today, in fifty years?

Will the four hundred acre lake to be built in two years in the Rush Creek Valley, to furnish Salem with a potential one hundred year water supply, still be in use, or even there? And will it be amply stocked with fish, as is now purposed?

Will the beautiful maples, ash, and black walnut trees that line our city streets all be gone? They probably will, for many have disappeared already—a definite loss of splendor from the Salem scene. Will wild persimmon trees still grow in abundance in the surrounding countryside, and even inside the city limits? Will people still be able to enjoy delicious persimmon pudding, or will they no longer know of such a thing?

So many things to wonder about.

Al Boling
October 1964

TO THE PERSON OPENING THE TIME CAPSULE

Please follow these instructions as to the disposition of this envelope and contents:

Give the entire contents to my Son and Daughter, Kenneth Max Boling and Mary Elizabeth Boling (or whatever her married name might be), should they both have survived. If one or the other is unable to attend the opening, then give the envelope to the one who is present, and ask that they hold in trust the half belonging to the other. If only one is still alive, then give the envelope to the one remaining son or daughter. If neither has survived, then my instructions are that these contents are to become the property of all surviving grandchildren, to share and share alike, one to own no larger share than the other.

If there are no grandchildren, then the contents may become the property of the nearest next of kin to my immediate family. If there is no kin into whose care these contents may be given, then they become the property of the Washington County Historical Society. If deemed unwanted by the Historical Society, then my instructions are that the entire contents of this envelope are to be burned.

I certify that I have arranged for the ownership of these papers in the fairest way I see possible.

Alfred L. Boling
October 4, 1964

The following story was submitted to the Time Capsule buried on the lawn of the Salem Public Library in 1964. Following is Alfred's explanation of why he believed it was necessary to do this:

Though the story was written by me, Alfred L. Boling, in 1961, three years before our town's 150 year founding celebration, without thought of its possible utilization during this period of celebration, it should have been worthy of publication at this time.

Having, however, been unable to arouse sufficient interest in those contacted to bring about its publication, I take this means of assuring the story will not pass into oblivion with the inevitable march of time.

Though lacking the capabilities so necessary to become a professional writer, I have for several years, written fictional stories for a Tree Hound publication known as *Full Cry*, a magazine published at Sedalia, Missouri by the Walker Publishing Company. I write only for the pleasure it gives me and for those who read my stories. *Full Cry* does not pay for its material. My stories are read from coast to coast and acclaimed by many, but at home, it is almost unknown that I write at all.

By the time the Time Capsule is opened and the contents of this envelope passed into the hands of my heirs, *Full Cry*, in all probability, will no longer exist. And so, my stories will have disappeared, along with all knowledge of their ever being written. This, then, is my one indulgence in self pride of something accomplished, and satisfaction in knowing it will survive. Though this story may even be considered as little more than trash by those who receive it, I will still have accomplished my purpose with its passing into their hands.

Written this day of October 4, 1964
Alfred L. Boling

Town on Trial

Foreword

An early history of Salem and Washington County, published by the Goodspeed Brothers of Chicago in 1884, has long served as a valuable source of information, concerning those hardy people whose determined, and sometimes desperate, struggles eventually materialized into the great, rich heritage we enjoy today.

Not only is history defined as something important enough to be recorded, but also as, learning by inquiry, knowledge, and narrative. By this very definition, then, it is conceded that, not only does the possibility of inaccuracies exist, but are probable.

Information relating to principal events in this story was gained, for the most part, by firsthand conversation with men who were there, who saw it happen, and who were a part of that violent period. One must agree that the stories of these men are as relative to the truth, if not more so, as certain events recorded in the history without even benefit of claim of authorship.

That certain tragic and criminal acts were lightly glossed over, if not completely misrepresented, is understandable. The history was written in 1884. Many people involved were still yet very much alive and their families prominent on the Salem scene. Why historians found transcription of the truth sometimes uninviting is obvious.

A close study of some events, as recorded in the history, will show that, in fact, the author contradicts himself. As if, at the very last, he decided to set the record straight, but again lost his nerve, leaving the reader suspended on the thread of his own confusion.

Though Washington Countians and Salemites have many reasons

to be proud of their heritage, we cannot shut our eyes to the fact that the history of our town and county is bathed in blood.

Though this is written as fiction, the main issues are based upon truth. As hard as it may be to believe, this was your town during one brief period, in July 1873.

Al Boling

Town on Trial

The 9:36 steamed into the station, came to a grinding halt, disgorged two bags of mail, one crate of chickens, and one lone passenger. In three minutes, it was gone—taking with it one bag of mail, two crates of eggs, and no passenger.

The young man who had alighted, surveyed the exchange at the baggage car and had a fleeting thought that, somehow, the train had been cheated. If he hadn't gotten off here, the trade would have been a little more even. But then, he would be climbing back on the 4:30 southbound that afternoon, so maybe that would even things up a little.

Before the last car disappeared around the stockyard curve, two hundred yards to the west, things had returned to normal on the station platform. The cloud of sparrows that had been disturbed by the swooshing of the engine descended again at the east end, to resume their pecking in the dirt. The shepherd dog returned to his reclining position on the cool bricks, in the shade of the overhang of the roof, and with a contented sigh, was instantly asleep.

The little, old, wizened station master slowly pushed the platform truck up to the door of the baggage room, hooked up the tongue to locking position, poked a finger into one of the chicken coops, and chuckled with glee, when he drew a squawk for his efforts. Then, as if noticing the young man for the first time, he turned away from the protesting chickens, and with shuffling steps, came towards him, mopping his brow as he came.

"Howdy, young feller. Sure is hot, ain't it? You up from the city?"

Lawrence Young, the pleasant-faced young man, smiled at the rapid fire of the old man's speech, and answered, "Yes, sir. Now, may I ask you something?"

The keen, blue eyes twinkled merrily behind ancient steel-rimmed spectacles, and his scraggly, tobacco-stained goatee fairly quivered, as he cackled in answer. "Sure, Sonny. Ask away. Not many people take the trouble to ask; they just go ahead and ask anyway. Besides, ain't nothing to do anyway, till the sun rises a little and puts that baggage truck in the shade, so I can unload it. Seems like its better that I talk to you than to myself, cause I cain't learn much from me."

Lawrence glanced at the three items on the truck and laughed out loud. "Well, now, that does look like quite a chore for such a hot morning, but isn't that sun rather hard on those chickens?"

The old man stepped to the edge of the platform and squirted out a long stream of tobacco juice before answering. "Oh, they'll do. It would take two hours of that sun to kill 'em; and in an hour, they'll be in the shade. You said that you wanted to ask me something."

As he looked at the old station master, Lawrence couldn't help giving a slight shake of his head. What a character, what an assignment. This town was dead, even this Old Timer, only he didn't know enough to lie down. As the word dead flashed through his mind, the purpose of his being there probed at him with insistent fingers. Slowly, he spoke, choosing his words carefully, and he hoped, wisely.

"I'm Lawrence Young, a reporter from the *Louisville Enterprise.*"

He paused briefly at the instant change in the old man's manner. The smile was replaced by a stiffening of features, while the twinkle in his eyes gave way to a look of wariness. Even more carefully than before, Lawrence phrased his next words. "It is my understanding that you had a little excitement around here last week."

Half statement, half question, it brought no response from the man who had been so eager to talk only minutes before. Taking a deep breath, he continued, "A hanging. Delow Hart, war hero turned killer. Taken from the jail by vigilantes, and tarred and feathered before being hung to—"

The old man's voice came harshly. "To the railroad bridge; that one right there, and then shot full of holes—seems like you know everything about it that there is to know. So there's no need for you to ask questions. If you'll take my advice, young feller, you'll stay right here and not go up town. You'll wait until the 4:30 train comes through and take yourself right back to the city. Folks around here won't take kindly to being asked anything about that hanging. They'd just as soon forget it. Best you had, too."

Lawrence, with eyes fastened on the wooden trestle a hundred yards up the track, had little time to waste on the old man's last words. "So that's the bridge where it happened. I suppose it's alright, if I go take a look at it?"

The old man's reply was curt. "Well, it's railroad property, but I don't reckon there's any reason why you shouldn't. Go ahead and look. Look all day. Look till the 4:30 comes in and then go back where you came from."

Then, in a more friendly voice, he added, "You're a right nice acting young feller and that's good advice I gave you; better take it." With that, he turned away and entered the station.

In a few minutes, the young reporter stood, looking at the north side of the bridge. Part of the rope still dangled from the sill. He watched, in fascination, as a slight breeze started it swinging back and forth. He could almost imagine a body swinging from the end; turning slowly, as the explosion of guns smothered out the sound of thudding bullets driving into the dying body, while little puffs of clothing flew away with every one that struck.

On the ground, below the swinging rope, dark blood was still in evidence. Boot tracks showed around the edges of the dried pool, as if done when it was still fresh, and over there, scuffed up sand, where he could imagine, the person who had stepped in it had tried frantically to wipe it off. He was unable to suppress a shudder, as he viewed the ugly, brown, dried-up blotch in the otherwise clean sand.

What kind of man swung here? Did he deserve to die? And in such a horrible way? Questions for which he must seek an answer. What had appeared to be just another routine assignment was no longer just that. He must know, for himself, if for no one else.

Suddenly, the spot where he stood seemed eerie. In spite of the hot July sun beating down upon him, the air had taken on a chill and the atmosphere, uninviting, as a shiver ran over him. A desire to be away from there prodded his numbed muscles into action. Quickly mounting the high bank, he walked back down the tracks towards the station.

The dog still slept and the sparrows were still busy at nothing, but the old station master was not in evidence, as he crossed the platform. For a moment, he considered approaching the old man again, but after short contemplation, he decided that it would gain him nothing. Without pausing, he headed up the main street towards the town square, a quarter of a mile away.

Walking slowly, he studied that which lay before him. Salem, Indiana—July 2, 1873. The street, unusually wide for a town that size, showed little signs of life. A few horses stood along the hitching rails, hip shot, and heads drooping. It struck him that maybe he was the only one with little enough sense to be out in the hot sun, by choice, that was. Take those horses now, they had no choice in the matter. They were there because they knew only to obey. But then, wasn't that the same reason that found him here? He had been ordered here on an assignment.

Once more, he went over his editor's words of that morning:

"Lawrence, you're one of my best men. I like your work, so I'm assigning you to a tough one. Here's a round trip ticket to Salem, Indiana. It will take you only an hour each way. You leave here at 8:36 and will catch one back at 4:30. That will give you eight hours to pursue your course, in any way you see fit. I'll bet you don't come back with a thing that we can use, anything new that is, beyond what we already know.

We know that a man named Delow Hart was taken from the jail there last Saturday night by a large band of men, tarred and feathered, hung, and then shot full of holes. We know that he was a war hero and an officer, a first Lieutenant in the 38th Indiana. But he must have taken a liking for killing, and continued to do so, after returning from the war."

Pratt, his editor, had paused briefly, frowning slightly in contemplation, and then continued:

"By last reports, he had killed three men. Each time, until the last one, he had managed to escape punishment, with nothing more than a few days in the county jail. Seems he had a brother, who being a power in political circles and also a good lawyer, always got him off on a self-defense plea. This time, however, there were those who decided that it wouldn't happen again, that he must pay for his crimes. They didn't wait for the law to turn him loose again, but took matters into their own hands. There must be more to the story than that. See what you can find. Good luck."

Well, he could vouch for one thing his boss had said. It would be a tough one, and maybe he could add something else. There was more to the story than met the eye. For why else, the sudden hostility of the station master, at the mere mention that he was a reporter?

Pushing the churning thoughts aside, he realized that the vacant lots next to the railroad tracks had been left behind. As he walked, the scene had given way to a solid row of buildings on both sides of the street. Buildings that were, for the most part, graced with identical swinging doors. From each one, as he passed, came the murmur of voices, mingled occasionally with laughter and the tinkle of glasses. Now he realized what it was about the street that made it so different from other streets in other small towns. It had taken awhile to dawn on him, but now he knew; the swinging doors, the saloons, he had never seen so many, all in one town, on one street.

Having progressed to a point about halfway to the town square, he drew to a halt. From there, he could see clearly both sides of the street. The swinging doors were all still now, because nobody came or went. Carefully, he began counting. It was incredible. Again, he slowly swept his eyes up one side and down the other. There was no mistake. In amazement, he exclaimed, "Fifteen! Fifteen saloons on one street of a hick town."

But there was no one to hear his statement of incredibility. As he resumed his slow pace uptown, he was still the only person in sight. He had a strange feeling of standing to the side, of viewing all this from another angle. Of seeing himself plodding along the side of the wide, dusty expanse of a street. Of a street that stretched endlessly on and on, one lined with swinging doors, as far as his eye could see. While back at the south end, by the depot, a scrawny, little, old man with a tobacco-stained goatee, jumped up and down, waving his arms, as he screeched, "Go back to the city where you came from. Git back to the city, where you belong."

Reluctant to enter one of the saloons, he continued on. If he didn't see someone soon, real soon, he would have to enter a saloon, but only as a last alternative. If the station master's attitude was any example, then it would certainly be like stirring up a hornet's nest to broach the matter in one of the saloons. The occupants were likely to be in a belligerent mood at this time of the morning.

Two pairs of eyes had, however, been following his progress for quite some time. From the shade of a large ash tree, in the courtyard, the men had seen him alight from the train and had waited patiently for him to reappear, as they had known he would. No greater contrast between two men could be imagined. Doc Caley, long, lean and lanky, with a drooping grey handlebar mustache and a thatch of equally grey hair. Faded, blue eyes peered from under drooping lids, at the lone figure slowly approaching from the south.

"Do you think he's had enough, Pot?" he drawled.

The one addressed, rolled over with a grunt and squinted down the street. Though he rolled sideways, his appearance would have lent strength to the suggestion, that perhaps, he might have turned over, end for end, just as well. Measured up and down or around the middle, it's doubtful that there would have been much deviation either way. Pot was a bald-headed man, with a big moon face that always seemed to have a worried look, a face that seldom smiled, yet hardly ever hardened in anger. Intense, dark eyes of an intelligent man, a thinking man, but also, eyes over which a veil of indifference was most often pulled, to be lifted only occasionally, and then, never in an unguarded moment.

A chuckle boomed out of Pot's expansive chest, as he answered, "Give him just a little longer. We'll look better to him that way. Pretty soon now, we had better move around a little, so's he can see us. And when he does, you can bet that he'll come running."

"Better not wait too long, Pot; cause from the way he's acting, he's about ready to bolt right back to the depot." Doc spoke in a surprisingly soft, drawling voice, and then added, "Read that letter again, so we can be absolutely sure of what Pratt wants us to do. Wouldn't want to make no mistakes and let our old friend down."

With another grunt, Pot fished in one shirt pocket with a stubby forefinger and thumb, coming out with a very crumpled sheet of paper, as he muttered, "Why do you want to hear it again, when you already know it by heart?"

"Oh, I don't know," Doc drawled. "Maybe it's because I like to be reminded that I know somebody who can read. Anyway, he sent the letter to you, so that means you're supposed to read it to me. Besides, Pratt knows I cain't read."

"He don't know no such thing," Pot snapped. "He sent it to me, because he knows you can read, but are too lazy to open the envelope. Now, shut up and listen."

Spreading the single sheet of paper out on the ground, he began: *Dear Pot and Doc, Old friends, I am in need of services, a talent for which you two have no equal among the vast expanse of my acquaintances. Knowing you two to be the biggest liars in the State of Indiana, it is only natural that I turn to you at this particular time. This little job calls for someone who is completely without scruples or principles of any kind. And whose manipulation of the truth, to suit their whims of the moment, is so artfully done, that even they believe it. So it was with pride that I remembered the magnificent ability of my two dear friends, Pot and Doc. From knowledge gained by my own past experiences with you two, I know that you stand alone at the pinnacle of proficiency. However, even though you are blessed with the golden fluency of natural-born liars, I must warn you that the utmost caution should be exercised at all times.*

Here's why. On Wednesday morning, a young member of my reporting staff will arrive in Salem on the 9:36 and will return on the 4:30 train. During the eight hours of his sojourn in your town, I expect him to be lied to more times than most people get in a lifetime. He is a very good reporter. So good, that I intend grooming him for my assistant editor. That gets to the main reason for my sending him out there to enjoy the wonders of your very unusual personalities. He has progressed so efficiently that, for some reason or another, he has come to believe that the whole human race can be trusted. You and I know better, don't we, Old Pals? But he doesn't.

In other words, his education will remain incomplete until he has to come into contact with the seamier side of life. And what better way for him to do that, than to bathe for eight hours in the sordid atmosphere with which you two almost perpetually surround yourselves? He will be after a story on the Hart lynching, which I realize is a mighty touchy subject up there. I think we already have everything that we would dare print, so I don't expect him to come back with a thing that we can use. But he will have finished his education in the mistrust of human nature. He will be informed by me, after his return, that you are two of the greatest liars in the U.S.A., and will decide, I'm sure, that if two gentle, kindly, old souls as yourselves can lie to him, then anybody can.

If you pull this off right, I will send you two gallons of the best Kentucky Bourbon that money can buy. But if he even suspects that you are lying to him, I won't pay you a thing. Not only that, I will run a story in the paper, telling just what did happen to Jed Herrick's ten gallons of whiskey that he thought he sent to Louisville. Now, I'd hate to do that, Boys, but if I have to, I'll promise you one thing. I will attend your funerals and give you a nice obituary in the paper.

I've done my best to prepare you, now you are on your own. Good bye, Dear, Dear Old Friends. I just don't know what I'd do without you. As ever, your most ardent admirer, Pratt.

There was a sigh from Doc at the completion of the letter. Almost reverently, he spoke. "Good Old Pratt. He really likes us. You know, Pot, it just kinda gets you right here," placing his hand over his heart. "Especially that part where he tells us how wonderfully sordid we are."

"Yeah, I know," Pot answered. "It gets me, too. But he really ought'n to brag on us so much, right to our face that way. It's apt to make you conceited."

Apparently, Doc hadn't heard too much of what Pot had just said, for he was looking down the street at the lone figure of Lawrence, who was now standing still.

"Pot," he said, "in another minute, that boy will head back to the depot in a high lope. He has had enough of being the only one kicking up dust out there this morning. Git up and move around, so's he can see you."

"Git up yourself, it's your turn, I moved the last time," Pot growled.

"Well, if you did, it sure must have been by accident, cause I sure cain't remember you doing it on purpose. But I guess it's better that he mistake me for a flagpole, than you for a balloon. One of us had sure better move, or there will go two gallons of whiskey down Main Street on two legs."

It was with a great feeling of relief, that Lawrence saw the movement of Doc's rising body in the courtyard. His feet, kicking up little puffs of dust, carried him rapidly in that direction. He couldn't shake the feeling that the deserted street was, in some way, connected with the hanging. As he drew closer to the inviting shade of the big ash tree, he was elated to see that there were two. For as he watched in amazement, Pot's rotund figure slowly rolled over and arose, as he pushed himself up from knees and hands position.

Side by side, they waited, giving no indication by their actions that they were aware of his coming. Doc spoke in a worried voice, "Pot, do you think Old Pratt would really tell about that whiskey?"

"You know durned well he would, Doc. Friend or not, he wasn't kidding, and Jed Herrick would shoot you, sure as the devil."

"Shoot me!" Doc wailed. "What about you? You're as guilty as I am. Besides, you drunk more of it than I did, seeing as how you've got so much more room for it than me. I guess that makes you even guiltier than I am."

"Now, Doc, that absolutely ain't possible," Pot snorted. "Jed knows that I'm too dumb to have thought up that deal. And besides, I just naturally look more innocent than you. Oh, you're the one he'd come after, alright. So just to save you, Old Friend, maybe we ought to play it pretty close for awhile. Let's sorta feel the kid out and stick pretty close to the truth for awhile, until we see how sharp he is. I sure would hate for him to catch us in a lie."

"Relax, Pot," Doc drawled. "I know the strain you'll be under, but after all, I've had some experience in telling the truth, and it's not so bad, once you've got the hang of it. So if you're worried, just keep that big fat mouth closed until I show you how. It won't hurt you a bit, you'll see."

The young man with the friendly face and keen, brown eyes was too close now for them to continue their argument. Falling silent, they allowed their gaze to rest on him, as if for the first time.

Not bothering to take the extra steps around to the gate, Lawrence climbed over the hitch rail that surrounded the Courthouse lawn, keeping on a straight line towards the two odd-looking characters standing in the shade of the big tree. Being already tempered by the strange events of the morning, so far, he felt no surprise at the odd sight presented by the pair who waited. It was, he told himself, to be expected. Nothing else had made sense there that morning, so there was no use to expect the pattern to change now.

As he pulled up short of the circle of shade, Doc said, "Come on in, son. It's hot out there."

Lawrence chuckled. "Thank you. It sure is."

Entering the shade, he extended his hand, and spoke gratefully, "This feels better. My name is Lawrence Young, from Louisville." As his experience with the station master had taught him, no use to tip his hand all at once.

Doc stuck out his big, bony paw and with a smile, said, "Glad to know you, Lawrence. I'm Doc Caley and this tub that walks is Pot Marson."

As he shook hands with them, Lawrence had a feeling of instant liking for the both of them. The one called Doc, he decided, must be at least six feet, four inches tall, without weighing much over one hundred and seventy pounds. While the other couldn't be over five feet, two inches tall, and surely weighed in the neighborhood of two hundred and fifty pounds.

There was, he decided, more to these men than their languid appearance would lead one to believe. In spite of their uninterested attention and veiled eyes, there was the uneasy feeling that he would never be scrutinized more closely.

Doc and Pot immediately dropped back to a reclining position in the grass, as Pot said, "Sit down, son, and enjoy a front seat to what goes on here this time of day."

"But there's nothing going on," Lawrence couldn't help exclaiming. "Why you're the only human beings I've seen, besides the station master. Where is everybody? Why are the streets so vacant?"

Doc shifted his position a little before replying. "Well, first I want to thank you for your generous way of referring to my old friend here as something human. It's not often that anybody pays him such a compliment. Although it wouldn't be good for him to hear that kind of talk too often, he might get to believing it; it's alright, once in awhile."

Doc paused long enough to turn a blank face to Pot, as if waiting for him to explode, but when no remark was forthcoming, he took up the thread of conversation where he left off.

"Now, as to your questions. There's just not much reason for anyone to be out on the street right now. Especially on this street, South Main or Tough Street, as it is called. Later on, after the sun goes down, it will come to life. She's wide open all night and a good place to be away from. The farmers hereabouts are all busy working in their wheat. Them horses you see down there belong to farm hands that had to come to town for something or other. They are in no hurry to get back to the hot, dirty, scratchy work that waits for them. So they're just nursing an extra drink along, hating to climb back into the saddle, and get back to the farm. The gamblers don't stir much this time of day, either. Son, that's just not a daytime street."

"But the saloons!" Lawrence exclaimed. "Fifteen! Why it's unbelievable."

Doc glanced at Pot, who took up the conversation. "Son, you could transplant that street into any western town, and it would be right at home. This is really a pretty good little town and growing fast. Most of the folks here are good, God-fearing, hardworking people. But the Street is a world into itself, with a floating population that nobody ever bothers to check on. Someday, it will all be changed. The saloons will give way to stores and shops, where decent people can enter, without fearing for their lives. Even the next generation, maybe, will find it hard to believe that their town was ever like this."

Lawrence was lost in thought, for the moment, and since both Pot and Doc seemed to be waiting for him to speak, he didn't keep them waiting long. A sudden decision to play his cards face up prompted his next remark.

"Gentlemen, I believe that I should be honest with you. I tried it with the station master, with not very pleasant results. However,

I have a feeling that this time will be different. I am a reporter from the *Louisville Enterprise*, out here about last Saturday's lynching. Now, do you want to run me out of town, too?"

Taken back somewhat, by his direct approach, the others looked at each other for a moment. Old friends, who needed no spoken words to reach a mutual decision. At a slight nod from Pot, Doc spoke.

"No, son. We don't want you to leave town for quite a spell yet. Not until we've done a lot of talking. First off, though, Pot, let him read the letter."

With a puzzled look, Lawrence took the letter that Pot held out to him. He read, with amazement, while the other two lay silently, drowsily quiet. When he had finished, he handed it back with a short question.

"Why did you show this to me?"

They both looked a bit sheepish, as if caught in a role unusual for them. Finally, Pot broke the mounting silence, "Son, we may be asking ourselves that for a long time, and maybe not so long either, if Pratt gets mad about us crossing him up this way. We didn't aim to show it to you. Didn't even know we wuz going to until the minute before we did."

There was a slight pause from Pot, as if there was need to search for just the right words. When they came, it seemed to Lawrence that he was really trying to explain it to himself, as well. "Maybe it's because me and Doc have finally decided to do something worthwhile, for a change. You see, son, we kinda like this little old town, and have had a belly full of what's been happening to it. We're pretty shiftless, don't work much, but loaf around town a lot. We've seen a little of everything that went on, and it sure hasn't been pretty. We've seen the fine, healthy, growing town it was, turn into a sniveling, whipped dog of a thing, that whines and cringes every time some tough from the Street lifts a hand. In a way, we have been just as guilty as the rest, by just watching it happen, and not lifting a hand to stop it. Maybe we've stood in shame as long as we can."

Pot seemed to have paused for breath, so Doc took up where he left off, his soft, drawling voice full of intense sincerity. "You see, everything old Pratt called us in that letter is true. We just mostly lay around swapping lies, winter and summer. When we make a strike, it's just another chance to cozy up to a jug until it's all gone. We're not married and are satisfied to be just what we are. We have a little shack at the edge of town that we call home. But even though it's clear across town from the Street, the stink still reaches us. Time was, when we got sick to our stomachs from watching the goings on here, we'd just hole up for a day or two, and forget all about it. But we cain't do that no more. And when it's too bad for us, it's more than too bad for the fine, decent folks in this here town."

Doc's voice drifted slowly to a halt, and after a respectful silence, Pot picked up the thread of conversation. "You see, son, this used to be a good town. A proud town in a proud county. Did you know that they used to call Washington County, the County of the Giants? Well, they did, and for good reason. There wuz more big, powerful men around here than about any place that anybody knowed of, I guess. If Abe Stover or Tom Denny, or a few of the others wuz still alive and in their prime, the Street never would have been allowed to take over like it has. They would have just walked down one side and up the other, and pulled it up by the roots as they went. Wouldn't have got up a good sweat doing it, either."

Again, as before, when Pot ceased talking, Doc took over. Lawrence marveled at how the other could start in where his friend had left off, and without a break in the trend of thought. It was almost as if they were of one mind.

"They used to call Salem the Athens of the middle-west," Doc said. "Because we had the first Institution of Advanced Learning in this part of the country. This has always been the home of proud people, ever since the Brocks settled here and started a mill. Some of the best Indian fighters of all times came from here. Fellers like Cagg Calloway, an old friend of Daniel Boone; fought the Shawnee and the Delaware to a standstill, and then ran them clear out of the country. He saved the forts around here, dozens of times, by scouting into Indian country and finding out about intended attacks before they happened. He spent more time in Indian country than he did at the forts. The Indians knowed and feared him, but he came and went, as he pleased. They tried countless times to catch him, but never did."

For awhile, all were quiet, lost in thought of what Calloway might have endured. Then Pot started in again, "It's sorta hard to say just when the change began, for it kinda slipped up on us. It must have started real soon after the War, though, for the boys were all heroes to the town's folks when they first got back. People just naturally overlooked a lot of rough stuff at first; figured that it takes a while to get killing out of a man's system, especially after he's had four years of it, like some of them had. But while they wuz overlooking, a bunch of riffraff was taking over, and all at once, they realized that things had got clear out of hand."

When Pot paused for breath, Doc nodded his head, and picked up the thread of conversation. "Take the time they hung poor old Uncle Joe. The outside world thought the town done that just because he was a colored, but twern't so. A bunch of no goods from the Street hung him one night just out of plain cussed meanness. Never did convict anybody for that either, though most folks knowed who it was. I guess it was about then that people began to realize that the Street had just about taken over the town. And there didn't seem to be enough guts in all the rest of us put together to try and stop them. By the time Hart had racked up his second killing, everybody knowed how it would be. The sheriff would arrest him and he'd go to jail for two or three days. In the meantime, his brother Horace would get busy and rush a fake hearing through, and get him cleared on a self-defense plea. It didn't matter whether the other man had a gun or not; it was always self-defense. Finally, it got to the point that if the men in this town were to ever hold up their heads again, they had to do something. So, they finally did."

Once more, Doc came to a respectful pause, giving Pot a chance to continue the story. "What Doc is trying to say, son, is that we know this town is on trial before the eyes of the world right now, because of what happened here. We are trying to show that world, through a story we hope you will write, that Delow Hart had a trial, too. He was sentenced to die, and not just lynched, like the papers said. Oh, he had a trial alright, for no man ever had more time to straighten out than he did. In fact, his trial lasted for years, and right up to the last killing, he could have gotten a reprieve. But he was so sure that nothing could touch him, that even after his last killing, he could have escaped and didn't."

Lawrence had stood, spellbound, until now, but as Pot seemed lost in thought for a moment, he prompted him with a question. "In what way could he have escaped? And another thing. Has the deserted Street got anything to do with his hanging?"

Pot answered the questions in the order they were asked. "Well, he was hung on Saturday night, but that afternoon, while the jail was left unattended, somebody got hold of the keys and opened all the cells. Most of the prisoners took off, but Hart just casually walked uptown and around the square, then returned to his cell."

As Lawrence was trying to visualize this, he was hardly aware that the story had again shifted to Doc's voice. "Oh, he was a cool one, alright. Always went well dressed and smoked them long, slim cigars, like most gamblers do. The Harts have money. Hear tell that the family offered to give five thousand dollars for a quick acquittal. He knew that his potbellied brother Horace would have him out in a day or two, anyway. He would have, too, only he just didn't have time.

"Now, about your other question. Yes, that's why the Street's deserted. You see, this town's just like a powder keg right now. It's split right down the middle, and neither side knows whether the other will light the fuse."

Lawrence's eyes hadn't left the speaker's face, but it seemed impossible to draw words from these two any faster than they wanted to give them up. And that was agonizingly slow.

"Do you mean," he asked, "that it is the Street against the rest of the town?"

"That's right," Doc answered. "Each side thinks the other is coming after it. Hart's friends have really raised Cain, and swore that they would get every man-jack that had anything to do with that necktie party. But at the same time, word is around the Street that the vigilantes aim to clean up the whole mess, now that they have finally gotten started. Don't know if there's any plans afoot to do that; kinda doubt it, though, cause we've had some word that the Governor is going to have an investigation. Hear tell that Hart's brother Horace has been bellowing all over Indianapolis for help from some of his political friends."

Lawrence interrupted, "Do you think that is true?"

"Could be," Doc replied. "But since that word got out, there has been something else added. Now there's talk of how the men who lynched Hart were from Jackson County. Feller tells how a man come up to him over at Seymour, and says that we are having far too many killings over here. And if there's any more, they would be over to dish out some justice. So there wuz another killing, and over they come, to do some justice. That's the way the situation is right now."

"Something impels me to think that you two know the true story," Lawrence said.

Pot flashed a wintry smile. "Son, me an' Doc have just been alaying here in the shade, awatching the whole thing. You see, we've always been kinda in the middle. The good folks trust us, cause they know we're too dumb and lazy to get into trouble. Besides, they like to hire us to work for them once in awhile. We cut a little wood, now and then, or something like that. That is, when I can get this lazy Doc in the notion of moving a little. Then the Street lets us alone, for we don't bother them none, and the saloon owners know that when we do get a dime, we'll spend it with them."

"Now, I'm beginning to see why the station agent got so excited when I told him why I was here, "Lawrence remarked. "Looks like just about everybody is uncertain of where he stands. Is there any truth in the story that it was done by men from Jackson County?"

"Well," Doc laughed, "I suppose it's possible, since they all wore masks. But it's funny that they had a man with them that stood head and shoulders above everybody else, and that one of our local citizens is just that same height. And it sure is a coincidence that the man who put the rope around his neck had curly hair, just like another one of our good citizens, who, by the way, just happens to be the father of one of the men that Hart killed. And it's downright ridiculous that another of our good men just happened to buy a length of rope, just like that used for the hanging, out at Harristown on Saturday afternoon."

While Lawrence pondered the incredulous story, Pot chuckled, and said, "Tell him about the accident down at the corner of Poplar and Water Streets."

Doc grinned under his drooping mustache, as he said, "Sure wouldn't want to forget that."

Turning to Lawrence, his eyes twinkling, and with an occasional chuckle, he began, "Even some of our most gentle people got all excited and done some unusual things. There wuz this one little round, fat feller who was determined to get in on the act. So he got himself a bucket of tar and a bag of feathers. He was too timid to take part in the real fracas, so he stayed at home, keeping the tar bucket on the fire, so it would be nice and warm when he got close enough to throw it on Hart. He waited until they got him out of jail and started down to the bridge. Then he grabbed up his tar bucket and bag of feathers and started down Water Street as fast as his short, fat, little old legs would carry him. Well, he was just about there, when he slipped on a wet cobblestone. His tar bucket flew up in the air and come down all over him. At the same time, the sack with the feathers busted wide open, and durned, if that little feller didn't tar and feather his own self right there. He turned right around and tore out for home, and crawled under the covers, tar feathers and all. His wife didn't know a thing about it, and told all the neighbors that poor, old Tom come home from town so sick, that he covered up his head and shivered and shook all night."

As he wiped tears of laughter from his eyes, Lawrence took out his watch and was surprised to see that it was thirty minutes past the noon hour. Quickly apologetic by his tone, he exclaimed, "Gentlemen, I'm sorry. I hadn't noticed that it was past dinner time. Is there a good place to eat close by?'

"If you like good, plain, home-cooked food, and all you can eat for a quarter, there's Ma Arnold's boardinghouse, just a couple of blocks from here," Pot informed him.

"Good," Lawrence replied. "Let's go. The meal's on me."

Doc quickly uncoiled to his feet, and between them, they managed to pull Pot to his feet, without too much effort. Together, they walked to the two-story weather-boarded house, east of the square. Meals were served continuously from eleven until one, his friends informed him, so all they had to do was hang up their hats and take places at the large table. Lawrence noticed, at once, a definite absence of conversation among the half dozen men already at work on the meal.

Ms. Arnold, a ruddy-faced, buxom woman of about sixty, hovered about, always at their elbows, ready to fill a dish the instant it was empty. She greeted them warmly, as they came in, and it seemed to Lawrence, was especially attentive to both his friends. That her undisguised interest made them both uncomfortable was obvious. As soon as they were finished, Doc suggested that he and Pot would make room for someone else, and told Lawrence that they would wait for him on the porch. Smiling at their eagerness to be away, he rose and went to pay for their meals. That done, he left the warm, generous atmosphere of the dining room and joined his old friends on the porch. He couldn't help ribbing them about being in such a big hurry to leave such a fine host.

"Oh! It's this durned Pot," Doc growled. "She wants to marry him, and it scares him so much that he's no good for a week after he's been close to her. So I didn't want to stay, for my old friend's sake."

"Don't you believe it, son," Pot snorted. "It's Doc, she's after. I've seen him shake for days just from her looking real close at him."

Even as he laughed softly at their obviously false explanations, he had no doubt that he understood their real reason. He was sure that each of them felt only fear that perhaps the other would, in a weak moment, succumb to the widow's charms, and that he would suddenly find himself alone. And with a feeling of warmth, he realized that either would be lost without the other.

But with the ominous story he had heard that morning ever present in his mind, he felt that every minute of his remaining hours in the town must be utilized.

"Say," he said, "can we rent a rig in this town?'

"A dozen, if you want 'em," Pot informed him. "Right down High Street at the livery stable."

The three of them were immediately headed in that direction, and within minutes, were climbing into the runabout chosen for the afternoon. With Doc at the reins, the fast-stepping bay mare left the barn in a rush. Letting her have her head for a few minutes, he then gradually began to pull her in, much to Lawrence's relief. The town was whizzing by much too fast to suit him. Finally, she came down to a good, fast trot, and he couldn't help remarking about her clean lines and blooded appearance.

"Yes, she's probably half thoroughbred, at least," Doc answered. "That's the one good thing that happened to this county when Morgan's Raiders come through. A lot of people called him a horse thief, and I suppose he was, but, for the most part, he only swapped horses with folks around here. Theirs wuz about played out when they got here, so they rounded up every good-looking critter they could find. Yep, they left some real blooded stuff here when they moved on, although folks didn't realize it, at first. The ones they left behind being wore to a frazzle and half-starved and all. But it wasn't long till they began to see what they had. A little grain under a horse's hide can make a lot of difference in a hurry."

As they talked, Lawrence realized that Doc seemed headed for some certain objective. But when he inquired as to their destination, the answer came from Pot. "To the cemetery, son. There's something we want to show you."

The young reporter marveled anew at his two strange friends. Without a word being spoken, Pot knew where his friend was going, for the information had been imparted with complete certainty. That he was correct soon became apparent.

The mare had been walking for several minutes; the hill to the cemetery was quite steep. At the crest, on the left, a beautiful grove of hardwoods graced the landscape. Towering sycamores in virginal white, kingly black walnuts of majestic splendor, and the abundant foliage of giant maples were all too breathtaking to the youth from the city.

"Ah!" he exclaimed, in wonder. "Such beautiful trees. They are truly magnificent."

"They sure are," Doc said. "But it's a shame the way good timber has been wasted around here. They're cutting it like it would last forever, and of course, it won't. Someday, they'll want all this timber that they've just piled up and burned. Take where the courtyard and square is now. Trees four feet thick grew all over there before they cleared it off. There's sawmills all over the county, everyone cutting as fast as they can. Someday, folks will wish their ancestors had thought a little more about the future."

They were fast approaching the end of the street that led directly into the graveyard. Surrounding it on all sides was a high iron fence. Lawrence hopped out to swing back the metal gate, hung between large limestone posts, while Doc tooled the rig inside. Quickly dismounting, they hitched the mare to the fence, after which Lawrence followed his old friends towards a grave, over which the grass had not yet grown to full cover.

A flat limestone marker sat at the head. The wording on it, brief and emblazoned. "Here lies John Cantle—Killed by Delow Hart—October 5, 1872—Cold Blooded Murder."

"Less than a year ago," Lawrence murmured.

"Yep," Doc said softly. "And he killed another one since then."

"But that's all," Pot almost whispered. "That's all."

"Tell me about this one," Lawrence urged. "Tell me all about it." He seemed to almost feel the presence of the others about them, as Doc began:

"Well, Hart had a way with women and they sorta went for him in a way that made things kinda easy. He was the love 'em and leave 'em type. He was, that is, until he got interested in one that he couldn't have without marrying. But there was one little problem. She was already married, to John Cantle there. So Hart found a way around that."

Lawrence knew what he was about to hear and a slight nausea roiled his stomach.

Doc finished the story, as Lawrence had suspected. "Hart just caught him over in town one day and shot him down. Pleaded self-defense and was out in three days. Cantle didn't even have a gun."

"What about the woman?" Lawrence felt impelled to ask.

Pot snorted scornfully. "Well, Doc told you that he had a way with women. She married Hart, what else?"

"Was she still married to him when he was hung?" Lawrence asked.

"Oh, yes," Pot answered. "But I reckon she didn't have much love for him by that time, though. Hear tell that she said if she knew the man who put the rope around his neck, why she'd just marry him, too."

As they climbed back into the rig, and left the cemetery behind, at a fast clip, Lawrence was engulfed with the realization that he was caught. Caught up in the same swirling, surging, current of emotions that were pushing so hard at Pot and Doc. Emotions born of love for their hometown and a desire to see it vindicated in the eyes of the world. Without actually saying, they were asking for his help, in the only way they could.

By placing him face-to-face with every event leading up to that terrible Saturday night, they could only hope that he would understand. No plea for sanction of a lynching, but a presentation of evidence proving that Delow Hart, duly judged by his peers, was found guilty and executed as legally as possible, under the circumstances. Elated by such a challenge, he found in himself only desire to see the thing through.

Content to follow their lead, he remained silent, as they progressed down a steep hill in the direction of the town square. Just a block short of it, the mare was reined to the right, down a street that Doc named as Water Street. Their destination was, at once, in sight. The rough-looking structure of part stone and part wood could only be one thing. The steel bars over the windows further attested that this was the county jail. The place from which Hart had been taken to his death.

A rather small building, that apparently contained no living quarters for a jailer. Finding the door open, they entered the one square room, which Lawrence decided must serve as an office. The cells were on either side, with two across the back, six in all, but cramped quarters at the best. All cells were empty, with doors swung open, but in the young man's opinion, still very uninviting.

"No prisoners!" he exclaimed. "Isn't that rather unusual?"

Doc spoke softly. "Who's gonna get excited about a house cat after the lion has been in the barn?"

Lawrence understood, at once, that which was implied. The terrible events of Saturday night were still too fresh. An air of violence still hung over the town, while the jail itself still seemed to echo with the furious sounds of struggling, cursing, and desperate men. For a moment, they gazed in silence, then Pot pointed to the cell in the right-hand back corner.

"There's the one he was in. See that broken chair. Notice that one of the upright posts is missing."

Lawrence stood in the open door and looked closely at what was left of the chair, while his keen mind grasped what must have happened. "Hart must have pulled the other leg off to fight with."

"He sure did," Doc answered. "He was a cold-blooded killer, but with plenty of guts. He asked the sheriff to give him his guns, when he heard them coming, but he wouldn't do it. So he tore that leg off, and as they stuck their heads through the cell door, he durned near knocked their brains out. Never would have got him out, if they hadn't shot him first."

"My God!" Lawrence cried. "Do you mean to say that they shot him down, the same way he would have?'

Pot answered him this time. "Son, they were out to get him and had gone too far to quit then. When they found out that he could hold them off with the chair leg, there just wasn't anything else they could do. So they just shot him enough to get him down, then went in and drug him out."

"And I know the rest, for I've been to the bridge," Lawrence said in an awed voice. "But where was the sheriff, while this was going on? Didn't he try to protect his prisoner?"

"Well, now," Pot said, "he was here before the mob, but then he just kinda disappeared. You might look at it this way. The sheriff has always been afraid of Hart. Everybody knowed that he never did really arrest him for the killings he done. Heck, no, Hart just come down to the jail and give himself up every time he killed a man. Not cause he was scared of the sheriff. No siree. But just because he knowed that old brother Horace would clear him anyway, all nice and legal like. Then he could start all over again with a clean slate. So you see how it was with the sheriff. By doing nothing, he could get rid of the most dangerous man in town. A man he was afraid of and also the man who was the leader of that gang of toughs on South Main."

As Pot finished with his explanation, Doc started towards the door. Lawrence was only too glad to follow. Anything to get back out into the sunshine, away from the foreboding interior of the jail and the smell he had noticed coming from the dank cells.

Climbing back into the rig, they were off again for an unspoken destination, but he couldn't help thinking that they had both decided where they were taking him. Someway, somehow, they had communicated.

Soon, they were back on the square, where Doc pulled the mare into the hitch rack, under the trees on the east side of the courtyard. While Doc tied the horse, Lawrence turned to lend a hand to Pot, but with a couple of grunts, he was on the ground almost as quickly as they.

Slowly, they walked over to the shade of the same big ash under which they had first met. Instead of flopping onto the ground, as he had thought they might, his old friends stood facing south, towards the intersection, where the Street entered the square. Pot's voice came out a little hoarse, as he took up the conversation. "Lawrence, imagine, if you will, a busy afternoon here on the square. A lot of people crossing the intersection there. Suddenly, a voice from the west sidewalk calls out, 'Cantle!' A man in the middle of the crossing stops, then slowly turns around and turns white, as he sees who called his name. Others see, too, and move out of the way fast. In seconds, just that man stands alone in the middle of that big Street. He tries to speak, but no words come from a throat that is too dry. Helplessly, he stands frozen, numb with shock of what he knows is coming. He tries to swallow, but cain't even do that. His hands go out in a kinda feeble motion of protest, as if trying to ward off the bullet that hits him high in the chest on the right side. It's only a thirty eight, so it don't knock him down, but just turns him around a little. Then the next one hits him in the left chest, right through the heart, and he goes down then, real slow like. Just sorta folds up, a little at a time. And all that time, there's that horrible look on his face that just seemed to say, 'Why?' I guess over a hundred people saw it and most of them knowed why. Hart wanted his wife, that's all."

Pot's voice slowly came to a halt and Lawrence wondered if

he had heard it all. He hadn't, for Doc added a little more. A few words that gave him more insight of the true character of Hart than anything he had heard yet. Forsaking his soft drawl, Doc spoke in an angry, clipped tone. "Before the eyes of all them people, that durned, cold-blooded killer blowed the smoke from the muzzle of his gun, put it back in his shoulder holster, then just sauntered out in the Street where Cantle laid. He looked down at him for a few seconds, poked at the body with the toe of his shoe, and then said sneeringly, to nobody in particular, "Get that thing out of the street before it starts stinking."

Shocked by the cruelty that had just been described to him, Lawrence was unable, for a moment, to withdraw his eyes from the spot where it all happened. Numbly, he could almost see it being enacted again, because their description was so vivid. A shudder ran over him, as he tried to shake off the spell that their words had spun.

Finally, he managed hoarsely to ask, "But how could any community allow a man to do such a thing, time after time, and do nothing about it?"

His old friends looked sharply at him, then brief smiles flickered across their faces. "Son," Doc said, "we wuz hoping to hear you say something like that. You feel it. You see, it was the only way. Now, can you make your readers feel the same way?"

For a brief moment, Lawrence stared at them, not quite comprehending their meaning. But, as his words came back to him, he knew. Without thinking, he had expressed his true feelings. Without suggestions, without insistence of any kind, they had shown him how it had to be. He, who had never condoned violence, and had never felt anything but loathing for a mob, was now sure that the lynching of Delow Hart was justice, long past due. A solution, for which there had been no substitute. Demanded by man's need of retaining self-respect, without which, there could be no survival.

Looking into their intense, old eyes, he said simply, "I'll do my best."

Doc's eyes shown, as he said softly, "That's all we ask, son, and I think it will be good enough. But you've not quite heard it all yet."

Silently, Lawrence waited. Prepared for whatever he might

hear, but that he could still be shocked more, he was to find out, as Doc continued. Pointing to the west of the intersection and about middle ways of the block, the old man said, "See them stone steps over there? Well, that's where Hart stood when he shot Tod Melvin, a week ago last Saturday. The last man he ever killed. He had actually signed his death warrant when he killed Cantle, but nobody had gotten around to serving it yet. That killing of Tod was the last straw. He was a harmless little guy and not very bright. Hart was always teasing him, every chance he got, and Tod would get a little madder every time. That just made Hart worse. Well, he caught the poor guy out in the middle of the Street that day and really got dirty, insulting him for no reason at all. Tod stood it as long as he could. Then he picked up a rock, about as big as his fist, and started walking towards Hart, with that rock held ready to throw."

There was a slight break in Doc's voice, as he stopped to swallow a few times, before going on with the story. "Hart stood there on the steps and yelled for him to stop, but Tod was so mad that he didn't know what he was doing. He just kept walking up to Hart. Even before he got close to the sidewalk, Hart pulled his gun and started shooting. Funny thing, how people just naturally take for granted that a killer is an expert shot. Well, maybe he was, maybe he was just off that day, but he stood right there and shot at poor old Tod five times, and missed every time. Everybody was yelling for Tod to stop, but he never heard a word they said, just kept walking. He was pretty close by that time. Hart just had one bullet left, but Tod was too close to miss. So with the next shot, Tod wasn't with us anymore. He was dead before he hit the sidewalk."

Doc had, for the first time, allowed anger to creep into his voice. His eyes flashed at the memory of what he had just described. For a short time, he seemed lost in thought, dark thoughts, as he relived Tod's killing. Then, getting himself under control, he went on with the story.

"Man, this square was like a beehive and mad bees at that. Hart knew that he'd gone too far, so he went right down to the jail and told the sheriff to lock him up. He was just gonna wait until Horace got him acquitted, as he had every time before. Well, as you know, he figured wrong. Some say that Horace had warned him, when he killed Cantle, that he had helped him for the last time. Don't know if that's so or not, kinda doubt it. Anyway, he didn't."

"There's one thing for sure," Pot said. "Unless the rest of the country understands the truth, this town is as dead as Hart. If that Governor's investigation comes off, and they really get to digging into things, all hell's liable to break loose here. The Street is tottering, and the next week or two will decide whether it falls. If Hart's death is recognized for what it was, a necessary execution, the Governor would probably call off his investigation. And that would be the end of the Street, once and for all. But if they don't understand, and the investigation takes place, then this town will be set back twenty-five years."

"You see," Doc went on with the explanation, "me and old Pot here would never live to see this town hold up its head again. And we would like to see it walking proud once more, like it used to. We would like to see a woman be able to walk down the Street again and know that she is safe. Right now, they don't even dare ride down South Main in a buggy, unless there's a man with them. I guess you find that mighty hard to believe?"

"Yesterday," Lawrence replied soberly, "I would have scoffed, if someone had told me such a story, but not now. You have shown me, in a way that leaves no doubt in my mind, that all you've said is true. I now feel as you do, and I couldn't change my mind, if I wanted to. I feel that my boss will see it our way, too. I hope that I'm capable enough to put it all into words, so that he will understand. For if he does, you can count on the full power of the *Louisville Enterprise* to back your cause. When Mr. Larder believes in a thing, he goes all the way."

"Son," Doc murmured, "we know that only too well. We learned it long ago."

Lawrence felt he had to ask. "Would you mind telling me how you became acquainted with him?"

There was a silence, a very long one, which was finally broken by Pot. "Well, it's kinda hard to say just when. Seems like we've knowed him all our lives, but that's not so, either. Something like that just sorta slips up on you. There you are, going along, from one thing to another and all at once, there's this feller, and you realize he's been there quite a spell."

Pot's voice trailed off rather wistfully, and silence hovered over the three of them again. It was obvious that Doc intended adding nothing to what Pot had said. Lawrence realized that he had been told absolutely nothing and decided to leave it that way. That his old friends had their reasons, he knew. That was good enough for him.

Suddenly, the thought of train departure time came to him. Looking at his watch, he was surprised to see that it was four o'clock. In thirty minutes, he would have to leave.

"Gentlemen," he said, "I'm afraid that my train is nearly due. Would you drive me down to the depot and then return the rig to the livery stable?"

"Sure thing, boy," Doc drawled. "Sure hate to see you go, and we are mighty glad you come up here."

"So am I," Lawrence replied. "I'll never forget the education I've had here today. Let's hope it pays off."

Reluctantly, they walked to the buggy, mounted, and let the mare jog slowly down wide, dusty South Main Street. Now, there was evidence of life about them, as they passed along, but the tide was still yet churning slowly. The mare's hooves, clop, clopping along were still making the loudest sound reaching their ears. Here and there, a man would step from the door of one of the saloons, and stare silently at them as they jogged past. From the clothes they wore, Lawrence knew, that for the most part, he was seeing the vultures of the swinging doors, waiting for night to drive their prey into town, the suckers into their clutches. The lonely, the desperate, to their gambling tables.

Ahead of them, to the right of the Street, and just across the railroad tracks, stood a large two-story weather-boarded house. Something about its appearance told Lawrence that it wasn't just a home. His question of its purpose brought a chuckle from his companions. As they exchanged sly looks, Doc said, "What do you think, Pot? Reckon we ought to tell him?"

"Well, now, he's pretty young," Pot replied. "Don't rightfully know if we ought to or not. Wouldn't want Pratt to think we wuz leading one of his reporters astray. I just don't hardly know."

Lawrence reddened, only slightly, at their good-natured banter.

Fully understanding their implications, he laughed, and said, "Gentlemen, you forget that I was raised in a riverfront town. I'm sorry. I should have known. That's where the girls stay."

"Yep, that's one of them," Doc answered. "There's a couple more, only they're in disguise. Hear tell that there's a real fancy one going up on North Main Street. Kinda like one of them southern mansions. But I don't know about it now. If the Street goes under, I'm pretty sure that the town won't allow it to operate. But if we have that investigation and our good citizens get kicked in the teeth, then the Street will control the town; there won't be nobody to stop nothing."

As they drew up at the depot, Lawrence's watch said four-fifteen. He was glad that the time allowed him a few more minutes with his friends. It hardly seemed possible that before nine-thirty that morning, they had been unknown to him, for surely he had known them all of his life. At least it seemed to him that he had. That he would never forget them, he was certain. He would be returning to this town, he also knew. He must see it in six months, a year, two years. He would do the job to which he was committed, fulfill the promise he had made to his old friends, and then return frequently, to check on the results of his work.

Pot and Doc climbed down from the buggy, and after hitching the mare, joined him on the bench in front of the station. They would wait to see him off. He looked at them with affection, as he took from his wallet several bills. As they started to shake their heads, he said, "You must take it. This isn't my money. It comes from an expense account that Mr. Larder provides for all his reporters while they're out on a job. And since he was quite liberal with mine, this morning, I feel quite sure that he intended for me to do exactly what I'm doing. In fact, I hardly believe that it would be safe for me to go back to the office with all the money he sent me out with. Here, take it."

Slowly, Pot extended his hand, as he said solemnly, "Well, that's a horse of a different color. We will be only too glad to spend some of old Pratt's money. In fact, he still owes me for, well—ah—well that's something else."

"Now, Pot," Doc said, "I always did think you was lying about that, and Pratt did, too. We both think you stole it."

"Danged, if I did," Pot retorted. "You're just trying to judge me by yourself. You would have stole it, but since I'm just naturally more honorable than you, I had to do it my own honest way. So I paid for it."

Their argument was interrupted by the sound of an approaching whistle. Seriously, Doc asked. "Son, how long will it be until your paper carries this story? If, that is, Pratt goes along with it."

"Well," Lawrence answered, "he may want to do a little checking, first. I rather think that he will give a lot of serious thought to it before he decides, either way. But it may even be out in tomorrow's issue."

"Son," Pot said softly, "just to be sure that it comes out, I want you to give Pratt a message from me and Doc. It's something that I never thought I'd ever be saying, but here it is."

Before continuing, though, he turned to Doc. As their eyes met and held for an instant, Doc nodded his head and uttered a brief "Go ahead."

Again, Lawrence marveled at the so complete communication that existed between his old friends. Dual thoughts, interlaced by bonds of long friendship, a window into the mind of the other, that eliminated all need of the spoken word.

Pot continued where he had left off, "Tell Pratt that me and Doc are ready to collect on that debt."

Puzzled, Lawrence studied the blank faces of his friends and realized that they would say no more. Nodding, he said quietly, "I'll tell him."

The blast of the engine sweeping past made all other conversation impossible. So, quickly grasping the extended hand of each, he yelled, "I'll see you soon."

Boarding the train, a minute before it pulled out, he dropped into the first seat he came to. He immediately took from his pocket a notebook and started writing.

So vivid were the events, as portrayed by his friends, that his pencil seemed to have a mind of its own. There was no need of contemplation, as words flowed from its end. Before the hour-long ride to Louisville was ended, the story was done. So intense were his feelings and so sincere his convictions, that he gave no thought to the fact that his boss might refuse to steer the *Enterprise* on such a course of campaign. This fact, was to him, completely inconceivable.

Hoping to find Pratt Larder still at the office, he lost no time in alighting from the train as soon as it pulled into the station. Walking quickly, he soon covered the six blocks to the large building housing the *Enterprise* and was relieved to see Pratt still at his desk.

Pratt Larder, looking through the glass partition separating his office from the news room, viewed the entrance of his number one reporter. Lawrence's exuberance was plainly obvious. To disillusion this boy would bring no enjoyment to him, but it must be done. His education would then be complete.

Steeling himself, he prepared to dash cold water on the boy's enthusiasm. Almost sadly, he visualized the disbelief that would sweep across his face, as he received the news that his source of information was completely unreliable, and his day's work all for nothing.

"Ah! Come in, lad. And how did you find things up at Salem?"

"It's a long story, sir. But I'd like to go over it with you while it's still fresh in my mind."

For the minute, Pratt hated himself for what he must do. "Sure, lad," he said. "But it won't take long. You see, there was a different reason for my sending you out there today, other than to get a story. In fact, I knew there wouldn't even be a story, but it has all been part of your training."

"But, sir, there is a story. And a crusading one for your paper. You see, I met these two old characters—"

His explanation was cut short by the raised hand of his editor. "I know. Doc and Pot. Well, I hate to tell you this, but that was all arranged. They are friends of mine and two of the biggest liars in the whole United States. They lied to you today on my orders. Even if I hadn't told them to, they would have, anyway. My God! Those old buzzards simply don't know how to tell the truth. Now, I'll try to make you understand why I did it—"

Now it was he who was brought to a halt, by a smile that flashed across Lawrence's face, as he held out the letter that Pot had given him.

"Yes, sir," he said, "I know all about that. Now maybe it's I who should do the explaining."

Pratt's face was a cross-section of consternation, disbelief, and anger, as his eyes fell upon and recognized his own handwriting. It was rapidly approaching the purple state, as Lawrence felt impelled to continue, "They were afraid that you would be angry, sir, but decided to chance it for the good of their town. They weren't lying to me up there today. They are asking for your help."

Pratt's face was slowly returning to a more natural color, and now, was swept by a look of amusement. It started with a chuckle, and finally reached down below his belt, before bouncing back with an ear-splitting roar. His laughter lasted long, as Lawrence stood uncomfortably before him. Finally, letting it subside, Pratt wiped the tears from his eyes, while shaking his head slowly from side to side.

In an apologetic tone, he said, "Son, how could I ever have doubted them? Why, they are even better than I thought. I'll sure send them that whiskey tomorrow. They have really earned it."

Again, Lawrence shook his head in disagreement. "No, sir. They didn't lie. It may have been the first time, I don't know about that, but I do know they were sincere today. Every word they told me was the truth; I'm sure of that."

Opening up his notebook, he took from it two sheets of paper. "Here, sir, is my story. Read it before deciding."

Pratt shook his head sadly. "Lad, there's no use. You couldn't have anything that is any good. You must believe me. They didn't utter a word of truth, not one word. I know them too well."

Suspended in midair, Lawrence's hand still retained the story. Pratt's refusal to even glance at it was a gesture of finality. Still holding the papers rigidly before him, his dark eyes flashing with intensity, he said softly, "There's one more thing. Something that Pot said just before I left town. He told me to give you a message.

He said to tell Pratt that he and Doc were ready to collect on that debt."

The laughter died at once in Pratt's eyes, as they widened in surprise. In a voice filled with awe, and one that trembled slightly, he rasped hoarsely, "He said that? Just that way?"

"Yes, sir. Just like that."

Slowly, Pratt's hand went out to grasp the papers that Lawrence still held before him. Shadows swept his eyes. Eyes that saw neither the papers, nor the boy standing quietly in front of him. But instead, dwelt upon something not of the present, of an era long gone, and a world of yesteryear, to which those few words had propelled him.

Amazed at the change in his boss, at just the mention of those few words, the young reporter remained silent—fully aware that momentarily Pratt was living in another dimension, a place he could not enter.

In a voice Lawrence never before had heard him use, he said, "Sit down, lad. If Pot said that, after all these years, then they were serious, very serious. I'll read your story."

As his eyes took in the heading and first paragraph, he raised them to Lawrence's face, as if to say something, but instead, returned to the paper, to read it again. The words stirred deep emotions within him, emotions that had long remained dormant, but were now whipped up by memories of his old friends, and full realization of their desperation in sending him the message out of the past.

The heading, stark, raw and emblazoned, hit like a battering ram. "I saw Delow Hart hung!" And the following words went on to new heights of intensity:

The town of Salem, Indiana stands on trial today, before the eyes of the world. Condemned by those without true knowledge of the facts, of having caused a man to be hung by the neck until dead, by mob justice, without benefit of trial. Such accusations are untrue.

Raising his eyes again to Lawrence's face, Pratt said, "A reporter's opinion?"

Lawrence's reply was instant, "No, sir. A newsman's belief in the facts."

Without further comment, Pratt continued reading:

*I arrived in Salem, four days after the death of Delow Hart,
yet, I still saw him hung. I saw legal justice administered and the
execution carried out. Prior to that, I was made witness to the three
cold-blooded murders committed by him. And I sat at his trial,
which lasted for five years; the verdict was death.*

For ten minutes, Pratt digested the rest of the story. Lawrence,
sitting quietly, waiting for him to finish, realized that he was tired—
emotionally drained by events of the day and wrung dry by the
words he had put to paper.

As Pratt finally laid the sheets of paper on the desk, he seemed
lost in serious study. Clearing his throat, as his words escaped
raggedly, he asked, "About this brother Horace. Are you sure about
his crooked political connections?"

"Sir, if we are to believe anything that Doc and Pot said, then we
must believe all. Yes, I'm sure. So sure, that I'm asking for a byline
on a front page box."

"I suppose you realize what this will mean, in case you're
wrong?'

"Yes, sir. The end of my career, maybe a lawsuit for the paper,
and the possibility of you losing your job. Sir, if I wasn't sure, do
you think I would ask such a thing?"

"No, son, I don't think you would," Pratt answered softly.
"Anyway, I have no choice, since Pot put it the way he did. I can't
refuse. Now, you go home and get some rest. I'm going to catch
number four up to Indianapolis tonight. There are a couple of fellows
I want to talk to. I'll be back at five in the morning. See you here
at seven. Today, you have become a newspaperman. Good night."

"Good night, sir," Lawrence answered. Turning to leave, he
paused and looked again at his boss. He just had to have the answer
to a thing or two.

"Mr. Larder, could you tell me how come you know those two
old fellows, and what Pot meant about the debt? I know I have no
business asking but—" his voice trailed off, as Pratt raised his hand.

"Under the circumstances, I think you're entitled to know. As
you know, I commanded a troop of Cavalry during the war. Well,

they were my scouts, and the best men I could have wished for. Pot wasn't fat in those days; just muscle. I guess he was the most powerful man I ever knew. Doc was like a whiplash. Tough and a hellion in a fight. Guns, knives, or rough and tumble, it didn't make any difference. They spent more time behind enemy lines than the Rebs did. Now, about the debt. They saved my life. I had taken a little spying job upon myself and was caught in civilian clothes. Of course, that meant the firing squad."

Pratt paused in reflection for a moment, then continued, "I don't know how those devils ever found me, but just in time, they broke out of a thicket and ran their horses clear over that firing squad. Killed every one of them, and brought me, four miles, back to our lines. That's when I made the promise. I know this must mean a lot to them or they would never have called on me to make it good."

Still Lawrence lingered, and finally, somewhat embarrassed, he blurted, "Mr. Larder, would you have told Jed Herrick about that whiskey?"

Pratt's chuckle was hearty. "I paid Jed for that whiskey a long time ago, but those old devils don't know it."

With a grin to match Pratt's, Lawrence started to leave, once more, but this time, it was his boss who stopped him, "I'll tell you something else, son. Both Pot and Doc called Hart out, one at a time, but he wouldn't fight them. As old as they are, either one would have killed him, and Hart knew it."

This time, he was through talking, and Lawrence left quietly, as the old man again picked up the story. Though he slept fitfully, he was at the office at the designated time, and found Pratt busy at his desk. Though the strain of a sleepless night was obvious, his eyes gleamed with unsubdued eagerness, as he greeted Lawrence warmly.

At the anxious look on the boy's face, he smiled, and said, "The political angle on Horace clicks, so we are going all out. Is there anything in your story that you might want to change?"

"No, sir," Lawrence's happy voice answered, "not a thing."

"Fine," Pratt answered. "It's all yours. We will hit the streets with it today. Brother Horace's fangs are pulled. When I showed your story to the right people and told them what we were going to do, they agreed to drop him like a hot potato. He's done, in his state politically, when the Governor sees our story. There will be no investigation, either. I've been promised that. So if that's all it takes to save Salem, it's saved. Now, get this to the composing room."

The following morning, the first copies of the *Enterprise* reached the depot, to find Pot and Doc eagerly waiting. There on the front page, in a black-bordered box, was the fruit of their efforts. Also, to their delight, were two beautiful gallons of Kentucky Bourbon, whose tags read merely, Pot and Doc. Hooking a long, bony finger into the handle of each jug, Doc said, "Bring the paper, Pot. I'll carry the valuables."

Grunting a reply, Pot folded the paper so that it would fit into his hip pocket, and panted and puffed his way up the Street in Doc's wake. Trying hard not to get too far behind, he growled, "Durn you, don't walk so fast. And don't you dare get out of my sight. Besides, I've got two free hands, so let me carry one of them there jugs."

Without missing a stride, Doc dipped a little and left one of the jugs resting in the dust. But not before hefting the two before him, as if to measure their contents. This little motion was not to go unnoticed by his companion, who immediately set up a howl. "There you go, cheating me again. You're just a natural-born crook."

But his tirade fell upon deaf ears, as Doc increased his pace, bound for the sanctuary of the courtyard and the shade of the big ash tree. He was sitting comfortably, with his back resting against the rough bark and jug tilted, before Pot puffed into the shelter of the huge branches.

Sinking down onto the soft grass, with a sigh, he lost no time in pulling the stopper and tilting his own jug. His companion, thirst quenched for the moment, slowly put the stopper back into his jug. A dreamy look encompassed his long, bony face, as he wiped the drooping handlebar mustache with the back of his hand. Looking at his companion, he said, "Come on, Pot. Quit that guzzling and read me that paper."

Without even taking the jug from his lips, Pot reached back and tugged the paper from his pocket. Tossing it into Doc's lap, he growled around the neck of his jug, "Here, read the danged thing, yourself."

To Doc's protest that he couldn't read, he paid no attention, but only flapped a hand and slowly let the bourbon slide down his throat in trickles, as if to savor it more.

Grumbling, Doc opened the paper and started to read to himself. There was a splutter from Pot, as he took the jug from his mouth, long enough to shout. "Read out loud, durn you. It's your turn. I read to you the last time."

"Well, alright," Doc answered. "But quit swallowing so loud or I cain't hear myself, and I'll be durned if I'm a'gonna read something I cain't hear."

Grunting in indignation, Pot lowered his jug and listened silently, as his companion read slowly. Pronouncing each word separately and apart from the others, each one to be relished unto itself, a triumph in every one, and each a jewel, to be tasted well before being released.

For twenty minutes, he labored through the story, and when he was finished, lowered the paper gently to his lap. Slowly picking up his jug, he took a long pull at its contents. Neither spoke for several minutes, each lost in his own thoughts. Finally, Pot broke the mounting silence. "Well, old friend, that ought to do it. I'm right proud of you. Before the week is out, the Street will begin to fold. The no-goods will drift away to some other helpless town that's not got a friend like Pratt Larder."

For a moment, Pot was silent, frowning slightly. Then, he continued, "Pretty soon now, you can squire the Widow Arnold right down South Main, without fearing some drunk will try to take her away from you. All the saloons will be gone, with the gamblers, the girls, and the killers. Yep, it sure will be nice. No more drunks flopping all over the place, yelling and fighting. When the saloons go, next week, next month, or whenever it is, that will be the last of that. Hurray! No more saloons, no more drunks."

There was a moment of terrible silence, broken finally, by Doc's quavering voice. "Pot! All the saloons?"

Pot's answer came very softly. "No. All, but one."

Feud Justice

INTRODUCTION

S omewhere along that thin line between boy and manhood must come a testing of the steel, before emergence is full and complete. None escape, for it is inevitable. Though it may suddenly be thrust upon him without thought, planning, or warning, he will recognize its meaning. Its coming may be both frightening and unwanted. As the blade is tempered, so comes the true worth of the sword, and the testing molds the true warp of the man.

This is the story of one such youth, Joey Taylor, and how he met that test.

DEDICATION

This book is dedicated to my wife, Stella. It could not have been completed without her patience with my detached presence during the months I devoted to writing this story.

And to Mrs. Estelle Walker, Owner and Editor of *FULL CRY MAGAZINE*, without whose willingness to devote valuable time to editing poorly-spelled and phrased script, this and other stories of mine might never have been published.

Feud Justice
Chapter 1

The dusty haze of late summer hung over the hill country of Southern Indiana. That Sunday afternoon in September, the Crawley brothers, Pete and Sol, paid a visit to Tab Taylor's home. They called to Tab to come out of his house. The tired leaves of sassafras and sumac, in the fence rows along the gravel road, had not ceased trembling from their car passing, when old Tab answered their call.

Striding purposely toward them, his lean, dark face hardened, as he saw too late that both held .12 gauge pump guns. Only the bleakness in his eyes gave indication that he was aware of a possible trap and that the time for talking had passed. Halting only a few feet away, he stared coldly, and waited for them to speak.

Pete's whiskey-soaked voice cracked out first. "Tab, we come fer the dog!"

"And I've told you before, you cain't have him," the old man said softly.

"Our bitch whelped him," Sol grated, "and he's our'n!"

"Now, I'll say this once more," Tab said piercingly, "you forfeited all rights to ownership when you shot her and left her for dead on the trail, with the pups yet unborn. But for my boy, Joey, that pup would have died, same as all the rest. You don't own him, never did, and never will!"

Even as they moved suddenly to get him between them, his hand flashed under his coat, to the gun he always wore. He must have had a second of horror, as he remembered, too late, that his holster was hanging in the house—before a load of number sixes from Sol's gun slammed into his back.

Knocked forward, but not off his feet, by the impact, the old man slowly twisted as he crumpled, until he was facing Sol. Only disbelief shown in his eyes, that he had been caught so easily. In an instant, the light in his eyes flickered out. The hand under the coat still twitched, searching for the gun that wasn't there. For a few short seconds, the Crawleys seemed stunned by the result of their violent action. They stared, in fascination, as the blood poured from the ping hole in the old man's back, and mingled with the dust of the roadside.

Molly Taylor's one short scream from the doorway brought their heads up with a jerk. Only then, as they viewed this delicate little woman, Tab's wife for fifty years, and the mother of his five sons, did the full impact of what they had done strike them. For an instant, they stared at her blankly. As whiskey nerve fled, they suddenly departed. While the cloud of dust rose high under the speeding wheels of their car, she ran to where her husband lay.

Born and bred to the Tennessee mountains, she was no stranger to violence. Tab's normally dark face was pale, as she knelt and tenderly took his head into her lap. Gently, she brushed dust from his gray hair and closed the still staring eyes. In silence, she slowly rocked back and forth; with head bent, the tears flowed unchecked down her wrinkled cheeks, and onto the upturned face of her dead husband.

Joey, sixteen, and Tab's youngest, found her there, when he came, on the run, from the barn. In his fair-complexioned face were the same delicate lines as his mother's, and in his slender body, all the marks of her side of the family; as an absolute contrast to the large-framed, rugged darkness of Tab and four brothers.

Struck mute by horror, he stood transfixed beside his mother, and then slowly allowed his knees to collapse, until he knelt beside her. An effort to speak brought forth only a croak from his dry throat. At the sound, she lifted her head, and looked into his white face, which with every straining feature, begged for an explanation, or even more, that she tell him it wasn't so.

With the iron will of the mountain woman, she forced her eyes to dryness, and her voice not to tremble, as she said, "It was the Crawleys. Go get Tom."

As was his habit to obey her without question, he rose at once, pausing only briefly to spill dust over the fast-coagulating blood around which flies had already started to buzz, even though his stomach roiled at the sight.

As his '29 Model A roadster left the yard with a roar, he knew that the shot would have already brought Dan and Arnie down from the still, on the run. Bob was with Tom down at the Cabin. Even then, with all the thoughts buzzing through his mind, he still experienced his usual feeling of distaste for Tom's roadhouse. Sure, Tom was the oldest, married, and had his own home. Sure, the Taylors made moonshine, as did most in the hills, since the big Depression set in. Man had to make a living some way, and besides, the law didn't seem to care much. But to him, there was something evil about the big rambling establishment of Tom's. It was called the Cabin, simply because it was made of logs. But it was an outlet for Taylor moonshine, better than having to deal with town bootleggers.

Most of the three miles to Tom's place ran between the foot of the ridge and the river. As he careened from one chuck hole to another, he had a sudden feeling that if he could just jump into the river, he could wash away all that had happened within the last few minutes.

To the flatland traveler, who suddenly found himself threading the many tortuous hairpin curves of the old state highway, as it wound its way to the bottom of the knobs, the sight of the Cabin close up on the right, with its large graveled parking area, was often a welcome sight.

Though innocent enough in appearance, with its single gasoline pump out front, and the large Coke sign on the porch, men who indulged, had a way of knowing. From long experience, Tom had learned to recognize their need, and to nod sympathetically, as their trembling hand sloshed out a little of the drink he had already poured before they reached the bar. He knew, too, as they tossed the first down and pushed the glass forward for a second, what their first words would be. "Gawd, I didn't know Indiana had these kinds of roads."

As Joey slid out onto the highway, turning left, he roared toward the Cabin, two hundred yards down the road. As he slammed into the graveled front, he dismounted almost before the car stopped rolling. He headed for the door, on the run. A large black bear, chained to the corner of the building, growled menacingly, but he hardly saw it, as he sped by.

The interior of the big room was darkly shaded and quiet, as he burst through the door. Pausing briefly, to let his eyes adjust, he felt relief in its coolness. No one was at the bar, but two men he knew from downriver, lolled lazily at one of the tables. They stared uneasily at the strain and horror in his face. Silently, one pointed to the back room.

"Bob! Tom!" Joey yelled hoarsely. Instantly, the broad, powerful figure of Tom appeared in the doorway, with the taller and younger Bob, close behind. They stared at Joey's white face, knowing that no little thing had worked the kid up that way.

Joey's words came hoarsely. "The Crawleys just killed Pa!"

The brothers stiffened as their faces whitened, but wasted no time on questions; that could come later. Tom whirled towards the back room, shouted the news to his wife, Nell, grabbed a belt and holster containing a single action .45, and strapped it around him, as he headed for the door.

Seeing that he intended taking his car, a low-slung, high-powered, black touring job, parked at the end of the Cabin, Bob and Joey mounted the Ford roadster, on the run. But less than a quarter mile from the Cabin, Tom pulled around them with a swoosh, and was soon lost to sight in the dust and distance that grew rapidly between them. Joey knew there was a reason for the type of car that Tom drove, but he really didn't like to think about it.

Tom was standing, looking down at his father's body, when they arrived. One arm was around the frail shoulders of his mother, as she sagged slightly against him, as if drawing strength from the great chest, where she rested her head.

Dan and Arnie stood a few feet away, scowling down at the body of their father, as they muttered darkly to each other. Joey was relieved to see that Tab was now covered with a blanket and that his head rested on a pillow. No flies were in evidence now, as all of the blood had been covered with dust. The job that Joey started had been finished by his mother or Tom.

Dan, always the impetuous one, stared angrily at Joey, out of stormy eyes. "It's all your fault," he lashed out bitterly. "If you hadn't brought that dog home"—but Bob whirled on him fiercely.

"That's enough of that, Dan."

Though equal in size and two years his senior, Dan had learned long before that Bob contained a wildness that he could not match. Too, he knew the reason that his brother had stopped him; a reason that he, along with the rest of the family, were in full agreement with.

"I'm sorry, Joey," he said softly, as he looked away. "I didn't mean it."

Puzzled and hurt by Dan's words, the youngest of the Taylor clan turned to his mother. "Ma, what does he mean?"

Love shown in her eyes, as she reached out and touched his tortured face lightly. Again, as so many times before, she was aware of the difference between him and his brothers. In him, no subdued violence to erupt at a minute's notice, as in the others; no dark burning fires of passion ready to flame unchecked, as was so much a part of the average hill or mountain man. The very gentleness of his nature had always drawn the two of them closer together, in a bond that the others both recognized and respected.

"It's alright, Joey. He didn't mean anything. Not a thing."

As his eyes searched their faces, he met only looks of sympathy, and would have pursued the question further, had not Dan, turning his anger elsewhere, spoken in a flat, cold voice.

"Well, what are we waiting for?"

Big, quiet, taciturn Tom looked at him steadily, and answered, "We're waiting for the sheriff and coroner."

Dan flushed, and said darkly, "You know what I mean!"

They all knew what he meant, and as the faces of Bob and Arnie darkened in agreement, Tom spoke sharply, "I know what you mean, and you can forget it."

As Bob and Arnie moved to his side, Dan's anger rose higher. "That's your pa laying there, murdered by the Crawleys. You mean to say that you ain't gonna do anything about it?"

With his father dead, Tom, being the oldest, automatically became head of the family. It was the law of the hill people. But he was only a few minutes into his new position of authority and yet to be tested.

Now, Bob spoke bitterly. "What kind of a Taylor have you become, Tom? I remember that time, back in Tennessee …"

Tom cut him off sharply. "This is not Tennessee and them times are past. We'll let the law take care of this!"

Arnie was a follower, but it was Bob and Dan's hotheadedness he must subdue. Dan spat contemptuously at Tom's feet. "I'm glad Pa cain't hear you. What do you suppose he would be doing this minute, if that wuz you alayin' there?"

Tom stared at his brothers steadily. He knew the fever of the fires that were running rampant through them; the violent urge to revenge a hurt, and the surge of pride to take care of their own. He, too, had felt those things when he was their age—before he learned restraint and the necessity of controlled emotions. He felt no anger at Dan's words, but only sympathy for the searing emotions they were experiencing.

Joey stood silently, watching and listening, in a complete state of confusion. Only six, when the family moved to Indiana, he remembered very little of their days before. Some vague stirrings of memory brought back pictures of his father and Tom coming and going, stern-faced and silent for days at a time, with their rifles over their arms. And the times when men gathered at the cabin on the mountainside, to talk in subdued tones for hours, then to break up into small groups and disappear into the darkness, every one armed to the teeth.

Out of deference to their mother, the others never talked about the days before Indiana. A new country, a new life, she had decreed, when they took up land in the Indiana knob country, and it had been so—until now.

The fires in Dan still burned high, as he stared coldly into Tom's steady eyes. Softly then, he said, "Get your guns, boys, and bring my .45." Tom moved swiftly to plant himself in their path. For an instant, they paused, and as Dan joined them, he moved forward with a growl. Molly Taylor's clear voice cracked out, with all the authority of the mountain matriarch she had become.

"Stand where you are," she lashed out scornfully. "I'll not have you fighting among yourselves, even before your father has grown cold." Fiercely, her blazing, blue eyes raked them, and they stood meekly before her. Then, turning abruptly, she knelt beside Tab's body, threw back the blanket, and thrust one hand into the side pocket of his trousers. Then, withdrawing her hand, she stood upright, facing them with open palm. On it laid four silver dollars. "Do you know what these mean?"

With pain in his voice, Tom said, "Ma, do you really have …?"

She cut him off. "Yes, Tom. It has to be said. There's no better time." As Tom remained silent, the others looked at each other, questioningly. Dan's eyes glittered. Being able to remember a little further back than the other two, he thought he knew, but was never sure. Bob and Arnie stared blankly, while Joey understood nothing. Tom knew, of course, but he stood now with eyes downcast, not wishing to interfere with his mother.

The big silver dollars, well-worn, seemed too heavy for her frail hand, but her voice was steel when she continued, "Count them; there's four, each for a man your father killed." Joey felt his senses reeling, but the others still stood unmoving; each face a dark shadow of disguised emotions. "Oh!" She added, "They were all fair fights; no murder like this, but they were gunfights."

Joey, half-blinded by a terrible sickness that gripped his stomach, gropingly made his way to a stump just inside the fence. Weakly, he sat down and dropped his face into his hands. He had learned more, he realized, about the past of his family in the last few minutes, than in all his sixteen years before. Through the fog engulfing him, their voices came clearly. Tom was saying, "But, Ma, Pa never murdered anybody. He never shot another man in the back."

For a moment she didn't answer, as the years rolled back, and young, vibrant, powerful, granite-hard Tab stood beside her, wearing the Taylor name proudly, as one both respected and feared throughout the mountains. Then her voice came softly, "I know, Tom, I know. Not legally, at least, but in a way, it was murder."

When they would have protested, a lift of her hand stilled their words. "It was a certain kind of murder, simply because other men were afraid of your pa and were half-beaten, even before they went up against him."

Slowly, Joey accepted that which had been and now was. As talking of the others droned on, the sickness in his stomach was being replaced by the slow-growing bitterness of shame in himself. Shame that he had not known before now, bore down with crushing impact.

True, there never had been a real closeness between him and his father, but then, the old man had always been fair. Though never really understanding his youngest son's unswerving determination to get an education, he had, nevertheless, gone along with it; even to the extent of getting him the Ford roadster, so that he could continue attending high school at the county seat in Sladen. He was aware that his mother had played no small part in that decision.

His refusal to help make moonshine, though, had been the one thing for which his father had never really completely forgiven him. To Tab, it was a way of life, and he saw no wrong in it; but for the interceding of Molly on Joey's behalf, he would never have let the matter drop. Joey was never aware of the respect that Tab had for the iron will that lay buried deep within him. An angrily-surprised, secretly-pleased Tab had listened with astonishment to Joey's vowed determination to take no part in moonshining. In the boy's white face and blazing eyes, he had seen that of Molly, when she had decreed that the Taylors were leaving the feud-ridden country of the Tennessee mountains, and realized, for the first time, that his youngest was not the weakling he had thought.

An exclamation from one of the others brought Joey's head up, to see a dust cloud in the distance. That would be the sheriff and coroner. Reluctantly, he dragged himself from the stump and eased over to stand beside the others, as the car drew to a stop.

Big, fat Sheriff Merlin dismounted and slowly approached them, mopping his brow with a bandana, as he moved toward the murder scene. The formalities didn't take long, for both Merlin and the coroner were perspiring profusely, and eager to get back to town. Molly's choice of the undertaker was noted and they promised to send him right out. They were ready to leave.

As he reached the door of his car, the sheriff turned wheezily, and stared at the group who stood, silently awaiting their departure.

The tip of his tongue flicked out to moisten fat, tobacco-stained lips, before he said harshly, "Don't none of you Taylors go trying to take the law into your own hands. We'll take care of this."

Bob's dark eyes narrowed to slits, as he murmured softly, "See that you do, Sheriff. And don't take too long; not too long."

A flush mounted into the sheriff's flabby cheeks, and he seemed about to speak, but the coroner's voice complaining about the heat apparently changed his mind, as he climbed in the car and left without another word.

Now that Tab could be moved, they gently lifted him, still rolled in the blanket, and carried him into the house, where he was placed on the bed. A feeling of utter uselessness swept over Joey, as he stood, looking at the still form. What had he ever contributed to the welfare of the family? Who was he to think that he was too good to make whiskey? And had his desire for the dog brought on his father's death, as Dan had suggested? He had to know! He had to know!

Feud Justice
Chapter 2

For the first time, since it opened three years before, the doors of the Cabin were padlocked. Still, they drifted in from out of the hills to sit on the porch in quiet groups, and talk softly of all that had happened. The old lion of the hills was dead and that took some studying on.

Would the Taylor boys run wild, now that the iron hand of Tab no longer held the reins, or would Molly be able to keep them in check? Older heads, realizing the steel within her, figured she might, with the help of big, silent, and level-headed Tom. With a shake of their heads, they all agreed that her work was cut out for her. The young'un, Joey, would be no trouble, for he was soft like his ma, but the others were something else.

Tom and Dan, having moved in with the family temporarily, took care of most of the arrangements, as directed by their mother. Tab was to be taken back to Tennessee for burial on Tuesday. Molly kept a steady vigil beside the casket all day Monday, and would not be persuaded to leave until late that night, when she had reached the point of complete exhaustion. Tom, unheeding of her protests, picked her up and carried her to the car, then home, and into bed.

Being practical, the family wasted little time on elaborate preparations. Nell, Tom's wife, would stay behind to feed the animals. The rest loaded into Tom's car and were on their way to the funeral establishment by six a.m. Minutes after they departed, a flat-bed logging truck rolled up, and before the startled eyes of a few observers, the over box, with Tab and casket inside, was hoisted up and chained down tightly. Within minutes, the grim trek back home had begun.

Molly, not being her usual alert self, had failed to notice the last-minute, hurried movements of her sons, just before they left the house. Before closing the trunk lid, Tom paused, to nod briefly at the others. Quickly then, Dan had again entered the house, to emerge, seconds later, with three tightly-rolled belts and holsters, a .12 gauge pump gun, and each carrying a single action .45. Though Joey's eyes widened as they were quickly stowed and the lid shut, a shake of Bob's head sealed his lips, when he would have spoken.

It was possible, though, that Molly might not have commented, had she noticed. Being the person that she was, it was not likely that she was completely without bitterness at the cold-blooded slaying of her mate of fifty years. Then, too, there had been no word of the Crawleys, and they did need to travel through Waverly, the Crawley's hometown, on the Tennessee/Kentucky border, on the way to Tab's final resting place.

They rode, mostly in silence, the first few miles. As her eyes sought the faces of her four oldest, the grimness of each told her that to protest might have, for the first time, been futile. They ate a prepared lunch on the way, stopping only long enough to gas up about noon. Around two o'clock, Waverly appeared, without warning, as they topped a high hill, and viewed it laid out along the highway in the valley below.

Within minutes, they reached the outskirts, and Tom pulled to the side of the road. For a minute, all sat silently, looking at the few old and dusty houses that made up the town of about fifteen hundred. Few signs of life were evident. A hundred yards down the street, on the left, a tired and sagging front porch graced the front of a small grocery store. Two lounging figures drooped in the shade of the overhang, while a skinny, long-legged hound sniffed around the rusty gasoline pump at the edge of the road.

Tom broke the heavy silence in the car with two words, but he spoke for all, "Let's go."

As Molly's worried glance took in the stern and cold faces of her sons, the question forming on her lips was stilled. She knew, and there was nothing she could do. Silently, she watched them get out and go around to the rear. When Joey would have followed, she grasped his arm, and with a shake of her head, bade him to keep his seat.

As Tom quickly handed out the rolled gun rigs to Bob and Dan, each buckled on his gear at once, and checked his gun. Arnie reached in the trunk and pulled out his shotgun, as Tom strapped his own .45 around his waist. The clatter of the action, as Arnie pumped in a shell loaded with buckshot, was the loudest noise made so far, since they had stopped. Inside the car, Joey failed to suppress a shudder at the sound. There was something uncanny, he felt, about Arnie's attachment for that shotgun. Scorning a rifle or handgun, he spent hours lovingly polishing and oiling that gun. All were aware, when the gun was loaded with buckshot, it made a formidable weapon.

Silently, the two inside the car watched. Fanning out, the others started slowly down the street, four abreast. Arnie walked on the left, with the shotgun resting over that arm; Tom, on the extreme right, with Dan and Bob rounding out the middle. Not a word was spoken, as they walked at an unhurried pace. The two on the store porch were on their feet now, as the grim-faced four came steadily onward. Finally, when about fifty yards away, the older of the two watchers shielded his eyes from the evening sun with his hand, and gasped, "That's the Taylors."

With that remark, he turned hurriedly and entered the store, with the other close behind. None of this was missed by the sharp eyes of the brothers, nor did they fail to see the faces now appearing at the windows, and from inside the door. But not until they were even with the porch, did they appear to notice, then they acted quickly. Abruptly, Arnie and Bob swung suddenly onto the porch and into the store. As he went through the door, Bob's gun was in his hand.

Only silence met their entrance, as the five men inside stood, deathly quiet, with all their hands carefully in view. Blankly, they stared back at the raking eyes of Bob and Arnie. Bob snarled harshly, "Where's the Crawleys?"

One man, who wore a denim apron tied around his waist, apparently, the proprietor, answered sullenly. "Ain't seen 'em. They ain't here."

For a few more seconds, the battle of eyes continued, and then there was an audible click, as Arnie set the safety on his gun. Slowly, they backed out, and not until they were back in the road with the others, did Bob lower the hammer on his Colt.

"They know?" Tom asked softly.

"They know," Bob muttered, through clenched teeth. "They know, alright."

The rest of their stroll was uneventful. Another hundred yards down to the end of the street, then retraced their steps. Only the silent faces with bitter eyes, stared at them from the store windows, as they passed slowly by. No one, however, came out. They didn't see another soul on their way back to the car.

Each paused only long enough to unstrap his gun, and Arnie checked the safety on his shotgun, before climbing back into the car. Joey suddenly realized that he was sweating profusely. Wiping his wet palms on his trouser legs, he stole a glance at his mother. She sat, with eyes closed, her lips moving ever so slightly. But at the click of a door latch, she abruptly opened her eyes and raised her head proudly to stare straight ahead, as the others were seated and the car got underway, without a word being spoken.

Joey noticed that the guns hadn't been put in the trunk this time, but rested under the hand of each, across their laps. Tom drove slowly through town, but picked up speed at the end of the street. The logging truck would now be close behind them with the time lost in the town.

Thirty minutes later brought them to the outskirts of Clayton, and then to the funeral parlor that was to take care of the proceedings. Here, in-laws were waiting to accompany them to the cemetery. Thirty minutes later, the truck pulled in, and willing hands quickly transferred its load to the waiting hearse. The small procession was soon winding its way to the graveyard, on a hill above the town. The service was brief; rendered by a young minister who hadn't known Tab or any of his family. He was not without insight, however; he was aware of the grim undercurrent of those attending the funeral. He could understandably be forgiven for his haste.

In a little over two hours after arriving, the nose of Tom's car was again pointed north, as they headed for Indiana. No less than a dozen men had offered to accompany them to help search for the Crawleys, but Tom had refused each offer firmly. His statement that the law would handle it, was met with blank looks and a shake of their heads. Was this Tab Taylor's son?

They sped through Waverly disdainfully, without even a glance at the old storefront. Joey rode silently, lost in thought of all that had happened in the last three days. So many things pounded through his head. He had refrained from asking about Dan's remark concerning his dog, but he would have no peace of mind until he knew the truth.

Feud Justice
Chapter 3

At the thought of his big hound, Raider, a warm glow stole over him. His mind went back three years, that fall. He had heard the bellow of a shotgun in the valley below him and the sharp howl of a hound, as he stood listening to the Crawley's pack drive a fox. The strange dog had opened sharply, only a minute before, in the vicinity of the shot. Joey had headed down the ridge, on the run.

He came upon them at the edge of the thicket along the creek. Pete and Sol Crawley stood looking down at a long-legged, speckled hound bitch. Joey's sorrowful eyes took in the small red spots dotting her neck and shoulders. Her heavy breathing told that she still lived, but just barely. Most folks thereabouts used number twos for foxes, and he figured the Crawleys no different. She was mortally wounded, he decided, and in a fury, turned to the men.

"Why'd you shoot her?"

Pete scowled and muttered, "It was an accident. Thought she was the fox."

Sol glared at his brother. "Danged, Pete, that's not so! You shot her out of pure cussed meanness, cause she cut through and jumped that fox, just when you thought you had it in the bag. Now we'll never know if she was any good."

"So what?" Pete growled. "She didn't cost us anything, and besides, she oughtn't to have slipped her collar. Cost me a fifteen dollar red fox, to boot. Come on, let's go."

Sol still hesitated. "The pups might have turned out good."

"Probably from some cur," Pete said. "Come on, come on."

Joey saw the whole story now. She was obviously a stolen dog, probably from Tennessee, and with pups due any time. The Crawleys had already disappeared around a turn in the ridge. As she made an effort to raise her head towards her flank, he winced with her moan of pain. Tenderly, he laid his hand upon her head and crooned in sympathy for her torture. But he knew the time had come to act.

Quickly, he jumped up and sped up the path towards the top of the ridge. Like a buck deer, his brown legs flashed, as they drove him like pistons over the hill and down the other side. He found his mother in the yard. "Ma! Ma! Come quick, come quick; you gotta help me, we gotta help her."

He was frantic, and under other circumstances, she might have found his actions amusing, but the desperation in his voice forbade that. His clutching hand caught her by the arm, as if to drag her bodily, to do his bidding.

"Wait up, son, suppose you tell me what you're talking about," she said, bracing her feet against his tugging.

His breath came in gasps. "The Crawleys shot their speckled bitch, but she ain't dead. Come on, come on."

Molly Taylor had never seen her youngest in such a state, but he still wasn't making much sense. But at the name 'Crawleys,' her face sobered. With a slight shake of her head, she said, "Now, Joey, you know we can't afford to aggravate the Crawleys. If it was their dog, I guess they had a right to shoot her, no matter what we think. It's best we not get messed up in it."

He was beside himself. "But, Ma, they shot her on Taylor land, and just went off and left her; only she's not dead. And, Ma, she's nigh to whelping."

Her small hand grasped his arm. "How close?"

"Any minute now."

"Lord, why didn't you say so? Get a sack out of the crib. Quick, now."

Impatiently, Joey trotted well ahead, stopping every little bit to allow her to catch up. Though small and sprightly for her age, she was no match for the wings on the feet of her excited son. At the crest, she bade him go ahead, and she would follow as quickly as possible.

Like a phantom gazelle, he leapt down the ridge. Before she was halfway down, she could see him in the small clearing at the bottom, kneeling over a smaller, dark object. When still yards away, she could see that he was crazily waving her to hurry—in a minute, she saw why.

The whelping had begun. Two tiny still forms lay pitifully to the side. Though Joey was trying frantically to rub some life into them, she knew that it was hopeless. Moaning, the female tried to help, but she was far past the limit of her endurance. In rapid succession, three more had made their appearance, and this time, with obviously needed help from Molly.

With dismayed eyes, Joey was sickened to see, that as she dried each one off and laid it carefully aside, it, too, was as still as the rest. But wait, that third one. Didn't it move? It did! It did!

With an exclamation of delight, he dropped to his knees beside it. "Ma, look, look."

Together, they brought it back from the very edge of darkness, that hovered so threateningly close. Breathed life into the small little mite of a thing, and at last, had their reward in a weak wail of hunger. Quickly, Molly thrust him to one of the swollen teats, and within seconds, he was sucking greedily. With all the pup's tugging, Joey still looked worriedly to his mother. "Ma, is he getting any milk?"

Her eyes were soft, as she gently moved him to another nipple. "Well, not much, Joey. Just the colostrum mostly, but that's what he needs right now. If she could just stay alive for a day or two, he might have a chance."

"We'll take her home and doctor her."

Sadly, she shook her head. "No, son, I don't think she's in any shape to move, and all the doctoring in the world will never do her any good."

As tears sparkled in Joey's eyes, seeking her face so beseechingly, she added, "We can't move her, but we can build a shelter over her, and take care of them both right here."

Smiling softly at the look of joy on his face, she quickly issued instructions. So eager was he to be off, that she had hardly time enough to list the things she needed. He seemed to fairly float up the path, and within minutes, was lost to view.

While she waited, she carefully moved the pup from one teat to the other, lest even one drop of the precious life-giving nourishment be lost. As he tugged valiantly, the female whined ever so weakly, and tried to raise her head.

Crooning sympathetically, Molly responded. "Sure now, old girl, you want to see your baby, don't you?" she murmured, as she picked up the pup and held it in front of the mother's nose.

Her efforts to lick the little fellow were pitiful to watch. Quickly, Molly shifted him to one hand, and slipped the other under her head. Lifted up in that manner, the task was much easier. When Joey returned, much sooner than his mother thought possible, she had washed him from stem to stern, while he whimpered with delight.

Molly placed him gently up against his mother's warm flank, where he instantly fell asleep. Joey had brought everything she had requested—several yards of binder twine, a hatchet, four gunny sacks, a quart fruit jar full of milk, and a pan.

Quickly, she poured some of the milk out in the pan and lifted the female's head off the ground, holding the pan up to her, as she did so. Joey stood, in fascination, as she lapped greedily, until his mother raised her head and indicated the hatchet with her eyes, as she said, "Son, you're wasting time. Get busy cutting the poles for the lean-to. Not big ones, now mind you, for it won't have to be but a small one."

Picking up the hatchet, Joey looked questionably at his mother. "Ma," he said softly, "it can't be too small, cause I'm gonna stay here, too." Being no stranger to the moods of her youngest, she detected the iron determination in his voice. Seldom did he seek to force his opinion upon others, but when he did, there was no changing his mind.

She did not argue, but sent him on his way, with a wave of her hand. While he was gone, she poured the rest of the milk in the pan, which she held until the last drop had been lapped up. The pup still slept, while his mother rested with a grateful sigh. The look in her eyes was payment enough to Molly for all she had done. She wasn't in any great pain, Molly decided, but was, apparently, slowly bleeding to death inside.

Soon, Joey was back with an armful of poles. Together, they set the corners in place and lashed the crossbars on with the binder twine. The top went on fast, but he had to make another cutting before the sides could be finished. A larger one for the back pole was cut, closer to hand, and soon, the job was done.

The lean-to had been constructed over the dogs, so they only had to lift her onto the gunny sacks that had been spread carefully over the dirt floor. With her well to one side, there was ample room left for Joey to lay full length.

"See, Ma, I can do fine here, just fine," he said.

Joey had been so lost in his reminiscing, that he had been unaware that they had passed through Louisville; but a splash of rain on the windshield, as they traversed the bridge across the Ohio, snapped him back to reality, but not for long. He remembered, only too well, how hard it had rained the first night he stayed in the lean-to. And if it hadn't been for his mother's foresight to suggest a tarpaulin cover for the shelter, and a ditch around the back and sides, he might have fared much worse than he did.

Bob had brought his supper, the lantern, and jacket, along about dark. Good, old Bob. He had even offered to stay with him. But that would have seemed too much like he was afraid. So he responded with indignation, and Bob, with a chuckle, returned to the house.

For two days, he had kept his vigil, and on the third night, the bitch had died. With careful, around the clock attention, the pup had hung on, steadily increasing in strength each day. Within two weeks, he was lapping milk out of a pan, and from then on, it was a matter of keeping him out from underfoot.

He had gotten his name from a bad habit. At about three months, he was raiding every hen nest on the place. It was then that Joey decided to call him Raider. He was broken of that, though, as Joey recalled with a chuckle, when he bravely, but foolishly, made an attempt to drive an old turkey hen from her eggs. After the beating she gave him, he never filched another egg.

As he grew in size and beauty, the story of how he came to be, spread rapidly through the hills, much to the chagrin of the Crawleys. They were often the brunt of wry remarks, concerning what they had thrown away. As his natural hunting ability developed rapidly, their feelings in the matter slowly turned to bitterness.

It soon became evident, that he had a little more than his share of canine brains, and was destined to become one of a rare type, an all around. At a year, he was not only treeing coon, but driving a fox with the best packs in the hills, and running at the front. But never did he mix his pursuits. He seemed to know just what kind of game the Taylors were after, and bothered nothing else on that hunt.

By the time he was two, the Crawleys were determined to have him. Their remarks concerning this were drifting back to the Taylors more frequently. Joey's family never discussed this within Joey's hearing, and for the most part, he was unaware of the growing tension between the families.

As Tom's car climbed out of the Ohio River bottoms, the steady beat of the rain on the windshield, and the monotonous swishing of the wipers, slowly lulled Joey to sleep, but not before he made a vow to himself. He would demand the truth of his father's death. He planned to take his place beside the other Taylor men in whatever operations they might choose to keep the family together.

Feud Justice
Chapter 4

At breakfast the next morning, Joey decided not to put off the showdown any longer. Tom and Nell were moving back to the Cabin, and he must speak while they were all together. He picked his chance, during a lull in the conversation, "Listen, everybody, I've got something to say."

Something in his voice commanded their instant attention. As one by one, they laid down their eating tools and stared silently at him, the presence of a new man in the Taylor family made itself known. This was not the same Joey of yesterday. And they waited for him to speak.

His voice came with clear determination, as his eyes went slowly from face to face. "First, I want to know exactly what Dan meant when he said I caused Pa's shooting. Second, from now on, you treat me like any other man in the family, and give me my share of the responsibilities. Third, I'll help run the still, same as the rest. And fourth," here his voice faltered, and he looked down at his plate as he spoke, "I'm not going back to school."

For a moment, there was complete silence, as they all looked at one another. Wise mother that she was, Molly held her tongue, waiting and hoping for the response she wanted to hear from the rest. She was not disappointed. Bob was the first to speak, "Joey, you're doing your part by going to school. You can't quit."

Joey shook his head violently. "No, I'm not. You've all been carrying me long enough. School is not important anymore. I've got to help with the work. I'm quitting."

Unconsciously, they all looked at Tom. Sympathetically, his dark eyes rested on Joey's face. He said, "That's where you're wrong. Your going to school is important. The rest of us, except Ma, ain't got no education, and the world is going to pass us by some of these days. We're counting on your learning to sorta help keep the rest of us from getting too far behind."

Tom paused briefly, as the others all nodded their heads in agreement. For the first time, uncertainty showed on Joey's face. He opened his mouth to speak, but Tom wasn't finished.

"You didn't know it, I guess, but Pa was glad that you wanted to get an education and be a preacher. He would have changed a lot of things that have happened, if he could, but since it was too late for that, he hoped maybe you might sorta make up for it."

"Pa really felt that way?" he asked hoarsely.

"Yes," Tom answered solemnly, "he often talked of it to me."

A bewildered Joey shook his head. "But, I never knew. He never let on that he approved."

"Well, he didn't, at first," Tom replied, "but he changed, and this last year he acted real proud about it."

Molly smiled, as she said, "Tom's right, son, it took awhile, but he saw that you were right, some time ago. He just couldn't come right out and tell you after being against it so long. He didn't know how."

At sixteen, the first stride into manhood is a long one; faltering, at times, as the boy occasionally exerts himself, then all forward momentum ceases, and adulthood must wait. And so it was with Joey.

Silently, they waited, as he sat with bowed head. Slowly, he raised it, until he was gazing into his mother's eyes. "Ma," he whispered, but efforts to speak failed him. No one else spoke, too many lumps in too many throats, and too strong the threat of wetness behind hard, brown eyes, as they saw the tears in his.

Nell made no attempt to hide those running down her cheeks, as she quickly went around the table to Joey's side. Bending to kiss him lightly on the cheek, she smiled, as she said, "See, Joey, it is all settled. You will have the educated brains for this family. Okay?"

The look of radiance that swept his thin fair face was a thing of beauty. "Okay, Nell," he said huskily, "okay." But then, he sobered at once, as the smile disappeared. "I will help with the still in my spare time."

All three knew how hard those words must have come. Though his voice was edged with determination, no one thought for a moment, that he had really changed in his opinion of moonshining.

"No, Joey," Bob said, "there's no need. Dan, Arnie, and I can take care of the still."

"But I want to do my part of the work," Joey protested. "I can never feel right again, unless I do."

"Don't worry about that, kid," Dan answered. "There's plenty of other work around here to do, cause Ma cain't near git it all done. Nope, Bob's right. We don't need you a messin' around the still. Besides, you don't know nothin' about it. You'd just be in the way."

Joey sat with flushed face, as Tom and Arnie nodded in agreement. When he would have protested once more, his mother silenced him with a lift of her hand. "There's no need to labor that argument any further, for it has already been settled."

Uneasiness flooded the faces of her other sons, as they looked at each other in speculation. "What do you mean, Ma?" Tom asked, after a moment.

"Simply that the still won't be running. The Taylors are finished with whiskey making."

Through the voices raised in protest, Dan's was the most indignant. "But we cain't quit, Ma. That's the only way we've got to make a living. It's all we know."

"Not quite all," she answered softly.

"What do you mean, Ma?" Bob asked.

"We'll open up the sawmill. It's just setting there, rusting away, while over a thousand acres of timber on Taylor land waits to be cut."

Dan's face flushed in anger. "No!" he exploded, "that's crazy. We've got orders for fifty gallon, and we've gotta make it."

Tom's black eyes flashed, as he said sternly, "Dan, don't you dare talk to Ma that way."

Dan read the shocked indignation in the eyes of the others, and his anger fled as quickly as it had been born. Sheepishly, he said, "I'm sorry, Ma. But gee, we cain't make half as much off the sawmill as we can the still. And besides ... well, you know."

As Molly gazed at this big, rawboned, twenty-one-year-old son of hers, a softness she atoned to, overwhelmed her. In his rebellious spirit, she saw again the fiery Tab at that age, and could recall, only too easily, that it had always been so with her third-born. As with the taming of a wild colt, the firmness of her must be tempered with the shrewdness, that knew when to bear down or when to give a little. And this was not the time for giving. Forcing a sharpness to her voice that she did not feel, she answered, "Yes! I know exactly what you mean. Running the mill is a lot harder work than tending the still. And as for money, the mill will bring in a decent living and you know it."

As Dan sat, red-faced, with eyes downcast, she directed herself to Bob. "Tomorrow morning, you see that the still is destroyed. Then, get the mill ready to go."

Bob looked questionably at Tom, whose dark eyes gazed back without expression. He was now outside the fold and had delivered himself from this immediate family problem. "Okay, Ma," Bob murmured, without spirit. "We'll get right on it in the morning."

Tom looked at his mother affectionately, as he said softly, "Ma, I hope you won't take it as my going against you, if I don't shut down the Cabin."

"No, Tom," she answered resignedly. "You're a man on his own for too many years. But the boys don't work for you anymore."

"But, Ma!" Bob and Dan protested, in unison.

They were stilled, however, as Tom responded to his mother. "Okay, Ma, whatever you say."

One by one, they rose from the table—Tom and Nell preparing for the return to the Cabin, and Arnie, Dan, and Bob withdrawing to huddle in the front yard to mutter in subdued tones. As Joey busied himself helping his mother clear the table, he suddenly remembered that he still hadn't gotten an answer to his question of why his pa might have been killed over Raider.

Feud Justice
Chapter 5

The faces of the three assigned the destruction of the still were darkly impassive the next morning, as they left the yard and headed up the path towards the top of the ridge. Concern wrinkled Joey's brow, as he watched their going. Only at his mother's insistence, had Bob reluctantly taken the axe along. He knew she was worried, by the shadows of emotion that swept her face. The sullenness of Dan bordered on rebellion. How much longer would she be able to keep them in hand?

The three, reaching the still site, stood, silently brooding, as they surveyed what they had come to destroy. Finally, with a shrug, Arnie put his foot against one of the three big mash barrels and pushed. The other two made no attempt to help, as one by one, he did the same to the others.

Wordlessly, they stared at the small flood, as it rushed down a short incline and gathered in a thick pool at the base of a large boulder. The air was pregnant with the sour stench that rose from the mash, as they watched in dismay.

The big copper cooker and worm were next. Bob looked down at the axe, made a half- hearted effort to lift it, but instead, let it fall from nervous fingers. Suddenly, breathing hard, Dan snatched it up and heaved it angrily down the ridge. Turning to the others, he said, "We ain't gonna do it."

A faint grin broke across Arnie's face, but only a bleakness stared at him from Bob's eyes. "You'd go against Ma's orders that way, Dan?" he asked coldly.

Dan's blazing eyes lowered a moment, then he raised them defiantly. "Yes, for the first time, I will. That's the best still in these hills. Pa brought it up from Tennessee, and by gum, we're not gonna take the axe to it."

Bob tried, once more. "Have you ever seen the time when Ma steered us wrong?"

The fires still blazed high in the impassioned Dan. "No! You know I never did, but even she could be wrong once. And besides, I'm twenty-one and ready to be my own man. I want this still. I'll move out. It's time for that, anyhow."

Suddenly, for a nineteen-year-old, Bob felt terribly tired. Too much had happened in such a short time. The vacuum in the Taylor household, left by Tab's violent death, was impossible to fill. His mother, he knew, had a much greater load to bear than any of the rest. Now, if Dan pulled out, the blow would strike her hard, maybe too hard; it must not be.

Arnie, he knew, would follow Dan's lead. Although twenty-three, and two years older than Dan, it had always been that way. He couldn't recall when Arnie had seemed to have a thought of his own. He had always seemed content to let the other do his thinking for him. He knew what he must do. "Okay, Dan," he said, "but I'll have no part of it. If Ma asks me, I'll tell her that I left you here to take care of the still, while I went ahead to the mill. I'll not lie to her."

Dan smiled crookedly. "Yeah," he said softly, "that's the best way. Get started on the mill. It only takes one to take care of this little job. I can beat it up real good without any help. Then I'll join you there. Oh, yeah," he said as an afterthought, "better take Arnie with you."

A pained expression swept Arnie's face, as Bob nodded. "But, Dan," he protested.

Dan's voice was firm, as he answered him, "Go on, do as I say."

In resignation, Arnie answered dispiritedly, "Okay, Dan, if you say so."

Bob said nothing more, as he turned in the direction of the mill. He knew Dan's reason for sending Arnie away. He just couldn't trust him to stand up under Ma's questions, if asked about the still. For years, they had realized that he was somewhat duller-witted than the rest, and in no way a match for their mother when it came to parrying words.

Bob walked a few steps, then paused. Turning around to face Dan, who stood, motionless, waiting for them to depart, he said, "There's one more thing. You stay at home and work with us at the mill for the next few weeks, just the way Ma said. At least until she has time to get over Pa."

Dan's face darkened in anger, but as he gazed at his brother, he knew there was no shaking him from the course he had set. It was either that or nothing. "It's a deal," he said, somewhat bitterly.

The mill was located about halfway between their home and the Cabin, at the mouth of a small hollow south of the river, and not far off the road, but safely beyond the high water level. As he pulled the tarp from the big table, he nodded with satisfaction, as he saw that his father had made sure that everything was well-greased, before standing it idle two years ago. He also knew it had frequent attention in between.

The boiler, he found to be in excellent condition. He ordered Arnie to fire up the old Ford tractor and take the water trailer to the river to be filled. The big circular saws and belts were stored at Tom's place and would have to be brought down that afternoon. Soon, there remained little to do, but fill the boiler with the first load Arnie had brought, and send him back for the second. A great stack of firewood was there in readiness.

By the time Dan showed up, shortly before noon, there was nothing more they could do at the site. Bob received his brother's report that he had fixed it good, in stony silence. He guessed that he had hidden the still in some remote place, on Taylor land, but he didn't ask. He didn't want to know.

As they walked the mile and a half, back up the river road to their home, Bob was well in advance, while Dan and Arnie brought up the rear. Lost in thought of the teams and teamsters they would have to hire, and the engaging of Ed Jibers as head sawyer, he didn't hear the brief exchange between his brothers.

"Dan," Arnie asked eagerly, "did you hide it someplace?"

Angrily, Dan turned on him. "I destroyed it, like Ma said. And that's all I ever want to hear about it. Don't you ever mention it again. Understand?"

Arnie's face blanched, before his brother's blazing eyes. There was a fury there, that at times, frightened him; a fury that he didn't understand. "Okay, Dan," he muttered sheepishly, "if you say so."

Their mother had dinner on the table when they reached the house. Bob was relieved that she didn't ask about the still. As he filled her in with talk about the mill, he couldn't help but wonder if she had refrained from asking, because for the first time, she had doubts about her control. Had it gotten to the point where she was afraid of the truth?

After they had eaten, all the boys but Joey loaded into their father's car and started seeking the help they knew they would need. It being Thursday, they agreed to start the following Monday. There was no need to advertise. When word got around that they were cutting, there would be orders enough. The railroad was always a sure market for decking.

Joey would have to spend most of the time the next day at the high school in Sladen, in order to get registered and receive class assignments. He decided to take Raider and go to the river for a swim. He found the big hound eager, as he unsnapped his chain. As before, he found himself speculating on just what kind of mixture Raider might be. Plenty of Walker there, Pa had said, some English, from the speckles on his legs, and just a touch of Plott, to give him that broad brindle head.

The sun was hot through his shirt, as he headed down the hill and across the bottoms, toward the line of sycamores that lined the river's edge. Raider kept well out in front, as he skirted around the bean field, for they had often taken the same route before. His booming tree bark came rolling back to Joey, long before he reached the riverbank. Raider had treed a fox squirrel.

As he had been trained, the big dog ceased his barking the minute Joey came to the tree, and stood, silently watching the top for sight of his quarry. The boy made no sound, as he waited for a moment, then tossed a small chunk he had picked up previously, to the ground on the other side of the tree. Instantly, as he had known, a big fox squirrel scratched its way around to his side of the main trunk, about halfway up.

A chuckle at its stupidity, broke from him. But as he carried no gun, the beseeching look in Raider's intelligent eyes had to go unserved. Instead, the dog had to be satisfied with crooned words of praise and a ruffling of ears, which to his way of thinking, was reward enough, since it came from Joey.

As Joey pushed through the remaining trees to the river's edge, he saw that a few dead leaves graced its surface. Soon, he knew, with the coming of October, they would lay there, too thick to see the water. It was a constantly muddy and sluggish river, whose slow-moving current seemed to take forever to move anything downstream.

The White River formed the line between Bolter County on the south and Jason on the north. As Joey stood, gazing across towards the other side, he was amazed with the absolute contrast between the two. Jason, as flat as a floor, as far as the eye could see, while less than a half mile south, steep knob country made up nearly the north half of Bolter County. Result of the glacier, he knew, but the very ugliness of the White River made one secretly wish that it could, somehow, be held responsible.

With its high muddy banks and muddy water, the river was actually a poor place to swim, but since it was the best he had close at hand, he and Raider made the most of it. And so, the afternoon waned away. At such times, Raider acted more like a farm shepherd than a hound, as he, too, enjoyed the water—swimming and playing with Joey, almost as another boy would have.

Finally, with much disappointment, he noticed the shadows creeping across the water, and knew that the sun had already begun its hurried descent. Still, he lingered, to salvage the most from the restful afternoon. Then reluctantly, with just enough daylight left to get home before dark, he climbed out, donned his clothes, and headed for the house.

It does seem that, at times, man has a premonition that he himself is unaware of, of things to come; a realization that something must be enjoyed to the fullest, as it may be the last. Maybe it was that way with Joey that afternoon. Why else would he have stayed so much longer than usual? The other boys were starting out to look for him as he reached home. Whatever the reason, he couldn't have known that it would be the last chance to ever experience the freedom of boyhood.

Feud Justice
Chapter 6

There was a nip of fall in the air the next morning. It was Molly's opinion that the dryness of the ground had held off a light frost. Joey left early for school, while the other boys lounged around the front porch, listening to his roadster roar away in the distance. A little after eight, the powerful motor of Tom's car could be heard coming up the road. As he pulled into the driveway, they were only mildly curious as to what had brought him to the homestead.

As he slowly dismounted and walked toward them, stony-faced, a feeling of apprehension tugged slightly at Bob. Something resembling a cold wind off the river rippled over him, as a shiver shook his shoulders. As he stood, gazing into Tom's fathomless eyes, wild thoughts raced through his mind, but there was no way he could have known that all hell had just broken loose for the Taylors.

Tom's voice came, cold and dispassionately, "They caught the Crawleys yesterday, over in Virginia. They're in jail in Sladen now."

Keenly, his dark eyes searched their faces for a reaction. It was instantaneous. Bob's face looked as if it was hewn from icy limestone, as he stared back at Tom, silently. Dan, too, remained silent, but as a storm built rapidly in his eyes, his sudden rapid breathing told, only too well, the range of emotions that were lashing him. Arnie licked his lips, in nervous anticipation, as he watched Dan and waited for him to speak.

Tom's lips formed one word, "No!" With that, he strode past them into the house.

His mother, having witnessed his confrontation with the others, stared worriedly at his stern face. "What is it, Tom?" she asked.

The eyes of her eldest softened, as they took in the new tired lines that hadn't been in that face a few days before. Had he imagined it, or had her voice, always before so firm and sure, contained just a slight quiver? He would, he told himself, spare her his greatest fear.

"Sit down, Ma," he said softly, "we have to talk."

Without taking her eyes from his face, and still without speaking, she slowly folded into her rocking chair. He wasn't surprised when she said, "They caught the Crawleys?"

Quickly, he told her all he knew. "Now, Ma," he added, "all we have to do now is go into town tomorrow and talk to the prosecutor. There may be charges for us to sign, I don't know. But I'm sure that's all it will amount to."

Her voice sounded tired as she answered, "All right, Tom. You can pick me up about nine."

He hated to leave her with all the thoughts he knew must be in her mind, but he wanted to study the boys. The next few hours, he knew, would be critical, as far as they were concerned. As he reached the door, her voice stopped him.

"Tom, I may need your help with the boys."

As he turned to look at her sympathetically, there was no surprise in his eyes that she had spoken of exactly the same thing that was on his mind. She knew, only too well, the passions within her offspring.

"Ma," he said, "I'll take care of them. So don't worry."

As she nodded silently, he turned again to the door. It was evident that she would worry, from the cloud of doubt in her eyes. Maybe he could control them, and maybe he couldn't. Ma knew that, the same as he. But she knew another thing, too. He would try his best, and if he failed, he would have at least done all he could.

Bob came to the door soon after Tom's departure, and called, "Ma, we're going down to the Cabin. Is it all right?"

"Yes, Bob," she answered, "try to be back by noon, though."

His "Okay, Ma," drifted back to her, as she heard the family car start. She watched through the window. With Dan at the wheel, they left in a cloud of dust. To keep from thinking of what could come, she turned her wrath upon the dust. How she hated it. It was everywhere and impossible to keep out of the house. After six weeks without rain, the very air was full of it, and with fall coming on, it would be worse than ever. The rain that had fallen on them on the way home from Tab's funeral had passed the hills by.

She knew why the boys had wanted to go to the Cabin; to talk the thing out; to see what others would have to say about it. But with Tom there to counsel, maybe talk was all it would amount to. As the possibilities of what could happen pushed all other thoughts aside, her tired, blue eyes closed, as the dust cloth dropped from her hand, and she slowly slid to her knees at the side of the bed.

There, with her face resting on the coolness of the bedspread, she asked God for the strength to face any ordeal that might arise, and for His help in guiding her boys. In the quiet of the shaded bedroom, she talked to the One, who above all else, she could turn to when mortal flesh seemed inadequate. And as the towering knobs looked down upon the plain, little weatherbeaten house, where she knelt, she felt His presence there beside her and was soothed.

There alone, head bowed by all that had happened, and the terrible fear of what the future might hold, she allowed herself the luxury of tears. Thus, for a short time, she was a mother who cried for her weakness as a woman, who must sometimes stand helplessly by, as fate deals as it will with those she has borne and loved.

By the time the boys had returned from the Cabin, all signs of her temporary letdown had been erased, and she was, once more, her usual calm and assured self. Soon, a typical, hot, late summer meal was placed on the table, and after a short blessing, they ate with the gusto that big, husky young men, born to the hills, seem to have.

Few words were said, as they shoveled in the shellout beans, sliced tomatoes, late corn on the cob, and new potatoes, topped off with sliced muskmelon. It had always given her pleasure to see them eat. Although they never talked much at meal time, they were unusually silent during this meal. She couldn't help being disturbed. That they all, even Bob, seemed to have trouble meeting her eyes added to her troubled thoughts.

Soon after they had eaten, they again retired to the front yard, where they, once more, engaged in conversation too low for her ears. About one o'clock, a cloud of dust heralded the approach of Joey's roadster. By the time he pulled to a stop and alighted, the others were preparing to leave. She only nodded tiredly, when Bob once more yelled that they were going back to the Cabin.

Joey, his arms laden with books, met them just outside the front yard fence. A smile of happiness lit his face, obviously born of anticipation of another school year, but it faded rapidly, as he viewed the bleak faces of his brothers.

"What's the matter with you guys?" he quipped, half-jestingly, half-seriously.

Bob would have answered, but Dan's bitter voice beat him to it. "They've caught the Crawleys, Joey, and if you want to join the rest of the Taylors, you'll find us down at the Cabin."

Joey's face whitened at the implication of Dan's words. Bob turned on Dan and said harshly, "That's enough, Dan."

Dan glared at him, but remained silent. Arnie only licked his lips and looked at Dan. For a moment, Bob fastened them with a stern look, and then turned to Joey, as his eyes softened.

"It's all right, kid. Don't worry about it. We're just going down to talk to Tom a bit. Glad to see you got all of your books." And with a wave of his hand, turned to follow the others to the car.

Not worry! Joey thought. How in the world could he keep from it? The cold savagery in Dan's voice could not be mistaken.

He stood watching them, until the car pulled out of sight, before he proceeded to the house. His mother met him at the door. She saw the worry in his eyes and tried to hide that in her own. But they were too close, and the one predominant thought between them had to be exposed.

Quickly, she mentioned the still warm lunch waiting for him on the back of the range, and busied herself with setting it out. Silently, he seated himself at the table, but made no effort to start eating. A light remark concerning school, made by Molly as she took a seat opposite him, only made the unspoken worry between them all the more obvious. Finally, he could stand it no longer. "Ma," he said, with eyes lowered to his plate, "are the boys planning to get at the Crawleys?"

For a moment, she didn't answer. The urge to evade his direct question was almost overpowering. There was that strange feeling that to put her uppermost fears into words might add to the possibility of them coming true. But communication between the two of them had always been complete, and they must be said.

"Son," she said softly, "I pray to God that they aren't, but I just don't know. They're a lot like your pa was at that age—wild and proud to be a Taylor."

A lump filled Joey's throat, as his eyes rested upon her tired and worn face. For the first time, he realized just how much she had aged since his father's death. This had hit her harder than any of them realized. The firm control that she had always exercised over them was gone, shattered with the blast of the Crawley's gun. They were all Taylor now, and there was nothing she could do.

As she sat there, silently lost in thought, he quickly finished his eating and got up from the table. There was Tom, he told himself, to keep them in check. They had always looked up to him. Surely, he thought, as he dredged up hope from the despair that weighed upon him, they would listen to him. But down deep inside, he was afraid—terribly afraid.

Joey felt the urge to stay close to home that afternoon. At his mother's suggestion, he picked the remaining green tomatoes and peppers, so that they could be used for slaw before the frost got them. Then, after helping her with the washing, slicing, and grinding, he realized that there was little else he could do, so he went out back to Old Raider.

Even the big hound was not his usual self that afternoon. Instead of his melodious bawl of greeting, whenever Joey went to him, he stood quietly while being unsnapped. He would ordinarily have broken immediately, in quest for a groundhog or squirrel, knowing that Joey would be close behind him. He now only stood, looking up with his intelligent brown eyes fastened on his master's face, while occasional whines broke from his throat.

The afternoon dragged slowly for the boy, but somehow, he didn't mind. He found the idea of a trip to the woods as uninviting, and didn't bother to ponder over the reason. On his many repeated trips to the house, for a few words with his mother, and to find if there wasn't something else he could do to help, Raider dogged his every footstep. Finally, tired from trying to fight off the heavy cloud of foreboding that hovered over him, he sat down against the big oak in the front yard, with the dog close to his side.

It was here that his brothers found him, when they returned from the Cabin. With his chin resting on his chest, he was sound asleep, but with his arm around the big hound. Bob took in the sleeping boy and the wide-awake dog, who sat ever so still, unwilling to move, lest he wake Joey. He knew how the dog's eyes had gone repeatedly to the face of his sleeping master, and then back to the surrounding landscape, in constant vigilance, but ever alert to the slightest change in Joey's breathing.

Raider's whine at the approach of his brothers roused Joey from slumber. Dan passed him rapidly, with only a grunt, while Arnie padded silently at his heels. Joey, at once, saw the look of suppressed anger on his face and the whitened tautness of Bob's. It was apparent that they had been arguing bitterly. He didn't have to guess what the argument was about, but he couldn't have known how close those two had come to fighting, for the first time since their boyhood days.

Though the hot Taylor blood in Bob left him no alternative but to go along and be a part of Dan's plan, the main cause of their trouble had been his determination that they would do no drinking that afternoon. And with Dan, it had been a constant battle. Arnie was no trouble, for he would do what Dan did.

Tom had watched them silently, as the afternoon wore on. Bob, by far the most level-headed of the two, seemed to be keeping things under control. But he held no delusions about Dan. Bob was all Taylor, and probably the most dangerous of them all, but he still had the coolest head. He had always kept a steady rein on the wildness coursing through his veins; while in Dan, it ran unchecked, ready to burst out in fury, at any given moment.

Saturday dawned clear and cool. Joey slipped his jacket on before going to the barn to milk at six. With this, the first day of October, winter was not far off. With the milking done and the horses fed, he returned to the house to find breakfast waiting.

As he washed up, his mother strained the milk, and as he returned to the table, he found his brothers waiting to join him. Only Bob made any attempt at conversation. There was no response from Dan or Arnie. Joey kept strangely quiet, his eyes constantly seeking the face of his mother. He felt the pain in her as the strains of worry gathered there. He wished that he could brush away every tired line, lines that had gathered fast these last few days.

The others ate fast, with eyes downcast. She sat quietly, watching them, as if to remember that breakfast for a long time, marking every line of their faces and every movement of their hands.

As if on signal, they all finished at the same time and rose to leave the house without a word. Slowly then, their mother rose to walk to the front door, where she stood watching them where they huddled under the big tree in the front yard. There, Joey joined her.

"Ma," he said hesitatingly, "Ma, it will be alright. Tom can handle them."

She answered him in the tiredest voice he had ever heard her use. "I'm not so sure any more, Joey. Not sure at all."

In about thirty minutes, they all three came back into the house, where they stood awkwardly, shuffling their feet under her searching gaze. Bob told her that they were going down to the Cabin and said goodbye. Dan and Arnie echoed his last words. Joey stiffened. Never before had he heard Dan or Arnie bother to say goodbye to their mother. Bob always, but them, never. Suddenly, Joey felt strangely cold.

As the family car left the driveway, with Dan at the wheel, Bob asked, "Did you get them all in last night?"

"Sure did," Dan answered, "sure did." Arnie giggled in the back seat.

For awhile after the others had left, Joey hung around the house, helping his mother where he could. A heavy cloud of gloom seemed to hover over them. Neither seemed in the mood for conversation, so finally, he went out back to visit with Raider.

In answer to the big hound's begging, he unsnapped his chain and headed for the river. Raider stayed just a short distance in front, and for some reason or other, made no effort to search out a squirrel or groundhog. It seemed that he sensed the boy's uneasiness. They didn't stay long around the water. Joey noticed that the sluggish White River was now covered from bank to bank with the leaves that had fallen during the last two days. So it would be, he knew, until the fall rains gave enough strength to the current to carry them away.

Slowly and dispiritedly, they made their way back home. After he tied Raider, he went into the house. There was no hustle and bustle of his mother, as in the past, as she flew to her tasks. For a startled moment, he was frightened by the strange and unusual quiet. Then, tiptoeing to her bedroom door, he saw that she was lying down.

For a moment, he stared silently, out of worried eyes. Never could he remember seeing his mother lying down in the daytime. Slowly, his tongue ran over dry lips. "Ma! Ma!" he whispered hoarsely, "Are you alright?" She turned her head to look at him and a wave of tenderness swept her face.

"Sure, son, I'm alright. Just a little tired, that's all. Better get your books out and read a little, hadn't you?"

"Sure, Ma, that's a good idea," he said softly. "That's just what I'll do."

Surprised that he hadn't thought of it, he quickly went to his school books and selected two. Then, quietly easing out the front door, he seated himself under the big tree in the front yard. So absorbed did he become in his reading, that it hardly seemed possible that so much time had passed, when his mother called him to get ready for dinner.

Though they waited until well after noon, the others did not make their appearance. So it was with heavy hearts, that they finally sat down and started the meal without them. The family had always eaten together and there was a great void at the table. Joey felt the food to be dry and tasteless in his mouth, and his eating was little more than a pretense. As his mother finally ceased all attempts at eating, and just sat there with head bowed towards her plate, he realized that she had fared little better.

Finally, he could stand the silence no longer. "Ma," he said, "they just forgot about the time. They'll be along in a minute." But even he didn't believe the words.

"No, son," she said resignedly, "they didn't forget. They're up to something, and we might as well face it."

He had never seen her so without spirit, so beaten down. The old fire was gone, and his heart ached for her. Suddenly, he felt a terrible anger at his brothers. Anger that they should add to all of the worries that had come with the murder of his father.

"Ma," he said fiercely, "if they don't come pretty soon, I'm going down there."

She raised her head and looked at him understandingly. "I don't think it will do any good, Joey. But you can try, if you wish." Later, she would bitterly recall those few words and regret deeply that she had ever said them, but at the time, she had no way of knowing the terrible chain of events lurking in the future.

When one o'clock came without the appearance of the others, Joey made preparations to leave for the Cabin. But at his mother's insistence, he agreed to wait one more hour. He didn't argue when she suggested it, but only sat quietly under the tree, hoping to see their car speeding down the road toward home.

When two o'clock came, and still no brothers, he rose and went into the house. His mother sat in her rocker with eyes closed. Quietly, he went to stand beside her. Placing his hand on her shoulder, he said, "Ma, I don't want you to be worrying this way. Tom is watching them every minute and he won't let things get out of hand. You just wait and see."

"Yes, Joey, I know that Tom will do his best. But they're grown men now. They've felt the bit in their teeth and like the way it feels. There's just so much that Tom can do, and I'm afraid it won't be enough this time. There's just too much Taylor in them sons. Too much Taylor."

The last words were uttered in almost a whisper, and as her eyes closed again, Joey knew that she was through talking. Gently, he patted her shoulder, then turned and left the house.

Feud Justice
Chapter 7

Minutes after firing up his old Ford, he was bouncing down the road towards the Cabin. Several cars of various makes were scattered around the parking lot, as he pulled in. Parking well to the side, he dismounted and impatiently made his way to the front porch. A hum of voices came from inside the big room, as he pushed through the door.

Again, the gloom caused him to stop for a minute, to allow his eyes time to grow adjusted. Most tables were full and several men lounged against the bar. As a helper served up drinks, Tom stood, leaning against the back wall, with arms folded. He hadn't seen Joey come in, because his eyes were riveted on the far corner of the room. Joey looked to see what held his attention.

They were in a booth, all three of them, along with a long-jawed man, whom Joey had never seen before. As Joey walked over, it soon became evident why they hadn't come home for dinner—the half-empty bottle on the table attested to the reason. Though Joey had known that his brothers did some drinking, he had never seen them when they showed the effects. The family had always adhered to two rigid rules: no drinking in front of their mother, and she should never see them drunk.

Dan looked up out of bloodshot eyes, as he walked up to the booth. "Well!" he exploded. "If it ain't Mamma's little boy."

Joey flushed and spoke to Bob, "Ma's awfully worried because you didn't come home for dinner. Bob, I think she's sick."

Bob's face flushed with drinking, sobered instantly. "I'm sorry, Joey, but we just couldn't come home. You can see why." A wave of his hand indicated the bottle.

Though Bob's eyes held a shadow at the mention of his mother, there was still an icy coldness in their depths that Joey had never seen before. Though he and Bob had always been close, this was a side of him that he had never seen.

"Bob," he pleaded, "won't you quit drinking and come home?"

"Not now, Joey. Maybe later. We have something to take care of first. You just go on back home and tell Ma we're alright. Tell her there's no need for worrying." Joey felt a shiver run over him at the strange tone of Bob's voice.

"But, Bob," he protested.

"No buts about it, kid. You go on back home now. Ma needs you with her. Now, git." Never before had Bob spoken to him so bitingly. Joey felt a hurt deep, deep inside.

Now, the long-jawed stranger leered up at him. "Say," he said raspingly, "ain't this the one who started the whole thing? Ain't this the kid what caused your pa's shooting?"

From the other side of the booth, Bob's right arm reached out, and his fist took the speaker on the point of his long jaw. There was a crack, like the snapping of a two by four, as the victim flew out of the booth and landed on his back in the middle of the room. Instantly, all voices in the place ceased, as Bob's words came with all the icy bleakness of a sudden winter storm. "That's family business, and it had better stay that way."

As the slugged man lay there, rubbing his jaw with a look of fear in his eyes, Bob allowed his gaze to roam around the room. Local hill men met his eyes and nodded in agreement. Strangers tried to face him down, only to quell before the intense fury they saw in him, and grow uncomfortable as they shuffled their feet aimlessly in the sawdust on the floor.

Bob's move had caught Dan by surprise. Now, he turned to him angrily. "Why did you do that? He didn't say anything that ain't so."

"Shut up, Dan! Shut up!" Bob retorted fiercely.

Arnie sat there, bleary-eyed, looking from one to the other. "Bob," he whined, "you know what Dan said is so. You know it is."

Bob's open palm caught Arnie flush on the side of the face. Instantly, tears appeared in his eyes. "Why did you do that?" he whimpered.

Bob ran a hand over his face. "I'm sorry, Arnie. I sure didn't want to, but you made me."

"But all I said …"

"I know what you said, and it was agreed a long time ago, that it would never be mentioned again. Guess you forgot, hey, Arnie?"

"Yes, I forgot," Arnie said humbly. "I'm sorry, Joey. I forgot."

As Joey nodded sympathetically to Arnie, Dan, his eyes flashing, spoke up. "Well, I didn't forget. And it's time the kid knowed the truth." Bob halfway rose from his seat as he reached for Dan, when Joey's voice rang out.

"No! Bob, let him talk. I want to know what he means."

"Kid," Bob said softly, "it won't do no good. Let well enough alone."

Joey's voice was just as determined as the others in their anger, as he replied, "No, Bob, I want to know now. I want to know right now." As Bob's eyes searched his face, he saw the whiteness, the strain of uncertainty, and the pain of worry brought on by Dan's words. The kid, he guessed, had just about reached his limit.

He shrugged. "Alright, Joey. I guess it is time you knew. Sit down first, though."

As Joey silently took a seat, his eyes remained upon Bob's face. He seemed to hardly breathe, as he waited for him to start. Then as Bob hesitated, as if trying to decide the best way to start, Dan started to tell it.

"Well, kid, it was this way…"

Bob cut him off sharply. "I'll tell it, Dan. I've told you for the last time! Shut up!"

Dan glared at him, but he slumped into a sullen silence, and Bob began. "You see, Joey, everybody knows how you saved Old Raider when he was whelped, and that he would have died, but for you. They know how the Crawleys shot his mammy and went off and left her. Everybody in these hills knows that he's your dog. They've knowed it all along. Everybody, that is, except the Crawleys."

Joey was breathing deeply, as he waited for Bob to continue. Dan opened his mouth, as if to speak, but Bob silenced him with a look, and then continued, "They was just sore losers, Joey. When they first heard that you saved a pup from that litter, they wasn't a bit interested. But when they saw what he finally turned into, then they realized what they had walked off from, and they just couldn't take it."

Joey was beginning to understand. He ran his tongue over dry lips. "Had they been to Pa about it?" he asked huskily.

Bob looked down at the table. "Oh, yes," he said softly, "several times."

"But I didn't know! I didn't know!" Joey said wildly.

"Of course not," Bob went on. "You didn't need to know. Pa wasn't about to let them bluff him like that. He thought it would die down. We all did. My, God! We sure never thought it would ever come to anything like this."

"But it is all my fault," Joey half-sobbed. "I killed Pa. I did it."

"Quit talking like that," Bob growled. "They pulled the trigger on Pa the day they shot that bitch in whelp. They set their course that very day."

"But if I had known how they felt," Joey said shakily, "maybe I could have done ..."

"Done what?" Bob cut him off sharply. "Turned Raider over to the Crawleys? Could you have done that, Joey, could you have done that?"

Joey stared at him out of pained-filled eyes. "I don't know," he whispered, "I don't know."

Bob went on, his eyes flashing. "Pa would have felt like a whipped cur if he had let them bluff him out of that dog. He just couldn't have done it, Joey. Couldn't have done it at all."

Joey slumped down into the booth and dropped his face into his hands. "But if I hadn't found him in the first place," he sobbed, "then it wouldn't have happened."

Bob laughed disdainfully. "Oh, it would have probably happened, sooner or later. If not from that, from something else. The Crawleys wuz a gitten purty big feeling around these hills anyway, kid. They stayed friendly to Pa, just cause they had to, but down underneath, they didn't like him none. I've seen the way they looked at him when he wasn't noticing. He knew it, too. Didn't none of us ever think they would have the nerve to shoot him, not even Pa."

Joey shook his head miserably. "But I still killed him. Any way you look at it, I still killed my own pa."

"No, you didn't!" Bob exploded angrily. "Git that through your head. We wuz all in it as much as you. Now, that's enough said about it. Go home to Ma."

They, all three, sat silently watching him, as he rose from the booth and shuffled from the room. Tom, watching, looked questioningly back to those in the booth, and then to Joey's slumped shoulders, as he passed through the door. Slowly, he walked across to his brothers.

"What's the matter with Joey?" he asked suspiciously.

"Little feller's worried he caused Pa's shootin'," Dan said scornfully.

Anger clouded Tom's hard, brown eyes, as he started a sharp retort to Dan. But Bob's voice interceded. "I think I straightened him out okay, Tom. He'll be alright in a day or two."

"Oh, say, Tom," Dan said softly. "Joey says that Ma's ailing pretty bad. How about you and Nell go up to see about her?"

Instantly, Tom's expression was one of worry. "Guess we'd better. It's a cinch that none of you can go home right now," he finished sarcastically.

They remained silent and unmoving, as Tom went back to his living quarters, and then, in a few minutes, returned with Nell. Stopping to say a few words to his bartender, who lifted his eyes in their direction, he then took Nell by the arm and steered her outside. The three remained where they were, not speaking, but listening for sounds from the parking lot.

At last it came, the throaty purr of Tom's powerful car. Their eyes glittered as the sound of meshing gears came clearly and the motor faded away into the distance. And still, they sat. Dan took a watch from his pocket. "Four o'clock," he whispered. "Too early yet. What say, we have another bottle?" As the others nodded, he rose and went to the bar. The man behind the counter was nervous. "You boys ain't up to anything, are you?" he said huskily.

Dan laughed coldly. "Just a little drinking. That's all, Rufe. Why?"

Rufe looked relieved. "Well, Tom said to keep an eye on you, cause you might be. I don't want no trouble with you boys, Dan. You know that."

Dan patted him on the shoulder as he picked up the bottle. "We ain't gonna cause you no trouble, Rufe, and that's a fact. We'll finish this and then go on home real quiet like, afterwhile. Okay?"

"Sure, Dan," Rufe said, relieved. "Didn't think you wuz, but you know how Tom is," he said, with a feeble attempt at humor.

"Sure, I know," Dan said, as he turned away. Good, old, worrying Tom."

For the good part of an hour, they sat there talking in subdued tones, and when the bottle was finished, rose and went outside. As they stood in the shadow of the overhang, they didn't see the small figure of Joey slumped down on the other end of the porch. From his position, he could hear their voices clearly.

"Are we goin' now?" Arnie asked excitedly.

Bob's voice spoke softly from the shadows. "Purty soon now, Arnie. Purty soon now."

Then Dan, bitterly, "Well, let's git at it. Tom will be back anytime now."

Joey, every sense alert, sat up, his eyes and ears strained to their utmost. Through the fast-approaching darkness, he could see them only as figures standing at the other end of the porch, but by their voices, he could easily tell which was which. Dan was impatient, Arnie drunkenly agreeable, while Bob's carefully-controlled voice urged caution.

They heard it the same time as Joey. The powerful throaty purr of Tom's car on the river road. Instantly, they were all galvanized into action. Going directly to the rear of their car, the others stood quietly, while Dan unlocked the trunk.

Even as Dan handed out the guns, Joey's mind was made up. Maybe he could still talk them out of it. He had to try, up until the last minute, he had to try. Standing up, he was ready when they climbed swiftly into the car and Dan started the motor. Not until it had started to move, did Joey move, and when he did, it was fast. As it swung in a looping curve past the end of the porch, Joey grabbed the left rear door handle, yanked it open, and swung inside.

He landed directly on top of Arnie, who was in the back alone. "Joey!" Bob yelled, as he grabbed the swinging door and pulled it shut. "You cain't go! You cain't go! Stop, Dan! Stop!

"Not on your life," Dan gritted. "He's with us now, so he can just prove he's a Taylor and go along."

As a spluttering Arnie pushed the thrashing Joey off him, Bob shouted again for Dan to stop the car. Dan's answer was to push the foot feed a little closer to the floor. A wild-eyed Joey looked desperately at Bob.

"Bob, I can't let you do this. You can't! You just can't! Think what it will do to Ma!"

Bob ignored him, as he turned his attention to Dan's driving. He was entering the first of eighteen treacherous hairpin curves that marked the two mile route to the top of the knobs. As the tires screamed around the first one, and the car rocked dangerously, his hand fastened tightly on Dan's shoulder.

"Slow down, you fool, or you'll have us over the cliff."

As the second curve came up fast, Dan tightened his grip on the steering wheel, but his foot eased up on the throttle. As the howling of the tires lessened, and the car rocked less crazily, Bob again turned his attention to their unwanted passenger.

"Joey, do you know what you are letting yourself in for?"

"I know what you are planning is wrong," Joey cried, "and you've got to stop."

"We cain't, kid," Bob answered coldly. "It has to be done."

"Then I'll join you. It's all my fault, so the least I can do is take part." Though Joey spoke with iron determination in his voice, it was without spirit.

"You'll do no such thing," Bob said harshly. "You're getting out at the edge of town."

Dan laughed bitterly. "Let him alone, Bob. I always wondered how much Taylor was in him. So, now we'll find out. Give him your pistol, Arnie."

"Sure, Dan," Arnie answered, as he shifted his pump gun to his left hand, and pulled a big frontier Colt from his belt.

Bob moved in a flash. As Joey's hand went out, hesitantly, to take the proffered weapon, Bob grabbed it violently from Arnie's hand. "No, you don't," he grated, as he pushed the gun down into his own waistband.

As Joey lapsed into a rather shocked silence, the rest of the ride seemed subdued. They sullenly sat, without speaking, as the humming tires ate up the miles. Then, almost without warning, the lights of Sladen appeared in the distance. As they started down the last long, gentle slope between them and the town, Bob said, "Pull up at the edge of town. Joey's getting out."

Dan didn't answer. Then, the edge was reached and behind them. It was obvious now, that Dan had no intention of stopping. Bob drew in his breath to lash out at him, but then remained silent. It would do no good, he knew. Dan was terribly stubborn, when he chose to be, and this was one of those times. Bob suddenly felt tired. Misgivings were fast setting in. But then he had tried. Tried his best to keep Joey out of it, and now, it was too late. They were all committed. But maybe not all, he thought, as his mind raced. Yes, that's what he would do. Maybe he could still keep Joey from becoming involved.

They were well down North Main Street now and approaching the old square. The Courthouse loomed large and ominous in the center. The usual Saturday night activity was in evidence. All stores and barber shops open, as they would be until nearly midnight, or until the crowd thinned out.

No one spoke, as Dan tooled around the west side and turned down South Main. In the half block to the jail, he drove cautiously. At the intersection of Main and Poplar, he slowed down to a crawl, as he turned left, and eased into the curb, just south of the jail.

Feud Justice
Chapter 8

Meanwhile, back at the Cabin, Tom was bitterly denouncing himself. It did no good that the bartender had told him the boys had said they were going home. They didn't, he knew, for he would have passed them on the road. There was only one place they could have gone.

"They've gone to Sladen to get the Crawleys. That's where they've gone. There's no doubt about it."

The bartender was apologetic. "Gee, I'm sorry, Tom. But when they said they were going home, well ... I thought ..."

"It's okay, Rufe," Tom replied, "it's not your fault. There wasn't anything you could have done. I doubt that even I could have stopped them." Then, as an afterthought, "My God! I hope they didn't take Joey with them."

"I don't know, but he left before they did," the bartender added hopefully. "He probably went back home."

Tom's eyes clouded. "But I didn't pass him, either," he said, as his shoulders slumped. "I wish now, that I had gone ahead and told them everything."

"What do you mean, Tom?"

Tom was silent for a moment, as if he hadn't heard Rufe's question. But then he shook his head. "About the real reason the Crawleys shot Pa."

"You mean," Rufe asked, "there was more to it than the dog?"

"Yeah," Tom answered slowly, "and it all happened a long time ago. So long ago, that we haven't mentioned it in years. These kids never even knew about it."

Tom paused, as his mind seemed to go back, way back, as he groped for words. "You see, it wasn't really the dog, at all. They just used him as an excuse. The real reason was … well … Pa killed old man Crawley back in Tennessee."

"But," Rufe asked huskily, "why did they wait all this time?"

"Oh, the law cleared Pa of murder, cause it was plain self-defense. The old man jumped him, but he just wasn't in Pa's class with a gun. Pa weren't but nineteen. First man he ever killed."

Tom halted again, then swatted the bar hard with his hand. "I don't know why they waited all this time. Maybe for just the right situation. Maybe it took them this long to get their nerve up. I don't know. I don't know."

Joey was feeling smothery and slightly nauseated, as he sat there, looking from one of his brothers to the other. They made no move, as they silently surveyed the front of the jail. Though many people were passing along the south side of the square, the sidewalk, from the corner down to the jail, was bare.

Then Bob spoke tersely, "Let's go."

As Dan opened the door on the left side and climbed from under the wheel, Bob emerged from the right. Arnie was already out of the back before Joey, reluctantly, reached for the handle. As he stepped out and stood upright, Bob turned to face him.

"I'm sorry, Joey," he said softly, as his right fist lashed out solidly against the boy's soft jaw. Bob's weight was behind the blow and Joey slumped, unconscious. Bob caught him, as he fell. The rear door was still open and he quickly lifted him inside, placing him gently on the seat.

Again, he said, "I'm sorry, kid. But it's best this way."

"Why didn't you let him go?" Dan asked angrily.

"Shut up, Dan," his brother snapped, as he stepped up on the sidewalk.

They walked quickly and silently towards the jail porch. Only Arnie's pump gun gave evidence of their intentions. The hand guns of the others were not in sight. They moved fast across the stone porch, and then smoothly through the door. No one was in the front office, but they could clearly hear voices in the next room.

Sheriff Merlin and his wife had just finished supper, and were walking into the living room, when the boys entered through the other door. At the sight of Arnie's shotgun, he stiffened, as his wife gave a little gasp of fright. And when Bob and Dan quickly produced their .45s, they froze.

The sheriff licked at dry lips, then croaked, "What ... what do you want?"

Bob's eyes gleamed, as he answered, "I think you know, Sheriff. We want the Crawleys."

At the disturbance in the living room, the jail cook, an elderly woman, came to the door. As she appeared, Dan quickly strode to her side. Grasping her by the arm, he propelled her into the room to stand beside the others.

Bob knew they must act quickly. "Where's the keys to their cell?" His voice was gratingly cold, and at its tone, the three hostages darted nervous eyes at each other. They each started, as the loud clatter of Arnie's gun pumping a shell into the chamber filled the room. The sheriff listened for the click of the safety being thrown on, but it never came.

One look at his wife told him that she was growing angry, and there was no telling what she might do when this anger really took hold. Though pint-sized, he had, on too many occasions, found that she could be a regular wildcat when roused. And he knew these Taylor boys were very dangerous. He had to do something.

In the interest of protecting his charges, and at the same time, do nothing to provoke the Taylors into using their guns; he began to search frantically for some way to stall. A thought crossed his mind and he grabbed it.

"The keys are upstairs," he said defiantly.

Dan shoved his gun into his middle. "Let's just go get them. Sheriff."

As the reluctant Merlin still hesitated, Dan's face hardened. "Now!" he shouted, as he pushed the gun barrel an inch into the sheriff's soft paunch.

Without a word, Merlin led the way to the stairs, as the boys herded the two women behind him. For awhile, they remained silent, as the sheriff seemed to hunt for the keys intently. From room to room, he moved, looking under this and under that.

Finally, Dan could stand it no longer. "Bob, he's stalling. They're not up here at all."

Bob turned to him fiercely, and as he did so, he saw the unset safety. Roughly, he snatched the gun from Arnie with his left hand. There was an audible click, as he slid it on. Arnie quailed under his angry eyes, and muttered, "I'm sorry, Bob, I forgot." Bob only looked at him disgustedly, and turned away in time to see Dan press his gun against the head of the sheriff.

"Quit stalling, old man, and give us the keys, or you die right here," he said harshly.

Mrs. Merlin was suddenly afraid for the life of her husband. The wildness in Dan's eyes lent terror to her actions. "The keys are downstairs," she said quickly. "I'll show you where they are."

Dan retained his hold on the collar of the sheriff's shirt, and kept his gun pressed to the back of his head, as they led the way down the steps. Stepping to the side, as they reached the bottom, he allowed Bob and Mrs. Merlin to pass him, as she headed for a desk in the middle of the room. Opening the drawer, she picked up a ring of keys and handed them to Bob.

As the procession, with the hostages in front, went toward the cell block, the Crawleys were moving frantically. They had heard enough of the loud conversation to know what was going on. They were not too surprised that the Taylors were there. Mountain-bred, as they were, they had only known what they would have done and guessed accordingly.

By the time Bob had unlocked the corridor to the cell block, the Crawleys had built a small fortress in the front of their cell. Beds were upturned and pushed against the bars. Chairs were stacked on top of this. Behind all this, the mattresses were set up edgeways, and behind this, they crouched fearfully.

Meanwhile, all had not been going well outside the jail. It was in the Crawley's favor that the Taylors had, unknown to them, been seen as they entered the jail. An old man, walking on the other side of the street, had noticed Arnie's shotgun. Grasping its significance, he scurried up to the square and into the first store he came to, announcing as he came through the door, that armed men had just entered the jail. There was no mistaking his report. Mountain people had lived among them for years, and all were familiar with their feudal law of an eye for an eye. There had to have been much speculation, since the Crawley's arrest, that it would happen.

Then began a tragedy of errors that only added to the fast-building horror of the evening. Someone turned in a fire alarm for the jail. As Sladen's only pumper truck careened around the corner towards the jail, dozens and dozens of sight seekers streamed after it.

Inside, the boys paused, as they entered the corridor. The siren, fast approaching, was an apprehensive sound. Quickly, Dan reacted. "I'll check outside," he said, and left at once.

Opening the front door, he looked out. To his dismay, several people were milling around at the foot of the steps, while some were already part of the way up. Dan was not one to be indecisive. Calmly, he walked out onto the porch and leveled his gun at the crowd. Instantly, there was a scramble, as those on the steps ran back down, and those on the sidewalk pushed frantically back from directly in front of him. Dan, as yet, hadn't said a word. His gun spoke plainly.

As the fire truck screamed to a halt at the curb in front of the jail, big Sam Harmon was sitting beside the driver. His job was to crank the old hand-operated siren. He gasped, as he saw the big bore of the .45 in Dan's hand, pointing in his direction. Many tales were told later about the speed with which he cleared the fire truck and scooted across the street and into the store there.

The total law enforcement for Sladen was one marshal, the sheriff, of course, who also served the entire county, and the one State Policeman who checked into the area occasionally, from the recently-organized State Police force. But on this particular night, with the sheriff completely outnumbered inside the jail, and the State Policeman not in town, it was fate that only Marshal Nate Harper was left free to enter history with the Taylors.

As he was quietly watching a western movie at the theater, across the street and down a block from the jail, he heard the fire siren whine to a screaming halt, only a short distance away. As was his duty, he rose to investigate the source of the fire. Leaving the theater, he walked quickly up the walk.

By the time he reached the intersection of Poplar Street, he was fully aware that something more than a fire was in the making. The many people peering from doorways across from the jail attested to this. Then a tremor ran over him, as he saw the figure of Dan, standing on the jail porch with a pistol in his hand.

He, at once, recognized the situation for what it was. His pace slowed, but he continued up the walk until he was directly across from Dan. Then he turned and stepped off the curb, slowly continuing across the street. With the fire truck between him and Dan, he reached the other side undetected. Marshal Harper had no need to prove his nerve to the citizens of Sladen. He had done this on several occasions before. He was a brave man and true to his character. He could have stayed safely behind the fire truck and picked Dan off, but instead, he stepped boldly out and approached him, walking slowly, and talking softly. "Put down your gun, Dan," he said.

Dan glared at the approaching marshal. "Stay back, Nate," he snarled, "I don't want to shoot you."

The marshal had not yet drawn his own gun, as he walked steadily forward. "Don't do anything foolish, Dan. Don't make things worse than they are. Come on, now, drop your gun."

He had reached the foot of the steps, when, with a loud click, Dan cocked his .45. Nate's guts knotted up at the sound, and as he viewed this young Taylor standing tall, proud, and defiant behind that big gun, he knew that one wrong move could be his last.

Again, as he slowly started up, Dan warned him to stop. Even as he took the first step, he observed how the long blond hair on Dan's bare head was slightly disarrayed by the slight breeze that was blowing from the north. His voice was soft, smooth, and gentle, as he closed in on Dan, step by step.

Dan watched his advancement with disbelief. There was almost a note of pleading in his tone, as he said once more, "Stay back, Nate! Stay back!"

Then Nate was up beside him and Dan still hadn't fired. Quickly then, the marshal attempted to carry out the rest of his plan. Before the horrified eyes of the onlookers, he made a grab for Dan's gun. Be he had not planned for the strength of that strong young arm. He was unable to wrestle the pistol from Dan's hand. Instantly, they grappled and rolled, locked together, down the steps of the jail. As they came to rest on the sidewalk, with Dan on the bottom, there was a loud explosion, as the .45 went off.

As the big hot slug tore through his middle, the marshal, for the first time, drew his own gun. Steeling every nerve in his body against the pain, he shot Dan three times. One on each side of the groin and the third straight through the heart. As their blood mingled with each other's, Dan died, as the marshal slumped helplessly across him.

The shots from outside came plainly to those in the jail who had just entered the cell block. Instantly, chaos was in the making. In a flash, the sheriff's wife flicked her hand at the wall switch, and they were plunged into darkness. Then, not to be outdone, the sheriff made a desperate, but foolish, grab for Arnie's shotgun.

As Arnie felt the sheriff's hand close upon the barrel, he reacted instantly. His left hand darted out to throw off the safety, as he held on tightly with his right. They struggled desperately in the darkness for possession of the gun. There was an ear-splitting roar from the .12 gauge. A scream tore from the throat of Mrs. Merlin.

To Bob's horrified ears, that scream was as cutting as a long-bladed knife. Nearly deafened by the explosion, he was just barely aware that both she and the sheriff were moaning that they had been shot. That, and fear of what the shots from outside might mean plainly told him that there was only one thing left to do.

"Come on, Arnie, let's get out of here," he rasped, as he threw open the cell block door.

As he held it open, Arnie flashed past towards the front door, pumping the action of the gun as he went. The light from the open door shown inside the cell block, and as Bob glanced back, a coldness such as he had never known gripped his insides. Both the sheriff and his wife lay writhing on the floor, their faces contorted with pain. The cook's body was a small motionless heap, a few feet from them. Arnie was streaking through the front door, as he sped after him.

It seemed that there was no end to the tricks that fate had in store for the Taylors this night. Abe Thorton, cousin to the Crawleys, had chosen this night, of all nights, to visit his cousins in jail. He had parked his car across the street just in time to witness the marshal's slow trek up the steps. Instantly, he recognized Dan and knew what was going on.

Being a hill man, the ever-present pistol was on the seat beside him. Instantly, he grabbed it up and jumped from the car. To men of his caliber, blood was a sacred thing, to be honored unto death. He knew, too, that it wouldn't bother him the least to use the fire truck for a shield, in order to get a shot at Dan.

It was over before he got across the street. Pulling up at the edge of the sidewalk, he stood, with gun in hand, staring down at the bodies of Dan and the marshal, lying in a rapidly-spreading pool of blood. The feudal blood in him ran hot, and he wished that it had been him who had pulled the trigger on young Taylor, lying there so still and white.

As his eyes remained fixed on them, in fascination, the youth of Dan was brought home to him. He didn't look at all formidable now. The harshness had left his face in death, and it was, in fact, only the soft lines of a boy's face that stared, sightless, up at him.

Arnie burst through the door and across the porch. As Abe raised his eyes to the rapidly-moving Arnie, he acted instantly. The old Colt .45 came up smoothly and he pressed the trigger, as the barrel lined up with the boy's chest. A look of shocked surprise swept Arnie's face, as the big slug struck home, and he staggered to his knees on the edge of the porch.

Arnie recognized his executioner. Rallying the last bit of life left in him, he raised the shotgun and fired. At such close range, Abe Thorton was a dead man. The impact of the .00 buckshot literally picked him up and cast his body like a rag doll, off the curb and into the street. He was dead before he hit.

Bob had just reached the door when he heard the shots. Horror met his eyes, as he threw open the door. Four bodies lay on the sidewalk. He took one glance at the terror-stricken crowd, looking on from a safe distance, and knew that he had nothing to fear from them.

Arnie lay sprawled at the bottom of the steps. Pausing, he knelt down and turned him over. The hot stench of blood rose to sting his nostrils. A dark stain was spreading rapidly over the front of his shirt. Bob spoke his name fiercely, and the boy's eyes opened. His lips moved, as he tried to speak, and blood bubbled out of his mouth. Frantically, Bob tore the cap from his head and wiped the lips clean. His breath came in short gasps and his eyes were glazing rapidly. In their depths, Bob could see the strain, as Arnie tried again, desperately, to speak.

"Bob, Bob—tell Ma … tell Ma …" The last words ended in a whisper. His eyes closed and his head dropped limply sideways, and Bob knew that he was dead.

Then, rising quickly, he went to Dan. Rolling the body of the marshal off him, his eyes searched frantically for some sign of life. But there was none. Beseechingly, his eyes begged his brother to speak, while in the pale face looking up at him, all the fierce fire of passion had gone out, and only the softness of innocence of youth remained.

Bitterly, Bob assailed himself. Two more Taylors dead. Poor Ma. Poor Ma. The crowd saw the whiteness of his face and the wildness in his eyes, as he rose and faced them. None there felt the least bit like being a hero in trying to detain him, as he walked on stiff legs to his car.

Stupefied, they watched him quickly size up the situation. Another car had pulled in behind the Taylor vehicle. And with the sheriff's car in front, they were tied in tight. Then with a gasp, their startled eyes beheld him yanking open the rear door, and half-pulling, half-lifting another figure from the car. They saw him slap the other lightly on both sides of the face and heard him speaking sharply the name, "Joey."

Another Taylor. My God! Was there no end to them? They saw, then, that he was only a young boy. His white, soft face flashed in the soft beam of the streetlight, as he raised his head and stared in their direction. They saw him throw up a hand in horror, as he saw the bodies lying on the sidewalk. And then he was gone, drug away by the other.

The stunned crowd stood silently for a minute, staring in fascination at the spot where the two Taylors had stood. Then the door of the jail was thrown open and Sheriff Merlin staggered out onto the porch. Holding onto the railing, he assailed the crowd, "Stop them! Stop them Taylors!"

They stared at him blankly, without moving. The picture of the wild-eyed Bob, with that big .45 in his hand, was still too vivid. Then, still without a word, they turned and began to drift away. Within minutes, the sheriff stood alone, staring down at the carnage in front of the jail.

But others soon came, as cooler heads prevailed. Quick examination of the marshal showed that he still lived, but with a terrible hole in his middle. They carried him quickly to the nearest store and laid him on the counter. A doctor, soon in attendance, arranged for immediate transfer to a Louisville hospital, with the hope that surgery might yet save his life. Not until he was safely in an ambulance, and speeding towards the proper medical care, was attention turned towards those lying dead on the sidewalk.

All three were carried to the same funeral parlor, stripped of their clothes, and laid out on a slab, with a sheet casually thrown over them. The big doors were left open, so the curious, the thrill-seekers, and just those with plain, morbid fascination, came in a steady stream, to view the terrible Taylors, now so still in death. They threw back the sheets and stared at the bullet holes and commented on the effectiveness of each shot.

It was such a scene that met Tom's eyes, as he came through the doors in the back. In disbelief, he heard the voices commenting on the wounds of Dan, as no less than a half dozen gazed down at the stripped body of the boy. A fury such as he had never known swept over him. Striding forward, he gripped the nearest man by the collar, and threw him heavily to the side. Scattering them like tenpins, his face dark with fury, he lashed out, "Get out of here, you buzzards! How dare you stand there, gloating over the bodies of those who were better men than any of you will ever be? My God! Is there no human respect left in you? Is there no privacy, even for the dead?"

They stared back at him with a blank look, frightened at the terrible glare in his eyes. Then, still without a word in their defense, they turned and fled. Slowly, the tautness left his shoulders, as a terrible weariness engulfed him. Tenderly, he pulled the sheets back over the still forms of Dan and Arnie. For minutes, he stood beside them, with head lowered. The thing he most dreaded now was telling his mother. He prayed that God would show him the way.

Suddenly, his shoulders straightened. He had things to do. Somewhere between Sladen and home were two more Taylors, alive and afraid. Those he could help. These he could not. As he turned to go, his eyes caught the thrown-back sheet of Thorton. Pausing, he gently lifted it into place, looking without malice into the still-bared face, as he did so. As he left, he went toward the front of the building.

He found the undertaker on the sidewalk in front of the establishment. The man appeared a little frightened, because he had overheard Tom clearing the townspeople out of the back. Tom pinned him with hard, dark eyes, and he swallowed, with a suddenly terrible dry throat.

"Get those doors shut and keep them shut. If I hear of one other person going in there to gloat, I'll come back and take you apart. Do you understand?"

"Sure, Tom. I'll shut them right away. I didn't think they … I'm sorry …" Tom fastened him with a withering glance of disgust, then turned and walked away, as the undertaker scurried towards the rear of his establishment.

Volunteers walked guard in front of the jail the rest of the night. A jittery town was spiked with rumors that the Taylors intended to return to finish the job of killing the Crawleys. Some were even being quoted as having heard Bob make such a statement, as he stood facing the crowd in front of the jail; all of which was untrue. But with people believing what they want to believe, the town of Sladen was on alert for several days.

Come Into My World :: 427

Feud Justice
Chapter 9

He knew that Bob and Joey had left on foot. He knew, too, that Bob was too smart to use the roads. But he would, on occasion, need to cross one, and with any luck, he might just be at the right place at the right time. With ten miles to go, it would be some time before the boys reached the dissecting roads, further north.

As Tom had predicted, Bob drug a bewildered Joey straight east, until they were well outside the city limits, and then set a course straight north, towards the knob country. Sick at heart, he only half tried to answer Joey's questions about what had happened. When Joey finally brought up the subject most prominent on his mind, about what it would do to their mother, he turned on him fiercely.

"Shut up, Joey! Shut up! We'll worry about that when the time comes. Right now, we have to concentrate just on staying alive and getting back to the hills."

Bob knew that a posse would be formed immediately. As he approached the state highway, which they must cross, he became especially vigilant. After that, there wouldn't be anything but county roads, and not many of them. Now, they were so close to town that they had to be extra careful.

Crouched behind bushes at the edge of the pasture next to the road, he waited. The headlights of an approaching car probed the darkness. It was moving slowly. At a point, scarcely fifty feet from them, it came to a stop. Gun barrels could be seen protruding from the windows, and the murmur of subdued voices came from inside. But he couldn't understand the words. An occasional rising voice gave indication that some kind of argument was in process.

With bated breath, he watched and waited. When Joey would have squirmed upright to get a better look, he held him down with a firm pressure of his hand. Finally, after about five minutes, there was a meshing of gears, and the car, with its armed occupants, pulled slowly away. When its taillights had faded, Bob rose, pulling Joey with him, and darted across the highway.

Though Joey's sobbing had ceased, Bob saw, only too plainly, that the bleak despair still remained in his eyes. He had to take his mind off the whole thing as quickly as possible, or the kid would collapse, and what better way than by action. Ahead lay nothing but deep valleys and steep hills, the shortest route home, but by far, the roughest. If the moon were to become hidden after they were committed to that route, they would be impelled to stop until morning. Too many slate bluffs, too many sheer drop-offs would make traveling impossible without light.

To the west, about two miles, lay a leveler route, longer, but easier going. More danger of being intercepted by the law there, but at least they wouldn't break their necks by falling over a cliff. His mind made up, he rose. "Come on, kid, we'd best be going. The sooner we reach the ridge road, the quicker we can find Tom."

As he headed west, Joey stumbled along in his wake. As he had feared, the moon soon became half-hidden, but slowed their progress only slightly. Bob's plan had been to parallel the state highway along a line about a hundred yards east of it, far enough out to avoid detection.

Reaching the approximate place where he desired to again turn north, Bob found their way barred by a nearly impregnable thicket of thorn, vines, and cedar. They would have to detour, even if it meant walking on the highway for a distance. Hoping that it might end short of the road, they continued walking west along its south side. But their hopes were in vain. The thicket ended only when it reached the fence paralleling the state road.

Discouraged, Bob, again, called a brief halt. Joey seemed to have put his complete trust in him, as he obeyed his every decision, without offering a single one of his own. Whispering for him to move softly and to remain alert, Bob slowly crawled through the barbed wire fence, turned to hold it apart for Joey, and then stepped cautiously upon the berm. There, Joey joined him, where they stood silent, for several minutes.

"Okay, kid," Bob finally whispered, "let's get going and walk fast. We don't want to stay on this road any longer than we have to."

Exhausted, as they hurried along the state highway, they realized that headlights were fast approaching from the rear. They ran for the ditch at the side of the road, and watched as the car moved toward them. To their amazement, they realized they recognized the sound of the car. Tom had come to rescue them!

Tom came to a screeching halt, when he realized Bob was standing by the side of the road. The brothers had never been happier to see one another. As they traveled the back roads, a plan formed, as they headed home to their mother.

They would park a mile from the house and walk in, just in case the posse had arrived before them. As they cautiously approached home, Bob and Joey realized that this might be the last time they would see their mother. That strong Tennessee mountain woman was becoming frail and weak. All the events from the past few weeks had taken their toll on her. They knew they would need to get as far away as they could, to keep their mother from being involved in their crime. Once they loaded up on supplies, they would hide in the surrounding hills, until all this blew over.

They parked the car in a secluded spot down a logging road. From there, they walked parallel with the road, but just inside the timberline, so they wouldn't be detected. Tom would approach the house first and signal to Joey and Bob, if it was safe for them to come.

Molly sat in the darkness, knowing that her boys would eventually return home. A friend from Sladen had called earlier to tell her what had happened in town. So all Molly could do now was wait and listen for the approach of her sons.

Tom stopped and waited to observe the house and the surroundings. There was no sign of a posse. As he proceeded toward the house, he kept to the edge of the woods, just in case he had missed signs that men were waiting to arrest Bob and Joey. Tom eased his way around to the rear of the house, then, realizing no one was waiting, he slowly opened the back door.

"Ma, it's Tom, where are you?"

Molly answered quietly, "In here."

As Tom approached the kitchen, he realized his mother had

been crying. She was grieving for the sons she had lost today, and possibly, the ones she might lose in the future. But in all her grief, she had kept a level head, and had packed two sacks full of supplies for Bob and Joey.

"Where are Bob and Joey?" she asked. Tom explained that they were waiting for a signal to come to the house. Tom would send Raider to find them, if the coast was clear. Raider was lying in his usual spot by the front door, and somehow, seemed to sense Joey nearby. Raider dashed out the screen door straight to the tree line, without a sound. Joey was ecstatic to see that wonderful dog!

As the boys approached the house, one thing was on their minds, saying goodbye to their mother; but they knew if they stayed, they would only cause more pain. There were hugs and tears, as they gathered their supplies and said a final goodbye. Just before dawn, they gave one last hug to Molly, and headed into the Southern Indiana hills, Raider trotting along behind.

Feud Justice
Chapter 10

Sheriff Trumble had little liking for the job at hand. And even less, because he wasn't even the real sheriff. He had been pressed into service, because of his past experience as holder of that office. With the present sheriff wounded, he felt bound to perform his duties to the best of his ability. And that, right then, meant capture of Bob and Joey Taylor. For the past two weeks, the posse had scoured the Southern Indiana hills, with no success. So today, there would be another trip into the hills to ferret out the Taylor boys.

The long row upriver had been hard, and all were glad for a chance to catch their breath before tackling the steep ridge ahead of them. Contemptuously, he surveyed his motley crew. Two pale-faced pool room hangers on, and the Thorton brothers, Jed and Ben.

Already, the early morning October sun had taken its toll of energy from the two from the pool room. Right then, he knew they were wishing they had never started in the first place. As he surveyed their sweat-soaked shirts and soft, paunchy middles, he was wishing the same. He doubted they would even know how to use the Springfields they carried. Those were two rifles that might as well not have been checked out of the armory.

The Thortons, though, were something else, again. Not only would they stand up in a fight, but would only be too willing to use the guns they had been issued. They had accompanied the posse on different occasions during the past two weeks. Their eagerness was becoming more apparent with each passing day. For that reason alone, he had allowed them to accompany him. With them under his command, he could curtail their vicious hatred toward the Taylors. He had no desire to see the boys hurt in any way.

Jed Thorton turned from the huddle with his brother, and spoke to the sheriff, "Well, Lon, we gonna stand here all day? Let's get on after them Taylors."

As irritating as the sheriff found the nasal, twanging voice to be, it was no more so than the leer on Jed's lean, evil face. Making no attempt to conceal the contempt he felt, he said, "Mighty anxious, ain't you, Jed?"

Jed looked at his brother, Ben, with a smirk. "Oh, I don't know. Just want to do my duty as a posse member. That's what we're out here for ain't it, to get us a Taylor or two?"

Though in his early sixties and a little on the heavy side, Sheriff Trumble carried his big body with an air of authority. Pushing his hat back from sweat-soaked gray hair, his usually florid face paled, and his eyes grew hard, as he answered with an edge to his voice.

"We're out here to take the Taylor boys into custody, and that's all. And you had better be sure that's all—both of you."

"Now, Sheriff," Ben whined, "that's exactly what Jed meant. We sure don't aim to hurt nobody. Ain't that right, Jed?"

"Why sure, that's right," Jed rasped, with a hurt look on his bony face. "Me and Ben, here, are just as peaceful as two doves on a rail fence. We're only here to do our civic duty, Sheriff, just our civic duty."

Without bothering to answer, the sheriff stared coldly at them for a few seconds, before turning abruptly into the trail up the ridge. "Come on," he said flatly, "let's go."

For the last several weeks, Raider continued to outsmart the posse, and today would be no different. Raider had been alerting the boys when the posse got close enough for him to pick up their scent. The big, spotted hound stood, poised on the edge of the bluff. With ears lifted and nose on alert, he studied the valley below. The muscles of his powerful shoulders quivered, as again, the faint sound came from the river. But still, he waited.

A fringe of willows bordering the high muddy banks of the deep, sluggish White River hid the source of the slight warning, but he mainly depended on his sensitive nose. Then, at last, a light breeze from the North skipped across the river, scooped up the scent, and wafted it gently up the ridge. A low growl rumbled deep in his throat as he tasted its fragrance. Now he knew, so he waited no longer.

With fast, ground-covering strides, he loped up the trail.

Reaching the crest, he turned east and increased his pace. Virgin poplar, hickory, and oak towered above him, as he ran effortlessly and silently over the deep soft carpet at his feet. Minutes later, he turned abruptly to the right, towards a stand of young pine that graced the highest point of the ridge, a hundred yards to the south. Alien though they seemed, amid their hardwood surroundings, they were but nature's way of healing the scar of a clearing some years before.

Quietly, he entered the thicket and padded on silent paws deep inside towards the center. Finally, he halted at the mouth of a small lean-to. Pausing only long enough to check for the smell of the two blanket-covered figures, he crept softly to the side of the smaller one. Gently, his cold nose nudged a pale cheek. The figure stirred briefly, as a hand went out to brush at the spot he had touched. As if impatient, he whined and nudged again, much harder. Instantly, the boy was awake.

Alarm faded quickly from the bright, blue eyes, as they softened at the sight of the dog standing over him. "What is it, boy?" he murmured, as his hand went out to caress the big head. Whining once more, he turned under the boy's hand, and faced the front of the lean-to. Again, a growl rumbled deep and low. Instantly, the alarm was back into the boy's eyes, as he quickly threw off the blanket. Rolling to his knees, he shook the figure lying next to him.

"Wake up, Bob, wake up, Raider's back! Somebody's com'in."

Instantly, the other was on his feet, with a grunted, "Let's git."

Because of constant practice, each quickly threw his pitiful supply of gear into the middle of his blanket, gathered the ends in, and lifted it to his shoulder like a sack. Picking up their rifles, they stepped out into the open.

The big dog stood rigidly, facing to the west, as growl after growl broke from him. The tall, lanky body of Bob stiffened, as bitterly, his dark eyes swept the density of the big timber.

"Must have come up the river," he said softly. "God, we're getting careless. But for Old Raider here, they would have had us sure."

Briefly, his hand rested on the hound's head, and then he turned.

"Come on, Joey, let's go hide this stuff, and then circle around to the crow's nest, and maybe we can see them."

With long strides, they rapidly bore southeast. No words were spoken until they reached a thorn thicket overhanging a shelf of rock at the lip of a small hollow.

"Let's stash it here," Bob muttered.

Quickly, he dropped to his knees, and taking Joey's from him, pushed both blankets well up under the shelf, to the dryness of the clay. This done, he rose, picked up his rifle, and still without a word, set out in a fast jog towards the southwest, with Joey close behind. Raider seemed to sense their desperation, for he loped well out in front.

Soon, they reached the south side of the ridge, where again, they turned due west, without slackening the pace. After a quarter of a mile had been covered, Raider, having reached a stretch of barren, rocky ground, stopped and waited. As they caught up with Raider, a wave of Bob's hand at once sent Raider stealthily to the right and up the slope.

Quietly, they waited, as Raider made his way carefully up the side. He seemed to know the need for silence, as he threaded in among the large boulders and around the edge of numerous shale slides. Reaching the summit, he slipped in between a cluster of large rocks, assembled as if by a giant hand, and disappeared.

Neither boy took his eyes from the spot, as they waited for his reappearance. At last, his big head emerged from between the rocks, and he stood again in full view, looking down at them with tail wagging. The shoulders of both sagged, ever so slightly, as they let their breath out in unison. The strain was beginning to show.

Carefully, they made their way up the slope. Reaching the nest of boulders, Bob, in the lead, dropped to his stomach and wiggled forward, while Joey followed close behind. From an opening between the rocks, they had a commanding view of a long stretch of the north side of the ridge, clear to the banks of the river.

Bob took a small, battered pair of field glasses from his shirt. Joey watched silently, as he adjusted them, and scanned the slope below. For several minutes, he raked the entire area from west to east, worrying silently, that he couldn't see below the riverbank.

"See anything, Bob?" Joey finally whispered nervously.

"No, Joey, not a thing. But we'll wait anyway. Raider's never been wrong yet."

A half hour passed, and still, they lay unmoving. Raider lay between them. With Bob's hand resting on Raider's back, he felt Raider stiffen, as his head lifted sharply. Hardly breathing, they waited, with unblinking eyes fixed on the line of willows at the river's edge. One minute passed, then two, and then their faith in the big dog's warning was rewarded. Even without the glasses, they could see them clearly, as they emerged from the trees. Slowly, one by one, they came into the open, five in all, where they stood for a time, as if unsure of how to proceed.

Bob's lips curled in contempt, as he studied the group through the glasses. Then, handing the glasses to Joey, he said harshly, "Everyone's packing a rifle and pistol, like they're really expecting a battle. Got half a mind to give them one."

Joey, in the act of raising the glasses, halted and turned fearfully to the other. "No! Bob, No! I told you I would have no part of that."

The fierce light burning in Bob's dark eyes softened, as he saw the look of strain in Joey's pale face. He had always been the gentle one, not tough like him and the others. Even Pa had said that the kid didn't take to the ways of the Taylors. Pa! Again, bitterness welled up in him at the thought of his father and of all that had happened in such a short time.

Placing a hand on Joey's shoulder, he said, "Don't worry, kid, I won't. Besides, they all have Springfields and I don't care to match our Winchesters against them."

Taking the glasses from the limp hand of his brother, he again studied the group below. Now that they had all spread out some, he could see each one clearly. Suddenly, he stiffened and a growl escaped him. The glasses rested on two who seemed to stand apart from the others. Those two—long, lean, and lanky, dressed in overalls and denim jackets, seemed to hold his gaze in utter fascination. Then, at Joey's insistence, he handed him the glasses with trembling hand.

"Go ahead, kid. Take a good look. Tell me what you see."

As Joey swept the group, he, too, came to rest on the two who had aroused the wrath of his brother. A shiver ran over him as the evil, bony faces under the old felt, battered hats came into clear focus.

"The Thortons," he exclaimed, "but why?"

Bob laughed scornfully. "I'll give you two reasons. First, they're cousins of the Crawleys. And second, they hate Old Raider here. They're so jealous because they don't own him, that they would like to see him dead, and us, too, for that matter."

Joey's arm went around the big dog fiercely. "They'll never get him, will they?"

Bob's face darkened, as he slid his hand along his rifle barrel. "No, kid, they'll never get him. I promise you that."

"They're mean, Bob, just plain mean."

"I know, Joey, I know. There's nothing they haven't done, short of murder, and probably that."

"Bob," Joey said, in a hushed voice.

"What, kid?"

"We might of ... we might of ... .if ... if ..."

"Yeah, I know, I know!" Bob rasped. "Don't think about it, Joey."

But for the next few minutes, it was a relief to have Joey interested only in watching the posse below. He didn't want to think about it either, but he had to. Was it possible that so much could happen in such a short period of time?

It seemed so unreal, even yet, with him and Joey being hunted day and night. Less than three weeks ago, they were as any other family in the hills, but during the last three weeks, their lives had been torn asunder. Pa, killed by the Crawley brothers; Dan, lying dead on the sidewalk outside the jail; the marshal and sheriff shot; Arnie dead; Ma stricken to her bed because of it; and now, he and Joey, hunted like animals. Where would it all end? As he thought about their situation, it seemed as if he were looking down a black tunnel, and all because of Old Raider.

Feud Justice
Chapter 11

As Sheriff Trumble and the posse made their way up the ridge, they soon were strung out along the trail. The eager Thortons had taken over the lead, with the long-legged stride of those born to the hills. The sheriff, not far behind, held to a steady pace, while the other two puffed and panted, well to the rear.

Suddenly, Jed paused beside a dusty spot in the trail. With a muttered curse, he pointed at his feet, "Well, there it is again, same as every other time."

The sheriff pulled up beside him and looked at the ground. The tracks of a large dog were clearly visible To see such a sign was becoming an everyday occurrence since the search began. The sheriff knew the trend of the Thortons' thoughts. Even before Jed spoke, he knew what he was going to say.

"There's that durn hound again. I tell you, we ain't ever gonna come up with them Taylors as long as they have that dog. He's awarnin' them, Sheriff, and we ain't got a chance."

Ben's eyes gleamed, as he squirted out a long stream of tobacco juice; he stroked the barrel of his rifle lovingly. "Ain't but one thing to do, and that's to kill that mangy hound. Me and Jed will do it, Sheriff. We'll just lay out here real quiet like, until he shows hisself, then, bam, it'll be all over."

Jed's evil face broke into a crooked grin. "Yeah, that's right, Sheriff, me and Ben'll git him fer you. Twon't be any trouble a'tall."

Lon Trumble was no stranger to the story of Joey Taylor and his big hound. Neither did he doubt the truth of the tale of how the boy and the dog had bested the Thortons one day on the trail, when they, assuming Joey was alone, attempted to rough him up out of pure cussed meanness. And if all the story was true, Jed still carried the scars of Raider's teeth on his forearm. The implication of their hate was too clear.

Angrily, he shoved his chin to within inches of Jed's bony face. "You dirty scum. That dog is about all that boy has left to call his own, and he'll not be shot. I'm telling you once, and you better listen. We'll get them in time, or they will give themselves up. They aren't bad boys, just scared. And if either one of you harm a hair of that hound, I promise you that I'll see you in jail, if I have to spend a year digging up evidence on every unlawful thing I've heard you both are guilty of."

Though the faces of the Thortons blanched at the sheriff's words, their eyes gleamed wickedly at his back, as he turned from them, and again, started up the ridge. Sullen now, they were content to stay to his rear. They were right, of course, about the dog warning the boys. It had happened many times before. But there still had to be a better way than killing the dog.

An hour later and a mile further down the ridge, he called a halt to the search. It turned out that he had known when the dog's track was sighted that the search was over. Sure, the Thortons had ferreted out the lean-to, and as he watched in disgust, they had destroyed it completely. But what did that accomplish? The Taylor boys could build another in twenty minutes.

Sheriff Trumble thought about the last three weeks. He knew that as long as Old Raider continued to warn the boys, there would be no capture, and that big dog was never going to leave Joey's side. So, he made a decision. No more posses. No more hunting for the Taylors. Hopefully, they would get tired of hiding, and come in on their own.

His decision made, he ordered a halt to the hunt. "But, Sheriff," Jed whined. "Where's the justice in that?"

"I'll tell you where, "Sheriff Trumble bellowed. "The boy's father and brothers are dead, and their mother's health is declining, as we speak. They're on the run for who knows how long. They've lost all touch with their family, and for hill people, that's justice enough. Basically, they're good boys, just a little wild, at times, and they act before they think. I know, in my gut, that they will eventually do the right thing, and turn themselves in. Until then, we do nothing."

It was an accepted fact that none of the hill people would help in their capture. Most believed that they had only done what was expected of them. General sympathy was with them throughout the county. Reports of them turning up briefly continued to filter in, all during the next few weeks. Winter was fast approaching, and as Joey and Bob grew weary of the hiding and living off the land, they finally turned themselves in.

Justice was swift for the boys. Since Joey had not participated in the actual crime, he was put on probation for commission to assist a felon, and returned home to his mother. Bob was charged with conspiracy to assist a jail escape, and given a term of five to ten years. After serving five of the ten years, he returned to his beloved Southern Indiana hills, desiring only to live as any other citizen. He became interested in church work, and lived his life as a respected member of the community. Raider was, once again, living the life he loved, being a constant companion to Joey, hunting coon, and just enjoying life.

As history often indicates, some families seem destined for tragedy. And so it was with the Taylors. It is only fair to assume that the Taylors were victims of circumstances resulting from the time in which they lived. Thrown suddenly outside the law by one passion-filled minute in the life of their father, they took the only recourse they knew in upholding the family honor; the code of the Tennessee hills that spawned them—FEUD JUSTICE!

Draft Card Burners ...

November 22, 1965—*Indianapolis Star*—Letter to the Editor

By Al Boling

DRAFT CARD BURNERS AREN'T FIT
TO WEAR THE COUNTRY'S UNIFORM

One's first impulse, upon reading Leon Smith's letter to the editor, is to agree with his suggestion that demonstrators against our presence in Vietnam be inducted into the armed forces. Further pursuit of that thought would, however, I believe, cause us to decide otherwise.

I believe this to be true for several reasons. This type of young man, who is so openly lacking in self-respect, so completely devoid of pride, and who has so little appreciation for the most envied privilege in the world, that of being a citizen of this country, is not worthy to wear the uniform of our armed forces.

As a veteran, who saw service in many countries, I would not want to trust my flank to one with so little principle. The taint would be unbearable. The most elegant dress uniform fades to insignificant drabness, when placed in contrast with the blood and mud-splattered battle dress of our real fighting men.

No man on earth is enshrined with more glory than our combat trooper. Filthy, ragged, bearded, and red-eyed, he crawls from his foxhole. On legs that have already gone too many miles without rest, he plows once more into hell, from which he may or may not return. But if he returns, and you look close enough to take a good look, you will see the proudest man in the world.

Look, as he stands, reeling, but erect, amid the gore and devastation around him. See the wildness in his eyes, that dies slowly after battle, and in some never does; see the horror reflected there; understand the sickness in his soul, because of what he's just had to do; and believe with all your heart, that he hates war as much as anyone; that he has, but recognized a call to duty, not because he loved life less, but he loved liberty more.

Yes, look at this boy/man, and if you are a draft card burner, hang your head in shame, with the absolute conviction that, but for him, you would be a slave. Look, but don't stand too close, for you are not worthy of standing in his shadow.

Please, let's not insult our combat men by asking them to entrust their lives to punks like these, who place so little price upon their manhood. Instead, perhaps, it would be possible to induct them into labor battalions; with an appropriate uniform, of course; say a bright yellow one, with maybe, a drop seat.

One more thing upon which Mr. Smith generalizes was the part played by our college students. I feel that he intended no malice toward the group as a whole, but he injects the following: "It makes me wonder if our young men and women are fit to run our country."

Mr. Smith, of course, you are aware, that only a very small percent of our college students were a part of those demonstrations, and for the most part, back our Vietnam War effort, 100 percent.

I wish that you could have been seated beside me, recently, at Indiana University during one registration day. I'm sure that you would have been as impressed as I was, with the seriousness of these young people, as they went about the business of selecting subjects of study, that would allow them to embark on their careers of choice.

You could not have overlooked the quiet, self-assured, and polite manner in which the boys conducted themselves or the calm beauty of the girls, as they reflected deliberate and determined detachment from others, as each sought only that which, for her, would be the right thing.

Yes, Mr. Smith, I'll trust these young people to run our country in the future, both those in combat and those in college. Best you had, too, for above all things, they need from us now our trust and confidence.

Dachau

February 26, 1964—*Indianapolis Star*—Letter to the Editor

Recently, the newspapers carried a small, inconspicuous story concerning the arrest of a self-styled Nazi leader, age twenty-five. Obviously, this young man is of unsound mind. Those who lived through that period of history, in which the Nazi Party dominated over half the world, would find it impossible to believe otherwise.

That any sane person would align himself to the degradation and shame connected to the Nazi Party is inconceivable—a party that will be forever recorded in history as having reached the pinnacle in man's inhumanity against man. A party, whose ruthless rise to power, introduced to the world the most hideous, horrible, and cruel methods of torture ever dragged from the deepest recesses of crazed minds.

Perhaps, if the young man arrested had been old enough to have seen firsthand some of the horrors of Nazi concentration camps, he would not now be living in a dream world of misconception.

Dachau should have been example, enough, had he been there one spring day in 1945. A company of infantry, sent in to capture it, went berserk at the sight of all the atrocities, so prominently displayed before their horrified eyes. So kill crazy did they become, that another company was sent in to quiet them. But they, too, reacted in the same manner. Anything that moved was mowed down. Many DPs died, because they didn't take shelter.

A moat of deep, swift-running, black water, separating the administration area from the compound, was soon bobbing with the bodies of vicious German shepherd dogs, used by the SS as guards and instruments of torture against prisoners. A top-ranking SS was wounded in the leg. After doctoring the wound, the GIs took him to the compound and tossed him over to the eagerly-awaiting hands of hundreds of prisoners. He died, screaming, under the fists and feet of those whose lives he had made a living hell. His lifeless and battered body was then tossed back over the fence, like so much garbage. Two days later, one of the camp commandants died the same way, when he was found inside the compound, dressed in the striped clothing of a prisoner. Cruelty only begets cruelty.

Typhus was running rampant among the DPs. An evacuation hospital unit tried their best to combat the disease. For days, many died hourly, until the epidemic was brought under control. Many of the survivors had no mind left. They looked at you with blank eyes. All intelligence had disappeared. In medical terms, they were all but human vegetables, moving bodies with no minds to command them.

The Nazis had killed faster than they could burn. Great stacks of bodies were corded up like square piles of fence posts, in front of the furnace building, and in surrounding corners, all waiting their turn in one of the five furnaces. Many bodies were covered with quicklime, that had not yet done its work.

Structures built of concrete blocks had recently been added on either end of the crematorium. Many more bodies were piled in these structures. One small, dingy, gloomy shower room, directly behind the furnaces, had served as the death chamber. A single, dirty showerhead had administered the gas.

The five furnaces were served by metal trays on rollers, whose long handles protruded outside the door. They were rolled out, a body placed in the oval bottom, and rolled back in. The bottoms were slatted, so as to allow the bones to drop through, to the bottom proper. These had not been cleaned out for some time.

An ingenious method of mental and physical torture was devised here, for those whose friends were being burned. A huge, wooden beam ran full length of the building, about ten feet from the floor, and directly in front of the furnaces. A large row of large, steel hooks, like hogs are hung on in a slaughterhouse, protruded from the beam. One giant Russian explained how he had been suspended there by the wrists, three different times, to watch a close friend burn.

On the wall of one of the end rooms were two bloody handprints. Bob Hope later wrote about these. From these pathetic prints, crimson trails streaked downward; a path of death marked plainly for posterity, by each bloody fingertip on its way to the floor and oblivion.

The sweet, sickening, stench of death hung over the entire area. One felt that it must have entered his very pores, in a manner that would defy all the soap in the world to wash it away. After breathing the air, so pregnant with the smell, he felt as if his lungs should be turned wrong side out and disinfected.

This then, was the true mark of the Nazi, a name to be spoken in contempt, and the worst shame ever to be placed upon the human race. How sad that there are those today, so uninformed, that they would consider the world of the Nazi glamorous. Nothing could have been further from the truth.

Yet, the rest of the world must accept some of the blame. We stood by, while the Nazi regime grew from a small nucleus of a few fanatics surrounding a crazy man, and did nothing. Every indication of its terrible potential was ignored, even laughed at. The world sneered at the raving little man with the funny mustache. He had written a book that clearly outlined his plans for world conquest. And before the sneers had faded, he suddenly emerged as the power behind the mightiest war machine that the world had ever known, and the course of history was changed forever.

If, as historians say, the only way to judge the future is by the past, then a few outstanding true facts of history should remain prevalent in all our minds. The Nazi Party, in the beginning, professed only to be enemies of Communism. Hundreds of thousands of Nazi Party members were in complete ignorance of the intended goal of their leaders, until they were caught up in its rushing momentum. They found themselves helpless to do anything, but go along with the horde.

The Nazi Party was only a small hate group, to begin with, not unlike several such groups that have emerged in our country, in recent years. Hitler did not introduce racial hatred. It was already there. He only fanned the flames and made it legal. There is danger of being lulled into complacency by the feeling that, because we wouldn't follow an organization with such tactics, then no one else will.

The Nazi Party practiced early elimination of important men in Germany, who were most in a position to lead opposition to them. This was accomplished by trumped-up charges, fanned hot by wild rantings, until public sentiment was such that they could be imprisoned or killed.

Bigotry lies just below the surface in all of us. In far too many, this can be brought into active being by the right persuasion. Any radical group draws its numerical strength from the unthinking, who like to be led by those who shout the loudest, and who are willing to follow blindly, without question, down the path to inevitable chaos.

And last, but not least, any organization that practices hate, that adopts the basic slogan, "Our Way the Only Way," encourages division among the people. It weakens the very country they claim to be saving, and bears false witness, with their cry that it is all in the name of Patriotism.

Alfred L. Boling
Salem, Indiana

www.ingramcontent.com/pod-product-compliance
Lightning Source LLC
Chambersburg PA
CBHW071343020726
47502CB00001B/222